Hound Dog's HOWL

Formatting Created by Atticus

Editing: Beth Hale @ Magnolia Editing

Cover Design Ebook and Paperback: @prettyinink creations

Interior Designs: Jamie Fritz and Canva

Ebook: ASIN BoD2VDPVFD

Paperback: 979-8-9867281-3-1

The Saint's Outlaws MC: Memphis Chapter

President- Hound Dog
Vice President- B.B
SGT at Arms- Twitty
Enforcer- Shooter
Chaplin- Reverend
Treasurer- Hank
Road Captain- Fender
Secretary- Otis

<u>Members</u>
Stray
Blue
Hellfire
Skaggs
Chameleon

<u>Prospects</u>
Woody
Waylan

Blaze

Here's to the ones that know their worth and bless the path it took.

But to those that need a Hound Dog to help them know they deserve so much... and that you're a good girl.

Before you start reading, I want to give a warning that this is intended for mature audience/readers. As I do in my day job, I want to give transparency. Here are the trigger warnings. Towards the end of this book, you will find a list of helpful phone numbers and websites to further help those who are seeking help.

Death of a loved one (past)
Anxiety
Drugs
Gun violence
Attempted murder and Murder
Organized crime
Trauma
Attempted sexual assault

HOUND DOG'S HOWL
JAMIE FRITZ

"Truth is like the sun. You can
shut it out for a time, but it
ain't goin' away."

Elvis Presley

Chapter 1

NASH

It was one thing to be screwed by the prettiest little thing in a bar, it was another to be screwed by someone you trusted. Especially when it comes to money.

Especially when they were the ones that were responsible for your career and making sure you made the lifestyle you earned. We're all human! We get back what we put in, correct? Or is that the lie we're all told at the beginning of life?

I stood in the recording studio, thumbing through the endless music that was written for me, because God forbid I didn't know what I wanted to sing or what I thought my fans wanted to listen to. When I signed on to the recording company, I wanted to be authentic. I was the young kid that was plucked from the streets because I grabbed the ear of the right person at the right time.

Fast forward a few years later, I had become a puppet that was controlled by money. My voice became controlled by those behind the scenes. I wasn't singing what I wanted but couldn't argue or everything I had earned would be taken away. I helped with my family, and Pop's health would be taken away. I didn't know where to go from there.

I scanned through the songs in my hands and nothing was jumping at me. That was until I found a few that had the same style that called to me. Between the words and the flow, it was like poetry; it was realistic.

It felt right.

I pocketed those songs because, call me a selfish bastard, but sometimes I took what I wanted.

If I was going to be controlled by someone else, play along with their games and their commitments, I was going to take something that they didn't deserve.

Over the years, I saw things that deemed me over exaggerated, too "pent up with nerves", or sometimes untrustworthy. When I spoke with my brother, Memphis, the night before he told me that I needed to take back control and regain my voice. He promised that he would help with anything he could.

I mean the man moved across the state and planted himself with a motorcycle club after leaving the youth shelter and "being called for a different purpose". What do you expect from the second generation of a motorcycle club member?

Only difference is that Pop's club decided to disband after too much shit went down with their president, and the club was beginning to be under fire. It was better to move quietly than fight to the death.

Pops told me the night before that he and Mama would be okay, they were grateful for the help over the years. Mama said she would miss being my biggest fan, but made me promise that I would sing to her. Pops said it wasn't my job to provide for the family, that he was going to work at the plant.

I knew his health was finally catching up to him, he tried to hide it. Between the club "business" and working in the factory, his back was giving out on him and sometimes his hands would spasm. The doctors said that they were working on a diagnosis, but we had no answers.

My brother was the dreamer, the one that was soft. Me, on the other hand, I had a hard, protective heart. Even when the studio wanted more from me, attempted to soften me up, it never worked.

Thus, I was given the "bad boy" of country music personification. I was still working on my "image", my name. I wasn't a "chart topper" but I was getting noticed more and more. But little things proved to me that no amount of money would be worth anything in the long run.

When I called a meeting with my producer and agent, I had every intention of making my demands and telling them the direction I wanted to go in. I had every notion to tell them that I noticed them not giving all the earnings I made and was contracted to have in my accounts. Their accountant had told me that everything was there.

But I knew it wasn't. They still had their teeth sank in me. They wanted me to make them the hottest company to work with, to attract other artists only so the studio would bleed them dry. They'd take the naive ones, the inexperienced dreamers for a ride that there was no getting off of.

I tapped my foot, waiting for them. They were making me wait, probably thinking that I would sweat it off and give in to them willingly.

I took one look in the mirror, and I didn't like what I saw. The pale excuse of a man. The shadow of the strong man that my folks raised me to be. I didn't look like I was, they thought I wouldn't see, but I had a sense. I did my own digging and flipped through the pages of my contract.

I could have consulted with Eric, but I didn't want to interrupt his busy schedule. The man would have done anything for me, he offered to help me with my contract while he was finishing law school, but I put too much damn faith that it was my break, a chance to change everything.

But there I was after so much "faith" for the people that believed in me, or so I thought. I believed so much, but when life gives you lessons and hints, you don't ignore them.

I waited for another thirty minutes before I was going to take out my phone and rip a new one with my agent. Jerry, my agent, was supposed to be there on time, as he promised that everything was going to be okay. I waited for Derek, my producer and part owner of this studio, to come with Jerry. No one else was to be in the building except us, no one else worked on the weekends.

The more time went on, I knew they were scheming. There were threats to my future, to my music. I started to pace the studio, enough to possibly burn a hole in the floor. My nerves turned into sparks of anger. I was about ready to officially walk out that door.

I was about to burn the image of "Nash Young" from the world and rip the history away from people. I wasn't an artist anymore; I lost that part of me when the music never felt right anymore. I had a higher standard of what I wanted to be, and yet it was never fulfilled.

Part of that was my own fault, allowing someone to tell me what to do and how to do it. How to feel, how to write, that's what they took from me. They took what being an artist, a musician was about.

As my hand reached for the exit, the twist of the knob stopped me. With a wide smile, Jerry walked in the room, arms spread wide like it was the best thing in the world to be in his presence. The man acted like he gave everything he had, like he was a god to worship.

"Nash, my boy, how's my little rockstar?" he asked, attempting to embrace me. I wasn't anyone's "little rockstar" anymore. Not when it felt like they stole the music out of my soul.

I took a step back, crossing my arms in front of me. Jerry dropped his head and signaled Derek to walk in the room, like the little lap dog he was just waiting for his master to call. Derek's eyes turned away from me as he tried to take a seat at the sound panel.

"What happened to professionalism?" I sneered. I was furious to the point of my blood boiling, creating a volcano ready to burst.

"We're a few minutes late, nothing to worry your pretty little head about," Jerry continued in his conciliatory tone. My eyes started to twitch, my fist clenched by my chest.

"I see, you're wanting to talk business." Jerry shook his head, deciding to brush past me to land his oversized ass on the couch.

"Didn't call you to braid my hair," I huffed out. "Jerry, Derek, I have been making a fortune for you all, and I think it's only fair that I get my correct portion of profits."

Again, I wasn't trying to be greedy, but no one was going to stiff me out of my money. Jerry leaned over, looking at Derek with a shock and confused expression. He pursed his lips. "You have been, Nash. I don't know where this is coming from. If it's more money you're needing, we can look into touring, opening for bigger names, but you have been paid what you're worth."

"Nash, I don't think you mean what you're accusing us of," Derek tried to gaslight me. The knife that severed into the final link.

"No, that's what I was accusing you of, stealing what's owed to me. You think I'm lying? Funny because it seems over the past two years, the amounts keep diminishing. The pay out should have been the same through my contract." I rushed to my backpack with all the papers that I printed off, showing the amounts that were deposited into my account, which I then strategically sent to other accounts for my own safekeeping.

I shoved the papers on the table in front of Jerry, showing him the truth behind his lies.

"I have given this studio the best years of my career, but every year I did more of what the studio wanted of me. I started to sing other people's songs. I became a version of myself that I'm not. Yes, I'm partly to blame, but other than that I have worked my fingers until they bled or I was on the verge of dehydration." I started to explode.

All the thoughts that I kept to myself to save face, appease everyone, just exploded out of it, and admittingly felt freeing.

I didn't shed light on the copious amount of addictions that could have been formed as they attempted to influence me.

Derek swung around to see what I had laid on the table. His eyes started to switch back to Jerry and then back to the papers. His reaction told me everything I needed to make my next move.

Did they really think that I wouldn't notice a few tens of thousands of dollars? That I was eventually going to be the "good little boy" and keep doing what they wanted? If you want something done right, you have to do it yourself. I was going to set myself free.

I couldn't trust my life, my career in anyone else's hands anymore. Between the thievery and lies, I needed to do things on my own.

"So, because you were all late and wasted what chance of civil conversation between artists you had, I'll skip to the next part. Either give me my money or I walk. I walk out of here and rip up the contract."

It was a risky move, but enough was enough. It was time to be a fucking man and remind people that they didn't steal from me.

"I don't know what to tell you, my boy. You have been given everything." Jerry leaned back on the couch. "If sales or traction was down, it wasn't on us."

"You're going to sit there and tell me it's my fault? I have done everything you wanted, what more do you want from me?" I asked.

Jerry folded his hands. "Nash, I like you, hell, love you like a son I never wanted, but you have to remember who found you on the streets, gave you a chance, even helped you in the beginning with your dad's health bills, with all his heart problems."

"So what, you're taking more of a cut for repayment instead of having a fucking soul?" I was seething with anger that it was steaming off my skin. There was a pounding in my ears, blurring out the world around me.

"Well, if you want to be greedy and look at it like that, sure. Just a repayment. We made you, we built you up. You should be thanking us. Right Derek?" Jerry said.

I twisted my head to see Derek nodding like a good puppet.

Music and artistry was long gone. Especially from me.

Before I could speak, he continued, "I'll tell you what. You do some tours, and a new album, the studio was thinking pop country this time, and maybe a few commercials, we can get that money back up to par."

Was he fucking for real? More work only for them to continue their ways. That was the straw that broke the camel's back.

The true explosion happened when I knocked Jerry to the ground as he tried to stand up and set me straight. My fist connected straight to his jaw, pummeling him to the ground. His groans were enough to bring a smile to my ass. I threw in a couple kicks to the gut. He had it coming, and in that moment, screw all the rules, because I was back in control, even if I was full of rage. Derek cowered in the corner, stuttering as I approached him.

Bending over to meet him face to face, I wrapped my hand around his throat. "If anyone asks, it was self-defense. Or better yet, don't say anything at all. You know who my father was associated with." Derek nodded at my empty threat.

"I'm walking away, Derek, and if I was you, I'd re-think Jerry. Be a fucking owner and stand up and toss the guy to the street. But this is the last time you will ever see me."

I grabbed my guitar case, my backpack, and took out a cigarette. I flicked a light to it, and for added dramatic flair, I flicked the lit cigarette in the next room. The studio was either going to be cleansed or burned in hellfire.

As I walked down the hall, someone bumped into my side. A quiet little grunt sparked my ears. I look to see a little auburn beauty with a notebook in her hand. She straightened up, adjusting her clothes before looking at me. Her hazel green eyes shined through her thick framed glasses. "You might want to leave the building and call the fire department, honey."

She fell silent as I turned away.

I hoped she did the same, if anything I hoped the poor little soul had a better life walking away from the studio.

As I walked away with an emptiness in my chest, I began to think about the next steps. I couldn't go back to music, not when I had no motivation anymore, and barely anything to produce. But I wanted, more like needed, to protect those that had a dream.

A dream is worth protecting, even if you have to fight everything in your way. Unfortunately, artists of all realms are easily taken advantage of.

My next steps were just a phone call away.

Chapter 2

NASH

Regret didn't set in until after walking down a few blocks, replaying everything that happened.

What the fuck did I just do?

I seriously did that. I set myself free, and in the ashes I planned to rebuild.

I called Memphis the moment I was free, the crashing sensation of not knowing what my next steps were causing me to crumble, mentally and physically. I had no back up plan. I had no way of helping the family anymore.

The only thing I had to my name was my dignity and the savings that I accrued over the years.

"So you set fire to your past and are ready to move on." His melodic, bass voice rang through my phone.

"What the fuck am I to do? A former rising music artist in a town that is also crawling with them. I have no other skills other than manual labor," I grunted out, while on my bike, on the sidewalk by one of the city parks.

"Afraid to mess up your pretty face?" My little brother laughed.

If it wasn't for the fact that he was in Raleigh, I'd would've kicked his stupid ass.

"No, what I'm afraid of is that there are too many others like myself."

"Like yourself?" he questioned. That's what Memphis did, he turned on that brilliant mind and rode along with you.

I sighed, darting my eyes around the sight of little families laughing and smiling and young teens by their lonesome keeping to themselves. "People who are talented enough that are left unprotected and used up until they aren't of use. It's not right."

"What? You want to be like a vigilante or something, staying in the shadows, coming to their rescue?" he continued to question.

"I want to take back this town, our town, and bring life back, run the city like it's ours," I finally said. I wanted the power back. I wanted people to be afraid of trying to take away or run a dream that wasn't theirs.

Memphis was quiet, a little too quiet for him. I didn't know if the man was shocked or out of words.

"Brother, you still there?"

He sighed. "It sounds like I may know a way that would help."

"Care to tell me, or do I need to beg you to do it?"

"You ain't never begged for anything; why start now, superstar?"

I rolled my eyes.

I waited for him to say something, anything. Mama would be so proud to know her oldest son was looking for help from the youngest son. If Mama could hear this conversation, she'd slap me on the back and say "about damn time you listen to him." I was hardheaded, I knew that, and I liked things a certain way.

"You're killing me here, Memphis," I softly said. Desperation clouded my voice.

He broke the silence. "I may know some people that could help you."

"Help me? Like get me a job?" I asked. I was worried that things would run dry, and I'd be behind.

"How about making your plan a reality," he answered. "It may take a few phone calls, and a favor but I think it will help you. Maybe help with your trust issues."

I winced at his implication, "I don't have trust issues," I snapped back.

"Really? So if you had to put blind trust and faith into a new group, you'd follow their lead, their rules, you'd trust them? In the end, to make your ideas a reality, and perhaps one day lead, allowing people to do things their way..." he returned to questioning me.

If you want it done right.

"I don't have trust issues," I grumbled. The words haunted my mind, after everything that had been in my path.

"I'm serious, the shit the studio pulled on you and what else they may have had in store, I understand. But if you're fucking serious about your cause, taking back the city, protecting the dreams of artists, and supporting your family, I might have the answer."

He wasn't wrong. Not completely.

"What did you have in mind?"

"Maybe you need people with power for the future?" he said plainly.

"Like the metaphor, like superheroes? What? You think I need business people with power?" I might have been overthinking it.

If an eye roll could be heard over the phone, it was then. "No, I mean you need to look into a club like mine." Memphis was in one in North Carolina, but he had said that they weren't going to expand, at least not anytime soon.

"How the fuck is that going to work?" I yelled, only to look around to see if anyone else heard the craziness.

"If you'd let me explain, before jumping my throat." He groaned, "I said that it would take a few phone calls, and I meant it. Rawlings, my Prez, knows a club that expanded over there. I mean if you're open, you'd prospect, prove your loyalties, and then build on your idea; a safe place for artists. I can't promise anything," he explained.

Another MC around here? Maybe I was blind to it, I never saw anything.

I thought about Pop's old club and that everything was disbanded.

"You really think that's a good idea? Getting involved with a club? Aren't there rules about legacies or whatever?" I retorted.

"If you plead your case and interest, they may be open."

"Oh yeah, a washed up, angry music star turning to a motorcycle club that one day hopes to help the community or the very least, take back what we are owed." The ideas were stupid. No one was going to be that open to an idea. It's about money and power.

I didn't have a true mind for business, but I had the passion to fight for power.

"You are the most creative bastard I have ever met. You can convince anyone, throw your charm. You bring to the table your intentions, show them that you mean business. That's if I can get you a meeting." Memphis was trying.

The poor sap of my brother with the bleeding heart.

I tossed around the idea. I was going to let fate choose for me. If Memphis were to get me a meeting then I'd entertain the idea and plan for the future and if not, I'd have to wait and see.

The Memphis chapter of the Saint's Outlaws MC was founded in 1998. They had settled and kept a lower profile. At least I didn't know they were in the area. And when Memphis worked a miracle and by the good graces of the chrome gods, I met with the Saint's Outlaws president at the time. And honestly, I was scared shitless.

They raised good questions. "Why now, pretty boy? Just because you know a person who knows a person, doesn't mean jack shit."

Memphis gave me a warning about what the process might be like to be a part of this club, but with how my life turned up, I was craving a change, and a way to take back the power over my life.

"Because there's something about power that was taken from me, and I want a second chance for that, but I have to earn it. But

I'm not the only one, this whole community as you've seen thrives on each other like artists, culinary arts, and history intact. And when outsiders get a hold of it and take from people, problems start arriving. One day it might come to the chapter, and then what? If you don't have like minded people, people who know this area truly and what it would take to keep the power in balance and in your hands, what happens? I hope to help do that for you, when I prove my loyalty to the chapter, to the club."

They started to tell me that I was too young, or that my "cute" speech didn't tell them enough for my reason. They even attempted to tempt me with being a nomad after prospecting until I was ready. I wasn't ready to leave my city.

When they repeated the question about why, then told me that I would be the only one that could see what I was talking about, I finally let loose.

I sighed. "Because I think I can help you with making more legit businesses that will help the community as well, creative souls that can become a part of the chapter, and help cover anything. Showing those that the Saint's own this city."

They looked at me like I was crazy, either that or they were actually considering what I had to say at that moment.

"You think I'm the only misunderstood, disgraced artist around here, people who are sick that the community is flooding with even more shady people, taking over things for monopolies? There's a number of people that you can band together and they'll show the town of blues that they'll sing their tune if you let them. Hell, they'll help rule this town if anything."

They thought for a moment before they finally told me, "You're lucky that you come recommended. You do realize that it's not that simple. You may have ideas, but it's going to take time, and you don't get a voice in the beginning. The club didn't get far without a fight, a fight that you can't fathom."

I replied with a widest grin because I knew the path that was ahead of me, and I started to believe that I would pay any price to one day make the club a true power name, one that would shut down anyone. One that fear would drip from the souls that attempted to cross us. I was young, a dreamer, and an angry soul.

With a curve of their smile, we shook on it and I was going to begin something new, something in my control. For once, I was back with my voice.

Before they left, one of the members embraced me, with a pat on the back, and said, "Sounds like a little hound dog is finding his bite."

The name stuck with me.

From there on, a new image began to form.

Before they left, they tasked me with showing them my loyalty by getting an additional soul on board, to prove to them that there was a band of people that shared why I wanted my reasons for wanting to be an Outlaw and what I saw in the community.

I had one person in mind. One that would charm the pants off of anyone, one that I could count on, and would step in to pick up the fight with me.

There were a couple of people I knew that would be on my side, a couple outlaws ready for a higher purpose.

I walked into a particular bar one night and saw a happy, go-lucky man tossing drinks like it was his art, Connor Davidson. The charismatic blues singer knew how to turn on the charm and the soul, but unfortunately was burned a few too many times, literally and unfortunately physically.

I grabbed his attention and he flashed a wide smile in my direction. I nodded to the back of the bar, he followed suit. I picked the most private table, one I could find in the busiest time of the place.

Connor walked toward me with a beer in his hand. "It's on the house."

"Like I was going to pay." I laughed, giving him a brotherly embrace.

Connor and I met in the wrong place at the right time. Well, depending on who was telling the story.

When I was testing the waters of the music scene and taking chances on different establishments, I made the wrong choice and booked myself in a blues lounge. I didn't know it at the time and when I went to the bar, a blonde, heavily tattooed, suave man greeted me.

At first I thought the man was coming on to me, flirting with me. But I later found out it was just his personality, a way to get people to trust him easily and ultimately get his way a time or two. When he told me that I looked like I didn't belong there, I was on the verge of laying the man on the floor at his insinuation.

He slid a drink in my direction and told me to look around. Only when I did, my eyes were opened to what type of establishment it was, a genre that I had no interest on doing.

As I attempted to leave, after being utterly embarrassed, Connor thought he would fuck with me and called my name to the stage. I tried to get him to take back my name but the bastard thought I was joking with him. When he ultimately realized that it was true that I made a mistake, he turned it into an impromptu performance for himself and having me as his accompaniment.

After that we became fast friends, where most days it was him being a sounding board to things going on with the studio.

"What can I do for you? According to my Nash Young calendar you should be finishing up new songs," Connor joked with me.

I gave him a half somber look at the mention of the studio. It had only been two weeks, but it felt like a lifetime ago. Connor thought I was still joking. But I think when he saw that I avoided any new news about the progress of the new album or anything about the studio, he shut up.

"Brother, what happened?" he asked. His voice grew worried.

I simply shook my head, reminding myself that what was done was done. "Nothing that wasn't already a plan in the making."

"Oh my God, you finally left. You put your big boy pants on and walked away." He started back up with his antics, pretending to wipe a tear away from him. "I'm so damn proud of you!"

I sipped on the beer in front of me and avoided his eye contact. "Oh no, what the fuck you do now?"

"I left, but probably almost killed someone due to setting a fire in the studio."

"You torched the place?"

"Cleansing by fire."

Connor just laughed it off, like it was the most normal thing to do. "So now what? What's next?"

"How about prospecting for a motorcycle club chapter with me?"

He cocked his head, assessing to see if I had gone mental, if he heard what I just said correctly. The bar's noise grew in our silence. Connor stared at me like he was waiting for me to tell him it was a joke and I just missed seeing him.

When my face became serious, his own laughter stopped. "You're not kidding."

"Nope."

"And that's what's next? A club."

"Connor, what would you say if you could take back something that was taken from you and your name was more feared and respected than looked down on?"

It was no secret that Connor hadn't performed in a long time, but he still cared about others doing what they love.

"I'd say that it's a pipe dream."

"What if it wasn't a dream, but reality knocking at your door?"

He shook his head in disbelief. "Nash, what good would it do?"

I looked at him dead in his eyes, all faith and seriousness in my voice. "The good would be taking back the city that is built on dreams and history, taking back the power to control the music, the art here. The good is we protect those that want to start here and be what they want, but gain more in our favor."

"So this is about money?" he questioned me.

I couldn't lie to him. "Partially yes, but money is power these days. But you and I both know what it's like when you get screwed by the people who hold your future in the palms of their hands and dangle it like it's a carrot and you're the fucking rabbit."

He took a deep breath and let it out slowly. I could see the wheels turning in his head. He was tossing the idea back and forth. He took one glance between the bar and the busy crowd, then looked me back in the eyes.

"What's next?" he asked.

After that night, it was like the path was paved in the right direction.

Chapter 3

HOUND DOG

10 years later

You never know what the top feels like until you've reached it only to look and see that there's more to conquer.

I was no longer Nash Lane or Nash Young in my world.

In the ten years that I made that decision and moved up in rank, we owned the city on our own terms. Sure there was some strife and hardships, especially when the Razor Hogs MC attempted to tell us that it was their city first. On top of that, the pandemic did not give any grace. Just like the world, we lost a few brothers and loved ones.

It was helpful to have Pop's guidance and reminders of how it used to be. The Saint's gave us a chance and thankfully through trial and error, things had been going according to plan. We opened a few legit businesses, night clubs, an indie recording studio, a few burlesque lounges, a couple art warehouses of rented spaces and other ventures.

When I set out to help create this chapter, I wasn't letting up on making the city ours in the way of artists. If anything it was also the perfect cover up for the unlawful things that kept us involved with the businesses of "moving" things that needed to be moved. And if that included a few drug runs, we didn't say no.

The only thing is I instilled rules like never selling on our property or to true addicts. It was too messy to try and cover up someone's mistakes or habits.

I hadn't touched music since I left that studio. Never had that inner muse and for the longest time it killed me. Time went on and that feeling disappeared. I surrounded myself with other distractions, some business and some pure pleasure.

The summer months were coming to an end which meant a few things; college was soon to be back in session, more last minute trips, and my favorite fall season coming. The fall nights meant better business with the temperatures dropping. Although every night seemed to be great with our businesses.

One of the first businesses we opened was the Blue Sax. I didn't pick the name, that would be courtesy of my V.P, B.B, who was once Connor.

B.B had a wild idea one night to make a bar and lounge a nod to his love of the blues and a big ass middle finger to those that thought he would never do it. Those people are eating their words now.

The Blue Sax was known for their open mic Friday nights. So when I walked in one Friday night, it was like a typical Friday or so I thought.

"Prez, what are you doing here?" Stray, one of my members called from behind the bar. The place was looking packed for the open mic night. People brushed past to meet with friends, artists drummed their fingers on the tables waiting for their names to be called.

"Just came to do a pick up. Just helping Hank and one of the prospects tonight," I told him as I went behind the bar as well, pouring myself a beer.

"What? The prospect screwed up the last drop?" Stray questioned as he served the patrons.

"Waylan is just a slow learner," I huffed out.

"Why did you think that allowing your cousin to prospect would be the best?" Stray laughed. I shot him a look to not push the subject. I knew that it wasn't the brightest idea involving family, especially young families to want to come be a part of the club. But Waylan was determined and still proving his worth.

I went to the back locked office to grab the partial deposits to bring back to the club so I could make the full deposits on the following Monday. I looked out at the Blue Sax, and the sense of accomplishment washed over me, reminding me that making the decision ten years ago had been worth it.

The system that I put into place worked, we made profits from the businesses, kept everyone happy and businesses a float. I did that. I took back control after all these years.

Everything was working and the club was thriving. I created that, I created this family, this community, and the name of the Saints struck fear to those that tried to take it away from me, from us.

Everything was blissful, the city was under our control and I couldn't have asked for better brothers.

Unfortunately, I didn't get very far that night. When I went to leave., Stray called me back over, his face twisted in annoyance.

"What now?" I growled out. His eyes darted between myself and whatever was behind me.

"Heads up boss man, had a few crowds coming in here harassing some of the singers. Had young Blaze settle them."

Great, just what I needed.

Privileged college students coming down here to cause trouble in our bar. My eyes rolled so far in the back of my head they might as well have been stuck there.

"Blaze have any trouble?" I asked. Stray shook his head.

A sense of relief flooded through me. I didn't need any trouble. I didn't want to test the boundaries between us and our cop friends.

I looked behind me and saw the crowded table of polo shirts wearing boys, bending down to hear what the others were saying. They were snickering at something. I was ready just to "politely" ask them to leave, but if it was under control then I didn't need to be involved.

"You going to go, or you staying for a few acts?" Stray asked with an empty glass in his hand, waiting for my answer.

With a deep sigh, I said, "Might as well since I'm here. Just let me go put this back." I lifted the bag of deposits in my hand.

As I hurried down the hallway and turned, I bumped into someone, throwing my shoulder back. With the fire of annoyance from the pep boys I fired out, "Watch where you're going."

Only when I turned, I was greeted by a pair of beautiful hazel green eyes that glimmered somehow in the dim light of the hallway.

"I'm so sorry, I didn't mean to run into you. I should have been more careful," her soft voice stammered out.

At that moment, I felt like the worst asshole. She had that angelic type of stunning in my eyes, one that stopped me in my tracks. I couldn't tear my eyes away from her. I tried to speak to apologize before she took off back into the bar area. I wanted to chase after her, apologize, only to just be around her a few more minutes.

I couldn't do that, I remembered that a man like me had no business with a pure looking soul like hers. She looked to be the type of person that needed a gentleman in her life, someone that knew how to be soft with her.

And yet those eyes stirred something in me that I couldn't shake.

Stick with what you know. One time. Get it and leave them.

I couldn't get attached to someone, especially not in the beginning. What kind of life could I have offered? Better to be single than think about the safety of someone else, much less be a bargaining tool. It was easier to live alone.

One by one new or local artists come up to the stage and each one of them were testing the audience as if they were figuring out their sound. It's a pure miracle when artists find their sound, their signature.

Sometimes it was like a drinking game, spotting the similar traits. Adjusting the microphone, going into a long monologue about their first love and how they wrote that song for them, or my favorite the young females that try to imitate the new younger singers of today.

I didn't miss those days, the days where you never knew what kind of audience you'd get, whether they were first time listeners or fans that followed your career. I didn't miss the days where you had to debate on the flow of your set.

A few were good, showing they had the passion for their music, as they fell into their comfort zones and were rewarded with the wave of applause.

I had about enough watching them all until the next performer caught my eye.

"Welcome to the stage Ms. Melody Rae," the announcer joyfully said.

A few claps and hollers followed as my eyes saw the little beauty that knocked into me. I couldn't take my eyes off of her. Her hands shook, her steps were light but rushed on stage. Her acoustic guitar swung on her back. Her little blue and white cotton dress showed off her voluptuous breasts and her curvy hips.

She looked like a forbidden treasure that I was tempted to find out more.

Melody Rae.

Fuck, even her name was a siren call.

She looked so small, like the stage would eat her alive.

She stood at the mic stand, her body trembling as she reached for the guitar. A cue for her background track to hit; as the music came on she fumbled with her pick. Her nerves were taking over.

She finally looked back in the audience, her voice shaking, "I'm sorry." Before I knew it she was off the stage and I was off my seat.

The crowd grew restless between the already drunk assholes and the ones going along with the crowd. A few were booing Melody, a few were heckling, throwing around the lines of what they would have done. Then there were the ones that spouted that she shouldn't have been on the stage to begin with.

Some people are born for the stage and some people are simply more for the background. But call it a hunch, I think she could be one of the pure artists that knew what she wanted, she just had the unfortunate stage fright that wasn't conquered yet.

I tried to track her in the busy bar but she vanished with her things and went out the back door.

"Tough luck. She seemed like a cutie," Stray commented behind me. "You good boss?"

My eyes spotted the swing of the side door to the alley, and unfortunately a couple troublemaking bastards followed her. Blaze saw what I saw, I just held up my hand signaling him to stay put. Seemed like my night was about to get interesting.

Chapter 4

MELODY

What the hell was I thinking?

I knew it was going to be a miracle to walk on that stage and perform. And yet I overhyped myself.

I mentally kept hitting myself, muttering to myself on how stupid I had been to think that I could do it, that I could conquer my fear on that stage.

I hated the feeling of failing, again. But looking in that audience at the eyes that silently waited to judge me, made the flood of thoughts too much. My heart traveled to my ears, humming so loudly that it was deafening. My breathing became harder and the sweat dripping from my neck was unbearable.

My voice was so shaky that simply saying that I was sorry wasn't enough. It wasn't enough for me to continue on. I just ran.

Not only did I feel like a failure, but I felt like a fool for being up there.

A few tears started to build up as I gathered my stuff and exited the building. I backed myself to the bricked wall outside the place, once I got out. I dropped my stuff, sliding down the wall, burying my face between my knees. The only other light was the dim light from the alley and the half moon that rose at night in the sky.

Breathe in. Breathe out.

For the longest time, stage fright had been my weakness, preventing me from rising through the ranks. I always stood in the background, watching all the stars rising in their own journey. To say I had stars in my eyes would've been an understatement.

I wanted more, I wanted to see the world, and do nothing more than to spread my words.

I knew that the first step would be to start small and move from there. But I couldn't even do that. The feeling that I was going to be stuck my entire life flashed in my mind. The words of my father telling me that the path I was on was a useless, childish dream that in the end I was just a disappointment echoed.

If he could see me at that moment, he'd taunt me and tell me he was right.

I wasn't ready, and maybe I wasn't ever going to be.

I sat there on the wall for a while before something startled me as the alley way, light started to dim. I didn't know if I was in danger or if someone was truly coming to comfort me. Which was still a ridiculous thought.

A demanding voice jolted me from my position, "Look what we have here, boys. A pretty little, scared thing. What's wrong sweetheart, those people scare you?" I opened my eyes, lifting my head to see a linen shirt wearing blonde man inches away from my face.

My eyes darted around me only to find that I was surrounded by a group of strange men. It didn't take a genius to realize that I was in danger. If the shiver down my spine didn't warn me, then what his friends did next seared the memory of their touch into my skin. His friends suddenly grabbed my arms, hoisting me up, almost floating me above the ground.

"Please. Let me go. I don't have any money. There's nothing I can give you," I begged, trying to find the strength to loosen their grip on me. Their fingers dug into my skin like a bruising claim. The pain radiated into my bones. If I shouted for help, who would come to rescue me? No one here was going to miss me.

"But I think that there is something you can give me." His eyes surveyed me like I was a thing, an object to have.

I didn't like it. I didn't like feeling like I was anything else. My lips trembled. I tried to feel anything but helpless, let alone worthless.

The blonde chuckled, gripping my chin hard. I did the impulsive thing and spit in his face. Not my best self-defense, but I didn't know what else to do. Fear took over like it was the only thing left in me. My eyes widened as the blonde man growled and his eyes turned cold, absolutely blank. He wanted to render me to be quiet and submissive, to be afraid of him.

He got off on the fear, and the pain. It encouraged him to continue, the thirst to break down everything I am. He could smell that I wasn't the strongest, that maybe I would put up a fight. Maybe he wanted me to be grateful that someone was paying attention to me.

My head fell to the side after his hand crashed into my face. I let out a scream, but it made my head spin. My head lulled back to see him.

"I see you still have some fight in you." His buddies came closer in, trapping me further down this darkness. "I'm sure we can get it out of you before we take each of these holes."

I shook my head, questioning why I was the target. I never spoke with them, never looked in their direction. I didn't know any of them and yet they picked me like a doe in an open field. I wanted to scream, but again who would hear me? Everyone else was too busy inside and there were no windows lending a view of the alley. And I couldn't rely on the people walking on the street. Beale street was the busiest with every nightclub and bar opening their doors.

I tried to yank against their hold again. "Please, just let me go and I won't tell anyone."

"Who would listen to you?" the blonde asked. The hot tears poured out like a flowing river down my cheeks.

"Are these tears for us?" He groaned out like he was enjoying this. I couldn't handle this anymore. I started to kick my legs in any direction, trying to get them all to back up or even let go of me.

As I started kicking, I was frantic enough that it spooked them. Their hold loosened on me as they were confused. They started to raise their voices and as soon as I got loose and dropped to the ground, my feet started to take off. I attempted to grab my backpack and my guitar case.

The goal was in sight, freedom was calling my name until someone grabbed my shoulder and dragged me back down. Another scream ripped from my throat. My head banged on the rough cement. I gripped my head trying to ease the throb radiating there. Suddenly a new kind of pain happened when a foot landed to my side, I hunched over, wrapping my arms around myself.

"I think it's time to break a little mouse," the same taunting voice echoed. His friends responded, agreeing with him.

I knew that this was it, everything would come down to this. Broken bones, a weakened body that couldn't protect itself, and worst, a dream that was fading.

The guys landed a few kicks, breaking down what existing barrier I had left. I begged and whimpered for things to stop, for someone to help me. My world was darkened and I wasn't going to find out if sunshine would ever warm my face.

If this was the end, at least Aria would be waiting for me at the gates, waiting for me to take her hand.

Wouldn't that have been nice?

I thought my world was ending when suddenly a thunderous *bang* brought everything to a halt.

Chapter 5

Hound Dog

Trouble followed us anywhere. If it wasn't the Razor Hogs, another troublesome and pain in my ass MC, then it was stupid assholes like those fellows.

I knew trouble was going to happen for that little Melody girl but when I saw the prep boys ushering out of the building I knew the night was about to be crappier.

What I didn't expect was to see them hovering over her like she was a piece of meat. And kicking a lady, now that is way too far on my scale. We never harmed women, even if they were a bitch sometimes. The sense of guilt flooded me seeing the little songbird in pain. I should have gotten there quicker.

I could hear her groan, her body hunched over. My vision blurred into a fiery red, blazing with pure anger.

I didn't think, I just acted, leading me to firing my gun in the air. It was more of a warning shot. But it got their attention.

The boys whipped their heads up as I pointed the barrel in their direction. Only two scenarios played in my head; one, they came quietly while we called the police or two, it wouldn't be warning shots anymore.

"We got a problem here?" I asked, not caring about what their answers were.

"Nothing to see here," one of the fuckers said, I think it was the dark-haired one, or the blonde. Honestly, I didn't care who said it, I wanted them out of my alley way and away from her.

"Well, apparently it is because you're in my alleyway and hurting *my* singer." It sounded possessive. Truly didn't mean to say *my* singer, but erring on the side of caution, I'd claim her as mine or ours, at least hoping that they were smart enough to realize their mistakes.

There was only so much hope for humanity.

"Didn't think she was yours, old man. Don't worry we'll take her off your hands." The blonde one actually laughed.

I cracked my neck; it wasn't going to turn out pretty. I stepped closer, debating on whether to call for backup. There were four of them and one of me. It was stupid not to call them, but this was one battle I planned on winning.

As I stepped closer, the boys charged as well. These pretty boys thought they could show up and "own" anything they wanted.

Not in my town, not in my business, and not to the poor soul they treated like a soccer ball.

"I'll give you a chance to make the right choice. Get your asses inside and we'll let the police handle it or I'll make you look unrecognizable." I clicked the gun, "Your choice."

They snickered back, like they didn't believe me. I gave them a chance to make it right, but my hope in human decency was out the window and had been for a long time.

"You ain't going to do shit, old man, you're not going to touch a hair on our heads unless you want your little business to stay open," blondie said.

"Is that a threat you little piss ant?"

"Not if it's a promise." He reached into his pocket, probably to get a small pocket knife that was supposed to scare me.

There was ambition in their eyes, thinking that I was easily scared off, but they must have been blind not to see the cut that I wore or the emblem that is patched on it. "Last warning, boys," I growled out.

The stupid blonde lunged forward, only to be elbowed in the back by me as he brushed past me. Another man tried to wrap his hands around me, only to be rewarded with a bullet to the foot.

The shot rang out and the other two lackeys that were left behind looked at each other trying to agree on what would come next.

Before they decided, I felt a heavy body collide with mine, wrapping me in a tight neck hold. He smelt of too much booze and sweat. His grip tightened around me, as his height brought me down for a moment, the force of weight bringing both of us down. I landed on top of him, the fall knocked the wind out of us, as my gun clacked to the side.

The two other guys came barreling, attempting to grab my wrists. The fight in me wasn't going to give up. As soon as they came in my direction, my feet kicked out hitting their shins and bringing them down to my level. My boots kicked each one of them in the face, shoving them down further to the ground.

Blondie rolled around on the ground again. His agonizing groans made me smile slightly. I bent down to pick up my gun, checking the safety on it before walking back over to him. I crouched down, tapping the gun to his leg.

"Could have had an easier solution, you stupid boy," I said. I holstered my gun.

I grabbed the slime ball by his shirt, bringing him up to face me. "You touched someone that doesn't belong to you. And now you'll remember this." I yanked his face to the patch on my cut, the one that said "president". "You'll remember next time, I won't lay your ass out on the street. You'll end up in an empty tomb, with no name. Fuck around with the Saints again, and there'll be no tomorrow."

"You don't know who my father is," he said, his voice weak.

"No, and I don't give a fuck." With that, my fist connected to his jaw and the man fell to the ground. He didn't move a muscle, laying there limply. "Around here, we're still gentlemen. Guess you lost your manners with that silver spoon in your mouth."

I didn't care what was broken, how much noise this would make, or even who they were. There were two things I worried about: my club and a hurt little bird that didn't ask for any of this.

I walked toward the woman, Melody. She hadn't moved since I arrived. Everything in me froze when I bent down to check her pulse, hoping that she was still breathing. My mind spun thinking of the next step.

I didn't know whether to get her to the hospital, which meant police might be involved or take her to my home, a safe place, and watch over her and allow her to make the next move.

Need control.

My hands ran through my hair. I had called her mine, made her feel like a possession to the bar or as a singer. I didn't know what the hell I was saying. I didn't know why I felt the way I felt, like she was reaching inside me and shining a light on the empty heart I thought I had.

I pushed her hair to the side, brushing it away from her face. The back of my hand grazed her cheek. A bit of dark red blood smeared across, probably from where one of them hit her. Seeing her like this boiled my blood. The thought that someone would harm her, rattled me and I didn't know why.

She was beautiful, that's what caught my eye in the first place. I wanted nothing more than to talk with her, keep her safe. The purity in her prescenes made something in me move in a way that scared me.

Snap out of it. It's just a woman. You're just helping a woman.

Only it felt like I was going to be wrong. This feeling was throwing me off. Everything in the past ten years has been planned and in order. One little birdie was going to throw everything into a tailspin.

I pulled out my phone and called Twitty, our Sergeant at Arms. Lord knew that if I called B.B he'd be either knee deep in pussy or planning to be.

After two rings, Twitty's bass voice pierced through the phone, "Prez."

"Twitty, I need you tonight," I looked around laughing to myself at the mess needing to be cleaned.

"What the hell you'd break now?" he growled. The roughneck was a former bouncer and bodyguard. The man was the epitome of brute strength. Yet when you got to know him, he reminded me of my brother, a hidden soft side. Emphasis on the hidden part.

"Let's see, possibly a broken femur, a couple concussions, a broken jaw, maybe a nose," I started to list off as I peaked at the aftermath and the light, barely audible groans.

"Went a little wild, did we?"

"Fuckers had it coming."

"Do I need to get Greene involved?"

I sighed. "Might as well give him a heads up." Last thing I wanted was to get him involved.

"What happened?" Twitty asked.

"A few drunk idiots decided on being monsters and assaulted one of the singers from tonight." I gave him the short version.

"Where's the girl?" he asked.

"I got her, don't worry about it." It came out a little harsher than intended.

"Want Shooter to come check her out?" Twitty asked.

I thought about it for a moment. Shooter used to be a former army medic who came recommended by Memphis's member D.R. One of the best decisions, but I didn't need him right away. I shook my head. "No, if I need anything then I'll call."

"Alright Prez. For now, then, clean up?" he asked, reassuring me that I knew what we were doing.

"Make it sparkling clean," I ordered before hanging up the phone.

I attempted to wake her up, enough to where she could consent. I didn't know if it would work or not. "Honey, I need you to show me a sign that you're listening." I gently shook her, listening for a groan or looking for some kind of movement. I tried again after no success.

After the second time, I heard a small whimper that tugged at my heart. Her eyes started to spring tears down her face.

"I got you, little songbird. Can you look at me?" I pressed the question, hoping I'd get a response before I scooped her up and took her to the truck. Her whimpers turned into groans as she attempted to lift her head, one of her eyes starting to open.

I couldn't tell if the other one was bruised or coated in dry blood. "Jesus Christ, hold on for me. I'm going to move, I'm going to help you. Okay?" I said in a soft voice.

Just trust me for a moment.

She weakly nodded her head, giving me the okay to move her. I carefully scooped her up, holding her close to me. "That's it, I won't let anyone else hurt you." Her groans vibrated into my chest as I quickly got her into my truck.

She started to stir more when I got her laying down on the truck seats. I didn't live far, only a few minutes down the road. She started to mumble something, her voice still ragged.

"It's okay, you're okay," was all I could say.

She mumbled again. I leaned over, straightening her head to glance at me through her one clear eye. "What are you trying to say?" I asked again, hoping for a clearer answer.

"Case," she whispered.

"Case?" I tried to ask, betting that I wouldn't get very far. Case? What did she mean by case?

"My case," she groaned.

Her case? Then it dawned on me. Her guitar case with a backpack next to it was still in the alley. I shook my head, knowing that I needed her out of there, quickly.

"We have to go, honey."

"Please," she whimpered, blinking at me. Her look gutted me. I tossed my head back and forth debating if I was going to pull the full knight in shining armor act that I know Mama would have wanted me to do at that moment.

I let out a growl. "Stay here."

I rushed back to the alley, still seeing the boys laid out on the ground. I chuckled at the weak picture I saw.

Idiots, all of them.

I found her black, rugged case and her backpack that was thrown on the ground. I started to wonder if she had a car and where it was. I rushed, my feet picking up speed, having a little faith that the men would be there soon to clean up and make it shine. I tossed the stuff in the bed of the truck, then I was back into my seat to drive off.

She was where I left her, like I would have expected her to run off in the condition she was in.

"Honey, I'm going to move you. That means I have to put my hands on you. Are you okay with that?" I asked sincerely before touching her, although she didn't have much of a choice. But it was the thought that counted right?

She slowly moved her head, tilting her head to glance at me again. She slowly nodded her head.

There's my little fighter.

My hands hoist her closer to me, resting her head on my thigh. I wanted her comfortable, I needed her to feel safe or else this wasn't going to work. I worried about internal bleeding and bruising, maybe I needed Shooter more than I thought. I didn't know much but I learned over the years what I could and especially when Pops was in his club at the time, learned to help patch him up a few times.

Part of me wasn't ready for the whole club to be involved. I needed her to have a low profile. I'd fix her up and she'd be on her way.

Chapter 6

MELODY

If I hadn't made the choice to leave, to bolt out of that place, I wouldn't have endured this much pain. Everything hurt. I wasn't sure about a concussion, but thankfully I didn't feel dizzy and I understood what the man was saying to me.

Whoever he was.

I could sense the slight hesitation, as if he didn't know if anything was a good idea. At that moment, I didn't care, I just wanted out of the nightmare.

It was too dark to see any other features to identify him, but his voice was something smoky and intoxicating, one that would lure you into anything you desired. I shouldn't have been so trusting after what happened, but he was the one that saved me, when I was too damn weak to do anything.

The street lamps passed us as we left the main street. He was at least careful of the turns and the twists, but I had no idea where I was going. I had no other reason to trust this man.

I didn't even know his name, where we were going, or how bad things back in the alley were.

And yet I placed my trust and life in his hands.

I didn't know what to expect. The last thing I thought would happen, happened.

Why me? I didn't ask for it.

The rumble of the truck quietened down, then came to a stop.

Where are we? It's not like it's my place. Not that I really have one.

My thoughts started to scatter everywhere, but the man paused. His breaths almost lulled me to sleep for a moment. It was comfortable, even if I was still in this moment of whether to trust him or not. It wasn't like I could run.

Everything hurts.

"I know, honey. I'm going to get you better," he said.

Did this sexy-voiced man hear my thoughts? Or did my dumbass actually say it?

He chuckled. "Yes, I can hear you. I'll take that as a compliment and comfort that you're a little coherent."

"Damn it, that was supposed to be my inside thoughts," I coughed out.

"Don't talk right now, just nod or shake your head," he told me. "Save your strength." he commanded, laying my head down on the seat as he walked to the other side of the truck.

The door quietly creaked open. The light from the truck inside shined as the stranger came into better light. One look at him brought me back to running into him in the hallway back at the bar. I was embarrassed not watching where I was going and even then one look at him made me forget how to breathe.

He was like a damn giant, his height towering over me. His golden brown eyes were fixed on me, and I could see the curve of a smile beneath his medium length beard. His hair was pulled back, but if I had enough strength, my fingers would have been tangled in it. He was a vision of strength and power, and I was the little mouse that walked into a lion's den.

He gently pulled me, gliding me off of the truck bench. The pain was still radiating through me, every movement hurt then eased up. My body couldn't decide whether it wanted to whither in pain or to simply settle down and relax.

"I'm going to have to carry you. It's not going to be pleasant but I need you to trust me." He stared at me waiting.

I nodded, not like I had other options. I prepared myself for the worst, the worst meaning possibly screaming in pain. As soon as

I nodded he guided me out of the truck and scooped me up into his arms. He cradled me, walking as if I weighed nothing. I wasn't supermodel thin, and God blessed me with more hips and thighs than a flat stomach.

He made me feel like I wasn't the problem, he didn't grunt in agony as if it was the hardest thing to do. I tucked my head closer to his chest, listening to him breathe, his heart thumping inside his chest. It was musical, comforting, and for the moment, the only thing I wanted to listen to.

I tried to gather any type of information I could and answer the unknown in my head. I knew I was still near the city because it didn't take long to be in the truck. But wherever we were, it was quiet, and somehow less neighbors.

The man opened the door to a single story family home. At first glance I couldn't see anything but he put me on the couch leaning me against the big, fluffy couch pillows. My eyes adjusted to the lights in the room. He started to walk away after taking off my boots for me as gently as possible.

I sank into the cushions only to shoot straight up remembering that I was possibly bleeding.

"Blood," I yelped.

He turned back around, doing a quick glance, "Don't worry about the couch, honey. It will be worth it in the end."

He disappeared around the corner and possibly down a hallway. My eye, at least the one that didn't have blood on it, could see the quaint home, barren walls that begged for a personal touch, and a couch that was too comfy and felt too new, and the smell that felt fresh.

I wondered if this was like a safe house, a home that wasn't his.

"You think you could sit at the edge for me, I can put the pillows behind you to help brace you," he offered when he came back. I simply nodded, still keeping his command to save my voice.

"Atta girl, come on. We'll get you back up and singing in no time." He sounded confident as if he didn't know the challenges that I was going to face.

He sat on the sturdy coffee table he pulled closer to me, his knees spread open, practically straddling me, holding me in place so I didn't bolt. Using a dampened cloth, he carefully cleaned my other eye. My face tensed at the tender touch of the cloth.

"I'm not much of a singer. I couldn't even get up there and sing." The words hurt more than the aches that shot through my muscles. The man's hands stopped for a second then a breath escaped him.

"It takes time," he admitted.

Yeah, right. Time was never on my side. It took more skill and confidence to stay up on a stage without the fear of everyone's silent thoughts.

His gentle touch returned to my face, cleaning the blood that crusted there. The slight sting from the disinfectant made me flinch. He was very sensitive around my eye, but thankfully he was able to clear it up. My vision started to become blurry, adjusting to the light that was hitting me.

He handed me an ice pack, adjusting it to my ribs; he could tell by my movement that the pain was coming from there. The instant memory of holding myself as those guys repeatedly kicked me ran through my mind. My body started to tremble, shaking at every moment that happened. He grabbed my hands, his thumb caressing my hand.

I glanced up at him; his eyes were warm. I just nodded, taking deep breaths, shaking off the feeling, the tortured thoughts. His eyes turned proud, his voice soft. "Atta girl."

He returned to cleaning up, he just couldn't clean the bruises that were forming.

"You got a name songbird?" he asked as I jolted at the nickname. I didn't know how I felt being called that. I didn't think it was an insult.

I found my voice again to answer him. "Melody."

"Seems fitting," he said, with a charming smile.

My cheeks flushed, how could he think it was fitting? I didn't see what he was seeing. Come morning, I would be a "fleeting" thought.

My voice was raspy, "What do I call my savior?"

It was only fair, he knew my name, and I wanted to know his.

"Hound Dog or Hound."

I knew from my own motorcycle club romances that it was his road name, not his given name.

"No seriously?" I asked again, hoping that it would be different the second time.

"Hound is what most people call me. Hound Dog seems too formal." There went the cocky smile, like he was charming me or something.

I formed the word, "Hound."

He froze at the mention of his name. His hand traveled across my face, caressing it. It was like sparks that lit up the sky on the Fourth of July.

He cleared his throat, dropping the cloth and the bandages that he used to patch me up. He looked around then met my eyes again. "I'm going to look at your abdomen, which means that I need to lift your shirt."

I froze as well. Feeling like I was already naked, vulnerable in his eyes, but to have him see more of me was frightening. "Easy. You control this. I want to make sure that you haven't gotten any additional bruising. I want to see if I really need to take you to the hospital."

Was he trying to keep this under wraps? Was I a secret? Or a part of a murder that happened while knocked out?

"Why are you doing this? You seem like you do whatever you need to?" I spat out.

That came out of nowhere and a sense of guilt flooded me. I snapped at someone that seemed to want to help. He didn't get mad, he didn't yell, his face didn't twist in regret.

"Because as much as I want you to report this to the police and go to the hospital, you need to make that decision. But know that, whatever you choose, I'll be there to help you. Don't need to ask," he said tenderly.

Well, holy shit and fuck me sideways.

Chapter 7

HOUND DOG

She was a little spitfire when she wanted to be. She looked at me like she'd never had someone give her a choice or give her an ounce of respect, let alone care for her. Whatever had happened in her life that forced her to turn into fight mode crushed me.

At that moment, I knew I was in trouble. She could have me wrapped around her like a clingy new puppy.

She nodded, agreeing to let me see her body.

"How about this, what if you just lift it up around your bra line and if I need to see more, you do what you feel comfortable with," I offered. As much as I was a twisted bastard and hardass, I could be a gentleman to those that deserve it. "Can you move that much?"

She nodded, resorting back to her quiet self.

"When you're ready, Melody." I waited.

She slowly leaned forward and inched her sweaty wet shirt up her body. She winced at every movement. Her soft looking skin tempted me to reach out and just touch for my own pleasure. She revealed luscious curves that outlined the already beautiful woman I saw before me.

Little red splotches colored her light pink skin. The imprints of the kicks left behind. If I could take them back, I would have. Imprints that overpowered the delicate ink that spreads across her skin. It was music measures that twisted along the side, it was gorgeous like her. A stark contrast to the ink that plagued my skin.

My mind wanted to read it, to play it, to hear whatever it was. What a little walking temptation she was.

"Stay where you are," I told her, getting to my feet and walking behind the couch to get a better view of her back.

My fingers softly touched her skin, and goosebumps met my fingertips. Her back was sprouting the same red splotches. None of them were darker telling me so far we were in the clear. I pulled out my phone, silently taking a few photos, sending them to Otis, B.B, Twitty, and Shooter.

My fingers returned to graze her skin, traveling toward the bottom of her neck. I didn't think she knew but I heard a small whimper, a pleasurable kind. Every little sound and movement she made tugged on my heart strings, when it shouldn't.

"What's your pain level?" I asked. I didn't see any bleeding or signs of extensive internal bleeding, she just needed to get cleaned up and rest.

"Like everytime I move, I'll break." she admitted, quietly. "But, I can handle it."

"I'm here to fix that." I smiled. "Do you think you can eat? I definitely need you to drink something."

I pulled her shirt back down, resisting the urge to cradle her into my arms for the rest of the night.

Fuck, what was she turning me into?

"I'm not very hungry," she protested, her voice was a little shaky. I called bullshit on her statement.

"You need to have something in your stomach for the pain meds I'm about to give you." I started to raise my voice, but stopped.

Her eyes widened, her body shrunk, then she laughed. "What are you a doctor or something?"

"No, but one of my men was. I trust him." I also trusted the ample supply of pain medications that Shooter stocked piled everyone. Only in emergencies, he said. And right now was an emergency.

I walked into the kitchen. I didn't have much in this house. This was just a house, not a home. I was at the clubhouse mainly, sticking close when times called. There wasn't much use for me to come here. I bought it on a whim, a dream for one day. A day that faded away from my mind.

"The guest bedroom is down the hall, and there's a bathroom in there. I laid out some clothes if you would like to change. Feel free to use the shower, I recommend it, it will help soothe the pain." I turned my back away from the open living room.

"Recommending or commanding?" Melody sighed, "Look, you've done enough for me, I need to go."

Go ahead little songbird, fight back.

"Melody, I would suggest you listen before I really take matters into my own hands," I quipped back. She still didn't have a choice, I'd get her to eat somehow.

"Be careful, Hound Dog, someone might take back the gentleman title."

"Honey, you couldn't handle my bite. Now, be a good girl and trust me." I turned to look at her, and her watchful eyes dared me.

It took so much strength not to rush to her side and do whatever I needed to, whether that was strip her bare and toss her ass in the shower and into my clothes or force feed her while she was in my lap.

Lucky for her, she did what she was told as she scurried out of the living room, and I welcomed the sound of the shower turning on. She wasn't going anywhere, she was going to rest her pretty little head here. And in the morning, she would leave and my world would return to normal.

Moments later, she returned, walking slowly back to the couch. She was a beautiful curvy woman, but even in my shirt, she looked tiny. And the shorts gave her plump behind little to no shape, though the temptation to palm it was strong. The sight of her became intoxicating, for a brief moment I knew I wasn't going to wish her out of those clothes.

"Eat and come take these meds," I called her.

She switched directions, making her way into my kitchen. She sat at the little two-person table I had. I handed over the grilled cheese, apples, and the water. She pinned her stare to the food and then back at me.

"I didn't poison it." I chuckled.

"That's what they all say." She raised an eyebrow.

I grabbed the other chair, flipping it around, grabbed the sandwich and bit the corner of it. She watched my every movement. She looked at me intensely, then wet her bottom lip. The warm sandwich melted in my mouth. I made a damn good sandwich.

As I finished chewing, I turned the sandwich back to her, holding it close to her mouth. She didn't grab it. She wanted to push a little bit, fight me a little. "Open."

One word. That's all it took for her to soften up, and open that pretty little mouth. She leaned forward, taking the sandwich in her mouth. "Eat," I told her.

With wide, soft eyes, she bit down and stayed there. Melody was waiting on something, something from me. She started to chew on the bite of the sandwich. Those beautiful eyes were pleading.

"Good girl."

She liked to be praised, the curve of her mouth told me so. I offered the sandwich again and she took another bite. Melody finally took the sandwich out of my hands. The woman couldn't tell me that she wasn't hungry, she scarfed it down like it was her last meal. I passed the two oxys her way. Hopefully she didn't have an allergic reaction.

"You allergic to anything?"

She shook her head.

She quickly grabbed the medication and the water and took it. A sigh of relief escaped me.

I would feel better in the morning knowing how she was going to get past all this and move on with her life.

She finished her plate. She curled up in the chair, looking around. I could see the gears twisting in her mind.

"I hope this is your place," she said.

"Well, if you wanted to come to my place, you didn't have to get yourself in all that trouble." I laughed. I was somewhat joking with her. She didn't laugh. "I'm kidding. I'm sorry that was horrible. Yes, this is my house. You're safe here."

She sucked in her bottom lip, she had this switch between fight or flight, I was sure she was giving herself whiplash.

"I wasn't going to take you to the clubhouse."

"Why not?" she quipped back.

"Because right now, you're mine to take care of, and having you enter the outlaw's compound, I'd have blood on the floor."

She jolted back, but then relaxed at the mention of *mine*. I had to be careful. I didn't know what kind of damage was going to be done.

"Thank you," she whispered.

Melody didn't need to express her gratitude. But it was appreciated.

"You need to rest," I quickly said. Her presence was doing something I hadn't done in years. I smiled.

She simply nodded, pushing the chair back. She stood up and walked away. But not before she bent down to kiss my cheek.

The tender sentiment threw me off. I brushed aside whatever feeling this was and shoved it down to the bottom of my core.

"Good night, Hound," she whispered as she went back to the guest bedroom. I hoped she would rest and dream of sunshine and of tomorrow.

My hands flexed, shaking the thought of one day she could be mine. I shouldn't want her, but I did.

I couldn't help but watch her later, chalking it up to checking to make sure she didn't have a concussion or trouble breathing.

Her little moans of content had me in knots. A few times she whimpered after she tossed and turned. I ached to be closer, to hold her. It was the protective instinct that all I wanted was for her to be okay. Hoping maybe she was dreaming of me.

This quick infatuation was not me. I took, I claimed, but not her. She deserved a happier ending than a deep dark path.

This is a new level of stalking, watching her sleep.

And yet, it filled me with peace.

Sleep begged me for peace as well. I carried my ass to my bed and stripped off everything. I was damn tired. Now that I had Melody resting in the other room, I could at least shut my eyes for a bit.

It felt like a blink, as a sudden creak down the hallway woke me up. Soft footsteps to match the sudden noises. Barely any morning sun shined through the windows, but enough to welcome the new day.

Little birdie is already trying to leave. I think not.

I sprang from the bed, half dressed, with sleep still in my eyes. I dared her to try to fight me, I'd entertain the idea. I leaned on the doorway, waiting for her reaction.

Melody had exchanged her sleep wear with her clothes from last night. She tiptoed out of her door, hunching over to quietly close it. She winced at every sound that came through the door. When she started to straighten up, her shoulders relaxed, thinking that she was going to get by with it.

She turned to her left, and froze in place. Like a teenager getting caught for sneaking out. I hid a tiny smile. She went speechless, but tried to find the words.

"Good morning, little songbird," I rumbled out.

Her eyes scanned my body, her chest heaved with surprise. Her mouth let out a troubled sigh, shaping it in an "o". She was speechless for more than one reason. She had me flattered. "You see something you like?" I said, teasing her. My voice was still rough from the morning.

"You're supposed to be asleep," she squeaked out.

I walked over to her, inching closer to her, her face forced to look up at me. Her auburn hair was twisted into a messy bun. She gulped.

"Trying to fly away already? Before we could even talk." I pulled a strand of her hair behind her ear.

Any closer and my lips would have been on hers, I wouldn't have complained.

She thought for a moment before saying, "Like ripping a band-aid, I thought this was easier."

I just shook my head, I wasn't completely ready to let her go. "What kind of southern man and host would I be if I didn't feed you before you scurry off?"

"Thought you said I couldn't handle your bite?" She folded her arms.

I leaned down, "Sometimes I'm wrong. Come on." I took her hand from her folded arms.

"Where are we going?" she questioned me.

"To the kitchen. I need to have coffee before I say what I want to say."

Chapter 8

MELODY

I should have escaped quicker. Or quieter. The sight of him in the morning was enough to get you on your knees and be at his beck and call.

When he scared me, I could have screamed, but the man was shirtless, his chest armored with enough muscles that showed me how easily I could be tossed around.

It had been quite a few months, almost a year or so. Shit when was the last time?

He was like a walking god, and the temptation to lick and taste everything was stronger than my will to leave.

He took care of me. He didn't have to, but the man wasn't ready to see me leave just yet and I wasn't going to fight too hard.

"Okay," I answered him. More like squeaked.

I wasn't going to say no to food, it would save me a few bucks. At least I know it didn't poison us.

I wasn't rushing only because whatever pain meds he gave me last night made me relaxed, feel at ease enough to sleep on a real bed. It was the most luxurious thing I've had to sleep on for months now. That was my barrier, my roadblock to overcome.

"I didn't think you had a lot of food here. Judging by the lack of decorations, or sense of home, you don't come here very much," I said as he began to find another pan.

"Someone must be feeling better or somewhat better." he chuckled.

"Merely observing."

"How's your bruising?" he asked, almost reaching over to see it while we were in the kitchen.

I stepped back, wanting to just show him that I was the lucky one. I lifted my shirt, revealing to him the somewhat darker coloring of my bruising.

The aches were still floating through me. They'd come and go with the radiation of the pain. I knew I would be sore, but nothing that my own pains or over the counter medication wouldn't take care of, but the way he looked at me sent more goosebumps over my skin.

He looked at me as a sign of desire, a look of longing.

"I see," He started scrambling some eggs. I'm not a breakfast eater to be honest, but I wasn't going to bite the hand that wanted to feed me. He continued, "Most importantly, how are you feeling?"

I thought about that for a moment. Did I still feel like I got run over by a truck? I sure did. Was I going to tell him I couldn't take care of myself? Absolutely not.

"I'll survive." I said quickly.

He clicked his tongue, like I said the wrong answer. "It's not nice to lie."

"I wasn't lying." I huffed.

"Honey, the way that you were moving, you look like you're tolerating the pain. If you need another day of rest," he started.

But I stopped him before he could think otherwise. "No," I said quickly. "No, you've already done enough for me. And I'm sure that any girlfriend or partner of yours wouldn't want to see me."

Where the fuck did that come from? He snorted at my response. My off the wall response.

"No need to worry about that," he let out before serving me eggs and some toast.

He only sat one plate down. He rested himself on his elbows, leaning over the mini kitchen island.

"Eat, and let's really talk," he said.

I nodded, taking the food and thanking whoever was listening for the man before me.

I ate in front of him as he just stared at me. I started to feel self-conscious, nervous of making the wrong choice. Jesus, I needed to stop acting like some young person.

"After you," I snarked at him, curling a smile in his direction.

"Do you want to make a report?" he asked plainly.

I swallowed a big gulp of food, surprised at his bluntness.

Did I want to make a report about it? I didn't remember what happened after I was stuck in a fetal position.

"I don't know," was my answer as I played with my food. "What happened after? Was anything done?"

He nodded his head. "I had my men take care of it while I had you in my care."

"Then I'm not. If it was taken care of and I don't have to see them," I started rambling quickly, hoping to move on from the subject.

"Wait now. Although I would have supported and probably have said to make that report, it's not what you think. They ain't buried, honey. But they are taken care of. They know who they messed with and know not to hurt nor go after one of our singers." he said.

I laughed softly. "Hound, I'm not a singer. We talked about this already."

I went back to eating my food, thinking that I might as well just go back to any of these studios and ask them to take me back and I'd just keep writing.

"What were you going to sing?" he asked me.

"Don't worry about it. It doesn't matter now," I said, stabbing my food as if the rage inside about this subject were to shoot out of me.

I felt his finger lift my chin, giving me no choice but to look into his eyes. "Tell me anyway."

"You're not going to let this go, are you?" I sighed. "Fine. One of my own songs."

I waited for a punch line or an "awe shucks" moment, but he didn't break away. He waited for more, so I continued, "I've been a writer for over a decade but never sang my own songs on stage."

Always behind the mic, never in the spotlight.

"Why not?" He kept pushing the subject. Why was he pushing the matter like he truly cared?

"You're going to think it's stupid." I tried to break away from his eyes. I was stronger than this, able to put myself in the best positions.

"Try me," he dared me.

I growled out, "I'm not good enough, okay." I paused to watch his reaction. Then I continued, "Well, that's what the studios tell me." And the truth was set free. "I believe I'm good, I believe that the music I create will take me places. But the way they see it, they'll take my songs, but not the voice behind it. I don't fit into anyone's world or style. Guess my mama was right, I'm just not special." I laughed.

If only Aria, my sister, could see me then, confessing a truth that I hid behind.

"That can't be true," he said, letting loose our gaze.

"Well believe it, Hound. That's the cruel world that we live in. There's not one place for Melody Rae Hart." I finished my food. I stepped away from the island trying to make my way to the living room, hoping my bag and case were there.

"How about for payment or a reward for saving your life to live another day, sing for me," he said, stopping me in my tracks.

I froze. This wasn't a happily ever after story where the girl sings and the man falls in love. I had my life to live and money to make to survive, or attempt to at least. I shook my head. "I don't think so. I will repay you for your kindness with anything else, but really, I can't."

I turned to look at him, and he was giving the most puppy dog eyes that beckoned to let him do whatever he wanted to do to me.

Or get on your knees for, you know.

"You really don't take no for an answer."

"Always a yes. So your answer is "yes Hound, I'll sing for you". Then we'll be even." He smirked.

I tossed around the thought of denying him again. I bounced back and forth.

"Ugh, okay. Fine. But can you please get a shirt on? I'm already nervous enough, I don't need your sculptured barbaric abs to make me sweat any more than I already have." I groaned, turning to find my case.

When he came back, he got comfortable on the couch and the rush of imposter syndrome flooded me. I already knew I couldn't sing in front of a crowd, what made him think that I could simply sing in front of him?

I couldn't stop my hands from shaking long enough to grab the guitar from my case. I had to quickly tune it. Hound stared at me like I was the most intriguing person in the room. Everything was shaking, my nerves got the better of me.

"Um, could you, um, turn around?" I asked, barely looking at him.

"Turn around?" he asked.

I nodded my head. He cocked his head. "I'm not judging you. I just wanted to hear you sing, give you a chance to share your voice."

I threw my hands down. "I know it's just I can't have anyone look at me. That's why people get my recordings of the demos, nothing live." The studios were always able to get my songs, just never live. Some didn't care as long as they got something they wanted.

He paused for a moment then adjusted himself to look away from me. I started to strum to a tune that was going to be my song that night.

I was down by the old oak tree,
The one where promises are born.
Where the names never fades,
Where the roots stay grounded.

Even after all this time,
Those memories were still.
Swingin' and kissin', laid out under the stars.
Dreamin' and lovin', fightin' until tears were shed.

Because after all this time.
I'll never say goodbye to that old oak tree.

I got carried away by the vision of young love that didn't know if they would make it or keep fighting for their love.

The melody swayed, sounding like the old blues country, where the emotions resonate the times of yesterday. The song reminded me of when we would be in Granny's backyard, back in the mountains.

Was it my strongest song? No, but it was a special song that meant more than I could say. I had closed my eyes when I hit the last chorus, singing that I'd never say goodbye to that oak tree. I played the last few notes. As my eyes fluttered open, Hound was looking at me with a big smile.

Instantly the nerves came back, knowing that this man saw me get lost and heard me. I slowly took off the guitar, setting it back down in the case.

He was speechless. He just stared at me in awe. Maybe that was when I should have seen the exit. Maybe he was lost in thought. Maybe he was entranced by the song. Maybe I unlocked an obsession for him.

"Please say something so I know that I'm not going to die at the end of this." I nervously laughed.

"I was right," he said.

"About what?"

"You are a little songbird. Where did that come from?"

I shrugged.

He tilted his head like he was being pulled back into a memory. "Your song sounds familiar, have you ever given it to someone?" he inquired. I shook my head, this was one song that was mine. No one else had it.

"Like I said, I write songs for others." I packed up the case, then didn't move. I didn't know what else to do. "Did I pay my bill in full?"

I crossed my arms in front of me. Hound eased himself off the couch, walked over in my direction until he was close enough to when our chests were close touch. He bent closer to my face. "You already did when you woke up this morning."

All the air in my chest faded.

I shouldn't want him, he was a stranger. He belonged to a world that wasn't very welcoming to people like me. People who were lost, people that had enough light in their heart, who wouldn't hurt a soul. He seemed like the type that would break my heart, maybe not from physically hurting me but something else I couldn't put my finger on.

"Come on, let me get you home," he said, before disappearing down the hallway.

Oh yeah, home. About that.

Chapter 9

HOUND DOG

I wanted to be selfish. I wanted to keep her longer at the house, hear her sing more, because what I heard and what I saw was an old soul rising with the voice of an angel. There was something that told me that this wasn't the first time our paths had crossed, whether here or another life.

Or I could just be crazy.

When I dropped her off at her apartment door, she offered me a smile and her appreciation. The car door slammed and echoed in my head. Her last words remained ingrained in my soul. "Thank you Hound, I guess I'll live to sing again."

I watched her enter the building, hoping that she'd turn back and see me.

I wanted her to soar, to spread that talent to people that would appreciate her. I wanted her to survive, maybe in the selfish hopes that she'd fly back to me. For a split second, I pictured her by my side, her barefoot in the living room with the guitar in her lap. A light to come home to.

Funny thing was, I hadn't kissed her. And yet, I knew it wouldn't be enough if I did.

I had to leave her behind, pretend that she was just another person in this whirlwind of a city. I had my responsibilities to my club, to my chapter.

I fought everyday to vanish the thought of her, and move on. How could one person affect you in everything you do? Your thoughts, your memories, your desires. I felt like a hopeless, lovesick fool.

It had been two weeks since I dropped her off when I started to feel even crazier, and I hadn't seen her around the club or any other clubs. I took it as a sign that she wouldn't come back, which was better for her. And perhaps myself.

But it was two weeks that would turn my world upside down again.

"Heard that a bigger shipment was coming through, might need to get the whole club or at least half with the trucks. Some of the men won't be happy, we'd get all the prospects together. They can keep themselves away from sweet butts for the night," B.B started to say before stuffing his face with barbecue.

I didn't hear him, my mind must have been somewhere else. I picked at my food, pushing it around with my fork. The sun was shining, the early fall weather was coming our way. Someone snapped their fingers, "Hello earth to Hound!"

I looked up at B.B's face twisted in confusion, "What?"

He curled his lip in his humorous way, "Saying that you need a sweet butt to screw you back into place."

This man was too much a ray of sunshine whether he was getting screwed or not. The man could get any woman he wanted. Sometimes the man would elaborate how he would make them scream and in the end, his face would meet my fist due to my annoyance.

"Ha ha,very funny" I pushed the tray of food away from me.

"I mean, say the word and I'll find you a nice woman," he offered. In the end I knew he cared about his family, his brothers.

"Not interested."

"Oh come on, one that would scream your name, begging you to go harder," he tempted.

"You really want me to mess up that pretty face of yours." I rolled my eyes.

He held up his hands, stopping the conversation. I continued, "Did Twitty get the last round of shipment?" We already had one shipment come in a week ago, it wasn't much, but enough to tie us over.

"And we're back to business, you're no fun," He pouted.

I let out a growl as B.B attempted to snag my food I had pushed away. "Jesus, you weren't going to finish it. Like you fucking need it, you giant." I waved him off, as he scarfed down the rest of the food.

Swingin' and kissin', laid out under the stars.
Dreamin' and lovin', fightin' until tears were shed.

Because after all this time.
I'll never say goodbye to that old oak tree.

That melody stuck in my head. Like a siren call.

"Did your mind leave the building?" B.B interrupted my thoughts. Melody's ghost voice faded away.

"I'm fine." I leaned back into the chair.

"No you're not. This about that damsel in distress from the Sax?" B.B inquired.

My eyes snapped to his face; the slightest smirk on his told me that someone blabbed a little too much about my life. My business was my business. The itch to fight someone was there, and boiling.

"You gonna answer me about Twitty," I growled out.

"You gonna answer about the little hurt singer that Waylon mentioned," B.B taunted.

"Drop it, B.B."

"You poor sap. Don't tell me you fell." he went to pinch my cheeks as I smacked his hand away from me. "I'm just saying, since when have you been hung up on a woman?" he asked.

Before I could answer, the grace of the heavens interrupted. My phone started to buzz, but the name across the screen wasn't who I was expecting, especially that early in the morning.

Lieutenant Howard Greene.

A cop under our protection, but still with the law. The only cop we could rely on, trusted, but always kept an eye on.

"Greene, what do I owe this pleasant phone call?" I said.

"Please tell me you can account for the whereabouts of your boys." he quickly replied. I shot a look at B.B. as he dabbed his face and started to get up. B.B knew it was time for us to go.

"Currently, no. Might need to be more specific," I told him.

"Last night," he said quietly.

"I believe so. What's going on Greene?" I stood up and started walking toward the bikes.

"You might want to come down here. I think that you might want to see this," Greene said.

Normally, our chapter is very low key, better to keep the law off our backs. Though it was nice to have Otis in the chapter, especially since he was previously an attorney. Greene was one of the happy encounters when more than one or two of our members got their asses handed to them. Greene and I had a discussion, knowing that the more backlash about our club, the worse for the city.

As the bikes started up, B.B looked at me. "Where we going?"

"Down south."

We weaved through traffic, even though the majority of it seemed to be tourism which should have been gone. We took the back neighborhoods and got down toward the scene but a few blocks away.

I had Shooter come meet us as well. If one of our men did this type of shit, he would be the one I needed with me. He stood proud, ready for any movement. The man looked like he had seen the sun for too long, always bronzed.

As we approached him, he grunted. "What kind of bullshit do they think we're up to now?"

We had picked the right person to be enforcer, his protective instinct was a force to be reckoned with.

"Wasn't much detail, but something tells me that whatever it was, it will land on us," I said.

"If it wasn't serious, Greene wouldn't have called," B.B offered.

Whatever was coming our way, I had high hopes that the men would be better than to be caught in something they didn't need to be involved with. They knew better than to test me and prove that they didn't need to be an Outlaw.

In the distance, Greene was in his plain clothes with someone in tow walking toward our meet up location, away from everything that was going on down the street. Greene kept looking back, as if someone else was following him or that he was hiding something.

Greene wouldn't have taken a chance on bringing in someone else if it wasn't serious. Would I have approved of it to begin with? No, I don't take chances in these situations and bringing in an unknown person is a greater risk to the club than a turf war with another club. Even worse, it was a greater risk than a lovers' scorn. But Greene had come far with our trust in him, fortunately, he'd never given us a reason to mistrust him or put him on a tight leash.

"You got a rookie or something there, Greene," B.B yelled out. I smacked his stomach before his mouth got him into more trouble than he was worth.

"Gentlemen, hated to make the call." He sounded apologetic.

"And yet we're here. Let's cut to the chase shall we," I said, straightening up, showing that time was everything at that moment.

"First, this is Officer Daniels, my trainee," he introduced the fresh looking officer, too pure looking for the dirt that might rub off on him.

"And you thought it was a good idea for him to come here? Looks like he quotes the rulebook like it's the pledge of allegiance." Shooter growled out. He took a step forward challenging the man to see if he'd back down.

Daniels stood his ground firmly and didn't take his eye off of Shooter.

"Easy, Shooter. You'll be happy to know that he comes from the club life." Greene vouched for him.

"Old man was a member turned Road Captain," Daniels started to explain himself.

I looked back at Greene. "Whatever your history is, doesn't mean jack shit."

He rolled his eyes and before I could address it, Greene cleared his throat. He dug in his pocket to pull out his phone. Once he found what he was looking for, he turned the phone in our direction.

What we saw wasn't something we expected. The three of us crowd around the phone, looking at a picture that would set off a new problem in our city. Shooter took the phone out of Greene's hands.

The picture captured a scene with a presumed male body with a bloody, foamy dried mouth. The person looked to have suffocated or choked. The question was how did it involve the club and why?

"What am I looking at?" I finally asked as the guys stood there gawking like there was more to find out, more details that we weren't seeing.

"Nathan Ewing, age twenty seven, resident of Nashville, but apparently was here for a gig in the city. Want to take a guess of where?" Greene said sternly.

"I'm assuming a bar or a stage," Shooter said bluntly.

I shot him a look to be careful of what he said next. But it didn't take long to put two and two together to make it make sense. The only other reason why Lieutenant Greene would make our asses come to him and why he was giving straight information, was if he thought we were involved somehow. The only connection the club could possibly have is that he was an artist in our city to work.

"Which one?" B.B asked, catching the information from Greene.

"Growler," Daniels cut in, delivering the truth we could agree on.

The Growler was a dive bar, something that B.B had thought of when we first got patched into the club. Growler would be the "hole in the wall" place on the outside only to reveal a place where sin and art came alive. We would get a range of heart broken, lustful sinners to the lost soul that needed a place to be theirs. A place that sometimes the darkest of art could come alive and still be supported.

I trusted B.B and a couple of members to take care of it, as it was one business that I couldn't see myself exploring, at least not yet. I turned to B.B, whose eyes were full of anger and shock.

"You think this person was murdered at the bar?" Shooter began his questioning, glancing back at the evidence in front of him.

"We don't know, but one thing was for sure, he appeared to have drugs on him and most likely in his system," Greene answered, throwing his hands in his pocket.

I shook my head, "A possible drug happy artist comes to perform and you think it's us."

Greene glared at Daniels. "Show him."

Daniels huffed out and reached into his jacket pocket, holding out an evidence baggie of some drug substance inside. But if you looked closely, it was a familiar bag to the club.

The evidence bag held a small blue bag with a tiny symbol of a devil.

It looked like the same product that was part of a recent delivery. Not that we got drugs all the time, but when we did, I had set rules and enforced them.

Our bag.

Our products.

Someone had to be setting us up. We didn't sell in our own establishments, but somewhere close. We marked our own product, no one would trace it back to us. That was the hope. Something inside of me said it wasn't us.

Our brothers nor our vetted sellers weren't stupid enough to go off base.

"There's no way one of ours was fucking dumb enough to break my golden rule," I sneered out.

I didn't have many personal rules outside of the charter and board. One, keep your noses clean even when you think no one is watching. Two, never forget to show manners to those who deserve it. We were southern and all. And lastly, never sell to addicts or near our businesses.

The last one was my golden rule. We never needed to fuel a problem, but fuel some kind of desire. But to sell at our businesses painted a target on our backs. Ones that were hard to get rid of for this very reason.

Something to trail back to us, painting us as the city's villains rather than vengeful protectors.

Someone had some explaining to do as Twitty and Fender oversaw a lot of this side.

"That's why I needed you down here. Because if it ain't you then someone is after you. Who knows if this was a one and done?" Greene took back his phone.

"How did you all get the call? And why here? There's not much over here, and obviously nowhere near our businesses," Shooter said.

"And why does this have to do with us?" I asked the most important question.

B.B's nerves got the best of him as he took out a cigarette, ones that he promised he'd quit. He lit one up and walked away to settle down. The man wasn't easily nerved, but shit had him worried.

"Call came in at seven this morning, a bystander out on a morning run. The 911 caller sounded like he was hyperventilating, the man could barely get out any words. The dispatcher had to ground him in order to tell her what was going on. What little details he gave, dispatch had a unit car go out, along with the EMS. But it was no use, it was more of a recovery and evidence call. There wasn't much to recover. He had his wallet, some cash, and his guitar case which had that little bag in there." Greene nodded to the bag still in Daniels's hands.

"Greene, you already know that someone is fucking with us. A dead body with signs of tainted product, and a bag that is similar to ours. After over a decade would we be that careless?" I got protective, defensive over our club.

B.B strutted back to having stomped out his cigarette. "You gotta get them off our trail," he said.

"My friend, the club hasn't been brought up, let alone the fact of this little present. But we both know that if I do turn up with this evidence, it's going to get found out and then there goes my job and your inside man," Greene whispered.

For a moment there it almost sounded like a threat and I didn't take kindly to threats. I stepped up his eyes staring into mine. "Is this going to be the one time that you play by the rules? You protect us, we protect you. Last time I checked, we never had a problem."

He didn't respond right away. He listened. He let the thought of all this time make his final decision before his fresh meat decided to speak. "I'll find it." Daniels spoke up.

"What?"

"I'll find it. It will make it look good on both ends, the fact that I found it under the guidance of my T.O. and it won't raise any suspicions about his loyalties." Daniels was a smart man. Maybe, for a brief moment, I could trust him.

"Hound, I have looked the other way and protected you all from serious jail time. You've taken care of me and helped my family. I'm not trying to place blame. I'm giving you a heads up that trouble is coming your way and you may have pissed someone else off." Greene took a step back and extended his hand to shake on it.

I looked down on it. Looking back at him, I reached out and gripped his hand. "You can't blame me. If this shit fucks with the club, then everything that this club has built, what it has started, would all go away."

"I wouldn't cross you," Greene tried to reassure me. But, unfortunately, some things were going to get handled by me. Sometimes, I still could only trust myself.

With a nod, Greene left with Daniels in tow. If the plan and trust worked then the club wouldn't be a moving target. Shooter shook his head, his blood must have been boiling. His fists clenched at his side. "Find out where everyone was the last two nights, I don't need any surprises. You hear me," I commanded.

"You got it, Prez." He took off without hesitation.

A beat later, B.B spoke up, calmer than before. "You really think it's one of ours?"

I rolled my neck from side to side, "For the club's sake, I sure fucking hope not."

I was ready to take flight and shed blood. No one was going to come here and make it as if we were cold blooded killers. If anything, we knew how to paint the town red and call it art.

Chapter 10

MELODY

The desire to go back and run into him again was strong.

My skin itched with the need to be impulsive for three weeks. Like it was on fire, like it needed to be fed with the fuel it craved.

That night Hound dropped me off, after he asked me to sing for him, he woke something in me. Call it motivation, call it a second chance, I didn't know what else to call it.

But he thought it was bringing back to my life, my home. Little did he know, it wasn't all true. I bet he viewed me as an "All-American" song writer that lived in a tiny studio, barely keeping houseplants alive, and sticking little flowers in my hair.

I wished that was a true dream. It would have been better than my nomadic ways.

"Come on, sugar. We need to leave in the next few minutes if we're going to see Mark perform," Sadie hollered from the living room.

I stared at myself in her bathroom mirror, trying to cover up the dark circles from the limited amount of sleep I was getting. Between the nightmares and sleeping in a makeshift bed, sleep had not been my friend. I was thankful that Sadie helped me out by letting me stay during the day, making it somewhat a home. But unfortunately, if her landlord found out that she was living here and not her uncle, whose name was on the lease, she would be screwed.

I wasn't going to risk her own struggling self to get in trouble. But she was a truer friend to me the past couple of years.

I didn't know how I got there, to the point where my home was a large van that housed everything I practically owned. Memories that were in photo boxes, important documents that were safeguarded in my backpack that went everywhere with me, and my guitar that was my life line in more ways than one.

Most nights, I had to find safety in a quiet neighborhood where no one would see me at the darkest hours of the night or the mornings. When I would have to leave or else someone would catch wind of me. And when the weather became unbearable, Sadie risked her housing for me to sleep on the couch.

I had survived a lot, and even that night I was going to survive, though it was going to be a long road to regain strength. It was more confusing when a man was sweet enough to take care of me and for once, I didn't have to bring up the shield on my life.

Hound Dog was always on my mind. It wasn't a pure coincidence that he found me. He never said, but I could tell.

"Melody Rae!" Sadie pulled me away from the downward spiral of thoughts. I brushed my hair over and over again. "Jesus, Mary, and Joseph, and the whole holy trinity. Are you daydreaming again?"

Guilty.

"Thinking about your knight and shining armor?" she asked, standing behind me. Her straight dark hair and tanned complexion was a thing of beauty. Made me a little jealous the way she was just effortlessly beautiful. Her kind smile spread across her face.

"No." I shook my head, packing my brush back into my little bag of toiletries.

"Liar."

"Am not." I stuck my tongue out.

She rested her chin on my shoulder. I told her everything about that night and she pestered me to go back to the club and keep "thanking" Hound Dog. I told her it was crazy as if I was the stalker. I was horny, but not desperate. No matter how many times I wished his soft touches melted into my skin.

"We are going for Mark," I reminded her.

I should have been reminding myself. She just looked at me with those caramel doe eyes like she knew I was kidding myself. If the universe was listening, I was sending positive thoughts that I might see him one more time. If anything to block him off my mind.

"Come on, you've written countless verses since you left him. And from the sound of it, he wasn't sure about letting you go." She pursed her lips.

I rolled my eyes, shaking her off my shoulders, grabbed my boho tote, promising myself that I would come back from supporting a friend and move on with my life. I wasn't going to stop my life or be hung up on a guy that literally showed me that there were still good people in the world, even the ones that swear they aren't.

In a blink, we met up with our group of friends at the Blue Sax. It was another open mic night, and it was packed. With the return of college students and long time residents, it was starting to become home again.

Artists were coming up and expressing their hearts and souls. Every chance I got, I would scan the room, thinking that I'd see that tall, brute of a man that made my heart beat faster at the mere thought of him.

Sadie's little crimson colored smile didn't stop, she knew what was happening. As much as I was going to deny it, she knew. To my own disappointment, he wasn't coming, nor would he return.

I mean, did I really expect a man that spent one night taking care of me to think about me, to want me? I wasn't made to be a romance book, I was made to live a life that I built.

I knew I was beautiful in my own way, I knew that I was a strong woman, it just took circumstances to stun me. I knew I deserved something good, but in the world around us, sometimes the possibility seemed distant.

But right there, sitting in the same place that I once had a chance to express my own voice, I was cheering on my good friend. I brushed off the last of the hope and plastered on a smile. And yet out of the corner of my eye, I thought I saw something, someone. I thought it was my mind playing games.

Or maybe it was the rum that was teasing my mind with the inner thoughts of what I wanted more, what I desired.

"I'm going to the bathroom." I leaned over to Sadie who was swaying to a song from a bluegrass singer on stage. She was trapped in the music, I didn't know if she heard me or not, but my feet kept moving.

I couldn't bear to confirm if I saw what I saw, my eyes averted any other direction but down. I trailed into a hallway that led to a couple of doors. But something told me to stop and slow down. That was when I heard the voice of a man that haunted my own melodies, that made me question my own sanity.

"Looking for something, little songbird?" His deep voice was enough to send me straight to an early grave.

I turned to find him, a few feet away from me, like he had been following me, waiting for the perfect moment to appear from the shadows. I saw him. My savior, someone who saw a piece of vulnerability that was a secret many didn't know.

His charismatic smile and alluring eyes put me back into a trance and I didn't know if I was going to be released.

My confidence was about to burst and yet, it was silenced. A simple question could render me speechless. My throat became drier than a desert in the middle of July. I had this whole plan of keeping it cool. But the way he was looking at me showed me that I was looking like a fool. That I was staring at him like he was the biggest monster alive and he was ready to eat me.

"No," I squeaked. Heat flushed my cheeks at the mere embarrassment.

Where the fuck did that come from?

He snickered. "You trying again?" he asked, looking at me up and down, taking a good look at my appearance. Everything from my faded ripped jeans to the deep v-neck one piece, giving him a nice view.

I shook my head, "No, supporting Mark."

He raised an eyebrow, "Mark? Boyfriend of yours?" His voice turned a little possessive, and angry. Maybe the fools were right, there was something like love at first sight. That would make one of us.

"What's it to you?" I played along, pressing every button I was allowed to break.

He stepped closer to me. The man continued to tower over me, his gaze setting a small fire inside me. "I'd like to know who else may have heard that voice."

"And what if he has?"

He quietly growled, stepping closer to me, our chests now touched. "I'd like to have thought I was the only one. One that simply asked, and you, like a good little songbird, obliged."

Now, who sounded possessive? Like he had a hold on me, and truth be told, the man didn't have to work that damn hard. If he asked me anything else, I would be happy about it. The ache to kiss him grew, the power of temptation.

What the fuck is with this man?

I gulped, not knowing how much longer I would put up the little battle.

"You wanted to be the only one? Seems only fair to know who you've sung for." I teased him. The long-awaited confidence reared her siren side. Then I started to stumble over my words. "I mean, if you do sing. I don't know why I said that."

He leaned close to my ear; a sweet smell of bourbon lingered on him. A shiver of goosebumps covered me as he spoke. "Only for you."

He pulled away as my eyes fluttered open. I nodded my head, "You've been the only one as well."

"Why's that?" Hound asked. He already knew the answer and I wasn't going to explain myself again.

"You know why." I glared at him, crossing my arms in front of me.

He walked me toward the wall behind me, trapping me with his arms. He wanted me alone, with all his attention. "Tell me why."

I'd never been impulsive, not to a degree. I'd followed the rules, played the games. But the way he looked at me tempted me to do everything others would tell me not to do. We were inches away and I couldn't help myself.

Get him out of my system.

Without hesitation I captured his lips, reaching to take his face, taking every reaction of shock to him. He didn't fight back, he didn't pull back either. He simply growled in what I hoped was pleasure. If anything, he kissed me back, pressing our bodies flush against the wall.

Our tongues tangled with each other, he fought for control. His pressed body was hard as stone, no matter where you looked. I should have pulled back, but it felt too damn good. He braced one hand on the wall, the other trailing up my hip to cup my cheek. The temptress inside of me was begging for his hand to go further up.

His kiss deepened if that was even possible. Almost possessive, like it was just us and no one else in the world. He felt warm, almost like light peaking through the early morning.

I couldn't help but just moan, the feeling was too damn good.

Impulsive, but damn good.

He pulled back, resting his forehead on mine. My eyes fluttered open, only to stare back into his. I bit my bottom lip, looking down and then back at him.

He growled, deep in his chest. "Mm, if that was a way to prevent you from answering me, then by all means do it again." He smiled like a damn fool.

I giggled. Me. Melody Rae giggled for the first time in my life.

"Well, it wasn't. But I'd be happy to do it again," I said. I almost begged him to kiss me.

He leaned his head back, looking around, probably seeing if anyone was looking, but his gaze fixed back on me. I got nervous, the high of my impulsivity fading away. My body started to tingle, a small sensation that intensified.

"Come with me," he said before pulling my hand, leading us through a crowd or two. He didn't give me a chance to protest.

He took us to the other side of the bar back, in a corner where the music wasn't blaring in our ears. He sat me down with my back toward the crowd and him in front of me.

I didn't know what else to do, but something in my veins craved him for a second longer. "You gonna answer my question?" he asked.

I sucked in my lips, debating on telling him no, but that didn't happen. "My stage fright?"

He nodded. I sighed, placing my hands in my lap, fidgeting with the rings on my fingers.

"Yeah, it's still a thing, and it's something I can't get over. I forget the music, I forget everything I worked for, and it vanishes. I can't look people in the eyes. If I try to sing, one look at someone and my voice cracks, I sweat, my knees give out under me. You saw what happened to me." I started to get defensive.

I knew I could do it, but the mind was a powerful thing.

I suspected that he would take pity on me or feel sorry. But his eyes, his body were soft and empathetic. I continued, "I can't get out of my head, I can't shove down the thoughts that plague me. I want to get out there and actually do what I want, but..."

"You're left feeling like you can't." He finished my thought. I nodded. "Been there before," he said.

I snorted, "Yeah right."

But his expression didn't change. He wasn't kidding. "Oh, well. Then you know the feeling of working yourself up to the moment, only to have your own body and mind take over." I said, leaning against the bar.

He shook his head for a moment, like he was tossing a thought around. "Do you trust me?"

What was this, a freaking princess movie where the hero reaches his hand out asking that question?

"Can I?" I asked in return.

Of course, internally I was saying yes I could trust him, but I'd only kissed him once and he took care of me in a dark moment. And yet, I could tell that others would have wanted me to say no.

"Honey, there's nowhere safer than around me. You wouldn't have given into the temptation of stealing my breath away if you didn't trust me on some level."

I hesitated, I didn't know where this conversation was going. Could I trust him, let alone could I trust myself? I took the chance and nodded my head. His soft smile returned. "Then maybe you trust me enough to help you."

I froze for only a moment before a burst of laughter escaped me like I found the punchline of the joke. But as my laugh died down, I saw the confused look in his eyes. The man wasn't kidding again. Jesus, I felt like an asshole.

I cleared my throat, "I'm so sorry! I didn't think you were serious."

He cracked his neck before pushing off the chair stepping closer to me forcing my head to whip back to gather in his height. "I want to help you. I think I can help you become something."

"Why would you want to do that?" I threw out the question.

The back of his hand caressed my cheek making me lean into his touch. Goosebumps pricked my skin, all innocent thoughts went outside the window. "You want the right answer?"

"There was a wrong answer?" I questioned again. One of these days my mouth was truly going to get me in trouble.

"The right answer is that I see the star, the artist you can become. I see the old soul of music flowing through your veins. I think you can do it," he said, without a hint of bluff.

This man believed in me and he never asked for anything else. He didn't know me, but my body already responded to him with such need. Maybe he could be a mentor, maybe he could help. I didn't question why a man of the club's life would do this, it was already known that the Saints were patrons of the arts, that they curated these venues to help folks like me.

The cut, the way he told those guys in the alley not to screw around with the Saint's, I wasn't blind, but he hadn't confirmed anything.

"What was the wrong answer?" My body shivered with sweet anticipation. I was already going to say yes, but curiosity got the best of me.

He smirked before brushing my loose hair behind my ear, leaning down to say, "Because after one sweet taste of you, I wanted more. I *need* more."

That did it.

He pulled away, and I couldn't help but release a small whimper at his words. My cheeks heated as pure embarrassment flooded me. He stared at me with pure heat. He licked his lips, glancing at mine. I could see his thoughts and my body squirmed under the anticipation.

"You need to stop looking at me like that," he grumbled.

"Like what?" I asked, confused at his words.

His face came closer to mine, freezing me in that moment. "Like you want me to devour every inch of you."

I gulped. I didn't think I was looking at him anyway. I wanted to protest, but damn it, maybe he was right.

"One can dream," I teased him.

He cupped my face before I said anything else, bringing his lips to mine, capturing it in a bruising, possessive, demanding kiss. The type that made you melt into a puddle only to get swept up again and do it all over. The type you wished would never end. The type of kiss where the man takes control and you sit there like limp noodle with your arms swaying by the side because you don't know where else to put them.

It's only when he pulled away that I remembered where I was. Everything was tingling, my vagina was beginning to have a little pulse.

"Let me take you home, and we can talk a little more in private." He grinned.

When my mind came back to reality, nerves started to come alive. Everything went from straight forward to worrying about my "somewhat" truth.

I bit my lip when he wasn't looking, but by the time he looked back at me, I stuttered, "We really don't have to, I'm okay."

"Honey, I only bite, if you ask," he winked.

"It's okay you don't have to help me," I started to say. I shook my head, trying to settle my nerves. Hound took my chin in hand.

"I said I could help cure that stage fright," he stared into my soul. I knew he could sense something, the man was taking over.

"I know, but can we go back to your house?"

He quirked an eyebrow, "You afraid to take me home?"

Fuck, he was going to make me break down a wall of pride, not needing someone else's help when I am down on my luck. "No, it's just... Maybe I'd be comfortable back at your home."

"If you have a boyfriend, you might need to tell me now," he said sternly.

"No boyfriend, I promise. Let's not go back to my place. Trust me, you don't want to," I stammered, feeling the sweat drip from the back of my neck.

"Melody," he growled in warning. "Your guitar is there, so we might as well go get it. Why won't you let me take you home?"

"I can't," I said firmly. His fingers tightened around my chin.

"Why not?" he asked again.

I felt one of those damn walls tumbling down. "Because I don't have one."

He stood there, silent. I just stunned him into silence. What came next was going to break down a lot more walls.

Chapter 11

HOUND DOG

After the day we had with Greene and his station questioning us, seeing her was the highlight of my week.

We had been bogged down with enough questions to make us question our own secured selves. It was bad enough that Graves advised us to deliver less and lay lower. He was confident that we would be okay but warned that shit never goes away.

Being the center of an investigation was not the way to go in this lifestyle. I couldn't say that I wasn't warned when taking on this club and this idea that I had. Being asked to come to the station for questioning, each man was prepared by Otis, being ordered to give the truth because there wasn't anything we were hiding.

No one would go against my rules of who to sell product to and no one wanted the consequences that would come with it. No one suspected me to be this leader but it wasn't so much the outward appearance but the power you possessed in the stares and demeanor you held.

There were a lot of people out to get the club, but none stupid enough to plan something like this, but then again you never saw a poisonous snake until they attacked.

When I got to the Blue Sax that night, all I wanted to do was drown my pain in cheap whiskey. B.B had already left my side to go flirt with someone and make face with the artists. A few other brothers surrounded the bar. We needed a night to blow off steam, a night to forget everything around us.

A clearer mind made for a dangerous one.

What I didn't expect was for Melody to return, let alone be in my presence. I didn't count on the fact of her eyes finding mine for a brief moment only to turn away like she was defeated. So, of course I went after her like a selfish bastard in the midst of a chaotic situation.

When she was close by, I saw that fire in her eyes, the one that dimmed that night. I saw her for her, her little movements, her mind spinning with thoughts of playing with my fire.

And this girl wanted just as much as I wanted, but never voiced it. At that moment, all I wanted was for her to be mine, even if it wasn't a full possibility. I wanted to give her anything and everything she wanted. I wanted to make her dreams come true, just so she could dream more.

How could one person, one woman make you feel this possessive? I guess like Pops always said, "When you know, you know." And with her, I just wanted to know more.

But what shocked me was that I knew she was hiding something when I asked her to let me take her home, she hesitated, her cheeks turning red.

Her answer made my heart drop.

"Because I don't have one," she said.

I cocked my head, seeing if she would turn it into a joke, like it wasn't true. There was no way this woman didn't have a place. A roommate maybe, the friend at least I thought was a roommate or something. Rent was expensive.

But to say she didn't have a place, didn't seem real.

"What do you mean?" I asked the question, hoping for a different answer.

She avoided eye contact until I lifted her chin to meet my gaze again. "Tell me."

Tell me that you're being taken care of and given everything you need.

"I don't have a place where I can take you to," she said with a little more confidence.

"And why is that?" continuing my questioning like a man possessed.

She licked her lips and released a heavy sigh, "Because I wasn't able to keep up a year ago so now I have my travel van."

She's been living in a van? Like she didn't have a choice. I was all for the nomadic life, but people choose that, not as the only option to avoid sleeping on the streets. It chipped away at me internally, briefly thinking about the community center that a sweet older lady, Mrs. Grace, ran for those that needed a place to get their life back on track.

"Honey, you've been sleeping in your van?" I asked, only to know more about her and if she'd let me help her or support her. I knew that most people would think that this was too fast, but it was never too much to be a decent human being and help those that asked for it.

"It's not so bad, over the past year I got to make it my own. Helps me just carry what is important and not carry too much. I mean it's starting to look more like a glorified van, like a custom made one," she calmly said, trying to paint me a picture of her makeshift home. Regardless, at this time, it would never be safe enough for her. "So, I mean I don't think you and I would fit, but if you're willing to make it work." She winked.

She was too adorable for her own good. And too cute to try to get me off track on the subject.

"That's okay, honey. You can stay with me, come on." I said, grabbing her hand to lead her out of the bar. She was going to protest, tell me that she didn't need my help or that she didn't want to put me out.

We weaved through the sea of people, I nodded my head toward the brothers.

As soon as we got outside, she tugged out her hand, "Woah there hotrod, don't you think I get a say in this?" She tossed her hips to the side, throwing a small tantrum.

"If I'm going to help you, yes," I countered.

"I didn't say yes," she said.

Oh, we have a little fighter.

"Honey, you'll say yes, because inside you want to say yes, but your heart is stopping you," I said, stepping closer to her. Under the street lamps she was still damn beautiful, her strong eyes glaring at me like she wanted to be stubborn and tell me "no". But she had a talent that I wanted to see her soar. There was something special about her, and I was thinking with more than my dick.

"I'm not going home with you." She crossed her arms.

"There's an extra bedroom," I attempted to make it look like it would be better. She was going to say yes, just needed to convince her more.

"I don't need your charity," she raised her voice at me. Her fight was back.

Her eyes looked hard, almost closed off. I imagined the anger boiling up in her body. I shouldn't want her like this but yet, I did.

"Let me let you in on a little secret. Saints protect their own, you haven't noticed we have a soft spot for creative minds." I leaned over, whispering in her ear, "And the more time I spend with you, all I want to do is help you succeed."

"Why me?" Her voice returned to a whisper.

"Call it fate, call it the right timing, but I know when there's something special."

She chewed on her bottom lip, itching to vanish.

"Please, only if it's just until I help you get over this little hurdle of stage fright," I said, hoping to put this to rest.

Having her at my house would mean her safety, my protection, and keeping her close without wandering eyes. If anything, she was going to be my secret. Question was, how long would that last?

I could see the answer at the tip of her tongue. I urged her, "Say yes. Let me help you soar, and then you'll be safe, free to rest your head without worry."

With that final temptation, Melody nodded her head. I clasped my hands on her cheeks, and couldn't help but smile. She definitely had a soft spot.

"Let's get you home, little songbird," I said, whisking her away from the crowds and back into my truck only to take her to her van and then back to the house. A house that was a lonely state, but with her light, it wasn't going to be lonely or unused anymore.

When we got to the house, she slowly stepped into the home, frozen as she looked at the house through a new set of eyes. Her way to form better memories than those of pain. I could still see the faint limp she had, her body was still healing.

"Welcome home." I smirked, helping with her bags. When she said she didn't have a lot, she wasn't kidding.

She started to walk toward the guest bedroom, but stopped, only to look at me. "Are you staying here?"

I wanted to say no, that I had my room back at the clubhouse property, but she made it damn hard to know how she wanted me to answer. I made up my mind. "I stay here, but you won't see me as often. Mostly you'll have the house to yourself. I'll stock the house with food so if you want to cook, you can cook."

She nodded, taking her stuff and placing it in her bedroom. I loved that she was being cautious. While I wasn't going to promise forever, I could at least have her start trusting me without blind faith. She turned back toward me in the doorway. I leaned against, taking up the entire space.

Her eyes turned up toward me. Her face was soft with pure innocence. I could see the little nerves in her movements. "You need to stop looking at me like that, Hound," she said, almost like a siren call that you couldn't ignore.

"Like what?" I tilted my head.

"Like you won this battle."

"I didn't win anything. Well not yet at least." I chuckled. I kept looking at her in awe. She floated between being easy-going and comfortable to cautious.

"You're still doing it."

"How am I supposed to look then?" I asked her.

Melody crossed her arms, only pushing her boobs up giving me a view of her cleavage. I should have looked away, but she was too tempting.

"Like you don't want to kiss me," she said softly.

"But I think you want me to." I leaned a little forward.

"This is supposed to be a business agreement," she protested.

I shook my head, "I think we both know that's a lie."

I pulled her closer, wrapping my arm around her waist. "Tell me to kiss you, Melody. Tell me that you agreeing to stay here was more than just pity or sympathy but that you believe I just want to see you succeed and make those pretty dreams of yours come true."

Her body trembled at my words, and she shook her head, "Shouldn't need to kiss if all you want to do is help."

Something low rumbled in my chest, "Honey, it's not, but it's about you and what you want and need."

Her eyes widened at the thought. "Kissing your protege, sounds tempting."

I was growing impatient, the need to have her lips on mine grew stronger.

"Tell me to kiss you," I growled.

"Kiss me," she finally whispered.

I couldn't kiss her fast enough. The way her warm mouth melted into mine. She was soft and gentle, holding back the inner siren she was, I'd follow her lead until such time.

Guilt washed through me, calling me selfish, knowing that in the end that I'd have to push her away. She shouldn't fall in love with me, because in the end it would end in pain.

But I could be greedy for a while. I could give into temptation, but reality sometimes had a stronger hold.

She pulled back, "Thank you, Hound."

I wanted to say, "anything for you" but the words didn't find their way out.

The sudden realization hit me, what I just did.

I brought a woman home and possibly just filled her mind with promises that I thought I was going to keep. Just like I thought I could keep her.

My hands trailed along her arms, she tried to grab my hands. I brushed past them, only to utter the words, "As much as I might want you, you shouldn't want me. I can't give you more than just this."

Her eyes softened at the sudden words that in the end I was there to help her, and anything else wasn't going to happen. No matter what. I didn't give her a chance to tell me otherwise, it was better this way, knowing that she deserved someone else, someone to grow old with, that didn't make a lot of promises only to worry if they would fulfill them or not.

She couldn't want me. Better to leave her with the image of a good guy than one that wasn't afraid to take a life for his own cause.

Those words would come back and bite me in the ass and own it.

Chapter 12

HOUND DOG

Melody settled in for the next few days, I kept my distance to allow her space, hoping that she would make it her own. I kept my distance primarily to allow her to not rely on me completely. She had gone out and gotten some things, worked with a couple record companies, and filled the house with life for once.

And yet I avoided her like I had taken my own word. Avoiding her to avoid the feel of retracting everything I said.

I barely looked at her even if she had emerged from the room. I made sure I was home late, only to avoid the late night wake up. I was going mad and looked like a maniac finding ways to avoid her because I feared that if given the chance, she might change her mind.

And as much as I wanted to be a part of that transition, watching her get a little comfortable in a safer space, it was for the better until we started working.

Our relationship, our partnership was going to be a friend teaching a friend. Or protege as she had joked that night. I laughed at myself at the foolish thought. Thinking that friend was enough. I needed her out of my head.

I sat in the living room one night, she hadn't come out of the room. I could hear her hum tunes and I ached to hear her sing. I hoped she was still writing during the times I left.

I would look up from my computer hoping she would stumble in, and flash me a smile. I could have talked to her but after I told her to come home with me, I knew the line I was tiptoeing.

Why did it feel like that was harder than patching into the club?

I was a seesaw that had no balance.

There was something off in the house, and it felt like strangers rather than something else. I had no one to blame but myself.

My phone pulled me from my thoughts, seeing that it was Fender. If Fender called, then something was wrong and I wasn't ready for what came next.

"Make it good, or make it worth my time, brother," I warned him, because as much as I needed to get out of the house, I wanted to be where I was.

"It's neither, unfortunately," he said.

My face dropped, I didn't want to hear that. It had been a while since we had heard from PD about the recent murder. Then again, we were trying to get them off our tails since we were innocent. After I had questioned each of the club members, I needed to know for sure that it wasn't them and someone wasn't testing my patience.

Was it excessive, sure, but I wasn't taking chances.

"What now?" I asked, looking to see if there was movement from Melody's room.

Fender let out a sigh before telling me, "Greene called, we're needed downtown."

Fender was right, it was neither.

"Get Shooter, send me the location and be there as soon as I can," I growled out before ending the call. I could feel my head pounding at my temples and tension in my shoulders.

I knocked at Melody's room, and she jerked her head back from the bed where her notebook was. Her hair was thrown into a thick bun, her bright face looking healthier than before, and her body looking damn tempting in her sweats.

"I just wanted to let you know that I have to go, and don't know when I'll be back," I said. Not that I thought she would worry about me, let alone talk to me after I was practically gone the majority of the time.

After barely speaking with her for weeks, I didn't know where that came from. My mind took control and impulsively knocked down a wall that I wasn't ready for.

I hadn't had time to help her like I promised, but she didn't push back. Something told me she was holding back thinking I'd kick her out.

"You didn't have to tell me," Melody said, softly.

"I just don't know what time I'll be back," I said, throwing my hands in my pocket.

She huffed, "You don't need to do this." She went back to writing.

I shook my head because now I was confused, "Do what?"

She sighed again like I had asked an obvious question. "Tell me your movements, you don't need to report to me. We're not dating, we don't own each other."

"That's not..." I started but she kept going. I quickly realized that my master plan of ignoring her, putting distances between us was working too well.

"A few kisses was enough to say and then tell me that there's nothing more, okay. I got it. You're helping me out, it's a kindness, not a relationship. You go your way and I go mine." She barely looked at me. She sighed, like hope was gone, "I think we got it out of our system. I understand. I appreciate the gesture. Hell, if you need me out just say so. If you're having second thoughts, I understand. Just tell me."

Obviously I didn't know what I wanted. It hurt a bit to hear it from her, the pain and almost sorrow in her voice. I caused that.

She thought I had second thoughts, but what she didn't know was that they weren't of regrets, they were ones of her and if I deserved a chance. I was angrier after she said it was out of our system because internally that would never be the fact.

Why was I expecting so much more fight, when my own plan worked?

I didn't like it.

I didn't have time to fix it, it would have to be later.

That was her defensive wall, to not expect the best, to only rely on herself. I saw that.

Before I could retort, my phone kept buzzing in my pocket. I already knew it was Fender blowing up my phone. My hands shot out of my pocket clenched into a fist, wanting to hit something.

My phone kept going off, she quickly looked at me.

"I got to go, but we're not finished with this conversation." I groaned, hating the fact that I had to leave when this was unfinished.

I was barely out of the room before she whispered, thinking I didn't hear, "Can't give more than that."

I knew I fucked up, but couldn't help the thoughts of wanting her but can't have her at the same time. I couldn't keep doing it. I couldn't keep tiptoeing around her. I needed to stop the damn pity party.

I pushed through the door, almost busting it off the hinges. I got on my bike, revving the engine loud. The roar of the bike vibrated underneath me, the power between my legs. I needed a few moments to get out of my head. The open air with the breeze in my face washed away any of the tension that was built from back at the house.

I dug that grave too early.

Weaving in and out of traffic got me downtown quicker than I planned. But when I pulled up a block away from the scene, I suddenly realized that the scene was down the street from. The Growler. Not that many people knew it was one of ours, our hands were in quite a bit of businesses.

The feeling it was getting closer to home didn't settle well.

Seeing Fender and Shooter at the corner welcomed me to whatever chaos was about to be revealed. Shooter flicked his finished cigarette on the ground as he cleared his throat. Fender started rubbing the back of his neck. Fender tended to be quiet, more in the background, more observer than talker.

Fender came to us through the grapevine but I knew him from back in my Nash Lane days when he played guitar until one night he paid a price with an accident and hung up the guitar. He started to have tremors that came in high stress. They were controllable and even for a road captain he didn't let that stop him. He couldn't keep himself safe, but he wouldn't let that happen to anyone else.

"Please tell me this isn't what I think it is?" I asked, joining next to them waiting for Greene and his puppy dog, Daniels.

"Well, don't think we'll be nominated for town heroes if that's what you were hoping," Fender joked looking at me, then noticing my stern, pissed off look before turning away. He stood a couple inches shorter than me, but still a tall motherfucker.

Greene came strolling over right on cue, with his nervous trainee behind him. "Greene, tell me that isn't a crime scene in the middle of the business district and damn sure not near our business."

He took a deep breath, unlocking his phone to show us what they had again. And suddenly my heart dropped in my stomach for the first time in years.

"Thirty year old, caucasian female. 5 '4, auburn hair, known to be a singer around here. Cause of death without proper examination appears to be an overdose, similar to the first one. Nothing was stolen from her, she was left in the alleyway." Greene started to distribute the information to us, but all my eyes saw was Melody.

I knew it wasn't her, but the likeness reminded me of her.

It was a coincidence. That's what I kept telling myself. What wasn't a coincidence was someone hitting too close to home.

The fear of ever seeing her like this, that it could be her was all I saw in this poor soul.

Shooter shook my shoulder. "Prez, you good? You look like you saw a ghost."

It was exactly that feeling, if it wasn't for the fact that the lifeless body in the picture was hours old and I just left the house with my eyes on her, I would have thought it was her.

"Something like that," I muttered.

I shoved the phone back at Greene. "I appreciate the heads up, but if you're not warning us about potential interrogation again, I fail to see the reasoning for us to be here."

Daniels interrupted, "Respectfully, he didn't have to call at all."

The man was ballsy. "Well, buddy boy, you can shove that back. You're still new here. We are not at some beck and call."

Greene interjected, protecting his rookie, "Don't take too much offense. Hound, this isn't good. There's only so much that I can push to get it out of your direction."

"That a threat?" Shooter growled out.

Shooter stepped up toward Greene, but Greene didn't falter, didn't even flinch. "I'm not a lackey either. But I am a man of my word. As long as I know that it wasn't you all, I have no issues."

"Doesn't mean that you wouldn't just rat us out when things got tough. Even to save your own neck," Fender retorted.

The tension between them was growing and if we didn't want any more blood to shed, someone needed to step in. The two men kept sizing each other up, never breaking eye contact.

"We didn't do this," I intervened. It did nothing to break the external struggle to keep things under wraps.

"Didn't say it was," Greene respectfully said. "But, it looks like someone struck again."

Another evidence bag filled with another small blue, devil printed bag. Someone did it again, pointing out the similarities between the first one and now the one that lay at the end of the road. There was no way it was us, but only so much could be done to show it wasn't.

I had nothing against the man but no one was completely true to their word, some loyalties aren't that strong and dedicated.

Fender cleared his throat, "We all may have a bigger problem that no one else is seeing."

Shooter and Greene stepped back and twisted their heads. When he saw that they were waiting for answers he continued, "If anything, it's not one of us, more like someone framing us."

"You think someone is getting sloppy and overlooking," Greene said.

"More like targeting, and doing something internally or second hand. I don't know. But nothing has been said to us about the department thinking it's someone else. Someone that knows about the business, about the bags."

Daniels and Greene fell silent at the notion. They simply shook their heads no.

"Well, if someone is then it seems you have a problem," Daniels interjected.

"Leave that part to us," I said, with a slight smirk. It was going to be a long night.

"I don't like cleaning up someone else's mess," Greene grunted.

"Ah, but that's what we pay you for." I laughed, lightly tapping Greene's cheek.

"Hound, if I see that it's one of your men, we're going to have a problem," Greene warned.

"Our problems are always your problem," Shooter said.

Greene looked the other way or kept everyone off our backs. It was the concern that some things were truly out of his power and we might not have the power to stop. I'd be damned if that were to happen.

As Greene and Daniels walked away, I turned and knew what the day was going to be like. I certainly wasn't going to be home anytime soon. And a certain conversation was going to have to wait, as much as I knew that it couldn't.

The club came first.

The club always came first.

"I want answers and I wanted them yesterday," I growled, rolling my neck.

"Boss, we can't predict the future." Fender came to defend the lack of answers or initiative to protect.

I didn't care, someone clearly from the beginning was sending a signal and I wasn't going to just let it go. I wasn't going to loosen up now, someone was coming for blood.

"I'll tell you what the future holds. That." I turned pointing at the scene surrounded by the red and blue lights. "That's strike two. I let it slide, thinking we were in the clear."

"We were," Fender started, but that shit wasn't flying with me.

I stopped, standing chest to chest. "I don't care if we were. I will not let our defenses down on pure thought. Next time you think, you remember what it's like to let your guard down." I sneered at him.

If you want it done right, then do it yourself.

"What do you want us to do, boss?" Shooter interrupted before I could break further. There were too many thoughts swirling around.

"Get Blaze to hack the CCTV footage, I want to know who was the dealer, or someone had to be watching and once he finds something, let me know."

"What do you expect to do?" Shooter questioned.

"If it wasn't us, then it was someone else targeting or selling. I think we have been too hands off. I won't mind spilling blood if that's what it means to get answers and end this crap."

"Sounds like Saints may be turning in the halos for a moment." Fender nodded his head.

"And church tomorrow morning," I added before it was fresh on my mind.

Shooter jolted. "Why not now?"

I shot him a warning before he backed off. "Because I'm meeting with Blaze tonight and then I got something I need to take care of."

Certainly, our halos were a bit tarnished. I had a little birdie that needed my attention before she wanted to fly and leave.

Chapter 13

MELODY

Do you remember the commercial where an older woman was beckoning for help and there was a device that would reach out for help?

After Hound left, that's what it felt like.

I already knew that something with him wouldn't be realistic, but it was damn nice to feel wanted and desired. Hell, I thought the feeling was mutual.

The man brought me home and wanted me to kiss him. His sweet words of wanting to help me accomplish my dreams felt like bitter lies at this point.

He said the word "friend" and even "As much as I might want you, you shouldn't want me. I can't give you more than just this." He said he was going to help me, but in the days I had been here, it was feeling like it was an empty promise.

This was nothing but a hot and cold treatment. I'd rather have been in my van and alone than being in this warm house and being alone.

I had called Sadie, I missed her voice and seeing her often. But I was afraid that with what I knew and gathered about Hound, I didn't know how much of a risk it could be. I had videocalled her. Her beautiful face popped up, and her lively voice made me smile.

I told her as much as I could, telling her I was safe. Telling her that sleeping here was great until Hound would ignore me or make excuses to leave. I had told her that I hardly saw him. She pressed about the hot kiss and his treatment in the beginning.

"Both of you have it bad. A knight in shining chrome." She giggled.

"I wouldn't call him that, really," I chewed on my lip.

Her eyes narrowed, she could tell I was more upset. "What's wrong, gorgeous?"

I huffed, "I picked an argument with him before he left and I may have guilt tripped him. Honestly, he deserved it. He went from the full welcome and support to high tailing it anytime he sees me. I wasn't expecting a relationship, fuck I don't know what I expected. Then he told me that he couldn't give me much more than "this". And what the hell does "this" even mean?" I rambled on and on, causing anger to flow through me.

Sadie tried to interrupt me. "Jesus. Melody, take a breath. You're in deeper than I thought. I mean you've said you hardly know the guy and now you're worried that he's changed his mind on you. Damn, this is better than my damn romance novel."

I could have left after that conversation, but the slight bleeding heart in me said to stay and hear him out.

I shook my head at her. "What the fuck am I to do? I feel like if I left, he'd find me and tell me to stay and possibly get back into the same habits he's got now. But he makes it hard to stay and believe. I'm starting to regret it."

She chuckled, "Damn, already got you dick-matized before he can even sink into you." I made a face, and she laughed harder. "Sounds like you both need to air out what you're both feeling and go from there. He'd be a damn fool not to listen to you and keep you, and who knows, maybe even fall in love with you."

Hound Dog? Fall in love with me? The man that has pushed me away saying that I shouldn't want him? Sure between this and the club, he has better priorities than to house a semi-homeless songwriter in his comforting home.

Internally, I needed to prepare myself for the possibility that someone changed their mind again and that it would be okay. I should have been more hesitant, not automatically taken his hand and said okay.

But there I was thinking about the man that had made it clear that while it was a moment of weakness and he was trying to be a nice person, nothing else was going to happen.

Just an intense friend or guardian or mentor? I didn't know what to call him. We hadn't worked on anything. You know they always say never take candy from a stranger. Well, I think I was looking for the whole damn Halloween bucket.

I sat there waiting for him, even when he said don't wait up for him.

I kept myself busy. Between circling the house, sitting outside with the sun in my face, even lying on the couch and sleeping, my mind kept wandering back to him. I was tempted to go into his bedroom or anywhere to gain insight on the man that was my roommate.

Nothing was giving me details.

The home was not much of a home. Still an empty canvas when he brought me here. I started to think what if I randomly found things and made it home. Add something every day to see if he would notice. The more I thought about it the more I felt it would turn into a prank.

Finally, I went out to my van and grabbed my box labeled "personal" to find something that would help me feel like the home was more than an empty prison.

A photo frame with a picture of Aria, my sister, and myself. The picture was worth more than anything. A reminder that there was sunshine that was taken away too early in life.

I placed the photo near the hallway table near my bedroom. I touched the picture like I'd done a hundred times. But unfortunately, she wouldn't sing anymore, she was gone for over eight years, taken away from me by a drunk driver one night. Her beautiful, smiling face calmed the nerves inside me. She had that effect when she was alive, and I missed her terribly.

After that, Dad stopped speaking to me, between his drunken rage and his "disappointment" in me.

I bided my time with cleaning my room, straightening up around me. I kept busy. Hours had passed since he left that morning. Night time was quickly approaching and I needed more distractions.

I couldn't get out of my head of what to expect with Hound and what was expected of me. Did I keep acting like there wasn't something between us? Did I keep acting like I was in his debt or waiting for him to tell me what we were doing? Did I heed his tone and warnings about not wanting him or that it was a one time ordeal?

I steered into the kitchen, playing blues music as I rummaged through the cabinets trying to find ingredients for baked apples. Each song moved me, listening to the words and melodies that could transport any emotion into an abyss of stronger desires.

The kitchen was filled with the aromas of apple and cinnamon and my secret of nutmeg and brown sugar. Something about apples and home was enough to ease any painful memory.

The music shifted to another genre, bringing a song that was meant for a duet, about a couple clinging on to heartbreak and drinking their sorrows from a bottle and how angels sing them to sleep. I couldn't help but harmonize with the male until the female lead came on. The song was full of heartache and sadness, I could feel it in my chest.

It talked about how the woman wanted to let go of the memory of him and she drank a bottle hoping it would wash it all away. I had closed my eyes only to chase away the harmful thoughts.

A tear threatened to drop down my cheek, as I took a ragged breath. The steam from the pan with the apples and ingredients burst in my face. I jolted as something else touched my cheek, wiping the sudden tear away.

My eyelashes bat open to see the rugged appearance of the blue-eyed, smirk filled face of Hound.

"You don't need the bottle, honey," he said, trying to comfort me, alluding to the fictional bottle in the previous song.

I jerked my head as I took the pan off the burner, turning away from him.

"Thought you weren't going to be home," I threw out.

His deep bass voice roared out, "I wasn't, but my thing can finish in the morning."

I grew curious. "Can I know what happened?"

I shouldn't have asked, didn't have a straight right to know. But something grabbed his attention early this morning enough to leave. He had a whole damn club to run, it was probably that.

"Better to not know right now," he answered with his own truth.

I scooped the apples into two bowls. I had no intention of sharing, but when I turned back to face him, his face was showing how much this thing had taken a toll on him. I passed the bowl to him as our hands grazed each other. The touch made me freeze, his eyes captured mine. The heat grew between us and I didn't know whether I was going to explode or shrink myself smaller.

He looked at his bowl, giving me a smile, before taking a spoonful of food and making a mouthwatering moan that wasn't the food's fault.

"Keep making food like this and I'll never let you go," he said, with the remnants of food left in his mouth. I shield away after that, knowing that it was about to be a conversation, but I didn't know if I was ready for it.

I cleared my throat taking charge, needing to get the answers to know my next steps. Did I stay or did I go?

"You said that we weren't done with a conversation, and now seems like the time to finish it," I said, taking a bite into my own comfort food.

The spoon clanked into the bowl; he finished chewing the apples before looking back at me. "Right, straight to it." He stretched his back, biding his time. "I think I need to apologize first."

I cut him off, "Think or know," I snapped.

His nostrils flared for a brief second, but calmed down before he continued, "I'm sorry, Melody."

"Sorry for what?" I crossed my arms.

"I'm sorry I haven't been myself and making you feel welcome. I can only imagine what you felt, and then having an idea that you weren't wanted," he said. It was only half of what I was feeling. But I wasn't going to step in and correct him. It seemed he had more to say.

He gulped, the man was a nervous wreck, "You have been nothing short of being perfect." I hid a snort at the word "perfect". And I treated you like the plague and I thought I could push what I was feeling and what I did down."

He started to step closer and my heart jumped into my throat, rendering me silent. I wanted to fight back but him being in close proximity, I didn't know if I was going to bolt or not.

If I did, I'm certain he'd chase me.

"And what's your honest truth?" I asked, waiting for his real feelings to shed some light on what was going on in that brain of his.

The closer he got, I resisted reaching out and doing something spontaneous. I forced myself to look up, seeing every detail of his face. The hard lines of his face, his full lips hidden behind his facial hair, the tiny red scar that went across the bridge of his nose.

"That there's no way I've gotten it out of my system," he said, as he grabbed my waist pulling to where there's no space. "And I have a few promises that I have to make good."

"Hound, you don't need to say nice things just to settle this. I understand that it was a brash decision and I just went with it. If I can't be here, then I'll leave and we can forget about this. It was sweet at first, but I know when I'm not needed and wanted or even when people have second thoughts. It's okay, we're humans, we get confused on wanting what we actually need in life," I started to ramble attempting to protect my heart. I threw everything at him that I could to not appear as the clinger people deem me to be.

Only after a period of time, I've come to do things on my own and never needed someone's help. I had something to prove to myself.

He leaned down, "Do you always run your mouth only to tell yourself you're not worthy."

I just blinked at him, because how was I supposed to answer that?

Before I fight and tell him that it was alright to do just that, just let it go and go safely in opposite directions, he grabbed the back of my neck. "I realized I was a dick, And I'm going to prove that I'm not."

I wanted to fight back, but when he pressed his lips onto mine, I was a goner. I couldn't hold back the moans that plagued me. It felt so good to let go at that moment. My hands gripped his arms, it was the closest thing I could grab. His kiss was like fire fueling my inside. It tasted of bourbon and sweetness.

He devoured me like I was the only one for him. He pulled back only to let out a pleasurable growl. I didn't say a word when he hoisted me on the kitchen counter where he didn't have to bend down to kiss me. I soon wrapped my legs around him, caught up in a lustful haze. He wrapped my hair in his hands to pull me to the side, he nipped and kissed my neck.

My hips bucked as he hit that one spot that made my knees weak. I didn't want him to stop but something nagged at me to stop him before I completely gave myself over to him. We needed to talk more about our situation and what was going to be expected.

All that was pushed down as our hands teased and taunted, itching to have what we wanted. For that moment, I wanted nothing more than him. Lust easily wiped away thoughts and power.

No wonder it was a deadly sin.

One of his hands traveled at the edge of my shirt, fiddling around until my body gave him his answer to do more. His hands were a mix between rough and satisfying, grazing over my skin until he found the lining of my sports bra. His rushed hand slid over the tender flesh as I let out a whimper.

"Hound," I breathed.

"Does this feel "out of our systems", little songbird?" he asked, his finger tracing over my sensitive, hard nipple.

"No," I answered as he kept teasing me. It had been so long since someone like him wanted to touch me, tease me. I was almost ready to combust.

He kept nipping at my neck. Every tease or twist of my nipple, I was close. My back arched, meeting his hips. The ache was growing stronger in me.

"Can you come with just me playing with your beautiful nipples with only just my hands?" He made it sound like it was the goal.

I didn't know if it was possible. "Please, please," I begged.

He did just that, playing me like his favorite toy and when I was ready to combust, it felt like notes that were unattainable were achievable.

Soon, I found myself flooded with bliss, every tingling feeling from my feet to my fingertips. He just held me there, allowing my body to revel in this new found feeling. If I could come with just him playing with my nipples, goodness knew what else he could do to me.

I bet it would feel freeing, vulnerable, or even an entirely new wave of emotion.

Maybe even belongingness.

My body writhed with pleasure, and he let go, adjusting my bra like a gentleman. He kept holding me like I was going to float away or something. I could still feel something hard pressing against him and I almost felt guilty that he didn't have the same release as me.

Well, he proved me wrong. It was definitely a possibility.

But then again, I was mad at him still, and we had gotten nowhere in our previous conversation. I started to unhook my legs from his waist until he stopped me.

"Hound, I can't stay like this all night," I protested. He just gave me a look, like he was still in charge. "I'm serious, and just because one orgasm was given doesn't mean we're finished here."

His darkened expression sent a chill down my spine with such dominance. "One will never be enough."

"Hound," I warned.

"I know, honey. Come here," he said, scooping me into his arms and carrying me over to the couch. He settled us into the plush cushions. This man didn't seem like a cuddler but what he was giving wasn't cuddling it was a brief reassurance. Reassurance that answers would be given.

He sat there in silence. I wanted to know what he was thinking, what was going on in that head of his. I also wanted to crawl off his lap with the tension between us, but I knew that wasn't going to happen.

"Hound," I started, more like I wanted him to carry on a conversation.

"Here's what's going to happen. Tomorrow night I'm taking you to a place where your lessons will begin," he started. I went to open my mouth, but he shook his head.

Yes, sir.

I didn't know where that came from, but it felt almost natural.

"I made a promise and I make good on my promises," he said.

"Then some," I whispered.

He squeezed my thighs in the most playful way. Who would have thought this gruff man had a softness to him?

"So, you don't want me to leave then?" I asked.

"Only if you want me to come find you," he said.

"Then what are we, Hound, because you tell me to stay away and then don't. It's college bullshit all over. I'm too old for games." I stood my ground. For once, I raised my voice for something that was going to affect my life. "I can leave, and try to pretend that this didn't happen. As much as I wish I won't have to, but that's what it is."

He sighed, "Would you accept the answer of "I don't know?"

I shook my head, "Then I would say that you don't need me in your lap, or you can't be kissing me or making comments about orgasms. I wasn't expecting a ring or anything, but I expected at least this." I gestured between the two of us.

"How about "I don't know" because I've never felt a strong connection with someone until you, so I don't know what to call it. With the amount of blood on my hands, there isn't a chance for a happily ever after," Hound admitted.

For once, I saw a hint of a truth.

"Fine, for now I can accept that." That was my truth. "You want to tell me what happened today?"

"I saw something that gave me a second thought," he said before kissing my cheek and bringing me close to his chest.

I had hoped that he meant what he said, because with this back and forth, I knew I wasn't going to stick around any longer if it meant that my heart was at war. But then again, what did I expect from a man of the club life?

Chapter 14

HOUND DOG

I had Melody at rest for now, and a plan for my promises to come true. But when I left her the next morning, I hoped that she would hear my answers and would stay. I would tell when I would pick her up for her first lesson.

Church was sacred to us. It meant business, it meant that sometimes we were at war and needed a battle strategy.

This time, everyone was going to tell me what the hell was going on and why we were lacking in protection.

I had trust in certain men, but some still had my weariness. I know that not every club would be truthful, though it was expected.

Coming to the clubhouse after my night with Melody had me wishing I was back with her, answering her questions.

"Lost in your mind there, Prez," B.B joked as he waited for me by the banister outside. I turned off my bike, cracking my neck from the stiffness it held.

"Wishing it was lost somewhere else," I muttered.

"Or on someone." He wiggled his eyebrows.

"Yeah, right," I scoffed, brushing off the fact that he was right. No one needed to know about Melody. I kept her safe, away from prying eyes. Soon, I'd bring her into this world of mine and perhaps make her my queen.

Well, that escalated quickly.

The sudden thought rushed to my dick. And those thoughts turned into tempting ones of seeing her on her knees begging for it. I shook my head.

She was my little secret, one I wasn't ready to share with the whole club. Even if it meant that she wouldn't be fully protected, she would still have me.

One step at a time, or at least that's what I kept telling myself.

"Can't play dumb with me, I know she's kept in your house, you dog you." he leaned about the post, crossing his arms.

I stopped dead in my tracks. Before I could say something, he continued, "Don't worry that pretty little head of yours, I'm a lover not a fighter, your secret is safe with me." He tapped his nose before walking back beside me.

"Is everyone here? I'm ready to get this started, so we can end the witch hunt internally and out there," I growled.

"Pretty much, except waiting for your little hacker genius. The man hasn't spoken a word since you told him to look into everything. I think you cracked his brain," B.B said as we both strode into the main meeting hall.

A welcoming sight of brotherhood, seeing all the members that helped create everything we built: a chrome, music filled empire.

Since my presidency, that had been the focus as well, the legit businesses. But now someone was making threats to our empire, and the club wasn't going to sit back anymore.

"Get the boy here now, I want a fucking name and I want it now!" I shouted. B.B was used to my tone, never back down nor questioned it. Well, not completely.

If I wanted certain things in my life, I needed to do it for myself. Pops said it best after I left the industry. "Sometimes the best things in life are the ones that you take for yourself."

He was right.

I approached the podium, the one that begged for attention. The roar of laughter that was once filling the meeting room died down as soon as I stood behind it. It wasn't much, but there was symbolism behind it, I earned my shot and my reign, and I wasn't going to let some rogue druggie take what I helped build, what the club owned away from us.

Dozens of eyes rested on me, waiting for me to speak. I had a lot on my mind, including wanting blood on my hands.

"Yesterday, Greene informed us that another body had turned up. Only a couple weeks from the last one. And nearby one of the businesses. I don't think I need to tell you all of this is completely bullshit. But I will ask, who was supposed to be at the Growler the past couple of nights?"

Brothers worked for an earning, a chance for work history to be built, not only part of the community, but for the money. I knew the answer to my own question but waited for the opportunity of truth to be revealed.

Stray and Chameleon stood up as soon as the question left my mouth.

Stray was a young buck like me, but was in the club earlier on. The man was the odd ball out of the club, whereas most of us come from some sort of entertainment business or creative mindset, he came from the boxer world. A reigning champ in his younger years but now helped run the gym and underground matches at Swing Low.

Chameleon was another good man. An older member but one from Pop's old club. When that club disbanded and others were lost, the original chapter president took precautions but needed the numbers. I'd known him pretty much since I was born. He was family and one of the few that I trusted when I got the presidency.

I looked around the room for one more, one brave soul that I knew, knew better. Waylan. My cousin on my mother's side. A wayward soul that needed a place to call home. He nervously stood up waiting for my reaction. I didn't show him mercy but I knew that he wouldn't let me down.

Shooter stood up in his seat, turning toward them. "And you didn't see anything?"

Shooter was straight to the point, and that was the way he wanted his answers. He didn't expect them to have time to think of another answer.

"It was a normal night, Shooter. Waylan and I were out front the entire night until close. Chameleon was in the back. We had our regular people inside the entire night. Nothing was happening," Stray stood his ground.

"Obviously, something happened. May not have been near the Growler but it was in close proximity," I continued the questioning.

"No outside bikes, no strange vehicles passing down the main drag," Chameleon chimed in. I looked at Waylan waiting for him to answer. But no prospect was going to step on anyone's toes. Well, no one was like me. I spoke my mind.

So if no bikes or other vehicles were around, did someone just dump and run without being seen? I needed more, because obviously my brothers weren't going to say anything that wasn't the truth.

One person better have something for me or else my temper might flare more than my bite. Out of the corner of my eye, I saw Otis brushing Blaze into the hall. Blaze looked like he was ready to crash any minute. The poor boy was lacking sleep, and I was guilty as charged.

I signaled Otis to bring him closer. Otis nudged him, giving him the okay to move closer. The kid was brilliant beyond his own good. He didn't get the name Blaze out of sheer luck. The fucker almost burned down a building or two doing experiments with pyrotechnics and lighting design. His way around the dark web came in handy.

I gave him a moment to tell me something before I addressed the rest of the group.

I let Shooter continue with any questions about other locations. I bent down to Blaze's face, waiting for him to tell me something good. I needed something good, or else I was about to hit the streets my way and maybe leave an actual trail.

Then who would protect our little birdie?

"Make it good, kid," I warned him.

He simply nodded his head. "I think I did, depends on if you think a name is important." At first, he had a cocky grin on his face, but noticed mine and quickly dropped it.

"Make it quick," I told him.

He handed me a piece of paper with a name, and quickly turned his tablet to show me CCTV footage of exactly what I was hoping.

Weston Farraday.

Yeah, I knew that name, and so should Fender. Weston was one of the dealers we worked with in the past, having been in the game for a long while. The footage only revealed that he had been in that area for the night.

It shouldn't surprise me, but we didn't deliver any product to him, as we had slowed down as per advice. So, what the hell was he doing in selling territory with nothing to have on his person? It smelled like a damn mole, or backstabber. Trusting him wasn't in the cards.

"Good work, Blaze," I commended him. He followed through and produced something helpful. The slight beam in his eyes told me that it wasn't a regret to have him prospect.

As I broke my attention away from Blaze, there started to be more grumbles from the crowd as Shooter was starting to piss people off with the accusations. He was on the verge of pressing his luck, looking for blood in the wrong places.

I cleared my throat as the crowd finally hushed. "Listen, I'm only going to say this once. We have a job and we take it seriously. Be on higher alert, because someone is out there making us look like murderers... this time."

I got a few nods from them. Something in my gut told me that whoever is behind this wasn't one of us.

"We're not shying away from our schedules, you hear me," I warn them.

My hope was that some normalcy would return and this situation would fade into the background.

As I dismissed them, thankful no other blood was shed, I signaled Fender and Shooter to come close to me and B.B. I let B.B in on what was found, and the twisted bastard curled his lips into a mischievous smile. More like a bloodthirsty look to me.

Shooter and Fender's look both combined with annoyance and exhaustion, but they would push past it. "Time to go on a field trip."

"Who we visiting?" Fender asked.

Shooter cracked his knuckles, "Do I need to bring any special tools?"

Oh to be in Shooter's mind, a dark and rough place. But his art spoke for himself sometimes. Sometimes I wasn't talking about the ones on his canvas.

"Weston," I said as I headed toward the door, back out to my bike.

As I passed through the main lounge area, the trail of sweet butts and ol ladies sent a sting in my chest. My mind traveled to Melody and if she would fit in. She was feisty, but sometimes quiet, she was a survivor. But something told me if she wanted to, she'd be possessive over me, staking her claim. The mere thought of her being possessive sent an ache to my dick.

I shook my head, bringing my attention back to the task at hand.

Being the leader that I needed to be. I needed to be the rough and ready, protective man that the club needed. Not the love-sick puppy I was being.

Chapter 15

Hound Dog

Weston wasn't easy to find by the time we got downtown. He was a mole that hid back in the ground, afraid to show his face.

When Fender knew that it was one of the "trusted" people, he was brewing inside. He wouldn't show it, he tried not to hold a lot of anger, but where Fender may lack in mental anger, Shooter made up for it when it came to his anger. The man expressed it in more ways than one.

The four of us made it downtown in time before night fell.

Weston was a self-made man, doing more business for himself and putting himself in the top. He started off picking from the bottom of the barrel when the Saint's gave him the chance when they started in the city.

It was then that safety was a thing, to not sell it to already known or suspected addicts. It was for pleasurable usage, not addictive. It was one death that we didn't want to be held responsible for, other than our own acts.

But thankfully it wasn't hard to find him; Shooter had surveyed the area and saw him. The crooked smile of my brother made me a lot more confident that hopefully this situation would end once and for all.

I wasn't going to break another promise. The quicker I could make this, the better. A few tourist groups were swarming around the area, making it a cover for Weston. When the crowd of people appeared in front of Weston, it acted like a cloud of smoke as the man bolted in the other direction.

The only reasons for a person to run from us were guilt, protection from a death wish, or a fun game of primal chase. Personally, I'm a fan of the last one.

As soon as the crowd cleared, Shooter went chasing him down with Fender on his heels. B.B chuckled as him and I hung back allowing the other two to nab him and haul his ass in an alleyway. "We think Weston actually did something?"

"I'm hoping that he knows or saw who is doing this and we can tell Greene who he can actually go after."

"Seems like a tall order." B.B just smirks like a damn fool.

We took our time, until we saw Fender grab him by the jacket and haul him into an alleyway. As we turned the corner, Weston broke free of Fender and gave Shooter one lucky shot. Though I didn't know if he knew it at the time, that punch probably was the signature on his death certificate.

Fender yanked Weston back to the brick wall. The corner of his mouth spewing with blood, like a mad man.

"Seems like an unfair fight," Weston bellowed out.

Shooter got his feet, ready to lunge at Weston, wanting his own turn for a spill of blood.

"Well, you ran," B.B chimed in. "Not a very good look for you, my friend."

He grunted as the men pulled him back. "Tell me, Weston, you wouldn't do anything to screw us over, now would you?"

The knife at my side was beckoning my name, to carve out the answers, to reassure everyone that questioned who was leader and ran these streets.

"Why would I do that?" Ge hissed out, he stopped struggling for a moment, twisting his head to look at me.

"A million and one reasons." I didn't hesitate. I continued, looking down at him, "Were you selling a couple nights ago?"

His eyes were dead, no sign of life. He was hiding something but playing it off as if his loyalties still lied with us. He slowly shook his head no. Shooter sensed his hesitation and knocked

Weston's head back into the wall. Weston let out a yelp, shaking his head back and forth.

"I don't know what you're talking about, I don't have a supply," he attempted to answer. But it wasn't good enough.

I tsked. "I think you're lying to me, Weston, and I don't take kindly to liars. You're the only one that can save your own skin."

"Best listen to him. He has been on edge lately, and is itching to get his hands dirty," B.B cooed as he warned that I wasn't in the mood.

Not a soul minded what was going on, someone people knew better than others. I pulled out my knife from my pocket, flicking open the blade. I stepped toward Weston's body, pointing the knife in his face. "Last chance before I take my own methods for a ride. I'll ask again, were you selling a couple of nights ago?"

He let out a deep whimper. "Only a small supply."

The knife traveled along the base of his neck, trailing along his collarbone. His body shivered under the blade, the nerves settling through his skin. "Where did you get the small supply? Last we checked, we hadn't given anything new in a few weeks," I pointed out.

"So you're either underselling and reporting back that you ran out, only to then pocket the rest," B.B tauntingly said.

"Or, you found yourself a new person and are selling for someone else," Fender finished the thought. The once calm man now tensed with his own anger of being double crossed.

Weston swallowed, debating what answer he was to give. I gave him a little more motivation to answer the damn question. The blade popped a few buttons, threatening to expose skin for easier access to slice. "Tick tock, Weston. Wouldn't want to damage a lot."

His body continued to shake. My patience was being tested and faded with each passing second. The sooner I could get an answer, the faster we shut it down.

The faster I can return to Melody, the safer she could be.

My knife poked harder at his abdomen, breaking the first layers of skin. His pathetic whimpers only made it easier to keep going until he sounded like he was going to cry out. "Wait, wait. Please don't," he begged.

"Why should I?" I growled out.

"You were the only one selling that night and a girl ended up dead," Fender accused him, passing along the judgment.

"I didn't do anything, I didn't kill anyone," Weston whined out, sucking in his stomach and attempting to free himself.

"And yet, a pretty young thing ended up dead down the street from where you were selling. So far the only cause of death is the drugs that were in her system and the drugs found around her," Fender continued out, his own passion powering his words.

Weston rapidly shook his head, trying to convince us of his truth. Enough blood and lives had been taken, and it wasn't any of my men. At least right now I could be confident in that.

"I didn't kill anyone," he kept repeating as if it was going to save his life.

"And yet you did. Answer the fucking question!" I pressed harder as blood was trickling down his skin.

He let out a loud groan, the sweat on this man was appalling. Disgraceful. But I was at my breaking point with enough people breathing down my neck like I was the one under the microscope. I had promises to fulfill to the club, previous presidents, and even the founding chapter. I wasn't going to let them down.

Weston struggled against the guys' hold. Fender's hand started to tremble. A flare up was coming on, I needed to be quicker.

"Answer. The. Fucking. Question." I gave him one last chance. Watching him squirm, panting for relief made something dark and twisty in me smile. I could be a twisted son of a bitch.

B.B's walked closer to me, a soft hand on my shoulder shook me away.

"Easy, Prez," he warned me, bringing me somewhat back to reality in front of me.

Weston grunted before releasing a sigh. "Someone else brought me an opportunity I couldn't resist."

"Start talking, rat, before I make it look like pumpkin season, spilling your guts all over this street." I pressed the knife harder into his stomach.

"Okay, okay. Someone gave me product but it had come with an added bonus," he began.

Greed is truly an ugly, deadly sin. Greed could touch every other sin, be the root cause of it all. There was an example in front of us.

"What was the bonus?" B.B questioned.

"Listen you have to understand, I've got things to take care of, the amount was going to be enough for me to do what I needed to do." Weston tried to reason with us.

"Does it look like I give a fuck?" I sneered.

I looked to the side to see Shooter's face twist in more anger; if the roles were reversed, we'd have a bloodier scene ahead of us.

"Someone came to me with a deal, I sell their product but it had to be in a different bag," he continued.

"What different bag?" B.B stepped to the side of me.

He gulped. "They asked to at least sell a product with one of your bags."

"Just one?" Fender asked for clarification.

He nodded his head. "I tried to tell them that I wouldn't use bags. I wasn't completely opposed to selling more if it meant more money coming in," he started to say as the urge to twist the knife was stronger than B.B's wake up call.

B.B cut me off before I could speak. "So you took a chance, thinking that it wouldn't come back to you."

Weston whimpered, "They said only one bag. They never said that they would do anything else. I swear, Hound. I just needed more money."

Needed more money, for what? The man did pretty well to continue to live in a tiny bit of luxury. He didn't have a wife or kids that we knew of, much less any family around the area.

"Well, let me let you in on a secret, something did happen. That one little bag landed a young woman dead and with the product in hand. You want to know what type of bag they found?" I challenged him to give me more excuses as to why.

He shook his head, whether it was true fashion that he didn't know or it was him buying time to survive this and tell the tale.

"It was the very blue bag that you supplied her."

"How was I supposed to know that they would go after her?"

"By not crossing us, and now, you're going to answer for what you did!" I shouted to his bloody face. And with one punch, he was out like a light. His deadweight body slinked to the floor. It took everything in me not to gut him there.

A confession was made and that was what I had to be thankful for because I didn't know if anything was going to work. Looked like some things needed to be handled a certain way.

Shooter and Fender stood by his body, the fucker was still breathing. At least for now.

"Had some restraint on you, Prez," B.B said as I turned to walk away.

"He's lucky that we need more information and he's not buried in the Mississippi." I growled.

"What you want us to do?" Shooter asked.

"Take him to the sheds, we'll give him a day or two to think about what he wants to do next," I commanded because as the sun had set I knew there was something that needed to be taken care of; a little birdie and her first flight lesson.

Chapter 16

MELODY

You've got to be kidding me.

I looked up and down between my phone and the place that Hound told me to meet him at for my "first lesson". A lesson I had no idea what to expect.

He had the desire to teach me the ways to be brave on stage and "fulfill my pretty little dreams". Honestly, I still wondered if he was delusional to think that he could teach me.

Hound texted me the address, after he finally got my number weeks later. But the address he sent me to was outside of the city, almost what felt like a warehouse district. Did I dare move into the building?

I'd seen too many suspense and horror movies to know you never go in a dark, spooky building. You get in your car, and leave.

"And yet I'm about to be the stereotypical woman wanting to go check it out." I gathered as much courage as I could as I walked closer to the building with my guitar in hand. As much as I didn't want to, a hit from the guitar would aid in my escape if this went sideways.

I looked at the message he sent.

Hound Dog

Time for your first lesson or two. Meet me here at 7pm. I want to hear you, little song-bird.

I had to admit that the nickname was growing on me. He had more of an admiring tone rather than a mocking one.

My heart raced as the darkened area was only lit by the warehouse lights inside. This abandoned warehouse was barren, I couldn't tell if there was once something there or something was being built.

I had blindly trusted Hound, growing from suspension and miscommunication to sincerity. We moved past the part where he was pushing me away or keeping his distances but his own foolishness had ended that.

I kept my mind from wandering into dangerous territory, not thinking about the way he could just touch me and I'd lose control. The way his words sparked a motivation to prove him right that I could do it, that my dreams could come true.

My steps echoed with each stride. My boots clacked on the cold concrete floor. The pure wonderment of the space and what it would be, the openings and the structures sent a chill down my spine.

I waited to see if Hound would come around the corner, perhaps with a small smirk on his face. But he didn't come. I walked further in the building, weaving in and out of the room barriers. It almost started to feel like a metal maze.

"What the fuck kind of deal did I make?" I whispered to myself.

"One with an outlaw that has some kind of beating heart for a certain woman," a deep voice rumbled behind me.

The small joke of being an outlaw reminded me of just that, that he was the president of the club. One that had eyes and ears on every street, they were one to behold. I turned to see the giant of a man invade the personal space bubble. He smelled like vanilla and bourbon, no wonder one could get drunk off of him.

"I feel like this was a test to see if I'd show up to a place that not even a cartoon crime fighting dog would enter." My nerves started up again, my hands were even trembling.

"No tests, but shows that you really want to do this, shows dedication," he replied, and with that my cheeks heated up. "Hi, songbird."

I gulped. "Hi Hound."

In that light, he eyes weren't just blue, it was like a midnight blue, darkened under everything around us.

It's amazing what can be felt when words are rarely spoken. It was somewhat skin crawling, wanting to fill the silence.

I cleared my throat. "As much as you look like you like what you see, it is a bit chilly. Could we get on with the lesson?"

I wasn't lying, the warehouse was feeling like a cold trap, even with the amount of layers I tried to put on. But the way he was looking was one that felt like he wasn't hungry for food.

He just smiled at me, "Yeah, we're gonna start tonight."

I looked down at the floor, "Okay, teach." I swung my arms out, "First, what the hell is this building? Is this where you lure all your obsessions and chain them to the wall until they beg you to take them?" I laughed.

He cocked his head, and in that moment I felt the heat rise again to my cheeks.

"Maybe." He cracked a smile at me, reaching to take my guitar and put it on the ground. "Maybe you're not wrong about an obsession."

"How can you be so intense then say such things that make a woman weak?" I looked at him, squaring up to his presence.

He chuckled as he smiled while biting his lower lip. "This is a new development. A legal development. B.B thought about a place for people to rent like additional art or creative spaces. It's in the early stages but for now, it will serve as our classroom. The acoustics right now make it feel like you're singing for a theater."

He trailed a finger down my cheek, "A place where you could be in the spotlight."

I leaned into his touch, trying to imagine this place filled with the creative souls he was talking about. Private spaces away from prying eyes or people judging you before you're ready to give it to the world.

"That's kinda beautiful," I admitted, walking away from him exploring the area. Mostly because if I stood in front of him any longer, the results would definitely have varied. "Will I ever get to meet this infamous B.B?"

He had grown quiet. "You sort of have."

"Apart from the Blue Sax. I wouldn't be able to point him out in a line up," I joked, but I got no response from him. I wasn't going to push.

"We're safe, right? Nothing is gonna come crashing down on me?" I laughed.

"Nothing's gonna happen. As long as there's no fire or something and we don't have to call the fire department, honey." He laughed alongside me.

You could say that I was like a cartoon character when their eyes widened when something drastic happened. But when I looked back at him, there was something that caught my eye, that small smirk. Like a memory waking up that was buried deep inside.

"You some kind of fire bug or something?" I cocked an eyebrow, nervous about the answer.

He shrugged. "Nothing too big, at least I think."

"Please tell me you're kidding."

It was like a memory had woken up and hit me over the side of the head. There was no way he... couldn't be.

"You gonna keep talking or you want to learn something tonight." he changed the subject.

But there was something. I wasn't blind.

He does something to me. I felt like I'd known him before. Something about his smile or his eyes when they lit up. The way he tried to make it easy to talk to me, like he was trying to fix something that was fixable.

Why would he want to help me?

I was a nobody.

I wasn't meant to stay in the light for long. I didn't fit into his world. And I wasn't going to change myself just to fit into his world.

He would have to take me as I was. I was somewhat strong. At least, I had to be.

He studied me for a moment. "I can hear your thoughts." He shoved his hands in his pockets.

"An outlaw and a mind reader," I joked.

"I asked if you were ready for your lesson," he said, stepping closer to me. I took a step back. "You keep looking at me like I'm kidding, like I'm going back on a promise."

"Well, can you blame me? The whole beginning of this has been the rockiest thing I have ever been through. And yeah, you made a promise. But I wouldn't blame you for taking it back." There I went rambling again.

His eyes darkened, "I beg your pardon?" He challenged me to finish my thought. The more I stood there, the more I couldn't take Sadie's advice anymore and a rush of reality hit hard.

"I'm sorry. I ramble like an idiot, not knowing how to shut up or accept help. Call it feeling like a burden. My problems are my problems and no one else's. Just like my music is my music, my path is my path. Things I called mine, and I can't let anyone take it away again."

There it was, a smidge of the truth. My own problem, I felt like I was the one that needed to get over it. Internally, I was a ball of self-doubt from the people that told me that I wasn't enough, that I was only good for one thing. Or even tried to turn me into something that wasn't me.

I was afraid of people helping me.

"I know what that feels like. Melody, you don't need to be afraid. You let go of the self-doubt. In fact, I have an idea."

He gently pressed a kiss to my forehead and dragged me further into the warehouse.

Chapter 17

HOUND DOG

"What do you mean you know what it's like?" she asked as I pulled her through the winding beams that made up the layout of the building.

If she wasn't loud and clear like before, I certainly heard her then. After being told she wasn't enough or that she couldn't accomplish things, it sounded like people tried to change her. I didn't fucking blame her.

What she didn't know was that I had gone through the same thing when I started off early in my career. So, I probably wasn't going to tell her as quickly.

Her feet picked up speed as I dragged her through the middle of the warehouse. It was just us, the way I needed it to be. Away from the club, away from prying eyes, a place where only I knew about, to protect her in some way.

When I set her in the middle, she crossed her arms, looking too damn adorable. "I don't think you do. Nobody dares to take from you. You're Hound Dog, the president of an infamous motorcycle club."

"And yet you're still here. Haven't bolted yet." I tapped her nose, taking a step back, I had an idea that would burst down those walls she built. The root of the problem, self-confidence. As an artist, you have to get to a point where you are pleased with yourself and embrace yourself.

If I could make her more confident between her presence on stage to her riffs to her confidently trusting herself and art, she would become an unstoppable force.

I wasn't going to change her. Hell the way she was part of the reason why I couldn't stay away from her.

But I wanted her to be open to anything, confident in her art. I wanted to see where the flash of bold confidence went. It was buried there somewhere.

"Well if I didn't, I have a feeling you would come find me no matter what," she joked.

She wasn't far from the truth. If she'd ran, I'd follow and drag her back. That was if she wanted to stay once something happened to her because of this lifestyle.

She started to tremble, between the cold and her own anxiety rattling internally. stepped closer, only to calm her down enough to get through this next part. "And I wouldn't want to give you back to a world that doesn't deserve you."

She was speechless for a couple of seconds, "You barely know me."

"Yet, you consume my every thought, even to put it in notes and measures." She consumed every inch of my mind, the way she was intense with her music.

"Why are you so obsessed with music and all of this?" She gestured toward the warehouse.

I'd share one of my truths only for her to give me all hers. I got her guitar from her case, watching her mouth drop when I started to strum a few chords, trying to remember a few songs that would give her some idea that I knew what I was talking about.

There was one song that was louder than the others, one that only a couple people had heard before. Something that wouldn't give too much of my past.

A past that I was no longer a part of anymore. A secret not many of my brothers knew. At least none of the newer ones.

If the sun burnt out,
Would you be there?
If I was lost in the stars,

Would you find me?

If anger flowed through my veins,
Would you keep fighting to save me?
If the world fell apart,
Would you stay by my side?

If the love was the only thing left,
Would you bind me with you
Never to let go, never to forget.
When problems grow and come in between,
Can we stand on hope,
Only to keep finding us.

Melody didn't say a word when I ended, her mouth was left dropped. The epitome of when a jaw hits the floor. I hadn't sang in a long time, but around her it was easy to get lost.

I barely sang after I started prospecting for the club even when I got patched in, it wasn't something that was fulfilling anymore. At least not until a wave of fate changed everything.

As much as I still wanted to push her away, it was evident that it wasn't going to happen. Little did she know that she was stuck with me.

"As much as I want to use that mouth for something else, you might want to close it, honey." I set the guitar back in the open case and strode over to her, tilting her face up to close her mouth.

Her breathing was even, but I could see the gears turning in her head. Her hazel eyes turned up, "You've been holding back on who you are." The way she looked at me was something to behold, like she was holding back a true smile.

"You think?" I asked her.

She nodded, she knew something. That little glint in her eyes sparkled under the warm lights. I gathered her in my arms, her hands traveled to my chest, playing with the collar of my shirt. How I wished that they would creep under my shirt.

"I'll trade you a secret for another one," she proposed.

"Careful, Melody.. That's not what we're here for. I showed you that I knew what I was doing to help you and that's what we're doing here." I tried to switch the direction of this night, but it wasn't going to go the way I needed.

"Please." She batted her eyes, her soft features melted me. "It won't take long." she cooed. She didn't wait for an answer. "When I first started writing, I worked for a lot of studios as a floating writer, the only way I could get my name out there without the stage. During that time, I wrote a song that a studio wasn't originally going to use, but then they had a young male artist that heard it and wanted it. Unfortunately, I never heard it recorded. Or heard it until now."

All color in my face felt like it disappeared.

"Later, someone told me who it was, the young artist that I wanted the song. An artist named Nash Young."

The sound of my past name crept through me like a ghost taking possession. The sounds of fate that weaved our stories together. She was the muse from long ago. The one that wrote with passion and grit, songs that were full of emotion.

I tried to say something but nothing came out. She smiled, like she couldn't contain it. "That's not the best part. I knew who he was before I knew he wanted my song. Because he was the same man that told me to call the fire department when I bumped into him in the hallway."

Now it felt like the world had shattered everything I knew. All the strings of fate finally untangled, because maybe deep inside that was trying to tell me she was mine for a longer time.

"You," I struggled to say.

"Me," she said. She waved.

"I guess I saved you," I mumbled.

"I guess you kinda did." She licked her lips.

There wasn't enough time to process all that I wanted to know, wanted to say.

"That's your song," I said again like a dumbfounded man.

"Well, I let you borrow it." The damn little minx winked at me. She was a ball of mysteries. "So, you're Nash Young."

"A long time ago."

"You're still him. Maybe not completely, but you are."

I shook my head. "I'm Nash Lane, but more Hound Dog."

That was going to be a conversation for another time.

I wanted her more than anything at that moment. Just her and me. In that moment, she accepted something in her that she didn't know.

"I'm keeping it, just like I'm keeping you," I growled out.

I had to tear myself away from her because any longer and I would have devoured her in a heartbeat, but I knew that before the night ended, what we craved would be satisfied until the morning.

"Lesson time, little birdie." I pushed away leaving her in the center of the room.

She hugged herself, not because she was cold, but because of her nerves.

"What's the lesson tonight? I thought I was just going to work on my singing," She somewhat pouted. The wheels were still turning in her head, trying to picture my first steps.

"That'll come soon, but first we need to get rid of those negative thoughts in your head that prevent you from being who you need to be, who you really are," I leaned on one of the walls, watching her squirm under the tension.

If I had it my way, she'd be in front of a mirror, stripping away all the things that hold her back. I'd save that for another time.

"You're going to tell me all that you have ever been told, every negative comment, every dismissal of your talent, every backhanded compliment, and you're going to yell out the right and truthful answer," I challenged her.

She rocked back and forth on her heels, hesitating to even start. "You think this will work?"

"It would be a start, but only you can know if it worked," I told her. Over the years, I thought I lost a version of myself to care for anyone other than family and the club. Most sweetbutts stayed away from me, already thinking that I was the cruel monster people made me out to be, but it wasn't far from the truth.

"Okay," Melody said, huffing out a breath like she had been holding it. She shook out her arms and her neck.

"What's the first thing that comes to mind that tears you down, what was first said to you." I tried to get her to think of where to begin.

Her face grew sadder at the thought, her eyes softening, her shoulders tensing up. "My dad telling me and Aria that the life of a singer wouldn't be a real career. That we wouldn't survive the real world, we'd turn into druggies or hookers."

Refraining from throwing my own fists into a wall was hard, because I felt the ounce of guilt that at least my folks and brother were there by my side. She didn't have that and it was where it all began for her. I swallowed my anger, "And what do you say to that, Melody?"

She whispered, "That I survived, that I'm in a career that I love, even when it tears me down."

It was close, but she still was focusing on a negative.

I pushed off the wall. "Say I'm a survivor."

"I'm a survivor," she said a little louder, but I wanted her to yell it to the point where the walls trembled.

I took another step. "Try again."

"I'm a survivor," she yelled out as it echoed in the emptiness of the building.

"That's my girl, what else." I started to circle around her, adding to the pressure that this wasn't going to end until she released a good amount of demons. The only demons that were allowed were the ones that I gave her, the ones that unlocked a true intimate desire.

She gulped, "The record companies."

"What about them?" I had some idea from what she'd already said to me.

"I'm told that I don't have the right image, the right sound, that it's better to stand in the background." She took a mental inventory of herself, touching her hips, her stomach, her legs. She was told like so many people that she wasn't the idea of beauty, that her unique and perfect external features weren't good enough to sell.

If she would have given in, she would have done anything from extreme dieting to changing her facial appearances to even become the person she wasn't. That showed strength that she didn't let greed overcome her.

I stood behind her, her back flush against my chest. I ran my hands along her curved side, running along her bottom of her stomach, caging her to me. I bent down to her ear, "And what do we say to that?" I said nipping at her ear.

She whimpered for a moment, getting lost in the sensation. Her little whimper went straight to my cock, twinging in my pants.

Her chest heaved as my fingers trailed along the edge of her jeans, the ones that made her peach like ass look good enough to bite. I kissed her neck, each kiss trailing along the curve between her neck and shoulders. I should have been hands off but I, myself, am a greedy bastard.

I'm also a Saint's Outlaw. I take what I want.

"Hound," she breathed out.

"What do we say to that statement, Melody?" I nipped at the midpoint of her neck.

Her ass ground against me, stirring something in me that just wanted to growl. "I am right for everything," she answered.

I shook my head, chuckling. "Try again."

"I am enough," she answered loudly, like my own little echo. With one hand wrapped around her waist, the other one traveled underneath her tank top. Which made me a little mad that she didn't wear enough layers for this cool weather. I made a little mental note for later.

"What else?" I asked. My hands trailed from her stomach to the wired contraption that was holding her luscious breasts. What I found made me smirk like a damn fool. Her nipples had hardened, and it wasn't because of the weather. I knew that if I reached down past her panties, she would be a puddled mess.

I wanted to play. But not until she unleashed everything and I could get her home. But tonight was the night that I would claim her as mine, I'd give her everything that I was, give into her cravings, worship her like the Aphrodite she was.

"I don't belong in the background." she rushed her words like they were buried deep down. I rewarded her with a tease of her nipples. I wanted so much to strip her and lick them, taste them for my own satisfaction.

"No, you don't, Melody. You deserve a huge, bright spotlight to show the world what a powerhouse you are," I growled out.

"Hound, please." She was in her own lustful haze. I wanted to drive her crazy, for her to submit.

"Tell me one more," I commanded her.

She shook her head no. I quickly released her nipples to grasp her neck, wanting to possess her.

"Tell. Me. One. More." I growled out, my voice rumbling against her back.

Her back straightened up, adjusting to my hold. "That's right, you're learning, never look down when talking about yourself," I said.

One more thing and I would believe I would had broken down those barriers.

"I can't perform on stage, because I'm afraid." she said.

"Why are you afraid?" I pressed.

I felt a tear drip down my fingers, wrapped around her pretty little throat. Her raw emotions were coming out. Her fears came alive.

"No one deserves your tears," I said softly, loosening my grip on her neck.

Her heartbeat was settling down. "I'm afraid that everything people have said will come true."

"But will it?" I let her loose, spinning her around, cupping my hands on her face. Those breathtaking eyes were filled with tears. Her brutal lies that once tore her down were no longer unspoken in her mind.

She rapidly shook her head, her warm tears dripping down her face. "I don't want them to. I want to prove that they were wrong."

I rested my forehead on hers. "And why's that?"

One final truth. "Because I am myself and I will prove them wrong."

There it was, she said she will, not she can. Her truth. For once, I ignored all the signs that told me I shouldn't and I went for it. I brought her lips to mine, capturing the rich feeling of a stronger, more truthful version of her.

She didn't fight me, she embraced it all. She embraced me. Her moans and her salty tears were delicious. It was tempting to take her now and not look back. But not there, not in the open where I could make her uncomfortable.

Her tongue slipped with mine, trying to take control over this kiss. This kiss that burnt deep in my soul.

But not here, I couldn't do it here.

I broke it, pushing away. Both of us were fighting to steady our breathing.

Her eyes looked lost and confused, she waited for me to say something. She tried to pull away from me, the look turned into rejection and hurt.

Oh no, my little songbird.

"Don't you dare think I didn't want this," I soothed her. "I can feel you. I want more and I would be happy to make that come true."

"Hound," she whispered.

"Go home, Melody. You're gonna spread your wings tonight," I said, grinning. Showing her that I wasn't going to let her go, never. "I'm giving you a ten minute head start."

I gave her another quick kiss, to feel her body once more before I truly devoured it.

Chapter 18

MELODY

The white lines of the road blurred between the tears I was still shedding and the speed of my van.

I couldn't fathom what happened between finding out the truth about Hound Dog. I mean Nash. I didn't know who I was kissing. At the time I knew it was Hound Dog, but then came the revelation that this wasn't the first time he had saved me from harm.

Then the man opened up scars of hurt done in the past. Every word that has torn me down, every twisted thought that told me I wasn't enough.

Then that kiss.

The kiss that told me he wasn't running and maybe I shouldn't either.

That kiss that I could still feel it ghosting across my lips.

He had awakened every desire, every thought of wanting to be loved and worshiped. He wanted me and wanted for nothing but to see me thrive.

Stronger.

I wanted him.

I wanted his damn fiery touch.

He even broke down my barriers and I didn't know how to thank him for making me do that. I was hesitant because I didn't know what to expect much less know how to feel. Emotions were built up between anger and frustration to devastation that I allowed words to tear me down and burn inside my mind.

Aria was always the strong one, my protector. But when she was gone, I started taking all the hits mentally.

I knew it wasn't an easy fix, those thoughts would come back even stronger and louder. If Hound wasn't going to leave, then maybe it wouldn't be too much of a fight.

But my van quickly got me home. Because tonight, I was going to explore this newly found version of me, one without all the chains of hurt and terror. The one that was somewhat more confident. Tonight I was going to be home with a man that was trying to free me.

Home. It was a strange feeling like I belonged somewhere where I was welcomed. Sadie was home too, but not enough to risk her losing it. My van was home, but Hound didn't think so.

I pushed every past memory of the cat and mouse game we had been playing and took another look at what I wanted.

Hound Dog would gladly satisfy every desire I had and make them come alive. My heart beat faster as the anticipation of seeing him grew. A thrill gave my feet life once I stepped out of my van. The more nerves played with me, the more I was starting to ache for Hound to step through the door and show me this was real.

Because for the first time, I wasn't going to let this feeling go. I was celebrating what was in front of me.

I was noticed. I was wanted.

And yet the awkward feeling subdued everything else. I could feel my mind starting to go in a downward spiral of never ending thoughts of what I was supposed to do or even look. Something in me wanted to please him, for him to see that this wasn't for nothing. I was sure that there were plenty of women that he could have been with, but for once someone was choosing me. I was going to show him that he didn't make the wrong choice, because I knew at that moment, I didn't either.

Sure, I had vanilla and that's all I thought I was going to get. Hound was anything but like vanilla, he was a whole ice cream shop. No one wanted to experience the dark truth of wanting to be chased, consumed, used for pleasure, and even praised.

Hound Dog wasn't that person. And I couldn't wait to see what person he actually was, the one that he hid from a lot of people.

Also, it had been so damn long. Then my mind spun to my body. I couldn't remember if I had shaved or not. I rubbed my temples as my mind spun with so many thoughts. Maybe if I had some time, I could have just stepped into the shower, a quick shave. Sure, that would solve all the constant thoughts.

No sooner than my mini panic attack came on, the front door slammed open and there stood the tall, muscular god of a man.

One look at him and my mouth went drier than the Sahara desert. Panic set in, was I supposed to be ready? Wait for him on the bed like a prize that he won? Or make it look like a boudoir session, looking like a pinup doll with the "come here" look?

Everything about him was a dream. From the short trimmed beard to his dark eyes set on me like a target to his cut hanging on him like it was made for him to even his jeans that gave you an idea of how powerful those legs could be.

He didn't let me continue with my wait, he marched through the hallway, pinning me against the wall, trapping my lips in a burning, searing kiss. The type that ran the burning feeling all over your body against the fighting cold. His hands gripped my hair, bundling it up in his fists. He gripped so hard that the slight pain only sent shocks to my pussy.

I tried to pull back, but he attacked my neck in punishing nips and teases. I wound my hands through his short hair, not wanting him to let go.

I fought to breathe, wrapped up in a passionate haze. "I feel like the ten minute head start didn't do me any good."

I could feel the slight smile on his face, the small chuckle he let out only made downstairs wetter.

"Time wouldn't have stopped me," he growled out.

"God help those that get in your way," I said as my body bucked against him. His knee slid between my legs, as it slid closer to my throbbing pussy. The pressure of his thigh was tempting, as my body begged for him to move it. But I was going to take just as much as he was giving. I rocked my hips to start riding him. I wasn't going to wait for him.

I was going to chase my own high, my own pleasure. Because that's what this man did, he drove me crazy between his "lesson" to him entering my life like a whirlwind to even then when I found out our paths had crossed in more ways than one. I wanted that crazy feeling.

He only pulled away to hover over me, giving me a good glance up and down like he was mapping out what he wanted to do. He rubbed his beard. "Someone's a little impatient."

He pulled his leg out from between me and I whimpered like a puppy dog. "No, please."

He put a finger to my lips, "We have all the time in the world, little birdie." He marched back down the hallway as he shut the door and locked it nice and tight, showing the true intention of not letting anyone else in, being just the two of us.

I started to walk backward down the hall, as he stepped closer to me like he was stalking a prey.

Come get me, big boy.

And yet instead of feeling scared, I was turned on. He had that obsessive, primal look in his eyes. It was a hungry look that would do it for anyone. But that look was only for me.

Every step he took made everything heightened. The anticipation of being spent and having my mind quiet for once. It was like I could hear my own heartbeat in my ears, I could feel every tingling sensation spread across my body. I bumped into his bedroom door frame. He trapped me, throwing his arms at both sides of my head.

He took a deep inhale, like he was smelling me. It should have been odd, but it was intoxicating. "Looks like I caught a little birdie."

"Yes, you did." That was all the brilliance I had in me.

His knee stepped in between my thighs, spreading me for him. "See, now this is the part where a man would say that he's going to ruin you for other men that no one would compare. But the sheer thought that someone else would have you, now that won't happen."

My back arched at the mere words he spoke, but internally something woke up and wanted to play. It was like a possession. "And what makes you so confident that it won't happen?"

The fire in his eyes grew, he gripped my chin forcing my face to be inches in front of him. "Because I won't let you go. You'll sing for me, you'll let me show you the world is yours."

And with that, Hound kissed me like he was truly never going to let go. His mixture of kissing me and nipping and tangling our tongues was enough to get on my knees for him. His hands explored every curve and inch of me. I threw my arms around him, anchoring myself to him. He got to the hem of my jacket and shirt, breaking apart the kiss.

I whimpered at the loss of his warm lips. I wanted more. I went to kiss him again, and he dodged me. He shook his head. "Oh no, honey. I have dreamed about this for the last few weeks. And these," he tugged on my clothes, "were not a part of that."

He pulled off my arms but guided me into his room. His bed was huge, and looked like a dream to get lost in during a great afternoon nap. The thought that he spent his nights alone here made my heart drop.

He sat at the edge of his bed, allowing me to stand. He sat there with eyes for only me, and part of me wanted to hide. He leaned back on his hands, enjoying his view.

"You want to make that dream come true?" He posed the question that reduced me to a heated mess.

I nodded my head. "Words, Melody." he growled out.

"Yes," I said with a breathy voice.

"Show me," he commanded. He waited for me to show him how much I wanted this, how I wanted him, even wanted to please him.

My fingers fumbled with the edge of my jacket, trying to shrug it off.

My jacket collapsed on the floor. My eyes dropped to the floor, my heart racing in my chest. A fire burned in my eyes as I glanced back up to see him entranced.

I wanted this. I wanted him to lose all control.

"Stop," he commanded before I could reach the hem of my shirt.

He licked his lips. "Honey, you are the most stunning woman. Anything you do makes me feral. You need to get out of your head. Let me help you, let me do this with you." His hands squeezed mine. "Let me," he said as he grabbed the hem of my shirt and quickly whipped it off of me.

Standing there, a cold chill gave me goosebumps that covered my body. "Mm, there she is. Feel my hands on you, Melody." And I did, the way they caressed every line and curve, giving them the attention they needed. His touch made me want to touch him the way he was, like he was mapping all over my body.

He leaned in and peppered kisses on my stomach, jolting me back, but only to be pulled back to him by the thrust of his arms around me. He trailed kisses along the outline of my bra. My nipples hardened the closer he got to them.

"I want to touch you, too," I whimpered as my head lolled from side to side.

"You will, but right now I want to worship you," he teased.

Before I could retort, he gripped my ass and hauled me on the bed, landing me on my back. He hovered over me. I reached out to fiddle with his beard, playfully pulling it, to bring his lips close to me.

"Hound," I breathed out before I took his lips with mine, sealing it in a heated kiss. His moans filled me with eagerness. His hand traveled to my jeans, he fumbled with the button. I tried to squirm away. He pinned my hips down.

He popped the button, then straightened up as he scooted back to the edge of the bed, ripping my jeans off my body. The force of it left me exposed, laid out like a feast.

"Oh, what a beautiful sight," he cooed before the feathery touch of his fingers traced over my thighs. He traced along the stretch marks that covered my inner thighs. But that's not where I wanted his hands. I'd show him impatience and I reached between us to grasp the pressing cock beneath his own layers.

He groaned. My own soft touches teased him. The man must have been thinking a lot if he was this worked up. My only hope was that he was so consumed with lust that he would skip steps three and four and go straight to step five.

I gave him one final hard grip, making him groan with pleasure. I couldn't help my little smirk. I reached for the hem of his shirt and whipped off his shirt like he did me. His abs would make a superhero blush. I couldn't help myself with my fingers tracing each pec.

"You like what you see?" he teased as his hot breath graced my ear. I nodded.

"Jesus, please just fuck me," I whimpered as my fingers kept roaming over his muscles. He shook his head. His body rumbled with the growl he released. I couldn't wait any longer or else my body would explode.

"I said that I dreamed about this woman. Can you just let me worship you? Cause all I wanna do is make every inch of this body tremble knowing that you belong to me," he retorted, sitting up, his knees spreading my legs apart.

I would have done it myself. But he leaned back on his heels taking in the sight. I teased him some more as my hands roamed over my breasts, rubbing them while picturing Hound Dog's hands doing it. I finally reached back, unhooking my bra. My breasts splayed out and my nipples hardened at the mere thought of him. My hands covered them, reaching toward my nipples giving them a gentle tug and twist.

All I heard was, "Fuck" as Hound slapped my hands away, pinning my hands in one gathering, above my head. He hunched over to latch onto my sensitive nipple. I was already ready to combust, the flood of pleasure waiting for a release.

"Don't stop." I whimpered at the sensation. "Please, that feels so fucking good," I praised him. Oh, that sort of unlocked a new level. Praising him made him play with the other nipple, switching between the one he was playing with his tongue and the other with his hand.

Just when I was ready to combust, my breath was fighting to even out. My own back arched up at the height of it all. The way he knew when I was close and pulled back, the way he listened for my breathing as he tried a rhythm or a sensation.

He looked up, grabbing my attention, the curl of his smile, the pop of my nipple, he smirked, "Let me take care of you, honey. I want more than a taste."

Well, so did I. I started to protest but the sound of a rip shook my attention. The man ripped my damn panties off of me and before I could mouth off to him, he gave me a long lick that made me throw myself back on to the bed.

"Just what I thought, you drive a woman to silence when you give her what she wants." He chuckled before licking and tasting me. The man made it feel like he was starving and all he wanted was me. I wasn't going to stop a hungry man.

I lifted my hips to meet his strokes, trying to drive my own hunger. "That's it. I'm only getting started and I'm not stopping until this pussy is dripping on my face."

"Yes, please," I whimpered.

And he didn't stop. The man latched on to my clit, sucking it, licking it until my hips decided to ride him. There was no other sound than our own breathing, and moaning, and a wet sound that should've embarrassed me. He held down my thighs as they threatened to close at the brink of my orgasm. It was only then that I lost control when he curled his fingers inside me, driving me to lose control.

I could feel it, I could feel the wall wanting to break.

"Oh, look at you. What a stunning sight. To think that my cock is going to stretch this tight pussy, especially when this pretty pussy is gripping my fingers." He kissed the side of my thighs as his fingers kept dancing and pulling me closer to the edge.

I damn near lost my mind right when his fingers curled a cool blow to my pussy and jerked my hips up.

"So sensitive. You're almost there. Give it to me. Give everything you have," he commanded and with one final stroke inside, my orgasm skyrocketed. When romance novels say that women see stars, well I saw the stars, the moon, and even the lost planet Pluto.

Most would call it a night after that, but Hound had other plans. When I lay there recovering from my orgasm, the sound of a zipper told me that I needed to be ready because one was not going to be enough.

Chapter 19

HOUND DOG

S he had me tripping over my own self. I rarely wanted to go down on a woman, mainly because it never enticed me. But Melody was different. Her little siren song put me under a spell. Everything about her from her soft skin to her gorgeous breasts to the sweetness of her dripping pussy.

This was a woman that captured a side of me that I didn't know I had.

Possessiveness.

I wanted to consume her. Bring her to the edge and back and have her moan my name when she came hard. The ache in my dick proved me right.

I couldn't wait any longer. I needed to sink into her, I needed my cock to stretch her and own her. Her little head popped up when she heard the zipper of my jeans pull down. In one swoop, my cock sprung free and was aching to unravel her even more.

She slowly leaned forward with her elbows and her eyes widened at what was in front of her. Her full lips parted slightly, and if you listened closely the word *fuck* came from her.

I started gripping myself, giving a slow, teasing rub. Without a moment to spare, she crawled on all fours, biting her bottom lip. Her irresistible hips with every movement, when she approached my hand glided over her back, bending over to grip her ass. I had all the time that one day I would bite it for being a damn distraction.

I looked at her, pushing her auburn hair out of the way. Those enchanting eyes looked soft and pleading.

"What do you want?" a small cruel smile appeared on my face.

"I want my turn," she said.

"Your turn?"

"Did you really think you were the only one that wanted a taste of something they've wanted?"

The little temptress.

"How could I deny you?"

She didn't need any other approval or direction. She leaned forward teasing my tip, with her slow, taunting licks. "Fuck, Melody." She kept going, making it known she wasn't going to stop. Little by little she took each inch, bobbing in and out. She wanted to bring me to the edge just like I did her. She wanted me to lose control. Well she was getting her wish.

Her moans vibrated my cock which only made it hard to refrain from groaning. She adjusted herself, spreading those legs apart. It was only then, in my own cloud of lust, that I saw a flash of movement. She had slipped her hand down to her already sensitive pussy.

She was getting off on my own pleasure. She had picked up the pace, still dragging her tongue underneath my cock. "That's it. Fuck. Melody. You keep doing that and..." I didn't finish as she opened her mouth wide and sucked me down until I felt the back of her throat.

I'm fucking screwed.

I bunched up her hair in my hand gripping it. Her moans continued as she looked up at me, locking onto my eyes. She pulled back, gasping for air. She was the first to try and I was going to make sure she was the last. Her back hunched as she was bringing herself to a second orgasm and I wasn't going to let that happen.

If she was going to come, it was going to be on my cock, buried deep in her, with my name screamed at the top of her lungs.

I jerked her hand off her pussy and pulled her up by her hair. I imagined that the pain would only turn her on.

"Such a good girl. Taking this cock, sucking me down. But little songbird, it's time to make you mine." I captured her lips as I leaned her back on the bed. I didn't know how much longer she and I would last. I was a damn teenager, ready to burst at any moment.

I rubbed the tip of my cock along her pussy lips, watching her mewl over the sensation. I wanted nothing more than to drive her wild, keep her in this bed. It wouldn't be too bad of an idea.

"Hound, please," she begged as I continued to tease her.

"Please what, honey? Tell me what you want," I cooed, putting the tip in her entrance. She bucked her hips, trying to make it go further.

I did something that I'd never done to a woman, much less a sweetbutt. I spanked her pussy. Something possessive stirred in me, and I'd do it again just to watch her jolt, and yelp in pleasure. "Naughty, songbird."

"I just want you," she whimpered.

"Want who? Hound Dog or Nash?"

She moaned. "Whoever wants to fuck me. I don't care who it is, I just want you."

"Want me where?"

I could see the little tears in her eyes between a need growing intense or the fact that emotions have been all over tonight. And for once, I wanted to make sure she didn't run.

"Shh, honey. I'm right here. All you have to do is tell me where you want me." I wiped the stray tear that started to run down her cheek.

"I need you to fuck me like you have dreamed about," she said breathlessly.

"No Melody, I'm going to fuck you like *we've* both dreamed," I said, as I thrust slowly into her, feeling all of her stretch, the breath she had now stolen away from her.

She was fucking tight, any tighter and I would have thought she was a virgin. Her wet cunt just made it easier to slip in and out just to drive her crazy.

Her breath hitched at every movement I made, thrusting ever so slowly. Her head lolled from side to side. Her focus came back to watching my cock disappear into her warm, wet pussy. The one that made a mess on the sheets. She was truly a vision as she squirmed underneath me. She went from moaning to growling at me.

What the fuck did I unleash?

In a shocking moment, she wrapped her legs around my waist then slipped toward the back of my legs. Her small frame was failing her at this moment. Her burning gaze made my heart sink and my dick harder.

"Hound. Fuck, please you can fucking be gentle with me on another time. We both know slow and intimate wasn't what you dreamed of. Make that another dream," she started to say in a breathless voice, then she pulled my chin closer, mostly by my beard, "Now fucking fuck my brains out, please."

What a damn mouth on her.

She wasn't the shy, meek type of woman that strolled into the Blue Sax, but a ravenous tigress, sinking her claws into me.

Then she kissed me hard.

To say that I wasn't harder than a rock would be a lie because for the first time, a woman that I craved, the one that I knew was down there in her soul had come to play, and she had claws. I'd let her win this round because that's what I wanted to do, fuck her hard into that bed, leave every mark that I could, claim every part of her body and soul.

"Hang on, honey," I said before I pulled out of her, flipping her to her stomach, wrapping my arm around her backside, pulling that juicy ass in the air. "Tell me, tell me that this is all mine?"

Thrust.

She whimpered.

Thrust

"Tell me that you're ready to stop running."

Thrust

"Tell me that you'll become the woman that I know you are to be."

Thrust

"Because while I'm not a hero"

Thrust

"I will be the damn devil revealing everything that you are."

Thrust

"Beautiful, big hearted, talented, and the only one that can drive me to this"

I picked up speed, hunching over to hear more of her breathing, her little moans that would set me off like a rocket to the moon.

"Hound. Everything. It's true, please, harder," she begged.

I angled her body to drive myself harder and faster, making us both chase our release. We were both lost in the sensation that was pure carnal desire. Between both of our sounds and me driving my cock into that sweet pussy, it wasn't long before we were both going to let go.

"You asked me days ago what I thought we were. And I said I didn't know. Well, I do now." I kept going, savoring each moment she watched me fuck her, being owned, being *mine*.

"Fuck, please. Ahh," she started to say as her pussy squeezed me like her favorite thing she couldn't let go.

"I know. You're fucking mine, and I don't plan on letting you leave." I craved this possession of her. Body, heart, soul, and mind.

Her pussy clung on to me with every thrust, she became louder and louder.

"That's it. Squeeze my cock," I commanded her. "Fuck you feel so good."

"Hound, please. Don't stop," she said, staggering each word.

"Never. But now I need you to give me one more orgasm, honey." I didn't hold back, I put everything into both of our orgasms. Her body started to tense and her pussy started to spasm, sending a final ripple through me as my cum started to bury inside her and my cock twitched from the release.

I collapsed around her, kissing her sweaty shoulders. Her auburn hair stuck to her back. The hidden little curls under the tangle of hair made me smile. Her heartbeat was matching mine, settling from the best feeling I'd had in my entire life.

If this was bliss, then I have found it with her.

We stayed there with my cock still ingrained there. The sudden afterthought that we got carried away broke through. I got closer to her ear and whispered, "Please tell me that you're on some sort of birth control." Her body was still sensitive, coming down from the high she climbed.

Her head turned to the side, a plastered grin came on her face. "What? Didn't you want to have kids right now?" She buried her lips between her teeth.

Mine.

"That could come sooner rather than later if you keep this up." I kissed her cheek.

The brief moment of seeing her barefoot in the kitchen, humming her tunes, while growing our kid sent both panic and a sense of bliss. Unfortunately, the thought didn't stay because right now, I wasn't ready to protect a fictitious child from the world we live in, especially my world at that current moment.

"Baby, your cock is still in me, you really want to talk about this right now." I raised an eyebrow. She scuffed, "Yes, Hound. I'm clean and protected. And if I wasn't already feeling like I'm out of my body I would be scolding you to make sure you're not the one with the diseased dick."

There was the little snark and confidence I was waiting for, she was the image of a box of mystery.

I pulled out of her, watching our releases mix together, and leaking out of that sweet pussy. "Next time you can scold me. But you're the only one."

I was raised a gentleman, of some sorts. I kissed her shoulder blade before walking to the bathroom to grab a warm, wet cloth. By the time I got back she had turned to her back, a glorious sight of her naked body in my bed.

If I wasn't holding back from breaking her, I'd make it a few more rounds.

When the cloth touched her sensitive pussy, her hips bucked, and she let out a little moan. I couldn't help but kiss her inner thigh, inhaling her sweet scent that would be burned in my own senses.

She reached out for me, my cheek caressed her hand. I crawled up her body, resting between her legs, laying my head on her stomach. Her nails combed through my hair, scratching my head. The pure innocence made me melt in her hands.

She whispered, "What are you doing to me?"

"Hopefully making you happy," I said, earnestly.

"Hound, you are doing so much more," her melodic voice said.

Chapter 20
HOUND DOG

What's worse than waking up horny with the most angelic woman in your arms when the sun barely has come up? Waking up like that and your phone blaring loudly.

Melody started to stir in my arms when I reached for my phone. I held her close, barely looking at the caller ID.

"This better be fucking good," I murmured in warning.

She had snuggled closer, like she didn't want the distance between us. The way her body vibrated with her soft snores. I didn't want to wake her but something told me when I relooked at the caller ID it wasn't going to be good.

"We need to talk. Meet me near the old Mud Island entrance." Greene spoke through the phone.

He clicked off before I could retort or tell him to fuck off for a while. I had just gotten my girl, I didn't want her to feel like I left her high and dry.

You could call me a simp now, instant sap because I got her and I wasn't going to let her go. No matter how much either of us wanted to run in the opposite direction.

With a deep groan, I tried to shimmy out of the bed undetected, but Melody stirred even more in her sleep. Her eyes fluttered open with that morning, blissful haze. She blinked a couple of times, looked at me, and sighed with a deep contentment. A slight smile appeared on her face.

"Thank God," she whispered, still in her sleepy voice.

"What, honey?"

"It wasn't a dream." She chuckled, her eyes fluttering closed again.

"No. More like a dream come true." I kissed her soft, inviting lips. I dropped my forehead to hers. "I have to go somewhere this morning."

Her body sank deeper in the bed, she let go of me and I straightened up. "Okay," she said. "I understand."

"My sweet songbird, I'm coming back. You know that right?" I caressed her face, hoping for a sign that she was okay with me leaving, only to come back to her.

Her eyes were still closed when she gave me a tiny nod. With a yawn, she spoke. "Yeah, I know. You got to do your job."

She was truly going to be the death of me, because I expected more of a fight. But not from her, not when most people left her or used her. Fuck the bleeding heart that started beating again.

"But I have someone worth making sure I come home." The sweet sentiment came quicker than expected. "Hey." I shook her a little bit. Her eyes opened up. "Kiss me, woman."

With a soft, yet stern look she scooted up, and met me face to face. Her warm lips planted softly on mine, giving me the guiltiest feeling that I had to leave. I pushed into the kiss with a little more demand, enough for her to crave more, to know that I would come back to finish what I started.

With a hushed sigh, she sank into it.

That's my girl.

With the small ache in my chest, I got dressed quickly, finding my cut and my keys. I sent a message to my board, keeping them on alert.

You could hear the birds echo their songs early that morning. Choosing the truck meant that I had more protection though I wished I had the freedom of the open road. Greene didn't leave much to know what would happen next.

My head was spinning with the endless thoughts of what was to come next. It didn't seem like the world was in balance let alone my world. There was someone out there framing the club for something we didn't do.

At some point I felt like I was letting the club down, but I was letting the mother chapter down too. When I got voted in as president I knew that it was meant to be. Some say all the tough roads lead to the smoother ones. I had done my time, I had proved my loyalty and more, and when they voted me in I knew that I was right for it.

But ever since the bodies had been dropping on Main Street, I had second guessed myself.

In the past couple weeks I had done nothing but think of how to turn things around, how to prove to the club that I was still the right person for this job. And now I had to add to the fact that I wanted to keep Melody safe from prying eyes that would do anything to see me torn apart.

That's why I had stayed away from all the sweetbutts and all the parties with the clubhouse. Because if I did get attached or someone thought I got attached it wouldn't have been long before even more trouble would come my way or the club's way.

If I was going to find answers I was going to put my nose to the ground.

And yet, as I drove through the backrest to Mud Island my thoughts reverted back to Melody and how I was a jackass in the very beginning, keeping my distance from her thinking that I could do such a thing.

And now that I had her I was never going to let go of her. But I wasn't ready to share her with the rest of the world just yet. She may not like it when I would have to tell her when I got back. The thought of her being my old lady sent straight pleasure down to my cock, the one she milked that night.

It wasn't long until I pulled up near one of the neighborhoods of Mud Island, a place where you could let go and hear music for days like echoes in a cave. What was once a treasured place was now just a ghost of the past.

But it served as a place to do business away from business. My boots hit the concrete gliding up to see Greene standing there in plain clothes, a lot better than a uniform but nonetheless. Greene had shoved his hands in his pocket looking at the coastline being able to see across the way about the Mississippi.

"This better have been good for getting me up so damn early in the morning," I rumbled out.

He had turned his head looking down at the ground. Something was on his mind and it wasn't going to be good. "I appreciate you coming out here, Hound Dog, I know..." he started to say.

I threw up my hand to stop him because all I wanted to hear was more updates and telling me that all was going to be well and that he had cleaned up whatever was messed up in the first place.

"Save the appreciation until after all this blows over." I pushed past the thought of just walking away. I didn't know if I was in the right mindset or not.

"Say whatever you need to say."

"There have been some things that have come, things that I've been hiding from the chief on this because it could involve another party of authorities." He started off. He piqued my interest, knowing that there was some kind of development.

"Keep going," I ordered him. I didn't like people wasting my time.

"There was additional DNA that was left over on the recent body. Either someone got sloppy or it was intentional. But I had my guy run it under the table, and it confirms one thing," he continued, "It wasn't the Saints."

I wanted to roll my fucking eyes because of course I knew it wasn't us. The amount of probing my own brothers and then second-guessing the people we had with us. I went down the rabbit hole when I asked Dolly, our manager with the burlesque, if there was something she was hiding. Other than a slap to my face, I deserved it, there wasn't anything.

"Get to the part that shows me that you're not wasting my time. I knew I had my club under control, so I turned over every rock." I was flushed with anger, teetering past the point of exploding.

He threw his hands up to show surrender, "While the DNA wasn't any of you, it was someone else that you may be of interest."

"Does the name Emerson McNealy mean anything to you?" Greene asked.

I shook my head. I didn't know whether I was supposed to or not. "Means nothing to me."

"Well it should," he said, reaching into his back pocket to pull out his phone to show me a picture, "as it's the name of a certain road captain of a club that you are very familiar with. I believe you know him as Indigo."

Greene handed me his phone to show me a mugshot of a man that some of us knew a little too well.

Indigo belonged to Arkansas's very own Razor Hogs MC, an MC that never wanted to expand but always wanted our territory. They had been around even when Pops was in his own club. They had been causing problems. But they were more like a failed cartoon villain. Whatever plot or scheme they had, it was rarely successful.

They weren't much of a threat until they came over to the various districts we were in and attempted to start fights. It didn't end well for them, but they were more of a nuisance. I stared at the picture a little too hard. I didn't know whether I truly needed to feel threatened or confused.

Why?

What had transpired to give them the inspiration to come after us.

"What do you think their reasoning has been?" I asked Greene, handing him his phone back before I let my anger get another chance to bubble up.

He shrugged his shoulders, "I don't know, man. Unless you and Slickback got into it recently or it's something to do with your shipping, I have no other idea. Shit I don't even think they've occupied the cells down there at Station 28 for a long while now that I think about it."

When he mentioned it, I knew he was right, we hadn't seen any activity from the Hogs in a while. While it was a blessing, it was definitely suspicious. But it would explain why Weston was hesitant to give up information. Maybe he knew who he was working for or but it didn't add up.

I was ready to burn their whole MC if it would solve anything but there were too many damn strings attached to this. They got to Weston; who knew if they had gotten to anyone else? Maybe it was time to set a trap or something, the thought was there, or maybe we set off a warning for them to stop.

Drop something or someone back off to them.

I thought it was time for Weston to return to sender. With a small grimace on my face, I looked back at Greene, extended my hand out. He reached for it, and I shook his hand and clapped him on the back. "You did good. Knew you would come through."

Greene tightened his hand, his eyes narrowed. "No you didn't. You're still trying to test me and see if I screw up. And it wasn't me that thought to check additional DNA."

I shot him a look, then it dawned on me as I withdrew my hand, "Little Officer Daniels." I sneered. I didn't like outsiders. The *club* didn't like outsiders in our business. No matter how much street credit the boy got.

Greene didn't let up on his expression. "I told you that I'd never pull one on the Saints. As much as I can't stand what you do, the amount you all have done, I look the other way."

"And the little bonuses you get helps too, right."

"Hound, you scratch mine, I scratch yours. But I've done everything to prove myself," he started to say before I cut him off.

"And what does that tell me," I warned him.

"That you can fucking trust me. I would have thought over the years and the past few you've been president that you let up." Greene squared up, challenging me.

As much as I hated it, he was right. The man never let us down, helping us when we needed it the most. I nodded my head.

"Yeah, I know. Jesus fuck." I rubbed my neck.

He cocked his eyebrows. "Anything else I should know?"

I shook my head, not his demons, but mine. His eyes softened when he saw something, call it wisdom with age, but he sighed. "You know it's okay to lean on everyone else."

I nodded, then he said, "I'll wrap up the investigation this week, don't worry about it."

He grasped my shoulder with a firm squeeze and walked in the opposite direction.

The weight of the club and being in this role could take a toll.

I just shook away any thought of self-doubt and shoved it where it couldn't be brought back up. By the time I had formed a plan in my head, I had made it to the clubhouse to wake up the men and decided that it's time to get off our asses.

I busted through the door, ready to give out commands. Call it revenge, or call it a warning, whatever it was, I was going to end it and we were going to get back to a normal life. Maybe a warning to the Hogs would shut them up and make them think twice before coming into our territory.

"Who ever is not fucking awake, someone better go wake them up, we have a rat to return," I bellowed out, a few members were scattered around, looking dazed and confused. "I'm sorry, did I fucking stutter, wake up the rest of the fuckers, now."

They scrambled out of their seats and went into the hallways to the rooms, pounding on every door, waking up the club. Because this was going to end and it was going to end how I wanted it to.

B.B approached me as he rubbed his eyes, the man didn't put on a shirt, but grabbed his cut. "What happened? You get dressed in the dark?" I held back my laugh as B.B ran his fingers through his hair. I continued, "I'm sorry, were you getting laid or something?"

He shot me with a stern look, and I just laughed. "You're in a good fucking mood."

More like I shook off doubting myself and my capability to do this job.

"For the first time, I think I am." I grinned, waiting for the other brothers to come. I wasn't calling church, we needed to move now.

B.B saw the look in my eye and knew that it was more than just a spark of happiness.

"Mm, did little Hound Dog get to howl last night?" he asked. He tried to cozy up like a damn cat, laughing at his own pun.

"Who howled last night?" Otis emerged from the hallway, wiping away the sleep from his eyes.

"Why was someone howling? I mean that's some kinky shit," Shooter said from behind with a twisted smile.

Some people were in a playful mood. The more people became awake, the more anxious I was to get this over.

When the prospects finally arrived, more like staggered in, it was time.

"Greene called me this morning and let me in on some news. Apparently the Hogs want to slither their way back over here. DNA from their own came back. So, I think it's time for our little rat to return to sender." I clapped the shoulder of B.B as he muttered something.

Otis leaned over to Hank, I could hear him, "I think boss man lost it."

"Maybe he's still hungover from whatever happened after yesterday." Stray murmured as well.

"Well, brothers, if being hungover from the feeling of ending this once in for all, you better believe it." I couldn't help but smile.

They all looked at me with confusion but Shooter stepped forward. "When and where Prez?"

"I'm glad you asked. The way I see it, the perfect opportunity is to stage our little friend in one of their businesses," I said as I walked through all the bed heads and early morning confusion. I brushed past Reverend who was by the bar, fiddling with the cross that was tattooed on his palm.

Reverend wasn't around much when it came to the turf wars or businesses. He was needed for other reasons but nevertheless the man always had an opinion, like the devil's advocate. But he simply nodded his head as I approached.

"Work with Blaze, figure out the timing of when they are least around." I snapped out my command.

"Got it all figured out?" B.B called out from the back. "Didn't want a second opinion?"

I shook my head, I had this under control, I wasn't going to let up on it.

"I'll tag along, I feel I need to rectify this," Fender ponied up.

He was a good man, a good heart, dedicated to the club, I had no qualms about this. I nodded, giving him approval.

Stray cleared his throat, "And what does that mean for the rest of us, oh Mr. President." he joked, bowing his head in sarcasm.

I banged my fists on the bartop, "It means we're back to business, boys."

I eyed the bushy blonde who walked and leaned up against the bar. "Figured it out on your own."

"I gotta do what I gotta do for the club."

B.B shook his head. "Five minutes, you could have talked with me for five minutes."

"I had it handled."

"Like always." He scoffed.

"What the fuck is that supposed to mean?" I pushed back.

He shook his head, "Nothing, brother. What do you need from me?"

B.B was holding back, but he wasn't ready to tell me or maybe I wasn't ready for what he wanted to say.

"Might want to give Dolly a heads up, business may be busier now that we're back in action." B.B was protective over his bars and his burlesque, something that Dolly and him cooked up. Lately, he had been more at The Feathers, but it wasn't my business to know every detail of the man's life.

All was going to be okay, I had to believe it.

Chapter 21

MELODY

"*Kiss me, woman.*" That's what he told me to do, and I followed his instructions. I had no idea what was going on, nor the time when I stirred in my sleep.

Everything was a blur, like waking up from a dream and trying to recall all the details because you didn't know how to react to the reality of everything that did happen.

The sun peeked through the blinds, illuminating the soft, warm light spreading through the room. His side of the bed was cool to the touch as my fingers traced where he used to be.

I knew that he said he would be back, but mentally I was always preparing for the worst. I attempted to find my phone because I wanted to hear Sadie's voice. I needed someone else to tell me that I wasn't crazy for letting go and entertaining the idea that there could be a "me and Hound" relationship.

Just weeks ago, I was a "traveling" songwriter that attempted to make her mark in the world of music, hoping for more artists to take a chance on my music. From there to where I woke up in a blissful state reminiscing the way Hound Dog made me writhe under his touch, the way he showed just how much he craved me, and most importantly that he showed his truth of his past and true intentions.

It was enough to make a hangover feel like a quick head rush.

I called Sadie, waiting for her to pick up.

"Hello?" a groggy voice answered.

"Good morning to you as well." I giggled.

I fucking giggled.

"You must have the wrong number because I don't know who replaced Melody Rae with whoever this is," Sadie joked.

I twisted the necklaces, gnawing on my bottom lip. I put her on speaker, finding a scrap of clothing to cover my well-loved naked body.

"We're calling her Melody 2.0," I teased as well. I found one of Hound's black shirts and I rummaged through his drawers to find a pair of gray sweat pants.

Of course they were too big, but knowing that these belonged to him filled me with a certain warmth and comfort.

"Please tell me that this giggly version of you means that you finally rode on that biker's dick." Her brash comment made me blush.

"You take the fun out of things sometimes, you know that right?" I grabbed the phone, taking myself to the kitchen to find some food, only to see that he fully stocked the kitchen. For the man that said he was rarely here, that was making a statement.

"And yet you love me all the same. Tell me..."

"Tell you what?"

"Tell me all the little naughty details." I could practically hear the smirk in her voice.

I knew that there was much to still know and understand, but I told her about him breaking down the barriers that she knew were built up. I went on about how he showed what I could become and that he wanted to be there to help me. I didn't tell her about his true identity, that was for me and he trusted me enough to not say anything. When I got to the part about last night's bedroom adventure all she could say was, "It's about damn time."

"It's crazy right? Tell me, Sadie. Because honestly I am a mess internally trying to stuff all the flight responses back inside." I started baking simple blueberry muffins, waiting for her answer, her opinion, a voice of reasoning if you will.

"Sugarbean, I think that this was the best thing for you. Sure, being a biker like him might not be the most sound choice, but obviously the man has shown that he's not going anywhere. And you, the fact that you're smiling from ear to ear and I imagine baking muffins," she said as I dropped the spoon in the bowl.

Guess I was predictable.

"There's nothing crazy about love." she finished.

I shook my head at the thought of love, I still hardly knew the man. "It's not love, Sadie."

She sighed. "Ah, but it's growing to be."

I listened to her continue on about her next gigs and the chances she was getting, and I was so happy for her. She told me that there were a couple producers that she was chatting up and wanted me to tag along. "Come on. Share some songs with them and I know they'll fall head over heels for you."

I got lost in thought as I put the muffins in the oven, turning my back toward the counter, folding my arms. I knew I needed to get back out there, needed the money to continue on this life, prove to dear old dad that he was wrong, prove to the world they were wrong.

"I'll think about it. I need a few more days to isolate myself and create some," I answered her.

She huffed. "Maybe I'm just trying to get you to come down from that tower of yours and see me. You know I miss you."

"You just miss me because I actually fed you."

She chuckled before hanging up, "That too."

What if we broke through the walls,
Into a sinners' lust.
Clear out the haze clouding me,
Telling me that it won't work.

What if we sang and we dance
Under the moon
Then sleep under the stars
Only to see the morning colors.

I didn't know what possessed me. I saw the tune weave the notes around me. I heard the fiddle in the background, making it feel like fireflies are dancing in the night sky. I felt the stupid, lovesick smile across my face.

My heart was still racing along with the thoughts that constantly flowed from my mind.

For the moment, I was happy.

While the tune in my head kept playing, a set of hands caressed across my waist pulling me into body heat. A body whose head nuzzled the crook of my neck, inhaling my scent, his beard scratching my skin. I reached behind, returning the caress. A shiver of vibration shook my body from him.

"Good morning," I whispered, not wanting to startle him.

This was the softer side that he hid from the world, from the club. I'd gladly take any side of him as long as he didn't leave me.

He inhaled one more time before replying, "Morning, songbird." I turned my head to see him, searching for his eyes. I leaned as far as I could to find his lips, surrendering to a soft kiss. When he deepened the kiss, I twisted around to face him. His hand gripped the back of my neck, pushing me forward to meet every taste of his tongue.

He broke it first, "Why is it, when I see you in the kitchen, all I want to do is splay you across the table and have my way with you?"

I gave him a cheeky grin, "I mean, there's no saying we couldn't." I reached back for another kiss, attempting to wrap my arms around his neck, claiming him in any way I could.

He growled within our kiss and I was ready to melt. But the brief smell of blueberry filled my senses. I pulled away from him, running to grab the oven mit to recover the muffins.

"Where did you go this morning?" I asked as I opened the oven door, the blast of heat soothing my soul.

Out of the corner of my eye, Hound fiddled with something, and a deep sigh escaped his sinful mouth. "Something I had to take care of."

No details. I wondered if it was more that he couldn't tell me or was afraid to tell me.

I set the tray down only to turn back and see a smile on Hound's face. It only sent a rush of heat on my cheeks.

"What are you smiling about?"

"Seeing my beautiful woman in my kitchen, with my shirt on, making herself at home," he said, smiling.

He walked toward me only to pop a muffin in his mouth. "They taste delicious, but I already tasted heaven last night."

Yep, that will do it.

Was it hot because of the oven still on or just me?

Nope, it was me.

I was at a loss for words. A man like that wanted to be around me. Fate must have been playing a hand in it.

I reached out to touch him, trailing my fingers along his cut, toward his somewhat exposed chest, mad that the shirt he was wearing was covering up a masterpiece. I could see him more in person, wanting to take my time to familiarize every curve of his muscles.

"Someone's a bit ravenous this morning," His deep chuckle startled me.

I withdrew my fingers quickly, slightly embarrassed that I got lost in thought and greed. But he took back my hand only to shove it under his shirt to his warm chest.

Fucking hell.

"You can touch all you want, honey," he invited me to keep exploring. Before I could wonder what he was doing he took his cut and shirt off in a flash. My eyes turned wide at the bare flesh.

I didn't realize the man had a little bit of chest hair that matched his dark hair. The rough cut muscles beckoned to be stared at.

"Oh my. You're very different in the daytime."

He laughed. "What did you think I was?"

"Not this. Not an Adonis even in the morning. I'm having serious thoughts here." I blew out a breath that puffed out my cheeks.

"Oh yeah, like what?" He mimicked my touches but inched along my bare thighs.

"That I was fucked by a man that could snap me in half and then go chop some wood after." The ridiculous things that came out of my mouth were truthfully cringe worthy.

"Mm, well I could say the same thing." He continued with his mind numbing capable fingers.

"That I fucked a woman that could stop a man in his tracks and melt. Only if anyone looked at you, they wouldn't have eyes anymore."

His fingers traveled up my leg, only to find that there was no other barrier other than the shirt. "Why, little songbird, did you walk out here, make me muffins, and not have any panties on?"

I gulped, "Well, I couldn't find them."

I stared back at his eyes, and caught the cocky grin on his face as he licked his lips, "That's because they're in my truck."

"You fucking took my panties? When you left?" I could have gotten mad.

"You could have gotten another pair from the guest bedroom," he retorted.

I tried to argue but the fucker had a point. "Why?"

He growled as one of his fingers slipped past my lips, and straight inside of me. "So I would be able to do that. Have myself in this warm, wet pussy that I knew would be waiting for me."

I whimpered as he slowly dragged in and out of my seeping wet heat. The man wasn't satiated last night, and apparently neither was I.

"I thought I'd get another lesson that would turn into another night like last night," I quickly said, trying to enjoy the pleasure I was getting.

"If you're with me, you better get used to it. I don't think this hunger will ever go away," Hound said before diving for another hungry kiss.

This was one of those kisses that you saw in a movie where the man and woman reunite and they felt like they were never going to see each other again before that. It was as if there was no one else in the world.

He backed me into the corner of the counter. I knew I wasn't going anywhere. Hound had slipped his finger out of me, only to cup my ass with his hands and scoop me onto the counter. I felt better because the poor man didn't have to bend down so far to compensate for my lack of height.

He pulled back from what our unbroken kiss was. "Wearing my fucking shirt, seeing that smile on you, makes you fucking irresistible."

"Keep talking like that and see where it will get you," I teased him, placing a quick kiss on his lips.

"I already got you where I wanted you." He smiled like a damn softie.

"Oh yeah? And where's that?"

"Here with me."

Fucking hell. Aria, I hope you ain't watching from the heavens.

"Hound Dog. If you could kindly let me off this counter so I can show you my appreciation for your sweet words, I'd gladly appreciate it."

And with that, the man turned into a mute.

Well, only until I drove the man to roar later as I swallowed.

Chapter 22

MELODY

H ound Dog never gave me any idea of what to expect when lesson two came around a few days later.

He had been in and out of the house "taking care of business", only to come home and not give me anything about his businesses or why there was a cut above his eye one day that I had to bandage up. He said it was to keep me from worrying, which only made it worse to think about when he left every morning.

Within those times, I submitted a couple songs that I had already been working on to a couple record companies. I needed more money, I was starting to feel like a free-loader. But the man told me not to worry about bills and that he would take care of everything.

"Don't worry about them, Melody. I'm taking care of you." he would say when I tried to pay for groceries or even when I went to go get us coffee one morning and I found that the order had been "taken care" before I got there.

The man hid things whether to protect me or not scare me off, but I was feeling like at some point I needed more than what he was giving me. He wanted all of me.

I wanted all of him. But I was only getting the side he wanted to show.

I needed to take the chance to take my newfound confidence and bravely tell him to give me more, to not hide from me.

Temperatures were dropping and if I learned anything from last time, layers were going to be needed. My boots clicked against the cement as I followed the lights to the center of the warehouse, seeing Hound Dog waiting for me with a wide smile on his face.

My heart beat fast enough to make my head pound at the same time.

It was just us, no instruments, no props. It made me feel even more worried about what to expect.

"I'm starting to think you get me out here to plot to kidnap me," I tried to joke, my fake laughter echoing between the walls.

"Didn't I technically already do that?"

"I mean depending on who you talk to, your brothers may say you did. That's why I haven't met them yet. But Sadie, she would say it's because you were playing hero." I went into his arms as he encompassed me with a tight hug until our lips met with a tender kiss.

I threw my hint out there, and got no quick response. I placed my palms on his chest, pushing back, focusing on my task at hand.

"Okay, teacher. What are we doing tonight?" I asked, backing away from him before we ended up tangled up with each other like every night since the first time.

"Straight to the point, okay then. Tonight I want to see where you are at with your basic skills." He pulled a stool randomly from the side, folding his arms across his perfect chest.

"My basic skills? At thirty, I have been doing this for ten plus years."

He raised an eyebrow, "And at thirty-seven, with more experience under my belt, you'll listen to me."

Fuck, he was thirty-seven, that tracked. He had been in the game when I was just starting. Age is just a number, but damn no wonder why the man was a gorgeous specimen.

"Yes sir," I sassed him.

"Careful, little songbird," he warned me, his stare freezing me in my tracks. "Sing your scales."

"In what key, sir?"

Okay, now I was just being a brat.

He trailed his tongue over his teeth before he commanded me, "Traditional, key of C"

I turned away from him, knowing that I couldn't see him while I reverted back to basics. That, and I didn't need him to see the eye roll that I did before singing the solfege.

"Again," he commanded when I finished.

I sighed, but did as he commanded. A voice is like a muscle, you train it well and it goes to say something about "muscle memory".

"Good, now do it a half step up," he said.

I didn't understand the lesson. I knew how to do this, I composed songs nearly every day. I was getting annoyed.

Taking his command, I sang the scale a half step. His lesson was turning into a warm up. I waited for him to tell me to work on my dynamics or even vocal placement. I was a mezzo alto, I knew placement.

Fuck, I knew everything. I taught myself and workshopped with some of the best voices I knew around the area. Now I was feeling insulted. I turned a quarter back toward him. "Work on your arpeggio," he barked out.

My eyebrows furrowed. And yet without a fight, I went into arpeggios. My voice filled every empty space between us.

"Good," he praised, still sitting in his chair.

"Anything else, *oh great one,*" I retorted. I was getting bold with every lash out I was giving him. I could chalk that up to the pent up madness that was stirring in me.

Hound had a stern look on his face, an expression of disappointment. "Something wrong? Something you want to say?" He was challenging me, testing my how long it would take before I broke down.

I looked away from him because I didn't know how much longer I was going to be before I broke for real.

"Other than blindly trusting you, when little has been given to me?" I let my chaotic thoughts free.

Hound cocked his head. "Little trust?"

"Yes, *Nash*. Because I don't think I can trust Hound right now."

His given name sounded weird coming from me, because I didn't know Nash.

I knew very little about Hound Dog, the president of the Saint's Outlaw MC.

His eyes grew a heavy fire, his nostrils flared. "You can't trust me?"

"No, and hell, maybe I can't trust Nash either."

He took a few steps toward me, but the coward in me kept my distance.

"Why not?" he asked, his shoulders tensing up.

I gulped, released a tiny breath. "I've given you more of me than anyone else. But when I ask you about where you've been or see the cuts on your hands, the blood or sweat on your t-shirts, it's nothing. But when I bare my soul about my imperfections or what was told to me, that's okay."

He didn't say anything, so I took the opportunity to keep going. "You've given me attention, food, a roof over my head, and those are fucking important and I'm grateful. But I thought we were getting somewhere, but be honest Hound, am I captive, a dirty secret, or am I someone that you actually want and aren't ashamed of."

The choice was his, and the way he answered would determine if I went back to the old Melody or stayed to become the person that Hound told me he saw. I also wanted to pummel him to the ground for making me feel like I was nothing more to him.

I let him approach me, but there was no sweet and gentle Hound Dog that I had gotten, there was a small darkness that roamed over him. For a moment, I saw more of the soul that was there cradling mine.

The warmth radiating from his skin was enough to make my own body sweat.

"You think I'm ashamed to see you, to show people who you are?" he asked.

"I didn't ask what I think, I asked you, what am I?" I thought he was holding back something that he was ashamed of, but not of me. He was holding back to be a person that he wasn't normally.

His hand gripped my chin in a possessive hold. "Mine."

Okay, instant wet panties.

"Yours to what? Hide, own, keep on the side, what, Hound? Give me something, trust me to take whatever you have in your life as well."

We stepped back to a wall, sending reminisce moments of the Blue Sax. My mouth was left gaped in a small O.

"How about you listen," he commanded. My once gaped mouth was now closed to prevent protest. I once said that he could kill me in an instant. His hands left my chin only to yank mine above my head, preventing me from running.

"My turn to talk," he said. I nodded.

"Being mine is a whole thing. Mine is a blessing and a curse and I'm trying to keep you safe. I am not ashamed to be seen with you, I am terrified of those around us that see you and know that you're my weakness."

My heart sank.

Weakness? Me?

"I don't want you to carry any darkness or anger that comes from my world. You don't need that."

I didn't stay quiet. "And how about you let me decide what I need?"

His grip on my wrists tightened, little shocks of pain shot down my body.

But Hound softened when I didn't back down, instead he nudged my neck to the side and placed soft trailing kisses there. I was supposed to be mad at him, but his touch was trying to wipe it away.

"Hound, you can't do that and expect to win."

His voice vibrated against my neck. "I can try, Melody."

I nudged his head away. "Ask me what I need."

"What do you need, Melody?"

"I need you to be you. I need you to let me in and not withhold anything you think will scare me away. What you're doing now will make me run."

"You won't like what you see, what you feel, what you'll know." He transformed his kisses to nips, trailing his one hand along my collarbone, pushing away clothing.

"How do you know?" I challenged him, bucking against him.

He bit my shoulder blade and the smallest whimper came out. "Don't push me, Melody."

"Then let me go," I hissed out. It wasn't doing any good, being held hostage. I was wanting more from this and obviously, I was the one willing to fall hard enough and want more than enough for the both of us.

At least, that was what it felt like to me.

"That's the thing, I can't let you go." His heated stare came back to me.

"Either you let me go or you start giving me all of you," I threatened him, the pure emotional rage building in my throat.

He kept fighting it. Fighting between wanting to give in or convince me otherwise.

I wanted to burst into tears at our struggle. How did we get this deep into something that barely started? How did I let myself fall for a man that was holding back so much from me?

He turned loose of my wrists, the fire in his eyes slowly died, and I was afraid I got my answer.

I cradled his face in my hands, my thumb rubbing his cheek. He was a good man but with a lot of weight that he was carrying for more than one person.

A strong man can only hold so much strength.

"Baby," I whispered, "don't hide from me." I threw his words back at him from the first time we met, the first time our eyes laid on each other.

He leaned forward kissing my forehead, which was my favorite, especially from him.

"What do you want to know?" he quietly asked.

"Everything you can give me tonight," I quickly answered before he could retract the question.

He nodded, "Let's go home then."

He stepped back, and before he could leave my sight, I joked with him, "I guess this means the lesson is over?"

Chapter 23

HOUND DOG

Yes, the damn lesson was over.

There was still so much I needed to press about her talent, but her heart needed more and I stood there wondering if I could appease that heart.

If I wasn't in control of my anger, I'd give her everything she asked in one violent thrust right there in that warehouse, where I'd hear the echoes of her screams of pleasure ripple through the abandoned building.

But I could do exactly that where I could keep her safe, for now.

But she had to challenge me to see what was behind all the smiles and the moments that she stared at me like there was more to tell.

I told her I needed to keep her safe.

But damn did it feel like shit when she compared herself in my life as a prisoner. I guess the little songbird felt like she was in a cage with clipped wings.

She ran through all my thoughts that day. Sure, maybe I thought I could keep her with me for a long while, before I could show her the way I wanted to show her.

She didn't need to see the darkness that I hid, I tried not to let it seep into the house, keeping her in a safe home, a safe mindset.

I didn't know what I was doing anymore, and I needed her to tell me what she wanted. This whole relationship was nothing but a test that I didn't have the answers for.

I reflected back to Reverend's wisdom that I shoved off so many times. "We all deserve the ounce of happiness, even when it hurts to get it." The bullshit I ignored shed some light. We were both chasing a happiness that was from both sides.

Her damn words, "Either you let me go or you start giving me all of you."

All of me was something that would scare her off. The darkness that bled from vengeance and power to the protectiveness of doing whatever it took to survive. The light that spread when she came into my life, reigniting the flame of music that was burnt out.

I waited for her, waiting for her van to come into the driveway. She wanted it all, she was going to learn it all.

As soon as she pulled in and shut off the old-time engine that sounded like it needed to be in the junkyard, I whipped the door open and before she protested, I hiked her over my shoulder like a man coming to claim her.

I felt the small fists on my back, her violent yelling shrieked into my ears. "Hound Dog, I swear, you don't need to be an ass."

I smacked her ass, and she yelped, fidgeting in my arms. I had a plan for this, I was taking back control over this, between us. It was the only way I knew to protect her and for her to remember who I was and what she was to me.

Her little furious temper tantrum continued when I threw her on the couch, caging her in before she could bolt or find something that would do some kind of damage to me. Her eyes narrowed on me, the fiery passion ignited in her. She tried to stand up, but my hand shot to grip her throat, not enough to cut off the air, but enough to get her attention.

"This isn't how it's going to work tonight," I growled out.

Her throat swallowed, her eyes widened.

"I have your attention now?"

She nodded.

"Good girl, now. You said I could let you go or I could give you everything. Is that what you want? You want everything that encompasses me?"

She nodded again, her attentiveness stirring my dick awake even more. There was a slight fear in her eyes, something that craved to be set free.

"But you said you were going to tell me everything," she started to protest.

I sat her back down, letting loose of her beautiful neck. I peered down into those lustful eyes, her head tilted to look up at me as I stood in front of her, then leaned over to brush against her ear. "This is what we'll do, for every question you ask to know "everything" about me, you are going to stand in front of me, not sitting and take off a piece of clothing."

A tiny whimper escaped her.

She wanted to play, she wanted everything about me. "And when your wet pussy drips down your leg, you'll beg me to fuck you like a demon capturing an angel, only to corrupt her. Only to use her for his pleasure."

She didn't say anything. She listened to every word that came from me. "Good girls please their lover, their everything."

"Hound," she whispered as a plea.

"Is that what you want?"

"Yes," she answered, only to hide that deep down between her wanting praise, she searched for a way to be craved by something that was only hungry for her.

My hand shot straight to fist her hair; gripping it fed into her desire. "I didn't hear you."

"Yes, Hound Dog," Melody said beautifully.

I didn't have to ask her to do what she did next. She glided past me standing across from the couch, as I sat sprawling my legs, leaning back to enjoy the next lessons.

To be prepared for what you started and to never hide yourself. Let alone hide from me.

The ache in my dick grew, wanting every inch of her and her submission. I was already a goner, I was just waiting for her to fall. Call me a sap, as long as she was mine to be a sap for.

"Whenever you're ready." I stared back into those baby hazel eyes.

She simply nodded before taking off the thick white sweater she was wearing, only to reveal a plain black tank up. A bit of a teasing disappointment.

She folded her arms across her chest. "Why haven't I met any of the other club members other than the ones you say were at the Blue Sax?"

I blinked because damn I wasn't expecting that to be her first question. But she was nothing but straight to the point now, a bit more comfortable than the woman in the alley. I leaned forward resting my elbows on my knees.

"Because very few know of you. I had my reasons," I started but her impatient ass interrupted, "What were those reasons?"

I shot a smirk at her, looking her up and down. I waited to answer until she fulfilled her end of the bargain. But tit for tat, she kicked off a shoe, and threw that attitude back in my direction. I liked the look of her riled up.

"I don't know if you'll like what you hear."

"Don't care what you think right now," she hissed.

I narrowed my eyes at her brattiness. "In the beginning it was because I didn't know if I could have you in my life, that maybe we'd go our separate ways. Then it was because I wanted you to myself. But now, I can't have people see you, thinking that I have a weakness, that I'd choose you over the club." The truth hurts more than we ever wanted. "And more than anything, some events happened and it happened to a woman that looked like you, and from then I knew that I needed to protect you."

There was a slight twinge of anger in her eyes when I mentioned weakness and choosing her. Melody's legs started to move rapidly, she took off her other shoe, bending down and chucking it at my head. I dodged in time for it to move the blinds behind me around.

I could have moved away from it or prevented it, but I couldn't stop laughing at the whole thing. A goddess of a woman tossing her combat boot at me. "And you thought that it wasn't important for me to know about this, the dangers that you were running into since we met. That maybe there was a danger almost too close to home? Hound, we've known each other for weeks, months at this point, you didn't think I should know? Didn't you think to trust me to know and choose for myself what I needed to do?"

At that point, I needed to decide whether to remain silent while hiding everything that I could have told her, or fulfill her wish of giving her everything.

"I couldn't risk losing you," I said, hanging my head, "You were happier, healthier looking, and safe with me."

"Which brings us back to this whole trust thing, Hound Dog." Her voice grew in a powerful wave of strength. The way she said my name like it was a curse, like there was no enjoyment in it, was truly indescribable. She wasn't backing down, nor was she running. "Without calling it a relationship, which we'll get to that mister, you couldn't trust me? Had I shown you an ounce of mistrust? For fuck's sake, Sadie doesn't fully know our situation, she just knows that I'm safe and gotten dick from you."

She bent down, grabbing both socks for payment. I loved seeing the little fire brewing, knowing that it could be used for destruction.

But again, she was right. Somewhat, not completely. "I want to trust you, because you blindly trusted me. I have issues I know, but I don't know how to do what you do. Blindly take on the word."

She shook her head, "It's about you opening your mind and allowing yourself to trust one person, someone that you feel close to."

She made it sound so easy to let someone know everything.

When silence broke, she unhooked the button of her pants and shimmied them off, tossing them to the side. "Why did you quit music? You vanished from the world." She took a step closer, at least it was a closer look at her thick thighs that beckoned me to bury my face in them. My mouth slightly salivated at the thought.

I shook my head, focusing on her. Mentally, I counted the amount of clothes that were left before I could see everything that was mine.

"Why I quit goes hand in hand with my trusting certain people, honey." I sighed. Her pleading eyes begged me for more. "The people that were in charge of the music I produced and my career, had different plans than me. They took more than I knew, taking a lot more of what I was owed, and the more they pushed the more my own voice disappeared. When I found out the truth, I took matters into my own hands."

Gave them the same burns they gave me. "Then you bumped into me," she added.

I smiled, "I did, telling you that you might need to turn around."

I could see the rosiness coloring her cheeks. She broke eye contact, glancing at the ground. But when Melody's eyes turned back to me, I noticed the little glint in her eyes like she wanted to start her own trouble.

She walked closer to the couch, around the coffee table, reaching to the bottom of her shirt, stripping it off, tossing it to me. As I threw the shirt in a different direction, she carefully straddled my hips. Her heavy breasts begged for attention, and she hadn't even asked her question.

I was halfway tempted to forget the rest of the lesson and feed the dark hunger brewing. Her fingers played with my wrinkled shirt, how I wished that she would just slip her hand under my shirt to allow me the pleasure of feeling her fingertips.

"Why me?" she whispered, watching her fingers dance with the fabric.

I tilted her chin for this answer. "Because I'm greedy and I want you. I saw an opportunity to coach you into a musician, then you surprised me. Your pure heart, your strength, your sweet melodies that you hum randomly, the way you care for others, I saw more than a damsel in distress. I saw someone that deserved to be shown the same kindness and more." Her eyes softened, hopefully hearing the truth I needed her to hear, "You're way more than I deserve and you deserve better than me, but I'm the selfish bastard that will do anything to keep you. I just may have some challenges right now."

Those hazel-green eyes teared, fighting everything to make it stop. In a twist of events, she reached over and threw her arms around my neck, wrapping herself in a tight hug. I threw my arms around her, keeping her close.

Then in the tiniest voice, she admitted, "I'm fucking scared, Hound."

My sweet little songbird.

"It's okay to be scared, because I'm fucking terrified."

I could feel her heart racing, pounding in her chest, so much that it felt like it was beating in mine. I didn't deserve anything she wanted to give me.

Her body sank into mine with ease. I wanted to know where her mind was at, and if she had given up everything internally.

She pulled back, reaching behind her to unclasp her bra. The way her breasts naturally fell was a vision to behold. Her eyes darted away, but her fingertips caressed her nipples, as goosebumps trailed her skin. "Am I still going to be your secret?"

That question burned my thoughts, the way she said "secret" like it was a curse. I couldn't keep her here any longer. She wanted everything, I needed to take it as her choice to see the world that is in my command, my responsibility. I wanted her to be a part of my world.

"Not anymore. You have to understand that this means my world would be your world as well. I want to call you mine, I'm going to, but I also want to see my name on your back. I'm going to try like hell to be the person you need, you deserve."

She interrupted, "And I'm going to try to be the woman you need."

I couldn't hold back, I slammed my lips on hers, shutting any other thought that would come from that pretty little head of hers. Yes, we both had work to do on ourselves, but not to the point where it was forced. She was perfect for me. I didn't want to change anything about her.

She gave into the kiss, sinking further into me. I gripped the back of her head, keeping her close. Her breasts pushed into me, her hardened nipples poking on my chest. Melody pulled back slightly, catching her breath.

I watched as her expression seemed lost, dazed. "If your world is my world, does that mean your darkness is mine too?"

A deep growl rumbled in my chest, the slight possessiveness succumbed to existence. I reached between us, finding the thin fabric sheathing her weeping cunt. In one swoop, I tore apart the flimsy fabric, leaving her completely bare.

"There's no going back now."

Truly, we weren't going to look back.

Chapter 24

MELODY

I was going down the rabbit hole, and I didn't care. I tasted what a whole new life with Hound would be like and I wasn't ready to be done with it.

I'd take a chance with Hound, any day. He could have stayed silent, or fought back that I didn't need to know anything but that wasn't the case.

The ripping of the last bit of fabric had my heart racing for the finish line. His world was going to be my world.

In one solid movement, Hound carried me through the house, slamming open the bedroom door, and the power within his movements shook me. And yet made me hungry for what was coming next. I welcomed it, I needed to feel like I wasn't a porcelain doll that he didn't want to break.

I had already welcomed a cruel world with the words that stung too deep to cover up.

"What a pretty little songbird," Hound cooed, making me want to do anything he asked of me.

In one quick move, his lips assaulted mine, showing me that he wasn't going to hold back. His mouth pried mine open in a hungry, bruising kiss. He carried me to the bed, laying me down before rushing to trail down my naked body, while the man was still dressed.

"So sweet for me, aren't you. The way your body craves me is a damn sin," he said, teasing me along my inner thighs. The sensitive flesh kept me squirming under his touch, like it was too much but too little. As I tried to beg for more, more movement, his two thick fingers slipped into me with ease. My back arched at the sensation.

I looked down, watching him play with me, his piercing eyes looked back at me. The wet sounds of my pussy filled the silence.

"Was this for me, honey?"

I nodded my head. "All for you, Hound." His fingers curled deep in me, stretching me, preparing me for his cock. He kept slipping them in and out. The ache kept growing, teasing to be released.

But Hound wanted to keep the pace slow, punishing, in his control pace. When I bucked my hips trying to find my own release, his fingers slipped and spanked my pussy.

"Fuck," I hissed, almost at a whimper.

"This is my pussy, to do what I fucking want. So if I want to watch you wither under my pace, edging the fuck out of you, you'll say thank you. If I want to continually watch *my* pussy squeeze my fingers and come all over it, you'll say thank you" he growled out.

His hot breath sent pleasure to my aching cunt, his darkness was true control, true usage for him. This was what he needed to center his world.

"Please, Hound," I whimpered. He didn't like that answer. *Smack.* Fuck, maybe I liked my pussy spanked.

"You liked that a little too much. You like a little pain, don't you?"

Truthfully, I didn't know it would turn me on to the point of explosion. He didn't return to my wet heat. He stepped away, unhooking his belt, crumpling it to the ground.

"Turn around, head hanging over the edge," he ordered. My heart raced harder in my chest.

I quickly scrambled to the edge of the bed, hanging my head exactly where he wanted. He let his pants fall to the floor, his thick cock bobbing in front of me. He stroked his cock, my mouth salivating for a taste, to please him.

Whatever he unlocked by entering my life, I wasn't ever going back.

I slipped my hand toward my clit, rubbing small circles, slowly teasing myself. It didn't last long as rough words escaped from Hound's mouth, "Hands off," I stopped, wanting to defy him, but didn't. "Slip your hands under your ass, like a good girl." So I did.

"That's my girl. Listening so good," he cooed, cupping his hand on my cheek. The anticipation was killing me. "Knees bent. You'll need to brace yourself as I fuck that pretty little mouth of yours."

With knees bent, I watched his movements, waiting for him to take control. Take what he wanted.

"Open your mouth," he commanded. I happily obliged.

His cock hit my tongue, his taste swirling around like it calmed everything. He slowly thrusted, teasing my mouth and into my throat. My body spasmed at the feeling, my hands itched to touch myself, touch him. His groan was my reward, knowing this would send him over the moon. He thrusted out, my lips teased him, sucking him as he hissed out, "Fuck".

That's right baby, only I can give you what you need.

Fuck, when did I get possessive?

"Fuck, do that again, Melody," he said. "Take all of me again."

I did, I took every inch of that cock that I wanted so bad to be buried in me. His cock hit the back of my throat, my body spasming again. My back arched up at the intrusion, accommodating for his girth and length. I was never one to like sucking dick but for him, it's all I wanted to do.

He stilled, waiting for me to gag a couple of times, before slowly leaving my mouth as my lips caressed him. He leaned over with a groan, his fingers tracing my inner thighs. He left the head of his cock at the opening of my mouth. My tongue swirled, tasting the precum that wept from him.

"That's my good girl, taking this cock like that's all she wanted," he praised. "Maybe next time, I'll have a little vibrator on this pretty little clit. Would you like that, pretty girl?"

I nodded my head, because the thought of losing control with him would send me over the edge.

He worked my clit, slowly teasing it. I felt like a wet mess that wanted to be cleaned up.

"Open your mouth, let me fuck it." I stretched my mouth wider, keeping my head still. At first he thrusted with a slow pace, but the more he picked up speed his finger followed suit, leaving me in a puddle as my orgasm started to crash over me. My scream was muffled by his cock. Small tears started to flood my eyes.

"Your mouth is a piece of heaven, but as much as I want to stay there," he said between breaths, "I want to come in that sweet pussy that keeps gushing for me. He didn't let up on my clit. My sensitive nerves were on the verge of coming again.

He pulled up, and brought me to sit up. The tears finally dropped down my face. He kissed every single one of them. "Look at you, such a pretty mess for me."

My body was recovering from the burst of pleasure and still, I looked at this man and needed more. I shoved the rest of his clothing off, leaning into a kiss. Our mixture of moans and groans, our bodies collided as if we were one. He nipped on my bottom lip, a thrush of pain surrounded my body.

He leaned back before flipping me to my front side. Hound's hand traveled along my backside. He propped my ass in the air, before he whispered, "Mine."

"All yours, baby," I mewed.

He dived in, savoring my pussy. I grabbed the sheets in front of me, muffling the screams of pleasure. He brought me to the edge, and I turned my head, "Don't stop, Hound. For the love of God, don't stop," I pleaded with him.

He palmed my ass, gripping his hands in a possessive, bruising way. I could feel Hound's fingers dig into my skin. The pain turned into pleasure in moments, leaving me wanting more of him than ever before.

Smack!

I thrust forward from the impact, only to be repositioned as he savored me. I could feel myself getting closer and closer to the edge. His tongue speared me, taking all that he wanted.

Smack!

"Ah," I screamed. The more I moved, the harder his impact. I'd take the blissful punishment any day.

I was right there waiting for the explosion. He must have known I was getting close because he stopped, pulling back leaving me to search for any kind of release. He leaned down to my ear, his hot breath on my skin, "You want to come? Tell me how much you want it." His voice darkened.

It took everything in me to catch my breath and gather up the words. His hand traveled up my neck and into my hair, he gripped tight to bring us up. His lips attacked my neck, waiting for me to say what he wanted me to say.

"Hound," I breathed out, but too captivated to speak. He drove me to the brink and back.

He kept nipping and sucking my neck. His other arm wrapped along me, palming my sensitive breasts. I wasn't going to last much longer. The pressure built up again, and all I could think about was him sinking into me where he belonged.

"Fuck, Hound please. Just fuck me like you want to, like you want to buried inside," I pleaded with him. His hand over my breast pinched my nipple making me buckle from the sharp pain.

His hand wrapped possessively around my neck, squeezing it, taking control of the air that I had. Pleasure was still rising throughout, building to the point of almost breaking. He released me, only to squeeze me again. His other hand trailed along my sensitive clit, circling around it. The mixture of pleasure and submission began to build in my head, like it was breaking free from the old version.

He released my throat and gave a deep chuckle. "You enjoyed that didn't you?" I moaned, still entranced by the slow, torturing strokes of my clit. My moans grew louder.

"Dirty girl, made just for me," he said sinisterly, before shoving me down to the bed, propping my ass back up.

Lost in the haze that he created, he teased my entrance with the head of his cock, and I was tempted to take control, but fought against it.

"There will be nothing between us, you'll take me bare," he announced. "Anything I need to know before I fill this little wet cunt." I shook my head.

Before I knew it, in one hard thrust I felt everything from him. Every fiber of me stretched to accommodate him. He was hitting every spot. There was nothing soft and sweet about his thrusts. Every fiber of my being wanted to collapse right there and then. It was real and it fulfilled any dark carnal need I had.

And when my orgasm flooded me, I thought it would have been in the end, but Hound never let up. Somehow he flipped me on my back, putting a thick pillow underneath me and resumed his speed.

Already spent and tired, I couldn't stop my eyes from drifting into a floating space. I heard the mumbles of Hound saying, "Hang on, songbird. This pussy is fucking heaven."

I screamed his name. Screamed "Hound" as if I was the one howling at the full moon. Every time I called out his name, it drove him to madness.

I reached for him, craving the touch of his skin. He took my hands and leaned forward. His burning lips pressing against mine into yet another bruising kiss. He held back for so long until his own orgasm took control. He buried himself in my neck as his cum mixed with my own release. His cock was still twitching inside as I circled my arms around his neck, holding him close.

His heart rate steadied, his contentment radiated by his touch. This powerful, strong-willed, infuriating man had released a bit of what has been pent up for a long time.

I stroked his back, my fingers trailing along his skin. I was coming down from my own high.

I kissed the top of his head. "Baby?"

He mumbled something. I caressed his hair as he nuzzled me. I couldn't help but smile knowing that this would change everything. "Baby?"

He finally turned his head, and the slight content smile on his face told me everything I needed to know.

The man was spent. "As much as I love that you're a weighted blanket right now, I need to clean myself up."

He moved down to rest his head on my chest, his chin resting there. His cock finally left my body, although the thought was there for a brief moment of what if it was still there.

Mind out of the gutter or the man may go for round two or three and you'll be seeing stars.

"I'd keep you in my bed if I could."

"I wouldn't put it past you, baby," I said, caressing his face with a sappy smile myself.

He laid there quietly before speaking. "You know what I realized?"

"What, Hound?"

He softly kissed my chest, distracting me from needing to get up and move. "I haven't taken you out on a date."

I sucked my lips between my teeth, not wanting to point out the obvious, but ultimately failed. "Well, that would have meant that you and I were seen together and not always fucking."

He sighed, which melted my heart. "Let me take you out, let me show you everything."

I gasped dramatically, "Oh my gosh, are you finally going to tell everyone your big secret?"

I joked with him, hopefully as a sign that I was ready to move past it and grow.

"Best secret that I've kept," he cooed. His big blues were shining back at me. "But I want everyone to know you're mine."

"Me?"

"Yes, Melody." He pushed himself up to hover over me, "You're mine now, too late to turn back."

I playfully pushed his chest. "Hey, that's my line."

I could say that we weren't looking back, even knowing what the roads would look like.

Chapter 25

MELODY

"Hound, where are you taking me?" I asked as he handed me a helmet to get on the slight death trap of a motor vehicle. I wasn't scared but I'd never been on a motorcycle. As much as the man had rearranged my guts, I was wary of the trust there on his chrome machine.

"Now why would I go and ruin a surprise?" he said cryptically. He saw the helmet in my hands, gripping it tightly. He pried it from my hands and fixed my hair to accommodate the helmet. Strapping it across my chin, he pulled me forward by the bottom of it. "Or I could just cancel it all together, and I could take you back to bed. There's a little red thing in the guest bedroom nightstand."

A flush of red spread across my cheeks. The fucker found it. "You wouldn't."

"You know the answer to that." He winked.

I wanted to be mad, embarrassed, but that turned me on too much. I crossed my legs as he walked to the bike and started it. I could understand the beauty of the ride, but nerves shook me. I looked up to watch him, my bearded alpha man, looking like a wet dream in his boots, jeans, and his cut. I lost all sense of speech just gawking at him. He swung his leg over the saddle.

"Alright, honey. Step over and swing your leg. Be careful of the muffler." he instructed. I took his hand and mounted the vibrating bike. The amount of power behind the vibrations were going to be a test, especially when I leaned back finding something to hang on to. But Hound pulled me forward, cradling his back side. He took my arms and wrapped them along his thick waist. My arms could barely come together.

What do you expect when the man was a damn mountain?

He huffed. "Where do you want to hang on?"

On the ground, preferably.

Without any other thought, my hands gripped the top of his thighs. He groaned. I started to retreat but he pulled them back on top. "You're going to be trouble."

I shook my head, but he just chuckled and soon we were on the road. Between the vibrations of the engine and my hands placed on his thighs, I was hanging on to more than just my life.

My heart beat hard in my chest; I wasn't ready for him weaving in and out of traffic, commanding the roads. I gripped his thighs the more he sped through traffic. And yet underneath me, the vibrations hit my center and a new sensation occurred. Self-consciously I got lost in the feeling to the point where I hadn't realized we were at a stoplight and I caught Hound's eyes in the side mirror.

I followed his gaze to my hand placement, I wasn't reaching his thighs, but cupping his cock over his jeans. My eyes widened and my hands retreated faster than I'd ever moved. I caught the small smirk on his lips.

"I'm sorry," I shouted before he took off again and my hands moved back to his thighs. I tried to fight off the growing ache of a pending orgasm. I tried to move and adjust my position, but it intensified. I was helpless and I didn't know how much longer it would be until we arrived at our destination.

My body moved along with the bike, turning and weaving. I mentally pleaded that the agony would leave as soon as possible, because I didn't know how much longer until I was going to combust.

Almost to the point of tears, we stopped in a small parking lot, outside of downtown where a parked food truck was housed.

But Hound didn't turn off the bike. Instead, he got off and sat back on it backward, facing me. His searing touch was almost enough to set me off. He took off my helmet, fixing my hair, only to put a strand behind my ear. "How did you enjoy your first ride?" He cocked an eyebrow.

I sucked in my lips because telling him that the bike was getting me to the verge of an orgasm and still building was embarrassing enough.

"Um, it was... Fine." I held back as best to not give it away, but the man wasn't born yesterday.

"Mm, just fine?" he said, scooting closer to me. "I think you may have enjoyed it a little more than you think."

"Hound," I growled out, but faded as the vibrations continued. We were in public for God's sake. I was in need like a damn wanton woman in a western film.

With a short chuckle, he grabbed the back of my head and pulled me into a deep kiss, one that continued to send that floating feeling in my head, like everything was wiped away. I couldn't hold back any more, and shortly found release from the pulsing ache. I melted further into his kiss, his mouth covering my moans of pleasure.

When my breathing evened, he cut off the bike, and softly transformed the kiss.

I pulled back and in a breathless voice said, "You cocky bastard."

He licked his lips, "Yes, I'm one *lucky* cocky bastard."

We got off, walking hand in hand toward the lot with the truck that was surrounded by other patrons and picnic tables. Alongside were heating lamps just in case the chill air crept in. Stopped for a second, I shook my head as I realized, "You're taking me on a date?"

The smug bastard turned, "For the first part and then we might have some visitors, who knows?"

"Hound Dog," I said.

"Oh, so serious?"

"Please tell me you're not killing two birds with one stone?"

"I like it when things go my way, most of the time," he said, pulling me along with him.

"If I had known I'd be meeting your friends or brothers, whatever you call them, I'd have dressed better you know." I started to complain, looking down at my jeans and long sleeve off the shoulder shirt, and an oversized jacket I found from a thrift store.

"You're beautiful the way you are, and my brothers will accept that whether they like it or not." His voice sounded so sure that it would be this way.

The man kept shocking me. I expected more fights or something, or a longer timeline. I started to think that I wasn't deserving of a man like this, one that listened and was completely obsessed with me. I mean you only read about it in books and here I was living that not-so-fictional relationship.

I smiled and went along with Hound.

And the date was just that, a date. Two people connecting in a shared place, opening up about the world they live in and how they see it. Conversations became easier with him. We talked about his brother, Memphis in North Carolina, where apparently they are completely opposite. He told me about his dad and mama, how he did everything he could to support them when he was Nash Young. He was a family man, a protective provider. It wasn't until the producers that his heart became hardened.

We talked about music, which only made me fall for him a little more. The scariest thought was that I was falling for him and I hadn't worked up the courage to tell him. But here outside the house walls, we were like two normal people sharing a weird bond that others might not understand, and that was okay. Because in my eyes, it was just Hound and I.

I kept noticing him staring at me. "What are you gawking at?"

He simply shook his head. "Just getting lost in you."

I threw my dirty napkin at him, "That was so cheesy, where did you pick up that line?"

"What? You don't like it?"

"Not when it sounds like that, coming from your mouth."

"Oh, I'm sure that you like something from my mouth."

There he went making me blush like a sinner in church.

"But, seriously, how did I get so lucky?"

I shrugged, taking another bite of my tacos from the truck. "Well, that's what happens when you save me from terrible men, only to bump into each other and you take me home only to then tell me that you were pretty much off limits."

"I did not tell you that I was off limits. I said that I wasn't good for you."

"Same difference. And you still didn't listen to yourself," I said, laughing at him and his casual nods.

"And yet, it was the best decision I made," he said with a mouth full of food.

I smiled softly, thinking that this would be our life. Most people would think that this wouldn't last or I wouldn't survive. But one look at Hound Dog and I knew for a fact, he wasn't looking elsewhere.

"So." I cleared my throat. "Is there anything else I need to know about rules or guidelines or history about the club?"

He gawked at me, as he put down the potential bite he was about to take. "Like what, honey?"

Little did he know that it would open the flood gate of words, "Well, like if I'm with you, am I supposed to act a certain way? Bake cookies for the club? Attend events? Am I supposed to stay quiet, in the background? How much can I tell people like Sadie or our friend group? If your brothers see me with you, what does that mean for them? Will I expect to see them show up now at our home?" I kept running off questions and I met his gaze to find a stupid smile on his face. "What? Did I say something wrong?" He just stared at me with awe and wonder. While I was being serious, he looked like cupid just shot an arrow at his ass.

He happily sighed, "My sweet little songbird." He chuckled.

"What?" I raised my voice. He shook his head. "I swear to all that's good and pure, if you don't tell me, I will be calling you by your first name."

He just smirked, before reaching for my hand. "You said our home."

I did? I tried to replay my words that spewed out of my mouth. *Our* home. Fuck, I was getting in deep with him, like wearing my heart on my sleeve. "I'm sorry, it's your home, I know." I took my hand back and started to rub over my chest as I got lost in thought.

I knew that this was what we wanted, but we had skipped so many damn steps that reassurance was something I needed.

There wasn't anger in his eyes, it was confusion.

He got up, moved closer to me, and straddled the bench seat, turning my chin to meet him, "It's *our* home."

Home wasn't an object, it's a feeling and it was leading towards him. He gently kissed my forehead, before a shadow casted over us.

My eyes widened as I was met with a smiling clean shaven, blonde man. There was a twinkle in his eyes, like a spark of pure happiness and yet a dash of mischief.

"Well, Prez, you finally set her free," blondie said. "Seems like a sweetheart, innocent, too good for you, you sap."

"How do you know she didn't break free, and Prez just happened to find her," another voice entered. When the man with the other voice came into view, I started to get nervous. Like meeting the parents only meeting your club members.

I was rendered speechless. Hound released a growl. "She's mine."

All the possessiveness he had just got me hot. I stood up to extend a friendly gesture, because being a quiet little mouse in the background wasn't going to go over well with me.

"And y'all must be the unexpected visitors he was talking about, I mean I was expecting someone more handsome-r, but you'll do," I gripped blondie and mystery man's hands to shake.

Hound busted out in laughter.

"Nah, she charmed him, that's why she's got the balls on her. Bet you got him wrapped around your little finger, don't you?" Mystery man retorted.

I turned to see Hound turned in our direction, so I slipped into his lap, wrapping my arms around his neck. "Why, whatever do you mean?" I pouted. Hound's body turned possessive as one arm wrapped around my waist and the other hand gripping my thigh.

"Okay, now y'all are just gross." Blondie winced. "You turned the man into a happy simp."

"It's that voodoo beauty. One look and you're under her spell." Mystery man commented.

Hound's hold got tighter, I glared at him. "Easy, baby, you might pop your favorite parts."

"Mine," Hound claimed.

"Yes, yes, you big grump, she's yours. Only a special woman would make you even crazier than you've ever been," Blondie joked.

He wasn't wrong.

Hound rested his chin on my shoulder. "Melody, I'd like you to meet two people that have known me longer than most people in the club."

They knew him as Nash. "The blonde jokester is my right hand man, B.B. Don't let the smile fool you, the man can be a cruel son of a bitch. But one the best people to help lead the pack."

I smiled in his direction. This was his best friend. Someone to help take the burden off of Hound. At least that was the hope.

"And this is Otis, too smart for his own good. Also our in-house lawyer and club secretary, if we are ever in a pinch," Hound said. "But don't play cards with him, the man will take your money."

Otis had caramel skin, his dark buzzed beard chiseled his features. But he had a softness to his eyes that were a comfort. Any woman would be lucky to have him.

"Not my fault you hadn't learned your lesson. Every. Time." Otis laughed.

The men shared a spout of laughter. I was a little lucky to see this side of him, a side that was more than what I saw. I eased into him, still sitting in his lap.

We carried on conversations as they swapped stories of the past, allowing a perfect stranger to know and hear them. They had gotten comfortable, joining in our lunch. Hound Dog had turned into a complete mush, as Otis and B.B kept reminiscing. Hound would kiss my shoulder blades, nuzzle into my neck, and never let me off his lap.

"You remember when Otis was prospecting and he had to go get Blue out on bail," B.B sparked a new story.

Otis had stuffed his mouth, looking up from his plate with wide eyes, he shook his head, almost pleading with them not to continue. But Hound joined in the story, "Yep, and he kept saying that it was a joke or a cruel task for a prospect." Hound's deep voice vibrated against my back.

"Why?" I asked.

"Because what he didn't know was that Blue was arrested in Bucksnort, Tennessee," Hound explained.

"And?" I asked, missing the whole joke.

B.B took a swig of his beer before answering, "Because we had given him directions to Kentucky and Otis was pissed because he had gotten pulled over."

"Wait, how did he get lost in Kentucky?" realizing that they were playing their poor friend.

Otis finished chewing, pounded his fist on the table, "Because these motherfuckers told me Bucksnort was in Ohio and fucking screwed up my GPS."

I shook my head. "How's that even possible?"

"I knew a guy," Hound answered, as B.B snickered.

"Hound got his little cousin's friend to mess with it." Otis scowled at them.

"You didn't think to consult like an actual roadmap?" I countered.

The men went silent, and B.B cocked his head, "Oh, well he didn't think of that before we left."

"You didn't tell her the best part." Otis jokingly shook his head, "That little cousin and his friend are Waylan and Blaze."

I bursted out laughing, "So motorcycle club is a family affair I take it."

We continued on until Hound's phone buzzed. When he took it out, it took everything in me not to fall on the floor. Hound shot up bringing his phone to his ear. I tried to stand but he gestured for me to stay with the guys.

He walked away, far enough where I couldn't hear the conversation. That's when I knew something was wrong, when Otis got up from the other side of the table and sat next to me. They weren't consoling me from my confusion.

They were guarding me.

Chapter 26

HOUND DOG

My girl was getting along with my brothers. She matched their banter and proved to me that she wanted to be a part of this life. That she was fine around them, everything would fall into place.

I would be lying if I said that I should have done that a long time ago, to show her the side that was the other part of my life. She couldn't be held, she wasn't like that.

Her laughter, the way she would sometimes squint when she laughed hard, the warmth of her smile when she was listening to the guys tell her stories of our antics when we first started in the club. For a moment, I felt content, like this was where my life was going to head in the right direction.

But that moment of bliss ended when an unknown caller popped on my phone. Normally, I'd ignore it, but something in my gut told me that I couldn't this time.

When I stood up and answered it, a deep chuckle graced the air. "Little doggie, finally answering phone calls."

I knew that voice all too well. Saber, the president of the Hogs. I did my best not to run into him, but there were times that it couldn't be avoided. I walked quickly away from the table, far away where Melody couldn't hear me. At least, not yet.

"Saber, I take it that you got our little gift. Sorry the bow wasn't big enough." I snarked.

"Funny, your little group thinks it's cute to dump a stranger in our laps." He tried to divert the conversation.

"Well, we figured you wanted your rat back. He got caught in one of our traps. Got a little messy with covering it up."

Weston was out of our hair, there was rarely any second chances when someone crossed us. It was either the river or the dirt.

"It was easy, for the right price." Saber said. He was trying something, I had no idea where he was going with it.

"What do you want, Saber? You call to tell me that you've seen the error in your ways?" I growled.

His venomous laughter was my response before he continued to talk, "I have no idea what you're talking about. We have been perfect little angels. We're not the ones that have been turning up dead druggies."

I wanted to ride across that bridge and strangle him and burn down whatever was left. This attempt at a cat and mouse game was ridiculous.

"You've already seen what we do to people who cross us. Call off your men, Saber."

"No can do, little doggie. Not when we had rule over Memphis until your little pathetic group came rolling in there." His voice rose.

The Saint's ruled Memphis back then and forever in the future. This was our town, our people, our kingdom. One that I wanted Melody to rule with me.

"You think one mess is going to scare us into leaving? Saber, how you do have any fucking brain cells left?" I wasn't going to react to his outburst.

"Maybe not, but I bet you wouldn't want anything to happen to your little bitch, now would you, Hound Dog," Saber threatened. Before I could retort, a ping came to my phone. I looked to see a new message.

What was sent made my blood boil like a volcano ready to erupt. It was Melody kissing me, holding me; it was taken while we were there on our date. That blissful thought that we would be okay and everything was under control vanished before it could even start.

He was threatening her. It was an empty threat, but one that I wasn't taking lightly.

"You so much as cross the state line and there will be a fucking bullet in your skull. Be careful of starting fires because they can easily be spread back to you." I warned him.

My thoughts were spinning, sweat dripping down my back.

"I'm sorry, Hound Dog, did I strike a nerve? How about this, your club gets the fuck out of Memphis, and we won't kill your little singer," he said so casually.

My eyes widened. They knew more about her than suspected. I needed to keep her and the club safe. If that meant going to war, I'd be doing it in a heartbeat. She would be going with me from place to place. I wasn't going to leave her alone. She was damn lucky I didn't consider placing a tracker on her or *in* her. But if she knew or found out, there was the risk of losing her.

I shouldn't have to risk losing her over her being killed. The second thoughts grew, the thought that maybe I couldn't have her in this life, I was bringing danger into her life when she didn't ask for it.

"Does this mean your darkness is my darkness?"

This was more than darkness, it was life and death. Could she thrive? Was I going to be enough for her? I could feel my mind spinning out of control, and I didn't know if I could regain it.

"I will fucking end your club, leave it in ashes. You threaten my club, my woman and I promise you'll ask for death when I'm through with you." I was seething at this point, impulsively ready to fulfill my promise.

I didn't give him a chance to respond. I hung up, taking a moment before storming back to the table. My eyes glanced at the photo that was sent, knowing that someone was here, watching us. He thought that his intimidation act would make me quit or run with my tail between my legs.

We had everything to lose, but the club had the ambition and the fight to continue to reign over our community.

I stalked back to the table, Otis had slid next to Melody, and his eyes darted to me as he quickly stood up. Melody's soft eyes followed my lead, her once smiling face turned into a frown of sadness. "Hound, what's wrong, baby?" Her soothing voice washed over me.

"We have to go. Looks like you'll be seeing the clubhouse after all." I tried to distract her from worrying but the grim look on her face told me otherwise.

"What's going on Prez?" B.B asked, matching my energy, feeding off the anger that was still radiating around me.

"Here's not the place. Otis, I need you to ring the board, meeting in twenty minutes," I barked. Otis nodded his head, pulling out his phone to do so.

Melody's soft hands gripped mine. "Baby, you're scaring me."

"Everything is going to be okay, you just have to listen to me," I told her, I thought she saw my body language and agreed.

B.B gripped my shoulder, he just nodded before he and Otis took off back to the clubhouse.

There was much I needed to tell her, but not in the open. Not when eyes were watching us. "Come on." I grabbed her hand, "I'll explain when we get there."

She was hesitant, I shook my head, "Honey, now is not the time for protest. I'm not opposed to slinging you over my shoulder and onto the bike." My tone sounded demanding, with a dash of pent up anger.

She trudged along, hanging on to me once we got onto the bike. I know I scared her, but this was a welcome into the life she said yes to. I had to keep telling myself that we'd get through it, that she'd understand eventually.

The ride to the clubhouse was a blur, but I wasn't hesitating about her safety. I pulled into the clubhouse as many eyes laid upon us. A few were whispering. The next part was going to be the brashest thing I've ever done, not including signing up to prospect for this chapter.

"Melody Rae is mine. You fuckers know what that means. She is one of us, and we protect our own." Her eyes widened at the claim. I wanted a little bit more of a romantic gesture, to give her her cut with my name on it, hear her actually say yes, and my brothers cheer for me.

In the end, it was always going to be her. My ol' lady, mine to protect and love.

Easy tiger, saying that too loud might be more dangerous.

At her blank expression, I turned her and gave her a possessive, searing hot kiss, leaning over and cradling her body. She allowed me control for that brief moment before I had to pull away and handle things the way I needed to handle that situation.

I pulled away, both of us breathless, "Melody, I need you to really listen to me right now." She gently nodded, "I need to speak with my board, figure out a plan, and when I come back I'll explain everything better. Please believe me when I say this was not how I thought today was going to go. But be a good girl, and stay with my cousin Waylan." I pinned my eyes in his direction signaling for him to come over, "Relax, play some pool, watch T.V., but if anyone touches you or is disrespectful, you will let me know. Got it?"

She was speechless; my little songbird was tucking her wings back in. A part of me was crushed to see her like this, especially when she had come such a long way.

I kissed her forehead, fighting the urge to bring her with me to the meeting, but there was no place for her in the boardroom. Not when there was an itch to fight.

Chapter 27

HOUND DOG

There was so much that as a president I was not allowed to do, one being out of control and making rash decisions. I needed to be a better leader, and hear from the people who are to use checks and balances. Rage could be ripping through my veins and yet there were other voices that needed to be heard, even if I didn't like the answer.

"Look I'm not saying that the Hogs don't deserve what is coming to them, but automatically jumping to fight without them throwing the first punch is risky," Otis tried to convince us.

"We barely have the cops on tail anymore, do we want to fucking risk them coming back when they see a turf war?" Twitty chimed in.

B.B stayed quiet for once, and yet it concerned me that he was.

"I think we know that this war is going to continue, whether we like it or not," Hank said. I had counted on Hank to convince the brothers to fight and end it all like I needed it to go. But for some reason he had wanted a peaceful end to things.

I waited for other opinions to take place, knowing that it would be a split decision. "Maybe we wait it out. If we do something now, it's only to trigger a war, one that we might not be ready for," Fender spoke up.

"As much as I hate to say it, Prez, we can't pull the first shot, how many times have you convinced us just that when we wanted to go on a rampage?" Shooter started to say, which I hated. The man thrived on the pain of others, some would say it was the only way for his own to subside.

I rolled my head from side to side, trying to stay calm and collected. But it wasn't working. I had felt rage before, but nothing like this, nothing like I was feeling. Then again, I never had a woman in my life that I cared about enough to go to war for in another area.

I couldn't think anymore, control was slipping from my fingers.

B.B lit a cigarette before speaking his mind on this matter. "If I had it your way, I could be compelled to start trouble on the other side of the bridge, but we have everything to lose, the Hogs do not. They are barely surviving as it is. We have to hold back. For now at least."

I let out a deep sigh, because clearly my judgment wasn't the best.

"I guess we don't need a vote unless someone other than myself has any lead on the other side?" I asked, already assuming that they didn't want to go to war over this. Could I completely blame them? They didn't want another Trojan War. Only someone put a target on Melody's back and I wasn't happy about it.

I felt the guilt in the pit of my stomach. That was my own demon I had to face.

Around the table, everyone else shook their heads. "Fine, we'll table any further action."

The brothers nodded their heads before taking their leave. I leaned back into my chair, a million thoughts rushing through my head and the majority of them were about Melody. A puff of smoke blew in my direction. I sat up and looked to see B.B hanging back.

"Got something else to say? Better say it now or drop it," I grumbled out.

He licked his bottom lip saying, "Well, there are a lot I would like to say, but worry that I'll meet the other end of your fist." He wasn't wrong.

"Floor's yours."

"There are times when you need to be the president and make the sound decision and there are times that you shoulder everything, taking someone else's responsibilities because you think that if you do it it will get done correctly. Or at least correct in the way you want it done."

"I'm not doing anyone else's job, but it's helping those when they can't do it." I said defensively.

B.B shook his head, "What I mean is, you don't ask for help only when you want something done your way and it's not asking, it's demanding."

"You've been around Reverend too long, go chase some pussy or something," I retorted.

B.B was taken back, "Pussy isn't going to change my mind, and if you must fucking know, I haven't been chasing anything for a long while now."

"Things have to be done to make this run smoothly."

He just shook his head, "Yeah, and what happened to trusting others who are in their roles for a reason?" He leaned on the table, snuffing out his cigarette. "Like me."

What the fuck did he mean like him? He did a lot for me, especially when I was trying to figure out Melody and how this was going to happen.

"What the fuck you mean?" I knew this was going to be a battle. B.B rarely smoked and when he did, it was a combination of a dramatic effect and to calm his nerves.

"When was the last time you allowed me to take things off your plate or to help you when you were knee deep in the trenches?" he pressed.

Fucker got me there, I couldn't remember, but he took my silence as his answer. "Exactly. I have always been here to help.

It's gotten worse the past couple of months and I think I know why."

Melody.

"She's not the reason why. She's the reason I found another purpose."

"You've fallen for her."

"I've claimed her."

"Which was shitty by the way, like she didn't have a choice."

"She had a choice," I shouted.

"No she didn't. She would have if you fucking asked logically. But it had to be your way," B.B snapped and his green eyes darkened with anger. "You may have said in bed that you claimed her as yours, but you and I both know that she would have liked it better to say yes."

He cared in more ways than one. "My way is the only way she's going to be safe." I pounded the table before standing up. "When she agreed to be mine, she knew what that was going to be like."

"Oh yeah, she signed up for you to control every aspect of her life."

"I know what she needs."

"How about what she wants?" B.B questioned me.

I knew that, I thought I did. B.B had me questioning myself and if I actually knew what my little songbird wanted.

"What does she want, Hound Dog? Hm? Because from where I'm standing, she's not going to like it, but she cares about you too much and the way she looks at you, she worries if you're coming or going."

I thought she wanted someone to be there for her like no one was after her sister Aria. I thought she wanted to be an artist that wasn't afraid to put herself out there. I thought she wanted a better life.

I thought she wanted me.

"I know what she wants," I responded with a slight doubt.

"I'd ask her again, because after today, you'd rethink that response." He started to get up and walk away. "If she knew any better, she'd kick your ass."

"Like you know what she wants." I sounded jealous.

"I'm just saying, think about what I said. Maybe there's some clarity in there that you didn't know," he offered as he left.

It was just me and the empty room, alone with the swirling thoughts that hadn't subsided. I couldn't let the club sink, we all had worked way too fucking hard to turn back now. For Melody, maybe this wasn't the life she expected. I thought she knew about the dangers of this lifestyle.

My head started to pound like someone took a brick and chucked it at my head.

Ask her again? Why couldn't we just fucking move forward? Figure things out later on in time.

I emerged from the meeting room, craving a smoke to settle my nerves before I went to find Melody and see how we could get out of this fucking nightmare.

As my hand started to rub the back of my neck, my eyes jerked to attention. Melody was engrossed in a conversation with my cousin and Reverend. I would be lying if I said that seeing her so close to them in a deep conversation made me a little envious, because it burned something fierce in me.

I walked up behind the couch she was sitting at, gently glided my hand to her shoulder, laying a claim to her, even though I already did earlier. Melody, my little songbird, leaned in my touch, leaning her head back to offer a small, soft smile.

"Hey baby," she whispered. I couldn't help but smile back, offering her a kiss on her forehead. I loved seeing her melt into me, like she craved me.

Just like I craved her with an intensity. Reverend and Waylan stared back, watching my girl making me smile.

"I'm going to steal her away," I said as I turned and scooped her off the couch and into my arms. She let out a squeak, and a blush of red clouded her cheeks. Her heart raced so fast that it vibrated against my chest. I paraded her through the hallways, weaving around others. I took her to the room that had been barely used within the past couple of months.

What changed?

I had someone worth coming home to.

"Hound, I can walk you know," she teased.

"I know, but I'd rather have my hands on you."

"You just didn't want me talking to your brothers," she said with confidence. Challenging me for a bit of the truth.

We approached the door and I nodded toward the handle; she picked up the hint and twisted the nob open. The door swung open and showed her the unkempt room, because I barely remembered the last time I was there.

The dark walls shed no light, no other personal effects, only clothes that I kept here just in case we needed to ride out for a whole other reason. She turned as I set her down, trying to find the light switch that beamed a harsh light until I could find the lamp light that I preferred.

Melody quietly walked over to the nightstand, her hand gliding across the furniture, taking in every rough and bump. She stayed quiet until her hand touched the bed and froze there. Her head dipped down. The sheets were still a mess from the last time I slept there. But her mind wasn't silent, and her shoulders tensed, her breathing heavy with a hint of madness.

"Anything I need to know about this room?" Her voice transformed from the once sweet one that was calling me baby to the harsh jealous tone that demanded answers.

"If you think there was anyone else, the answer would be not for a very long time, way before you flew into my life." I slid behind her, trying to take back control of this moment.

She looked over her shoulder, her eyes softened but her body remained defensive. Maybe she needed the moment to collect herself while I was gone. Or maybe her words were true that she was going to remain by my side no matter the true ugliness.

I started to rub her shoulders trailing along her upper arms, she leaned back into me. "What do you want, Melody?"

"You know what I want, Hound. I'm pretty sure we've discussed this already." she said, but I knew that she was confused. She twisted around, facing me. "Is this about what happened before the meeting? Your little announcement?"

She was playing with me. I could hear the teasing, little brat in her voice. There was nothing little about claiming her in front of the club.

"Melody," I warned her before she continued to derail what I needed to say. "I think you need to understand everything before you say anything else."

She shook her head. "I don't think so. I think you need to listen." She was poking the bear, the hidden beast that she got a taste of before. The temper that flared deep.

"Melody, listen to me." I commanded her, bumping my chest to hers.

She spread a cocky grin. "Or what?"

"You don't want to do this."

"Oh but I'm yours, baby. Right?"

"I'm not playing."

"Me either." She sneered. Okay, maybe I was poking the bear. "Either you tell me what is making you this crazed man or I'm going home. I'd like my Hound Dog back please, if you don't mind."

"What the fuck are you talking about?" I shook my head.

She sighed, her hands palming my chest. "Let's recap shall we. You and I were having an amazing time, and then I met Otis and B.B, which side story, I need to talk to you about something B.B recommended," I started to protest but she put a finger to my lips. "Nope, I'm still talking."

I needed to sit down for this. Was it wrong to wish that she was back to her timid self, where she kept to herself, guarded? Yeah, it was wrong. I sat on the bed, she edged herself between my legs, her hands under my chin forcing me to look up at her.

"I met your friends, then a call came in, and judging from that call, you changed. I went along with it, not arguing. Then when we got to the clubhouse, which wouldn't kill y'all to clean it every once in a while, you made a claim and showed it before talking to me. But I knew what that meant. I stayed quiet until I could process it. And thankfully you have some good men here because apparently I could lean on them, just like you can. At least that was what Reverend and I were talking about."

Well, fuck me sideways and smack me like a piñata. I was wrong about it, and so was B.B, which reminded me that I needed to rub it in his face that my girl didn't need to be underestimated. A few weeks with me and she'd blossomed.

"So, lover, please ask me again what do I want?" she challenged me. My hands started to grip her ass before I rubbed it.

"What do you want, Melody?" I growled.

She inched closer to my lips, just barely touching them. She smiled like a little vixen. "You. I've already chosen you."

Chapter 28

MELODY

I 'd choose him over and over again. I would never know when the man would stop acting like I was running. Maybe when we were first figuring things out, but I wasn't running. Not anymore.

I'd still have questions, but if this was going to work like we both wanted it to, I would have to have patience. Or less, I'd push him too close to the edge, and I wasn't going to make him start regretting anything.

He started to protest, but I stopped him, "If you ask me if I'm sure, you will be sleeping on the couch and no sex for a week."

He cocked an eyebrow. "That also means you won't be getting orgasms too."

Cheeky bastard, so fucking smug.

"That's why they make dildos and vibrators. I've used them before you, I can use them again. Plus, in your old age, your stamina may not be too high."

He didn't like that answer as he softly grazed my backside, sending goose bumps down my spine. I didn't know if this would either bite me in the ass figuratively or literally.

"That's a bold statement, awfully cute for someone that could be getting a spanking right now," he said with a grin. My body started to loosen up, all the tension released from his muscles.

"Well, look who decided to relax," I cooed, wrapping my arms around him, only to lightly scratch his head through his short curls.

"Knowing that you're safe right here," he said leaning into my chest. His hands snaked back around, sliding under my sweater. His rough hands skimmed over the soft curves of my stomach, cupping my breast. He was trying to distract me or tempt me, more like taking back the dominance. I loved the way his hands could silence me from the wild thoughts that edge to my mind.

"Hound," I started to say, losing the words as his hands started to reach back for the hem of my sweater. He hummed in response. "About next Friday."

He whipped the sweater off, only to trail kisses along my stomach. "What about next Friday?"

I started to get weak in the knees. My knees started to buck to the point of straddling him on the bed, almost submitting to him, forgetting my own words.

"Um. Well. Oh fuck that feels too good." Hound Dog's hand reached around to grip my hair to allow him access to my neck to tell me who's in charge.

"Keep going," he said.

I swallowed but my throat was dry. A traitorous moan escaped as I gathered my words. "B.B said that I should try again on Friday night. Ahh shit, Hound, please don't stop."

My hips ground against his cock, which pressed against his jeans. He nipped my neck as soon as he heard his friend's name on my lips. "Oh, did he now? What else would you like to say about my friend?" He pulled harder on my hair.

The little act of jealousy only heightened my need for him. He wanted me. "That I should try again, that's all. Baby, take out your cock, please. Just, ahh," I whined as he held me down to prevent me from rubbing against him. Denying me the pleasure.

"I see," was all he said, though he continued his pace of hungry kisses. I reached for his cut, but he stopped me. "You want my cock, you don't want to play? Such a pretty little thing so needy. Aren't you?"

I nodded. Yes, I was so needy for him. This was what the man did to me, drove me crazy for him and only him.

"My little songbird wants it rough and quick?" he teased, in between kisses along my collarbone. "She knows what she wants. Right?" His playfulness was also mocking. Something was wrong with me because it just made me wetter to think about it.

"Hound, this was supposed to be a conversation, not a fuck fest." I whined, then grabbed him by the hair, yanking him from my neck. I pressed against him so I could devour him the way he was devouring me. We both fought for control, but I lost in the end when he grabbed my throat, controlling the air I breathed.

He pulled back, his hand still gripping my throat. "We will, but one thing I will get right now is my girl, in my club, screaming my name, laying her claim on her man."

I struggled within his hold, but the tightness and adrenaline only fired more desire in me. "I knew you liked it when I squeezed this beautiful neck. Don't worry, you'll learn from breath control." He winked. The smug bastard winked, which only excited me more at the anticipation of his meaning.

Okay, he could be in charge. Because I wanted that too. I pleaded with him. My eyes begged him to let me claim him.

"There she is." He grinned, "Tell me what you want this time."

"I want you."

"Want me to do what, use your voice," he kept teasing, as he loosened his grip.

"I want you to fuck me hard while I scream your name, for everyone to hear," I nearly whimpered.

"Whatever my woman wants." He placed a punishing kiss to my lips sending all thoughts away, leaving only room for him. "I think you're a little overdressed, honey. In fact, so am I."

The hunger in me took his hint and scrambled off his lap, shedding my clothes. His gaze set a fire in me, leading to my nipples hardening under his stare. He watched me like I was the only person in the world for him. He leaned back on his hands, gawking at my every movement. I teased him back, caressing my skin with feathery touches, my hands traveling down my body, edging myself with my own pleasure.

My fingertips grazed over my sensitive clit, the building release begging to come undone. I heard the faintest "fucking hell" from Hound Dog. I saw his cock swell beneath his denim. It took everything in me not to bend to my knees and crawl to him like a little kitten wanting to play. I waited for his command. His eyes grew with passion.

He couldn't wait anymore, the teasing was pushing him past his point. "Come here, now," he boomed. I sashayed over to him, stepping between his thighs. He gripped my ass, giving it a rough smack. The pain sent me close to the edge of my release. "Take what you want, Melody." He eyed his pants that were ready to be busted out of, my hands started to tremble from the excitement.

As soon as I pulled the zipper, he helped to take everything off from the waist down, leaving his shirt and cut on. He wanted me to lay claim, and I was going to as I watched his thick, big cock bob from movement.

"Let me see how wet this pretty pussy is," Hound said before plunging two fingers in. He got his answer as his fingers went in with ease. He stole my breath as he worked his fingers in and out of me. The sloppy wet noise he created from his thrusting only made me wetter. "Fucking perfect. Soaking wet, easy for this cock to fuck you deep."

His words only made things hard to think to stand firm on convincing him that maybe I was ready to try again. But his tantalizing touch only washed away any ground I was standing on, I was just putty in his hands.

I was there on the edge when his fingers escaped from the soaking heat and I was left with the feeling of emptiness.

He grabbed my hips, adjusting me as he lifted me to straddle him, I lifted as his cock found my entrance. I lowered myself slowly on his cock, feeling every inch of him bury inside me. The stretching of my pussy made my head loll back.

Hound's deep grunt as his own pleasure was building just made me smile internally. To see him let loose, even to use me as his escape, was part of the reason why he was worth it. I felt safe with him, I felt encouraged to live out my dream, I felt alive compared to the life I had.

I felt full from trying to be seated, but his chuckle grew as I tried to push further. When I said this man was big, it seemed to get bigger or something like he had some magical dick. "You trying to take me, honey?"

I nodded, and before I knew it, he had thrusted further in me, so deep I could feel him everywhere. I yelped with a twinge of pain but there we were connected in his own room in his clubhouse, in the safety of his world from whatever was out there.

"Take what you need, Melody. Come whenever you want, but only if you scream my name," he commanded as his hand came back to my throat, not tight, but enough to place his own claim on me.

I did just that. I moved my hips and my body to my own pace, just enough that I was rewarded by the sounds of his grunts and moans that encouraged me to keep going.

I felt a fire in my senses, in my core burning for him, and when I rode him I let myself go. His other hand palmed my breasts. He brought it up to his mouth only to suck on my nipple, then to nip it sending shocks of pain and pleasure.

"That's it, keep going. Being such a good girl riding this cock. Taking it so well," he cooed once he pulled from my nipple. His grip tightened around my throat as his eyes gazed into my mine with power and force.

I couldn't hold back any more, I screamed his name, as my body sparked like a burst of lightning through my veins. It continued as if there was no end in sight. His name never left my lips. But his own release never came and through my lustful haze I whined.

As my body slowed down, I went limp. He pushed my wet hair out of my face. "My little songbird already tuckered out? You looked so beautiful coming around my cock." He kissed my forehead, my favorite little slice of heaven.

I slowed my breathing. "But you didn't come."

I squeezed around his cock, and he growled, "You want me to come, Melody? You want me to pound this sensitive pussy until my cum coats it?"

His dirty words made me agree, agree for him to use me for his own needs. "Yes, but you have to scream my name."

Whatever I did turned him into a feral beast that flipped me to my stomach, gripping the sheets as he re-adjusted at my entrance. He hoisted my ass in the air, only to appease his love for it.

"I'll scream your name over and over if it means you'll never leave me," he whispered in my ear like it was a possibility that I'd leave him. Not after everything he opened in me, and I connected with him on so many levels.

"Then you better howl for me, Hound Dog," I said with a cheeky smile.

Every thrust was a mixture of punishment and salvation. Every thrust was a connection that was only built stronger.

"Fuck, don't stop, Hound, please," I kept begging him as the animal in him continued like he truly wanted to be buried deep in me.

Every groan and moan this man let out caused me to chase a second climax that.

Shortly, we both came crashing down. Hound repeatedly screamed my name like it was a song, his howl. Sweat dripped from both of us, surrounded by the smell of his bourbon and smoke like a campfire, one that you wanted to be around and sing songs.

Hound kissed my bare shoulder, his head nuzzling my back. Our breathing was returning to normal. When his cock stopped twitching from his climax, he slowly left my dripping cunt. His contented deep sigh vibrated against me, probably watching his remnants drip out of me. There was something erotic about a man happy to see his cum drip out of someone he cared about only to wish to do it again.

Slumped on the bed, I twisted my head to see him admire the view. While I thought my mind was empty from his attempt to derail me from my purpose of conversation, it was brought back to the front of my mind.

I flipped back over onto my back, adjusting myself to lay back on his pillows. I reached for him, only to get us entangled within ourselves. I saw the little smile on his face as he brought me closer to him.

We stayed like that, basking in each other, molded like we were made for each other. I started to believe that he was the other half of me, the strong, defensive, brave side.

I needed to get out what I needed to say, or else it would never happen.

My fingers played with his dark chest hair, his even breathing told me it was now or never. "Baby, I think I should try again this coming Friday," I whispered, but calm with sparked confidence.

His deep breath concerned me as his chest rose and fell. I worried that he was going to say no, or tell me that I wasn't ready to go back on stage. I was basking in my newfound confidence that I wanted to try.

"Is that what B.B was talking about with you?" he questioned.

I nodded my head. "We got to talking about music and he remembered me from that night and said the stage would be open for me."

"I'm not sure that right now is the right time," he answered, but his voice gave little confidence nor encouragement. Internally I didn't know how to process, like I was waiting for his permission or his blessing. I mean I didn't need it, but I guess I needed the extra boost of encouragement, or something.

My chest felt heavy with disappointment. But there was a fire still aching to fight back, "And why not? I think I have worked hard on my songs, and your "lessons" have helped me open up." I was determined to do it, I already set my mind to it.

"Melody," he started to say.

"Hound Dog," I mimicked back.

In one swoop, he pinned me underneath him, having taken my hands, pinning them to the sides of my head. "Are you going to let me finish or continue to be a brat? Please pick door number two because I promise that your ass will be redder than a spotlight."

I could also be a brat.

"If memory serves me right, you did finish, I have the evidence still inside me," I mouthed off. Which in hindsight, might not have been the best when a giant brute was hovering above me with my hands pinned to the bed. I could have cried for mercy, but it was his fault. He was the one that woke something inside me, not the timid, "doormat" version of me.

His cock gently pressed against my entrance. He could have been ready to fuck the sass out of me. "Same question, little songbird," he growled.

My eyes widened and I nodded my head submissively.

"That's what I thought. All I said was right now might not be the right time. I never said it was a bad idea or you couldn't do it." His tone was smooth, sincere.

"Tell me why. I think after everything and being called yours, I should know. Because if I'm going to be a prisoner or captive, I need to understand."

He shook his head in the beginning, but muttered something. I encouraged him, rubbing my body against him, two could play that game. He groaned, fighting back the advance. "Melody, please, listen to me."

"Make it good then."

"Fucking brat."

"You wouldn't have it any other way."

"Part of being mine, being a part of this club, means I can either completely leave you out and you completely trust me or you can know everything. You can't pick and choose the information I give you. One option is peace of mind and the other option is shouldering everything we are."

He was still trying to scare me, thinking that he knew completely what was best for me. I knew he cared for me, maybe to the point of very strong feelings, but he didn't believe me when I said I wasn't running and that he could give me everything and I could handle it.

I bucked against him, hearing him hiss, knowing that I wasn't backing down.

"Give me the burden of knowing everything. Give me your darkness." I wrapped my legs around him, pinning me close to him. His cock was rubbing up my clit. I whimpered at the sensation.

"There's no going back."

"You can stop saying that, I didn't ask for a way out," I snapped back.

"Where did this mouth come from?" he teased.

"I was Pandora's box, baby."

He sighed, letting loose of my wrists, unwinding my legs from him. He sat back against the wall next to his bed. "I said not right now because another club has been pinning murders on us from drug use, claiming it was ours, but we found evidence against that claim and we thought we shut it down."

I turned on my side, finding a scrap of blanket to cover me up to listen to him. I asked for it, so I was going to listen.

"Actions have consequences," he said, but it sounded more like a warning.

But a warning for who?

Chapter 29

HOUND DOG

I knew that opening this can of worms could resolve some but not all of what had been happening. She watched me with watchful eyes, she was truly listening. Gone was the slight attitude.

"Actions have consequences," I said. *My* actions always had consequences.

She scooted closer to me, not saying anything. "It's hitting too close to home, it's involving people outside the club."

I didn't know why it was getting harder to express the truth, why I couldn't say it. But she knew. Her eyes darted for a moment, then back to me. "They threatened you with me."

I didn't need to confirm because I think she saw it, the way my body tensed up like I was brought back to protecting everything that I had.

"You don't think I'd be safe?" she further asked.

I nodded. "I can't risk losing you, not when I just found you."

Her face dropped with sadness. "Would they actually hurt me? Even if the city is your territory, your claim?"

I wished it was simple and that people would just respect that, but it wasn't like that. The Hogs were relentless in their attempts. We weren't ones to harm children and women, but they wouldn't bat an eye.

With Melody, you'd best believe they would try anything. She'd be used as a pawn against me and the club.

"They would, and they wouldn't have any remorse," I said bluntly.

"So going back to the Blue Sax would be," she started, but I finished, "A bad fucking idea. You know I'd do anything for you. That's all I want for you. But not right now."

If I had any other ideas, I'd make it a possibility. Hell, I was just proud of her for not shying away from the chance to get back on that stage.

But what she said next had me in a state of confusion. "Could we try? I mean, just have protection around just in case? It would be like you're just protecting your business, I just happen to be there. You know, I can be by your side," she began to barter with me.

She was trying every which way to make a deal. I didn't have it in me to say no or anything. It was like watching a teenager trying to convince their parents to allow them past curfew before they planned to sneak out if they said no.

She had a way to wrap herself around my finger because I couldn't tell her "no" nor did I want to. I knew how serious the situation was, a threat against an ole lady is also a threat against the club. She didn't wear my name yet, if I had it my way I'd tattoo her in a heartbeat. That was what my brother, Memphis, said his club did.

"Honey, I'm not sure," I started to say but she pouted.

The little brat pouted those perfect lips that made my dick twitch under the sheets. I groaned. "Oh no, you're not going to do that." I gripped her chin, bringing her close to me. "Don't forget who you belong to."

The vixen curled her lips, "You sure about that? I know I can be very convincing. Do I need to show you again?"

"I don't need convincing, your pussy weeps for my cock. What else you got there little songbird?" I challenged her.

"I'll cook for you... naked.. Every night for a month." Oh, she was really bartering here.

I chuckled. "Melody, I don't need you to play housewife. You're a remarkable woman with a huge caring heart. You cook because you want to. But if you were to be naked, I was already going to hide your clothes anyway."

I let loose of her chin as she playfully shoved me. "Please, *Nash.*"

She spoke my name as if it was her secret too, like she was protecting me. She was appealing to a soul that had been long gone before she popped in my life. But the way she said my name breathed a little fire in me, awakening something from a deep sleep.

"Melody, you're making it very hard to turn you down." I inched closer to her face.

"Because you know I can do it." She grinned, her lips grazing against mine.

"I never said you couldn't, I just said it wasn't safe," I corrected her.

Her fingers caressed along my chest, and I was tempted to rip my t-shirt and cut off, but we'd be here all night, even though the idea of fucking her to sleep played in my mind.

"Then keep me safe, baby." she cooed. "Let me try one more time, and then you can keep me safe in *other* ways. I'll be a good girl."

"Oh, you'll be a good girl whether I say yes or no." I growled.

It wasn't a completely bad idea. I just didn't trust enough people to do it.

Her enchanting hazel eyes pushed me over the edge. I closed my eyes, the words clenching my jaw. "If I say yes, you stay by my side the entire night and once you're done singing your heart out, we leave."

Before I could tell her more stipulations she smiled, capturing my lips in a soft, plush kiss. Her smile beamed through our kiss and the satisfaction that I made her happy was the best feeling. Even if I didn't know what would happen next, I only hoped that she truly was ready and that B.B didn't plant a seed that wasn't ready to be watered and grown.

She pulled back. "Oh baby, thank you. Thank you." She continuously kissed me in different places on my body, still expressing her gratitude.

"You're lucky that..." I stopped myself from quickly saying in the heat of the moment, "you have me wrapped around your little finger."

That wasn't what I was going to say. But she didn't need to know that. At least not at that moment.

Her face lit up like a Christmas tree. Her smile was so bright that I wished it never went away.

"I can't wait until you hear the song I want to try," she squealed, jumping off the bed, gathering her clothes.

"Why's that, little songbird?" I got myself off the bed, following her rushed movements.

I stood behind her, as she bent down to grab her jeans. "You'll just have to wait and see," she teased. She popped back up, brushing up against me. She yelped. "Where you going?"

She stammered, "Back home, with you I hope."

I shook my head. "We're staying here for a couple days. Then once I feel that no one is coming after you, we'll go back. You understand?"

The little temptress nodded her head and said, "Yes *sir*."

"Brat."

"Yours," she added.

Yes, she was mine, and I was the selfish bastard that would tear and destroy anyone who would threaten me and mine.

First, I needed to make it official. Well, even more official.

After a few days of having the prospects and Shooter watch the house, I let her go back to the house, but until we could minimize the threat of the Hogs, the house would be guarded by the club and if she so much as tried to escape, I would know.

Though, I think I gave her plenty of reasons to make her stay without a fight.

But in a blink of an eye that Friday came too quickly, and I wasn't one to break promises, especially to my little songbird.

I could see her nerves rise and fall from that morning; her hands shook while she was in the kitchen making breakfast. I had her do some deep breaths with me. For moments she was calm and then others she would go back to her downward spiral. I worried that she was pushing this too much and between being thrust into this world and wanting to make me happy, she was pushing herself.

By the time she was calmed down, thanks to a few orgasms and listening to her sing some of the other songs she was working on, her smile returned, and she started to build herself back up.

The Blue Sax was its typical rush of artists and patrons. The place more on high alert because I wasn't fucking playing with her safety or the business.

She slid out of my truck with ease. Her long sleeve western dress made her look like a dream, like I could see her on a ranch as the sun went down cascading its golden rays on her. Her waves of auburn hair were twisted up in a loose bun. She looked delectable and made me whine inside to keep her at home.

With her guitar in hand, we pushed through the doors and she stuck to her promise that she would stay by my side. Though I didn't go anywhere throughout the night. B.B and Otis came through and joined us for company. Their normal chirps and quips at each other made Melody comfortable.

Her body was relaxed as they kept distracting her from the pending stage performance. I was proud of her at least, she made the first step which was to sign up at the back to be added to the list.

Her friend Sadie, whom I finally met, sat near the bar. She leaned in for a hug and said, "You're the one who made my friend a little sex maniac."

She did not miss a beat. The guys chuckled at the comment, but clinked beer bottles when I responded, "She might surprise you, she was the one that made me speechless."

"You naughty boy. You treat her right and she'll love you for a long time." She winked, before grabbing her a drink.

I had hoped her presence made my girl less nervous, but it didn't.

I leaned over while we were waiting. "You know I'm proud of you."

She turned with her bourbon in her hand. "What for? I haven't even started."

I took her hand that was placed near my upper thigh, more like gripping it with strength, and brought it to my lips, kissing her there "Because this was all you, you could have ignored B.B."

B.B cut in, "Ouch, no one ignores me."

"Except one person," Otis joked.

B.B mimicked laughter before punching Otis in the shoulder. The lightness of her laughter burst out.

"I feel like I'm missing something," Melody said.

If only she knew that our very own VP was being a love sick puppy to a woman that he claimed was playing hard to get. Our lover boy was head over heels for her.

We were interrupted by Twitty leaning down and letting me know if there were any troubles. Thankfully he had said there were no other worries, for now, but we weren't going to take it easy just because there was a calm in the storm.

Melody's legs bounced up and down like a rabbit thumping the ground. Her hands were tucked between her thighs. If I stuck her outside in the cold weather, she would still be sweating up a storm.

I was lucky that she hadn't bolted to the bathroom to puke her brains out. I would have had more reasons to worry about that one.

I rested my hand on one of her bouncing knees. "Honey, you're going to be great." I attempted to ease her mind, but she just nodded, flashing a small, fake smile. I was going to try one more thing to calm her nerves and prevent me from getting seasick from the earthquake of her legs.

I leaned closer to her ear, keeping my voice low to where she was the only one to hear me. "My little songbird is going to make me so proud of her. She's going to show everyone that she is a talented soul, but get jealous when they see me with you, because they'll know that I'm yours."

Her legs stopped.

That worked.

"Does that make you happy? Hearing such praise from me, honey?" If I couldn't calm her nerves due to performing, then I would distract her the only way that would get her attention.

"Hound," she started to whimper.

"Say my name again, and I just might show everyone here how you're mine." A bit too far, I wasn't much of an exhibitionist, but she wasn't going to know that.

Her cheeks flushed a beautiful pink, "You wouldn't do that."

"You want to find out," I smiled.

She couldn't answer because she was being called.

"Give it up for Melody Rae." Our announcer bellowed her name.

All color washed away from her face. I gripped her sweaty hand. "You can do it. Just sing to me."

Chapter 30

MELODY

S ing to him? He was kidding right? Fuck, was I kidding myself? What did I get myself into by agreeing with B.B that this would be a good idea? Hell, I expected Hound Dog to keep fighting me on this and turn into a caveman.

I mean there was still time. I could have made a quick exit. But the man whispered naughty words in that voice that made me shiver with pleasure and desire.

When my name was called, my world went quiet. I saw mouths moving, but there was only ringing in my ears. Ringing and my heart beating deep in my chest.

Hound's hand traveled along my back, pressing to get me off the chair. Sadie stood at attention, waiting for my next move. I couldn't hear what she said, but she handed my guitar and gave me a simple nod.

I couldn't remember how I got close to the stage, but it felt like everything was shrinking, like I was back in wonderland, waiting to see what food or drink would make me feel normal.

Aria, if you're watching over me, please darling girl, give me strength.

Aria would have been the one on stage, she wasn't afraid of anything. I mean, I wasn't afraid of a lot, but the stage was the seventh level of hell for me. Being in the spotlight for everyone to watch me and judge before I made a first note.

Hound and Sadie were the only ones to hear me, other than Aria, and I wondered if that would be enough, make me feel content. But it wasn't enough. Or at least I thought so.

I found the cord to plug in the electric acoustic, hoping that if I started somewhere my nerves would settle. After the crackling of the feedback rang my ears, I searched in the crowd for friendly faces, hoping that everything could be overcome.

The bright lights warmed my face, my back sweated even more if that was even possible, my heart raced causing my hands to shake. All thoughts of failing overpowered the ideas of success, it felt like a train wreck. My fingers fumbled with the pick in my hand, and managed a few strums before the pick fell through my fingers. There were a few snickers.

It wasn't completely silenced, but I could feel the watchful eyes over me.

I knew I was fucking it up when I saw the quickness of Hound rush to the stage side, waiting for my next move.

I wanted to bolt and forget everything. I made myself a fool, once again. I whispered into the mic an apology and ignored the consequences. I could feel the bubble of emotions in my throat, threatening to surface.

I crashed into Hound's arms, my body still shaking like a leaf.

He walked me away from the stage, toward the back, through the darkened hallway.

I knew that I should have just stuck to songwriting and remaining in the background. That was what I was good at. And the disappointing factor, I had a special song that I had been working on that I had hoped would make Hound happy to hear. Something that would make all confusion about where we were in our somewhat twisted relationship.

But tears fell down my cheeks, a stream washing off the makeup that caked on my face. I felt weak, like a shadow of doubt clouding over me telling me that I was weak for Hound, for being a part of his world. Who would want to picture me with him now?

His arms tightened around me, holding me close to him. His warmth felt like home, a place I never wanted to leave.

"I'm so sorry," I muttered into his shirt. But he didn't hear me. I didn't think he cared.

In past relationships, if I failed in their eyes, I'd hear "well, I told you it wasn't a good idea" or "I could have told you it was going to happen". Not Hound. Not my Hound Dog. He just held me like a weighted anxiety blanket.

Hound's body straightened up in an instant. I pushed off of him, turning my head to see Otis shake his head. He wasn't coming to check on me, us, something was happening. His face turned up when I caught his eye, his expression was full of apologies. His way without words of saying that the moment was over and Hound was going to have to let me go.

I turned back to see Hound, and one thing I would have to get used to, disappearing without a word or indication of what was happening.

He captured my cheeks in his hands. "Honey, I'm going to have Sadie take you back to the compound."

The compound? We were just at the house last night. He had told me we were safe. At least, I thought we were safe.

"What's happening? What should I know?" I pressed.

"That is a very good question that I don't have the answer to right now." He tucked a loose hair behind my ear.

His tenderness melted my heart but made it ache at the same time.

"Tell me you'll come back to me?" I pleaded.

He only smiled, avoiding the original question. "You want me to come back to you?"

I rolled my eyes, blinking through the leftover tears that hadn't fallen. I wiped them before telling him off. "No, I want you to never return so I can have the whole bed to myself."

"I can quickly fuck that brattiness out of you." he threatened.

"Save the good times for the bedroom, baby." I huffed out.

He just leaned down and kissed me hard and quick. He rested his forehead on mine, "I'm coming back. And when I do, I expect you naked under those blankets, waiting for me. And then when I've fucked you nice and good, we'll talk about tonight."

I sniffed, clearing my sinuses. "You'll come back to me in one piece?"

"When I have you to come home to, I'll fight even harder." He promised before pressing one more kiss on my cheek and leaving me alone in the darkened, quiet hallway.

I pressed my back against the wall and slid down, taking in the loneliness that I craved for a long time before. Now, I hated the feeling of being alone again.

You are a brave bitch, you are not afraid anymore.

Not anymore. Like Hound said, I had a reason to keep fighting. I wasn't perfect and that was what this man appreciated about me, I wasn't weak, I just needed time.

I felt a hand on my shoulder, Sadie's soft smile brightened my world. She got down on my level. "You have one caveman boyfriend, babes."

Caveman. Well, that was one way of describing him.

I sniffed. "I know. And yet, I love that about him."

She sat down next to me, bumping my shoulders. "Love, huh? Said that a little too easily."

And yet it felt natural, normal even. Love wasn't linear, we all love differently and our timelines of when we start feeling it is never the same. Like a snowflake.

"And I'm okay with that." I rested my chin on my knees, turning to peek at her. I laughed at her shocked expression, "What?"

She only smiled, then said, "Just admiring this outlook on you."

Me too.

The rest of the night I had to wait and see if Hound would keep his promise to me. After Sadie dropped me off and checked out the compound, she left and told me to message her when things settled down.

The one thing about Sadie was that she did not give me pity attention, her friendship had been one of the truest in my life.

I hated waiting around, repeatedly checking my phone to see if anything came through. I was too anxious to think about anything else. I paced the bar, lounge area, there were a couple of girls that B.B had introduced me to previously, telling me that these were the good ones. Ginger and Posey.

They were truly sweet. They kept me company, telling me that everything would be okay, that the guys would return and in the end peace would be back.

Night had turned pitch black, and I couldn't sleep when he wasn't there. I circled his room countless times, and when I was distracted, I pried into every crevice of the place.

I mean tit for tat, he snooped in all of my things, it was only right.

He didn't keep much here other than phone charging cords, change of clothes, odds and ends, some condoms, and completely random items. It barely looked like it was lived in. I started to think that maybe he once did, but then I smiled thinking that he had a reason now. I went to his closet, anticipating that there wouldn't be anything in there. But when I turned on the light, there were a few shirts, but what caught my attention was a black jacket that smelled like new leather.

My fingers traced the fabric taking in the feel of it. I pulled it out and my eyes grew twice their size as I noticed the patch on the back.

"Property of Hound Dog"

Chapter 31

HOUND DOG

Nothing was ever too good to be true. When a night was clear and safe it turned into a man hunt. And it came at the worst time. I truly wanted to strangle someone. The look on Otis' face when he had to give me a look to sign that we had to go. Leaving her wasn't the solution.

Seeing her on stage should have warmed my heart, should have been beaming with pride. But one look and a few strums later, her mind wouldn't shut off. Seeing her like that broke me.

Let it be known, I didn't want to leave her nor did I think she was completely ready, but only she could tell me that she was and I listened to her.

After Sadie found her, I knew whatever was happening, it must have been damn trouble if I got pulled away and no one else could handle it.

"Someone start talking now," I ordered, looking around at the guys.

"Blue called, he noticed something weird at Grunge," B.B said before putting on his helmet and starting up his bike.

"Explain something weird." My anger started to flame.

"Cameras went out and Blaze can't explain why." That was all I needed to get out of there.

If the kid couldn't understand why the cameras were out, then we were screwed and someone was going to pay. I had enough of this cat and mouse game. If they wanted a fight they were going to get one. It took a coward to keep hiding behind antics. If they were so fucking smart now, they knew how to find us.

I whipped the truck in and out of traffic, didn't care if there was a trooper or not. One way or another I was going to end everything. Bury people in the Mississippi if I had to.

Tell me you'll come back to me.

I would come back to her, even if I had blood on my hands. I'd shelter the burden of my sins to keep her close and the club safe.

Grunge was one of the most hole in the wall places that we owned. It had been one of the oldest, an institution if you will. One of the places that gave me the ideas for the places we had now. B.B and Otis weren't too far behind as I pulled up, halting the truck to a stop. I slammed the door, reaching for the piece that was strapped to my side. I had half a mind to get Greene down here, but he had reassured me that cases were closing and arrests were being made.

It was the aftershocks that apparently we had to worry about.

Blue had emptied the place, airing at the side of caution. He stood there waiting for us. The street we were on wasn't occupied, like a ghost town waiting for a showdown.

"Boss," he acknowledged.

"Blue, now would be the time to tell me we didn't waste our time." I warned him.

"Kid is trying to recover any video from before the cameras went out, but I don't like this feeling," Blue said. Blue was one of the older members, I could trust him as much as anyone else. But if he was saying that he wasn't getting a good feeling about something, I wasn't going to negate that.

There was something in the air, other than the cool breeze that caresses the goosebumps on the back of my neck. It was as if my senses were on higher alert. An eeriness spread across the area. Like something or someone was hiding. I signaled for no one to make a sound as I pulled my gun from the holster.

I stayed along the sides of the business, staying out of the street lamp that was flickering. I heard the clanking of Otis and B.B's guns following me into the darkness.

I walked past the business next door to find the alleyway, crowded by the dumpsters. I kept low to cover me. Across the alley was another street, filled with businesses, but streetlights weren't as bright.

The wind whipped back and forth, but there was nothing but the sound like scraping across rubble that broke my attention. I turned the corner of a trash pile and saw nothing, but felt a blow to my head that made me crash down to the ground. My gun was knocked out of my hands, clattering to the ground.

Shots started to fire from someone else because my attacker threw himself on me, pinning me down further to the ground. The fucker's weight was heavier than expected. Shots kept firing as my men started to yell out. I tried to buck the person off of me, then found a knife at my throat.

"We'll make this quick," the voice bellowed out like it was a game or a prize from a hunt.

I thrust my head back, which made me a bit dizzy. The man staggered back, I finally was able to stabilize myself and turn to get a look at my attacker. I couldn't make out a certain face but I knew those patches anywhere.

It was what I expected for them to do, a sneak attack. And what's worse was that they wanted to butcher us, more like butcher me. A slower, painful death.

The flash of the metal from the knife gleamed in the dim light. I grasped the fucker's hand, attempting to pull the knife away from my throat. The knife flung from the man's grip and went as far as it could and I rushed the man before he could make another move. I didn't need a weapon, just needed them out of his reach. Shots kept ringing around me, and soon cops would be surrounding us if we weren't careful.

If anything, they would find dead bodies near the business, still wouldn't be a good look on us. I didn't know how much Otis would be able to get us out of this mess legally.

I had the man pinned underneath me, he squirmed trying to break free of the weight that was crushing him. My fists started to connect to his face. Shots kept firing behind me, I wondered how long it took for them to finally knock the other attacker off their feet.

I shouldn't have turned my head to look at the scene behind me, but when I did I ended up back on my back, with his fists connecting to my face. My head was thrown back, the pain starting to radiate like a thumping heart beat.

My attacker's hands wrapped around my throat, squeezing it tight.

My hands searched for his face to push him off, I went to pry his hands off my throat, wanting to find some way to get off of me. The shots stopped, a *thud* hit the floor. Suddenly my body was moving alongside my attacker's movement as Otis and B.B's hands pried him off. Air returned to my lungs as I coughed, gasping for air.

"Hold him back," I coughed out. Anger wasn't the emotion I was feeling, whatever I was feeling felt like it needed a new name.

I could feel the warm blood trailing along my cheeks, staining them with the remnants of the fight that happened, a failed attempt to take me out.

My mouth tasted the tang of copper. I hadn't lost a fight, but I never expected a gutless man to jump me from the side. He truly had a death wish.

I wiped my mouth, the darkness in me swirled with the need to end a life.

My attacker went feral, trying to bust through his hold. Blue came up from behind, yanking his head back. One look at him and I could tell that he had taken some sort of drug that would have gotten him in this rage, all adrenaline rushing toward him.

"I'm not going to waste my time and ask you who sent you because I know. How does it feel that you were just a failed pawn to your president's plan?" My voice cracked a couple times, but I wasn't going to stay quiet.

"Pussy whipped for a president." He laughed.

I threw a punch to his gut and the fucker kept laughing like he was a demented soul with no remorse.

"Go ahead, piss me off some more," I growled. But the rush to my head was coming, and I could feel the world around me start to become unstable, like my feet could come out from underneath me.

Pull it together.

"I hope that your president knows that you won't be returning home." I grinned like a mad man.

"Cowards," the man spat.

"Funny, we were thinking the same about you." Otis sneered, gripping the man's arm tighter.

The man was still bleeding from his mouth from the few shots I was able to land. He grinned showing his bloodied teeth.

"I told Prez we should have gotten your little girl. But he didn't want to waste time with a weak woman, too easy to kill," he taunted me. Throwing Melody in my face. She wasn't weak, she was a fighter.

My blood began to boil, everything inside of me twisting like a whirlwind.

"The easy kill is your fucking throat." I sneered as Blue handed me one of his knives as I slid the blade across his throat, watching the blood spurt out like a flowing river.

He struggled, but it didn't matter how much fight he had in him, the light vanished in eyes. Two rats down and more to go, but this wasn't going to end quietly.

I stood there watching the blood stain the ground, and I thought for a moment. In the past I would have thought that Melody was the problem, not me. But I was going to protect her, even if she decided to run. A threat to her was a threat to the club.

B.B and Otis let go of his arms, throwing the lifeless body on the ground. B.B turned with his phone in hand, probably calling the cleaning crew. I leaned against the wall, my vision started to blur for a moment. Muffled voices came into my blurred vision. All I could remember was total darkness.

Atonement for my own sins and darkness. A twisted punishment.

I didn't know how much time had passed but the strong scent woke me up, and I thrust myself upright. There was still a pounding in my head, like a throbbing pain. Certain noises made me wince. The fucker gave me a concussion that felt like a migraine.

"Well, I'd joke that the dead has arisen," That annoying voice that could only be B.B.

"I had Shooter come and take a look at you," Otis said from somewhere around me.

A bright light came into my eyes, I swatted it. "Easy there, Prez." Shooter kept going with whatever he was doing. My stomach was in knots like if I were to eat something it would not be good.

"Prez, I need to test something. I need you to tell me what you did this morning," Shooter ordered as he checked my neck.

He needed my ability to concentrate and recall. Only problem was this morning was a bit more detailed in my memory as flashes of Melody whimpering as her legs were up and over my shoulders. The way her nails scraped across my back. Her soaking wet pussy tightening around my cock, squeezing the life out of me. The way her moans sounded like echoes of a true melody in my head.

That was more detail and privacy than my brothers deserved to hear.

I could lie on the spot, make up a whole new story, but if I was going to be back in one piece to her, then I needed to talk to the good doctor.

"I settled my girl's nerves this morning. She had rested well, and was making breakfast this morning. French toast from scratch, said it was her grandmother's recipe she was making. She's an amazing cook, responsible for a few more pounds on this body. She was babbling about the "what ifs" and what could go wrong. And I may have quieted her mind for an hour or so."

Well, it wasn't a complete lie.

Shooter nodded his head. He patted my face. "I think you'll survive but I'm afraid you won't be settling anything for a good week or so."

I scoffed. "You ordering bed rest there, Shooter?"

A few laughs roared. "I think bed rest would be more trouble than good. But your head will be sore for a bit. Might need to have your girl keep you busy differently."

"Basically keep it in your pants. Distance makes the heart grow fonder," B.B joked.

"Not if someone makes something else harder," Otis retorted, hiding his laughter.

"I give it two days, and if anything Melody will make him break," B.B continued.

"A hundred says five days and he breaks all by himself." Otis extended his hand, B.B shook it.

Fuckers. All of them.

But I only had one thing on my mind, and that was to go back to Melody.

I wouldn't break a promise like that. I wondered if she was exactly where I wanted her to be. And when I opened the door, I saw the most beautiful sight. Something that revived this non-existing heart.

Chapter 32

HOUND DOG

My girl was gawking at the last thing that would make her mine, a warning to heed to others that she was protected, loved, and respected.

She didn't notice that I was standing in the doorway. Which was better, knowing the state I was in, her own anxiety would rise to the roof. No, I wanted that moment of peace, an image to engrain in my mind.

I loved her.

I loved her hard.

I loved her and I kicked myself for wanting to fight it all.

My little curious creature turned away from me, but took the jacket off the hanger, and slipped her arm through it. My heart and my cock ached so hard. Fuck the concussion, I'd risk anything to fuck her right there, wearing my name for the first time.

Her cut looked like a dream on her, she had smoothed it over. She was getting used to the way it felt, and when she opened the closet door to reveal the small hanging mirror, her eyes shot open.

All I could do was grin. "There's my beautiful girl."

She twisted quickly, rushing into my arms. Her heart raced fast enough that I could feel it through my own clothes. She clutched onto me, I gripped her tight, cradling her head like the precious cargo she was.

"I told you I'd come back."

"You did."

"You miss me that much?"

She nodded as her head nudged into my neck. My fingers trailed along the leather material, and I was grinning like a happy man. "You know this wasn't how I wanted to ask you. I had a plan and everything. Surrounded by the club, presenting this to you, and asking you to officially wear it."

"Sentimental are we?"

"Maybe a little bit, maybe a bit romantic. But are you just wanting to try it on? Or do you want to keep it like you want to be with me and be a part of this club?"

She looked up at me, smiling. "I guess since I want to keep you, I'll keep this."

She jumped up, wrapping her legs around me, and I fought back the urge to show her just how much I missed her.

I walked us to the bed, only because I didn't want to drop her from the dizziness I was feeling. The small twinge of pain in my head made me hiss. She jolted back, silent for a moment.

But when I looked, there was a blood smear on her palm. Her fingers started to peel through my hair and my beard. I pushed off her hands, but kissed her palms.

"Oh my baby." Her sincere voice warmed me.

"I'm okay. Songbird, I'm okay. I promise." Just going to be out of commission for a little bit, but I didn't tell her that.

"What the hell happened?" she pressed.

I shook my head, but started to tell her about the Hogs. Her eyes dropped at every mention of where I was hit. And then tried to repress her laughter as I told her that Shooter told me limited physical activity.

"I'd rather "no physical activity" if that means you'll be okay."

"He said *limited*, he didn't say turn into a monk." I leaned in for a kiss and she stopped me.

"If he said what he said, then the doctor's orders. And that means no late night snacks," she said with her little attitude.

I grinned because she would be the one suffering that consequence, the one where she wouldn't wake up with my head between her thighs. I wasn't sure about that at first, but the little minx opened up that she wasn't against it, it was hard to say no to that.

My hands cupped her ass, hoisting her closer to my cock that was pressing against my jeans. "I hope that you're ready for your next lesson."

She snapped back, "We're still doing that after all of tonight?"

Under my protection, I couldn't contain her in this club. I nodded. "The only way to show that it didn't rattle us is to continue on. And I'll have Stray and Hank teach you to protect yourself."

She interrupted, "I have my pepper spray and knife."

My hands traveled to her hair, gripping it to silence her, "A knife to a gunfight, Melody, you'll be at Heaven's gates before you even think straight. I want you to have a fighting chance."

She sighed. "Fine. only because you asked."

"And you love making me happy, don't you?" I nipped at her neck.

Much to my attempt, she cockblocked me the entire night. I couldn't keep my hands off of her. I knew soon she would need to talk about what happened on stage, but I'd work that out of her.

I still had a few ideas of how and it would appease Shooter that I wasn't doing "excessive physical activity". But the raging hard on the rest of the night as Melody had pressed her plump ass on my cock did not help the cause.

When I woke up, I reached for her side of the bed. It was cold to the touch, she wasn't there. I started to panic, bolting out of bed and finding any scrap of clothing and my cut. I burst through the hallways in a whirlwind. She couldn't have gone far and I was certain none of the guys would actually let her leave.

Well, that was my hope.

Early morning murmurs filled the open area, the guys were too busy stuffing their faces with breakfast.

I tilted my head, because it wasn't just any breakfast. It was homemade breakfast with the familiar scents that I knew too well.

The kitchen. Usually one of the guy's ol' ladies would come and make breakfast and sometimes their kids would help out.

I was welcomed by the sight of a little songbird humming while Reverend stood watch with a cup of coffee in his hand. Dressed in my shirt and my sweatpants, she was smiling as she started to serve scrambled eggs and homemade fried apple French toast.

That was her love language, doing for others and feeding them. It felt good to see her smile and do what she loves to do. I think she worried about where she would fit in, especially when she deemed herself not the strongest.

Reverend gave a small nod to me as he filled a cup of hot coffee, sliding it in my direction.

"I always said there's nothing sexier than seeing you cook in the morning," I said.

She startled as she turned around.

"Why didn't you wake me?" I asked as I sipped the coffee.

She shrugged. "You were sleeping peacefully and needed it more than me. I couldn't sleep anyway, so I found the kitchen and Stray and Twitty were up and grumbled about where to find breakfast. So I said I'd make something, it's the least I could do for the club."

Thoughtful. I didn't fucking deserve her.

"They would have been just fine with the diner down the way," I countered back.

"Well, then you can go to the diner, and this plate can go to one of the prospects because y'all run them to the ground," she sassed, grabbing the plate to walk out.

"That's their job, honey. They get most of the grunt work." I stepped in her way.

She raised onto her tiptoes and placed a soft morning kiss on me. She pulled back. "All the more reason to give them the fuel. Now, be a good boy and sit over there and wait for your plate."

Sassy little thing. She walked past me, her hips swaying as she left to deliver some of the plated food. A warm sensation floated in my chest. Happiness. Even if it was brief.

I turned around to see Reverend just smiling away.

"What's got you smiling?"

He just chuckled, slapping a hand on my shoulder. "Just glad to see that not all hope is lost. Especially you, Prez. Between you and Shooter."

"Worried about our souls? I think we're a little too late for that." I stated the obvious. We weren't the most stand up citizens. But we had a little heart to ourselves.

"Never too late to be a person in love," he said before leaving.

Just watching Melody interact with the guys, watching the guys with their wide eyes like they couldn't believe that another person wanted to take care of them. I started to have more confidence that she would fit in just fine.

I wasn't kidding when I told her that we were going to continue with our lessons, I needed her to open up about what was going on in that head of hers. Only she could tell me what was going on, all I could do was listen.

"I didn't know this was up here." She touched the ivory keys as her eyes gazed upon the hidden second floor of the Blue Sax. No one would be around until later in the evening. I would have taken her to the warehouse but there weren't enough security measures there. At least not yet.

"Not many do."

She turned back. "Well then, teacher, what are we doing today?" Her fingers kept tracing over the keys, urging to play a little something.

"Walk me through last night," I commanded.

She started to shake her head, but I voiced for her to stop. Our dynamic was trust, trust me that I knew what she needed. Physically, mentally, and emotionally. She was mine to care for, just like she did with me.

Her shoulders slumped. "I tried, I froze, I ran. Did I miss something? Can I play on this?"

"That's one," I simply said, keeping track of how many times she would talk down about herself or avoided the conversation.

"One what?"

"For me to know, and you to find out," I challenged her. "Try again."

Her face hardened, almost a little spark of anger there, "I got over confident. I overhyped myself and then standing on that stage, it felt like it was washed away. Too many faces, and the heat from the lights didn't help. I don't know how to fully explain it. I mean how did I manage to strum a few chords."

I held up a hand to stop her, "Because you are improving."

She laughed. "Yeah, right."

I darted my eyes. "Two."

She rolled her eyes. *Three. Just because I felt like it.*

"You are. It wasn't the improvement you're hoping for, but enough that it's a start." I said, mesmerized that she was so damn talented, she just second guessed herself.

"Maybe singing on stage is just too ambitious for me. You know that Aria was the star, I was the one with the lyrics".

Time for her to unleash her potential. She wasn't her sister, her sister was just a part of her journey, her inspiration.

"Four," I started to say, she was about to protest, but one look and she stopped from speaking. "You can't expect things to fall into place. I never said it was an easy process or a fast one."

"Easy for you, rockstar. You had people eating out of your hands. Your Knoxville gig, I remember playing that video over and over again." She reminisced about a time where it was a great night for performing.

"So then tell me what is stopping you?" I asked.

She sighed. "Maybe I'm scared to fail, and it's easier to give in to defeat than to fight. I don't know, Hound, we can keep working and working on things that you think will help. But I still see everyone's faces, the people turning to whisper and wonder if I actually have what it takes. I still feel the sweat drip from my face because I'm already scared I'll mess up. I guess what's stopping me is that I don't know how to stop feeling like that. Offstage, I'm a powerhouse, I'm more confident because you believe in me. But the moment I walk on stage, I'm not that girl anymore."

Something clicked, too many eyes on her. She saw all that.

"What if you never see any of them?" I started to form a plan.

"That would require that no one be there." She chuckled.

I could be mad, but it was an idea nonetheless.

"You said with the lights you feel the heat, you see the people. What if you didn't have to, and you were just singing to me." I tried to coax her.

"How hard did you hit your head? You're not making sense." her fingers started to fidget again. Like she always does. Twisting her hands, her nerves starting to form again. Another idea popped in my head.

"Then leave that to me," I said, walking around to find a piece of sheet music that I could use for my next lesson.

"Okay then, great and crazy mad man, what are we doing here?

"Let's see." I started to walk around the piano. "We worked on knocking down those barriers, those thoughts that kept telling you every negative thing about you, that wasn't true. You already proved that you can do different dynamics. But you know what I've noticed?" I questioned her.

Her delicate little fingers started to move from fidgeting to letting her fingers dance on the keys. A slow tune played.

"That your lessons turn from productive to seductive?" She continued to play.

I hummed in agreement, "Yes, but not the answer I'm looking for. You fidget a lot."

"Well, mister teacher. I have a milder form of ADHD, they used to call it ADD, but I digress. Between my own anxiety and attention span, my mind needs to fiddle with something or else the thoughts keep getting louder. Busy mind, silent thoughts." That explained a lot actually. I'm pretty sure Memphis was diagnosed with that, but he wasn't medicated.

"Again you fidget. Today, your task is to not move other than playing that piano and this music," I said, plopping a familiar song sheet on the stand. "I have a working theory that when you focus on the music and not what's going on around you, it will help with the nerves."

She tossed me a look like I was the one confused, a sense of doubt. "Just trust me."

"So focus, and don't move?" she asked.

I nodded. She turned back to the piano, eyeing the music. "Alright, wise one, sounds like an easy task."

That's what you think.

Chapter 33

MELODY

I had serious concerns about how much damage was done to his head. And yet out of all the times he was teaching me, something always came out of it, whether it was an orgasm or a true lesson.

I studied the music sheet, I knew the song, it was a classic, one that many from Memphis knew about. It was a part of history. A promise to give a lover's heart today, tomorrow, and forever.

It was hard not to sing along, but I focused on the dynamics of the piece, imagining an acoustic guitar picking the melody, and a symphony from a chorus. The piano piece was always my favorite.

Hound slowly walked closer, pulling a chair to what I imagined was behind me. My body tingled with the knowledge that he was watching me, and the curiosity of what he really meant by his intentions.

But I kept playing until the very end. I stopped and waited for him to do something. Hell, I was waiting for him to pounce on me. But simply said to start again. And I did, following his instruction. I replayed the song, barely looking at the sheet music, knowing my mind had it already ingrained.

By the first chorus, a brush from Hound's hand caressed my neck. I flinched, ending up creating the wrong note.

"Start again, songbird," he said, but his hand never left.

I followed his order again, restarted the song. I suddenly felt his hot breath on my skin, right above my right ear. I tried so hard to not think about how close he was and continued to play. It was hard not to move, but his touch was so damn addictive that I couldn't.

Then he lightly brushed my hair to the side, allowing him to plant kisses from my neck to my shoulders.

I accidentally let the melody build by taking it in my own hands. Between the mixture of the music building between us and the warm sensation of my body, internally I was ready to explode. But part of me wanted to make him proud that I was strong enough to do this, strong enough to overcome things that he thought I could.

His low groan as he kept exploring every inch vibrated against me. "Mm, such a good little student."

I replayed the piece, my body set on fire and fueled with need, wanting to move and touch him. I knew that he would drive me crazy, but it felt like torture.

"Please," I whimpered.

He shook his head, as his hands glided down my body, caressing my breasts. The sudden feeling made me jump out of my skin causing me to make a few sharp notes. I grunted in not only agony but disappointment. I was doing so good.

"Again, little songbird," he whispered in the shell of my ear. A little nip at my ear had me on the edge ready to throw in the towel. "You were doing so well. And you know what good girls get right?"

"A reward. And it better be something better than a milk-shake," I joked. The craving had been strong for a good thick chocolate milkshake. But I wasn't going to be disappointed if I got something else that was thick.

"This is what I'm talking about." His hands cupped my breasts before diving into my shirt through my bra to pinch my already sensitive nipples. "When you're focused on something like your music, like the notes that you can see without the sheets, you will soar."

It wasn't his words of lust and need that broke the rule, it was his damn words of encouragement that made me turn around to kiss him hard and deep. The sounds of our breaths and our groans were music to my ears. His weight pushed me to sit on the piano keys where the cascading notes made him chuckle.

He pulled back, "Naughty, Melody. You were so close to completing the lesson."

"I moved, so sue me. Take that back, fuck me." I groaned before pulling on his cut, pulling him back to kiss me like he meant it. "I understand what you mean. If I ignore everything and focus, allow my fingers, my mind to fidget with the music, it could help with easing my mind."

It wasn't a completely bad idea, just not one to automatically pull out of the hat when I needed it.

"Belief in yourself, and yes, focusing on something else with your nerves. We'll keep working on it. Even if we have to repeat this exercise." He brushed a front piece of hair behind my ear.

Hound's warm eyes casted this look like he was full of happiness and full of control. "You know it's a shame that you didn't last longer. I was fully ready to dive deep into a soaking mess."

"I mean you can still do that; after all, you said I've been a very good student today." I tugged on his beard.

He slowly reached for my shirt, tugging at the material attempting to take it off. "Yes, but you failed, which means no reward."

Before he could say anything else, I pulled away and backed away from him. "I don't think so, mister. You are on doctor's orders! No heavy activity. And let's just say, I can outlast you."

He sat on the piano bench, leaning on the front, "You think so?"

I knew this was about to earn me more trouble than I was worth, but what's the fun in that? "Oh yeah, let's see, I'm younger than you, so I have more energy."

"Keep talking." Hound smirked.

"I know that I have lasted longer without sex and proper orgasms than you. And don't try to deny, Shooter and Twitty are very chatty when you feed them." I kept going. Maybe sometimes it was funnier to get the punishments than rewards, especially if the punishments turned into rewards.

Hound still had on that smirk, one of his many killer looks. "Such a pretty little mouth on you."

"Only to suck you better, baby."

"You're just racking up that number you owe me," he said, standing up to come toward me like he was stalking his prey.

"I'm not scared of you, Hound."

"You never have to be scared around me, but you might hate me when I return to full activity."

He was some sort of magician with being under his touch, his demand. It was freeing. For brief moments, I didn't have to make a choice, I didn't have to think about my next steps.

"Is that why you were counting? Keep track of something?" I circled around the piano, edging him to continue his little game. I loved seeing his playfulness, his side of giving in to the lighter side of his life.

"Perhaps. Guess you'll have to find out soon." He continued to stalk around the piano.

"I never thanked you, Hound," I said.

He stopped in his tracks, looked at me inquisitively.

It was true, I didn't thank him. Sure in the beginning, but after, for him believing in me, protecting me, and maybe even loving me the way he did, even if he hadn't said those words yet.

My baby shook his head and flashed me that smile that made me weak in the knees, "Wasn't looking for appreciation, maybe it's me who should be thanking you."

My dirty mind sparked a little bravery when I uttered the words, "I'm sure we both know how to express gratitude. Question is who's going to be the first on their knees?"

He burst into a roaring laughter, covering his face from the redness in his cheeks. He rubbed his face and let out a boisterous groan. "Woman, you're going to kill me from your sassiness and temptation."

Oh, there were ways I wanted to express that toward him.

Unfortunately, my little ploy to give in and win my own bet with Otis and Twitty didn't go as planned and Hound wanted to get back to the compound.

I buckled my helmet, zipping up my cut, his name spread across my back. I looked over to Hound, flashing a soft smile in his direction, but his face said everything I needed. From soft and easy to high alert.

"Hound," I softly said, hoping that it was just him being cautious. "What's with the face, baby?"

He revved the engine of his bike, taking no time to tell me what was happening or what he saw. "Get on, now," he demanded, almost like a subtle plea. I thrust my legs over the back, hanging on for dear life. I could barely make out what he was saying, but I knew he wasn't talking to me. He had a way to call the club.

"I need anyone we can spare, 23rd and Jackson, now," was all I could hear. The bike sped through traffic, ignoring all the beeping and people shouting in their cars. I turned my head back noticing a large black SUV moving alongside, following our path.

I gripped around Hound's waist tighter, holding back the panic in my body before I caused us to have an accident. I feared the worst, I feared that we weren't going to get out of this, that Hound and or myself wouldn't make it out.

I prayed to whoever was listening for help or the very least safety.

I could feel Hound's holster from my arms sliding down his body. The intrusive thought of whipping it out and trying to distract them should have been buried deep in my mind. I could feel Hound's racing heart and the sweat that dripped from his neck.

The sentimental in me allowed one of my hands to slide over his heart, tapping it, letting him know that we'd be alright.

As Hound turned the corner, I saw two bikes over his shoulder. But as we passed them they weren't the clubs, but another patched club. When they noticed us, they swooped around idled cars attempting to catch up with the black SUV that we hadn't lost.

Hound's body heated up like an inferno. He kept watching for an opening, I didn't know what was going on in that brain of his and maybe that's what should have been the part I was scared about.

Chapter 34

Hound Dog

E very moment that I thought we were out of trouble, it was the same knocking like a family member you don't want at holiday celebrations.

Melody gripped me tighter and tighter as I looked for some sort of plan or opportunity. The Hogs were relentless, driven with the greed of claiming something they lost years ago.

Melody's hand slid over my chest, right where my heart was pounding ready to burst out of my chest.

She was still with me, hanging on for dear life.

As we went out of main traffic, I led them through the back-roads, when it was all clear they would speed up tailing us. If I could reach to my side and pull my piece out, I could get off a couple shots until my backup arrived. Shooter told me that there would be a couple of the guys along the back road near the compound.

But the Hogs were getting closer and I didn't know how much longer I could hold them off. One of them got out of my blindside, riding close to Melody. Melody jolted, shocked by a man close to her. Her body tensed up, her hands gripping me tighter.

Where the fuck was my backup?

"Get the fuck away from her," I growled out.

They crept up closer, trying to sideswipe me.

Protect the club, protect her.

The bike started to wobble as I looked in the mirror to see Melody being grabbed at like a piece of meat. She started to fight them back, yanking back her arms, clawing at them. I didn't know what they wanted, whether it was to scare us or take her or take me out.

The other bike beside me inched closer and closer, making me whip the bike from left to right. If they wanted to throw me off balance, they were relentless.

A flash of metal met my eyes, a gun shining danger.

Melody's hands returned to me, tucking her head close to my back. I had one thought and I prayed that it would work. Or at least work until I could get closer to where my brothers should be meeting up with us.

I tapped her hands, grabbing her attention, her worried eyes blinked in my mirror. "Honey, remember the short lesson Shooter gave you on gun handling?" More like two and a half hours, but with no target practice. She nodded her head. Good girl. "I need you to grab my piece and start shooting."

A bold decision but time seemed to be slowing down instead of rushing. She hesitated, probably replaying the command I just gave her, in disbelief that she would be needing to start shooting. It said a lot to me that I had faith that she would be okay for the time being.

Her shaky hands reached for my side as I continued to battle the bikes trying to edge me out. I kept pulling back, slingshotting their bikes forward. But they would mimic what I did.

Fucking hell.

Melody finally grabbed my gun, cocking it back. This was the most dangerous thing I could have asked of her. Without a second thought, she let a shot ring out. It missed the bike on the right, but not by much.

"Try again. The guys should be here any minute. You're doing well." I tried to praise her, but she let out a piercing scream as the man on the right tried to yank on her. She fought back, giving the man a shovel, eventually kicking at him. The guy swerved, pulling back a few yards, trying to readjust before trying to pull back up.

I was too busy watching behind me, and finally noticing a shine in the distance. But it was too late, Melody had yelled, "Hound Dog, watch it."

The remaining man on the left pulled out his piece, waiting to aim at me. He practically had a lock on me.

They're not wrong when they say that your life can flash before your eyes. I sensed the failure in my scream, overpowering moments of being with family, moments with Memphis, moments of being on stage, then being patched in, and even the moment I laid eyes on Melody. I failed at the moment of being the president I wanted to be, I put everyone in this position, or maybe I didn't fight hard enough.

A shot rang in my ears and I jolted the bike to a halting stop, my breathing a little heavier. I looked for the entrance wound, only there wasn't any.

I turned to see Melody. Afraid to find what I found.

A heated Melody holding the gun, with no entrance wound.

No way.

I turned back and saw my brothers slowing down. She had shot him. We all saw the bike wobble down the road to finally crash to the ground. And the surviving bike turned away and high tailed it out of our sight.

Blue, Shooter, and Twitty stood there with idled bikes in awe and wonder. Melody was frozen in place. The gun was still in her hands, her hands were shaking after the fact. If I had doubts before, they were washed away. If she had doubts about being in this life with me, in this role, those would be washed away.

I cut the engine, putting the bike on the kick stand, and she looked at me with those hazel doe eyes. I reached my hand out for the piece, waiting for her to break out of her frozen mind. It was like she was trapped between overthinking and quietness, like stuck between the before and after. Blue rode closer to us.

"I got this Prez," he said, before focusing on Melody. I stepped aside, unable to help for a split second.

"Melody," Blue calmly said. Melody's eyes darted to Blue and his soft expression. "Hey, little darlin'. You're okay. Just focus on my voice."

I itched to get closer, but Blue, unfortunately, had a lot more experience in handling the aftermath of events like this. Especially with his ol' lady and his daughter.

"I'm going to take the gun away, okay. It's all over. We got you." He inched closer, slowly taking the gun out of her hands. "I know it's a lot but your man and the club has your back."

Melody's blank stare kept looking through Blue. Shooter and Twitty stood watch, and if I didn't know any better Shooter was calling Greene, at the very least to start the cover up. No one would know she took a life.

I never wanted to darken her soul like this, no matter how much we convinced ourselves that we did it out of love and protection.

Blue was centimeters away from her trembling hands, he shot me a look to get ready for what happened next.

As soon as she let loose of the gun, Blue stepped back and Melody's eyes started to flutter, her body going limp. I thankfully caught her in time, her heart steadied, her mind was shutting off. "I got you. I'm not letting go," I cooed, hoping that she heard me. "Get a truck here, now."

It wasn't long before I loaded her in the back of a truck, and followed them to the compound. Twitty clasped his hand on my shoulder, once I parked. "She chose you."

Yeah, she did. I carried her small body back to the exam room to have Shooter check her out before I laid her out on the bed, because the aftermath of the first kill was going to be a rough road. And for an innocent soul like Melody, my Melody, her mental strength would be put to the test.

"Hound, Greene's in the office." B.B crept up behind me as I let go of Melody in the exam room.

I nodded and shuffled toward the office, which wasn't used often, but in moments like meeting with Greene and out of the eye of the men, it was better to use that room. B.B stayed close behind.

Greene stood there waiting for us, giving a subtle nod in acknowledgement.

Suddenly there was a twinge of annoyance that washed over me, the look on his face was with a mixture of unpleasant news or uneasiness.

"Not one for house visits, don't know whether I need to feel honored or concerned."

"I don't know what happened," he began.

"You said you were making arrests, obviously you either didn't know or you're too slow to do your job," I roared out. My own annoyance didn't disappear.

Greene's eyes darted to me. "You think it's fucking easy to make arrests in another state? Yes, our jurisdiction but a whole other fucking state."

"Sounds like a personal problem," B.B muttered under his breath.

I held up my hand to tell me to stop before he said something he would regret. "Someone was dragging their feet then, because if you said you were making arrests when you said you were, I wouldn't have this situation on hand."

Then Greene's slight guilt appeared on his face. His body softened. "Shooter said your ol' lady shot someone."

"Between you and the club, yes. To anyone else, I shot the bastard." I'd protect her from any blame or sideways looks from people if they judged her for protecting me, for taking a chance and succeeding.

"With all due respect, if you're looking to pin this on someone, Hound, it's not me," Greene warned.

B.B stepped in front of Greene, squaring up to him. That was one thing about B.B, he was all sunshine and rainbows out of his ass, but the minute that someone challenged us, it was like he would turn into a whole new person.

I stepped around the desk, my boots heavy on the floor, I clasped a rough hand on Greene's shoulder. "Make the fucking arrests or you won't have to worry about them."

"You going to wipe them out?"

My voice boomed off the walls, "That's what they are doing to us. That's what they have been doing. If it wasn't for the fact that the club has respect for you and what you do for us, we wouldn't be having this problem."

"A scorned lover makes for a ruthless killer," B.B chimed in.

Greene heavily sighed. "They are happening."

I nodded. "Good and when they do, you let us know."

"What so, you can make sure I'm doing my job," Greene snarked.

"So I know that I did the right thing. So I know that my club is protected. So that woman that I fucking love and would burn the streets of downtown for if that would make her happy know that she won't have to worry about nightmares." I gripped his shoulders tighter.

Too much had happened and everything felt like it was spinning out of control. Like a severe level twister was trying to ram through my life and take everything I loved and I worked for up into the cyclone. Of course I was mad at myself, blaming myself in every direction.

I couldn't look at many others. My own adrenaline was coming down and all the fire in me burned something fierce. When Greene left I sank into the office chair. When I could hear my own heartbeat in my ears, I exploded.

In my own rage, I swiped everything off my desk, not caring if there was something important or not. I knocked over anything I could, trying to take the pain of failing away. I punched a wall, leaving a dent in its path. I felt arms gripping me, pulling me away from the path of red I was feeling.

I busted from those arms pinning the owner's throat to the wall with my arm. In the haze, my eyes focused on a struggling B.B. calling out my name.

"Hound Dog. Brother," he kept calling. He didn't call for help, but enough noise was made for people to become alarmed.

I felt another pair of arms grab at me from behind, hauling me away. "Someone fucking hold him before he actually rampages through the state of Tennessee." I heard him cough out.

B.B straightened back up and faced me, staring into my eyes. "Are you going to listen to me?"

What a stupid fucking question in a time like that.

I yanked off whoever was holding me, setting myself free.

B.B didn't back down. "Are you going to listen to me?"

"Speak your mind then," I growled out.

I may need to calm down.

"Whether you actually hear me or not, but what happens after is what I care about," he started. "For too long you have taken all our mistakes, mishaps, and incidents on your shoulders. You drop everything to handle a situation rather than allowing us as a club, as a board to do what we were voted in to do. You are not the savior, you do not have to prove yourself."

I could feel my body ease up on the tension.

"It's your way or the highway. I get it, after you took over, you had the vision, I remember our talks. I know you. Stop trying to take blame for everything that had nothing to do with you."

"You say it's easy to just let go and hope that no one walks over me, take everything the club has worked for?"

"Have you looked at yourself? You really think that someone would be that brave and stupid enough to challenge you?" B.B challenged. He leaned closer to me, saying the one statement that might have snapped me out of it, "This isn't the record company."

No, the club wasn't the record company. Far from it. The club was an escape, the club took me in and challenged me to be more vocal, to become powerful. They showed me how to take charge and remain loyal.

B.B was right. I spent years in a shell of protecting myself from making another mistake and showing complete and blind trust like the record company. When I gained back my life, my control, I put up a barrier that I didn't think was one. I protected myself from getting hurt again.

Just like Melody did for years.

A knock interrupted us and I found Shooter at the office door, confused at the scene before him. "Um, I was just coming to tell you, she's awake, but if this is a bad time, I'm just gonna come back."

B.B sighed. "No, this is the perfect time."

Trust and let go. That's basically what he said to me. What he'd been trying to say.

I scanned the room, looking at all the evidence of destruction. As much as my mind told me that there was more to think through, there was only one person on my mind.

Chapter 35

MELODY

I didn't know when I started crying or why, but my cheeks felt wet, coated in salty tear streaks. But I had done one thing I never thought I would do.

The echoes of the yelling, the engine rumbling underneath me, and the sound of the shot rang in my ears like an endless loop. When I thought they were over, my mind would replay the sounds.

I could still feel the grasp of the man yanking me, trying to pull me off or knocking us over. The way his fingers gripped me, leaving an unpleasant sight. There was an ache in my neck and shoulder. The only thing I could remember last was Hound Dog staring at me in disbelief like I actually did something.

I laid there in an unknown room where Shooter had hooked me up to machines.

One thing was for certain, I killed someone.

I physically pulled the trigger on a gun and killed someone. Their blood was on my hands, their own soul taken from this world.

That wasn't me. I wasn't a killer. I didn't think of myself as a protector either. The ache in my chest turned into panic. Why did I do it?

Because he was going to hurt the one person that loved me.

The pain of knowing what I did and the compromising factor of why had me in a spin. Was that enough to justify what I did?

I needed Hound. I needed to know that it wasn't true that it was all a horrible dream and really the world would keep on spinning.

I wished that someone was there to sedate me so I couldn't feel anymore.

Hound would have done the same thing.

Yeah, he would have, but he seemed like it didn't bother him as much. He protects, that's what he did.

And you didn't?

I felt like there was a war in me, fighting to know who was right. I heard heavy boots strike the floor at a hurried pace. I knew by the racing of my heart it was the one person I could trust to soothe me, as he often did.

My rugged man's face hovered over me. "Hey there, little songbird." he cooed. A spread of warmth hit me.

His hand caressed my face, his thumb tracing the path of wetness on my cheek. He pulled me to sit up, where he could step in between my legs so I could look up at him. He radiated heat which only compelled me to face plant into his chest.

His hands rubbed down my back in a tranquil sensation. The light pressure felt so good that I could have fallen back asleep. And yet for a moment when I lost myself to peace, darkness slipped back in. My chest started to heave with panic.

And in that moment, Hound Dog picked me up from underneath my ass, hoisting me to the point of nuzzling his neck. I allowed the tears to flow down, I couldn't stop. I didn't know the true reason, but there were many speculations, I just couldn't choose.

My legs clung to his waist, I was like a child in his arms.

"Shh, I'm here, I ain't letting you go," he softly said.

I had hoped that was true in a lot of manners. All I wanted to do was apologize like a small sliver of this situation was my fault or made it worse. I kept apologizing, murmuring against his neck. How would I get past this?

Next thing I knew he had carried us to his room, shutting the door. He had sat me down on the bed, only to strip off his cut and shirt. He grabbed me as he put us on his bed. But not before he had stripped me down bare and dressed me in one of his shirts.

He laid me on top of him, pulling the blankets over us. I made him get softer ones and a bunch of them. I noticed one thing.

This was like my aftercare. When I gave out or when I had reached my limit, this would be what he would do. Ground me and surround me with warmth. A little haven for me to feel like I could escape.

The tears still flowed.

"It's never easy, honey," he said, "My first time was during my second run with the club as a prospect. We had run into trouble and I didn't stop to think I let my instinct take over. I was shaking, I knew it would be a part of the club life and I had shot before when the family would go hunting or go to the gun range for fun. But that all meant nothing compared to the first time."

I burrowed myself further into him. His fingers stroke my hair, lulling me away from the worries I had, the uncertainty I felt.

"Melody." Hound beckoned me. I couldn't look him straight in the eyes, not when I wasn't my best. "I know you're spinning. But thank you for saving me. Thank you for being the woman I don't deserve."

I interrupted him. "Not true."

His hands stopped running through my hair. "What?"

"You deserve it all. We deserve it all." Now I was crying for a different reason, and yet the words weren't ready to come out.

"Yeah, we do." He kissed the top of my head. "I know right now you don't feel it, but you are an angel."

An angel? The hidden joke was there, but he didn't say or maybe he didn't know it. But an angel of death. A fallen angel.

His heartbeat was steady, it was like a lullaby to my ears and before too long I was lulled to sleep. Wrapped up with a man that was meant to be with me. I promised myself that one day I wouldn't let this keep me from being in the moment with him. If he was going to remain alongside me, maybe it wouldn't hurt as much as it did.

I'm safe. We're safe. That should be all that matters.

My first night wasn't horrible but it was the next two that I ended up screaming, then begged Hound to sedate me, give me something that would make my sleep dreamless. I was aching from the mental drain of the incident and missing our home, one that I wanted to be my safe place. Though, anywhere that Hound was, was my safe place.

He promised that everything would end, yet he said that from the beginning. I had blind faith to know that he would follow through on his promise. By day eight, I was less numb, and not panicky. That morning I couldn't go back to sleep but Hound was sleeping like a rock and the dead couldn't wake him.

I slipped out, finding my shirt and sweatpants and padded down toward the kitchen. I needed something to idle my mind, especially when music felt lost and gone. I wanted nothing more than to write and find that music again. But it felt hopeless.

I poured myself into an apple and cinnamon coffee cake, allowing my hands to follow the recipe that I had made several times before. The sweetness of the apple and the sugary goodness of a brown sugar cinnamon just felt like home.

As I found my rhythm around the pantry, something alerted me that I was no longer alone. I turned with a mixing bowl in my hand and I found a beautiful, older woman with purple and maroon hair staring at me with a small smile. Her blue eyes almost reminded me of Hound Dog's. She looked like she worked in the sun and it kissed her with enough love and admiration.

I'd never seen her before, made me think that she was one of the ol' ladies like me.

Shit. I am an ol' lady, aren't I?

"Um, hi," I sheepishly said, trying to wave with a wooden spoonful of cake mixture. It splattered in a few places and embarrassment hit me. I was standing in the kitchen, staring at a woman I had no idea who, looking like I rolled out of bed.

"You sure are a pretty thing," she cooed, spreading a bigger smile. She walked toward me, cradling my face in her soft hands. "Like the heavens sent us their best angel."

Oh now she had me blushing. "Thank you."

"No need to thank me for just telling the truth, sweet girl." Her smile never faded.

Normally, I would tuck and run from the extended contact, but something in my soul told me not to, that I was safe with her. Her eyes darted to the mixture in the bowl. "He wasn't kidding about you feeding the boys."

He?

She let go of my face. There was something about her warmth that just oozed out of her. Only a brief conversations and I could tell that she was a good person. At least, I was hoping so.

"What can I do to help?" she asked, walking past me to the counter where the rest of the ingredients were laid out.

I fumbled over my words, trying to figure out what I needed. Hound normally would gawk at me in the kitchen, trying to tease me. And yet the sudden memory of our other special memories were creeping up. I needed to get the thought of Hound bending me over the house's kitchen counter, teasing my throbbing pussy, out of my head.

I finally spoke, telling the mysterious woman to butter the pans I had out.

She started to hum before diving into conversation. "Being in a kitchen just takes your mind away, right? Just to think that simple ingredients can make something so mouthwatering. Or even the simple way that baking or cooking allows us to busy our minds when we don't know what else to do."

I just nodded.

She kept going, "Or a way to get close to family."

That hit harder than any punch I'd taken. Family. I sighed. "Unfortunately, not everyone has a family."

"Family doesn't mean blood," she said simply.

She was right I guess. She started to chuckle. "Family can also mean future in-laws."

Oh, she was a friend of the club, which made it better. "Oh, I mean sometimes you get lucky there."

"I'd like to think so, she has not made that boy shut up about her. And I couldn't be happier," she said as I scrapped everything into the pans before baking them.

"She must be really good to your son then," I said, grabbing my coffee cup.

She reached for the coffee pot and poured her a cup as well. She leaned back into the counter and kept smiling. I'd never met a parent in the club before. I figured most of the guys were free spirited or ran away from their previous lives like Hound when he was Nash to the world.

"I like to think so, especially when she not only cooks for him, but cares for his brothers. He goes on and on about her singing and all. He didn't realize it, but he called her his songbird. That mush of a man." She peered at me, holding back her laughter as my eyes widened. I was talking to Hound's mother. Then my stomach hit the bottom when I realized she joked about future in-laws.

"Double fuck," I muttered.

She couldn't contain her laughter and sputtered out words. "Oh, sweet girl." She kept laughing. "I didn't mean for you to think... You are too adorable... Please don't think this was mean.. I was kidding." She saw the panic in my eyes.

I shook my head, "If I had known you were coming by or something I would be..."

"Not in Nash's clothing."

My cheeks reddened. I nodded. "Oh Melody, you are just a peach. And even more beautiful than he described. He doesn't know. But I talked to B.B and Reverend, and they thought I'd be best to come talk with you." She said.

"So he.." I gestured to the hallway.

"Nope, he might not be happy, but he loves his mama."

It took me a second to readjust, replaying the whole conversation, I thought it was a coincidence. "You're his mama. I'm so sorry, Mrs. Lane. This is not how I want to... make an impression."

"You can call me Ms. Mary." She pulled me into a tight hug. "Or Mama Mary, whichever."

I was so sick of crying and feeling all of the emotions, but her hug reminded me of being hugged by my mama long ago. The type of hug that envelopes you into a sense of warmth and love. I sank into her hug, never wanting to let go.

"Oh sweet girl," she cooed, pulling away, brushing my hair out of my face, her soft fingertips tracing over the skin. "No more tears."

"I'm sorry, it's just," I sniffed, "you know when you don't realize how much you miss something until you get it again and you wonder why you went for so long without it."

She chortled. "That's just the power of a mama bear hug." She sat us down at the island table, gawking at me. "I'd ask you how you are doing, but I have a feeling that's a loaded question and not easy to answer."

I nodded. I truly hated those questions because however you answer, people look at you like you were going to keep breaking or maybe you're actually okay.

"I take it you know what's going on?" I asked, she nodded her head. "Numb, some days. Others I'm okay until when my mind goes quiet and replays those memories and grasps me so hard that I can't shake loose. And I don't want Hound Dog to keep worrying about me, he has enough on his plate."

She took my hand in hers, and her thumb started caressing my skin. This was what it was like talking to someone like her, someone like Mama, where you could unload like it was their job to be there for you. Again, not everyone was lucky.

"Mrs. Lane," I started.

She squeezed my hand, "Oh don't call me that, I'd be afraid my mother-in-law was standing behind me or something. As I've said, Ms. Mary or Mama, whatever makes you comfortable."

I sheepishly nodded. "Ms. Mary, when I met your son, I was a completely different person and somehow he saw something in me that wanted to come into this world. We both pushed and both felt like we didn't deserve the chances we have with each other, but he never gave up on me. I don't want to revert back to feeling like I have to have walls around me. I'm not a murderer."

I could feel the tears starting to well up again, threatening to release, to be vulnerable again. These were my problems, and I'd already roped Hound Dog into my life, I didn't want to get anyone else hurt.

She wiped a stray tear. She offered a small smile, telling me I wasn't alone. "When I met Nash's dad, I mean Hound, I never thought that I would be a part of his lifestyle, then he chose me. Loved me for me and dreamed of giving everything I wanted. Then I was in your shoes once."

I nervously laughed, my voice cracked. "What, you shot someone because they were going to kill the person you loved?"

Mrs. Mary stayed quiet, Her blue eyes darkened and yet remained soft. I could see the fight in her eyes, one that had been going on for years.

"You did?"

She nodded. "I did, more than once."

My heart sank. She didn't look like she was the type of person that could harm a fly. She started to tell me the first time she shot someone, and it was for the protection of her family. Then proceeded to tell me about the times that rivals or even people looking for her because of the connection she has with the club. "I don't regret any of them, because in the end I did what I needed for the people I loved and the protection of my family, which also meant the club. Melody, it's hard for the first time because there is no perfect timing."

She was right, of course. In the end there was no perfect timing, nor any way to ignore it. "When did you start to be okay with what you did?"

"Well, that depends on you. Are you going to let the memory haunt you, preventing you from living your life? Or are you going to power through and remember who you are?"

Who was I?

I was a person that was pushing every negative voice telling me that I couldn't do anything, I was the one with the big heart that loved a few people in her life but opened up to love more. I was the beautiful soul that captured the rough and rugged man in her life.

I wanted to choose to move on. I was going to be the strong woman so many people believed I was. I was the person that deserves everything good in her life and accepted the love from Hound Dog.

Ms. Mary's warmth and comfort was maybe what I needed to be pulled from that funk. After that I waited for Hound to come find me, but not before she revealed stories of young Nash, especially the story of Christmas and the little cowboy boots.

And the rosiness of his cheeks when he found me later, laughing at the home photos that Ms. Mary was showing me, made me feel lighter.

I already loved being with Hound, but being accepted by the club and his family, I knew I wasn't going anywhere. Not that Hound Dog would let me go anywhere.

Chapter 36

MELODY

Day by day I didn't let the memory win. I didn't let the memory take over my days, the nights were getting better. Of course, Hound had an idea that would help. He called it "replacement" therapy, I called it midnight orgasms.

Half way waking up to Hound's face buried in my pussy, easing the cries that I belted out, turning them into pleasure cries were better. He would lick and suck his heart's desire, turning into a little monster. He would trap my thighs so I couldn't move them, he controlled every aspect.

In the end, I'd return the favor. We took care of each other.

When December came around, I couldn't believe that time had flown. We weren't at the clubhouse anymore, and returned home.

Our home.

Our bed.

Little by little, music slowly returned to me. Any time the memory would creep up, I'd bring out the guitar and let the memory turn into an outlaw ballad. Sadie was proud, even after she cooled down from knowing what happened. I could trust Sadie, just like she trusted me.

The fork in the road.
Between a life with or without.
I'd never turn a world red.
But I'd rather live with.
Never without.

I'd take a chance with the trigger
Than the fear of the screams
Or broken promises.

Hound tried to make things normal. He'd taken a break from collecting shipments or checking on businesses to take me from the city.

The man even took me to Graceland. My Hound Dog in the home of the original Hound Dog. I loved every minute of it. At which time, he said that one day I'd give it a try again. He kept telling me that I was going to be great, that I was going to get there.

"You're a star, you are a marvel of talent." He kept uplifting me. "You can do it."

That man just wanted the best for me, and I wanted to let him. I wanted to show him and my sister that I could do it.

One afternoon, we were relaxing, which was more of a treat for him. Something happened in those few weeks and Hound was home a little more. Which I wasn't going to complain about.

I had my feet on his lap, he was watching something with football, I wasn't paying attention. I had my book in my hands. When it got to the spicy part, I couldn't help but fidget. I tried damn hard not to have him notice. But his hands would travel up my calf and back down. I could feel myself getting wetter by the moment.

"You keep moving your feet and I'll have you in my lap reading to me." He snickered.

I waved him off, barely taking the book down from my face. "Just watch your game."

"Hm, I'd rather watch you," he teased.

I shrank down further into the couch. I peeked over the book finding his eyes staring back into mine. "What are you doing?"

"Thinking that something's got my girl super excited over there, and I can't help but wonder what's getting you worked up and if I could do it."

"Stop being a book boyfriend."

"What the fuck is a book boyfriend?"

I scoffed. "I'm not explaining that to you."

He reached over and tried to pry the book out of my hands. I tucked the book closer to my chest. He curled his lips. "Oh honey, we can play that little game."

I shook my head. I knew what that meant. Someone would be reduced to a puddle and all bets were on me. "All because I won't explain what a book boyfriend is?"

"That, and I can smell your arousal, so something has you excited and I want to know."

"You're not a bloodhound, you cannot smell when I'm turned on. Weirdo."

But Hound insisted that we were playing a little game. In one solid movement, he yanked me further across the couch until he was hovering over me, pinning my hips to the plush couch. His raging hard-on pressed harder against me. "So if I slipped my fingers under these sweatpants, I won't find you wet."

I licked my lips. "Only one way to find out."

"Oh honey, I plan to find out and more," he whispered. He rested his forehead on mine. One hand traveled along my collarbone. Goosebumps fleshed my skin, my back arching into his touch.

"Oh now that you'll win the bet, you think you're going to fuck me now?" I challenged.

The man would not let his brothers win the bet from when he had a concussion. He said that he wasn't neglecting my needs, and when I begged him to actually fuck me, he'd shut me up with orgasms after orgasms.

At one point Sadie bought me a dildo, though it was smaller and shorter than him, that I was tempted to use it. Until Hound threw it away and literally growled at me and said I needed to be patient and the only dick I needed was his.

He slept on the couch that night, which didn't last very long until I found out where he ended up the very next morning when I was getting hot flashes from a surprising presence.

"Keep being a brat and I'll edge your fine ass," he growled.

"Do you enjoy sleeping on the couch? Because the next step is that I'm getting a dog to cuddle with in the bed while you sleep on the couch," I threatened him. Edging could be pleasurable but I had just come off my period and I was in a good place mentally again. I wanted him and I was desperate to have him my way.

"Feisty, mouthy, and needy. There's my girl. I was wondering when you'd make your way back." He nipped at my neck. I wanted more, I craved more from him.

"See what happens when you make me wait? Making me desperate for you, practically wanting to just grab your cock and do it myself." I cupped his face, bringing it to my lips, pressing hard into him. I wrapped my legs around him.

He groaned as our tongues tangled with each other. Something came over me and I was praising whoever for it. He grasped my throat, pulling himself from my lips to attack my throat. Hound licked and sucked on the little spots that he knew I liked.

"Yes, baby, right..." I attempted to say, but he started to lightly squeeze as he pulled my tank up, allowing my breasts to spill out. This is what my body wanted, what it craved. His undeniable dominance to take over, to revel in the haze of need.

"Every inch of you is a fucking dream. One I know I never want to wake up from," he murmured into my skin. His hot breath caressed my skin, trying to find which nipple he wanted to tease. I looked down to see him lick his lips, only to look back. "Maybe I want to see if my little birdie can use those breathing techniques. Maybe if I squeeze a little harder." It only made me buck against him, a little delirious dizziness floated in my mind.

He let go, sitting up straight, gawking over me like I was his prize he had won, his pretty little thing.

"That's my girl. But you know you're wearing too much clothing," he said as he ripped my tank up in two, then popped my bra off. "Mm, getting there." He didn't waste time taking off his shirt and my pants. When the man wanted something, he went for it and took it with no mercy.

He palmed his cock that was still pressed against his jeans, he stared at my seeping wet pussy. His stare was demanding, hungry, and it just made me even wetter.

"What a pretty pussy. Is that all for me?" his hands skimmed around my pussy, teasing it, thinking of all the ways he wanted his way with me.

I shook my head. "Maybe not all of it."

It was like waving a red flag in front of a bull. In retaliation, he shoved two thick fingers in me, making me cry out. "Really? What else, Melody? Tell me? Was it your book?"

His slow, agonizing strokes only made me want to beg for harder, faster.

"Were you imagining yourself in the character's shoes? Wishing it was you?" His taunting only made things painful, itching for more.

I whimpered as he continued his strokes. "I imagined it was you."

"Naughty girl. Getting ideas."

"Please, Hound. Fuck me rough, hard, I don't care just hurry up." I pleaded, which only rewarded me with a sting to my pussy. I was on the edge, but he stopped, giving me a couple more slaps to my sensitive heat.

Those blue eyes darkened, Hound pulled me up sitting up. "Never tell me to hurry up. When you're with me, I may use you, tease you, make you see stars, but never to just get off. My woman will be given what she deserves." His hand shot up to my throat. "On your knees, but sit up, and legs spread apart."

I was his, and he was certainly mine.

I scrambled to my knees, still sinking into the couch. He got up and left, leaving me waiting for him to return. Only when he did, he didn't come empty handed. My eyes bugged out of my head because he was going to prove that he knew exactly what I needed.

"We're calling this a lesson in breath control. We're gonna count from one. My hand is going to be wrapped around this pretty little throat while this little vibrator is going to remain on your clit. Understand so far?" he commanded.

"Yes," I said, while my mouth started to salivate.

"Good girl." He smiled. Hound trailed the vibrator along my naked body. "When we count, the vibrator will be there along with my hand on your throat. Use those lung muscles. If it gets too much either say your safeword or if you can't speak, tap your thigh or grab my wrist."

The anticipation was enough to make me come right then.

"Yes, *sir*," I teased.

"Tell me why you think I want to do this," he asked while nibbling on my jawline.

"Because you like lessons." I said while his hand without the vibrator palmed my breasts, grasping it, the heavy weight felt freeing.

"Maybe," he continued.

"Because you know what I need." I answered.

"I know you very well, just like you know all the buttons to turn me on." He pressed a hard kiss on my lips. "You ready?"

"Please," I pleaded.

"Such a good girl, asking nicely. Oh, and Melody," he said as he turned on the toy, "You can come as many times you want."

I felt like there was supposed to be a clear cruelty in that, but death by orgasms didn't sound like a threat, but the best way to high five Jesus. I went from barely knowing what it should feel like, to being a little sexual monster.

"Last chance, do you want to continue?" he considerately asked me.

"I want this," I said eagerly.

His hand grasped my throat and squeezed.

Chapter 37

HOUND DOG

She amazed me everyday. Months ago she would have had a second thought or I'd be afraid she would run away. But she looked like a goddess, and legs spread waiting to be worshipped by me. I had all the intentions of being nice and slow for her, making love to her like the true goddess she was.

But that mouth, waving a challenge in my eyes. If only she had this sort of confidence on stage.

She was getting there. I knew that one day she would, and I would be there to see it and celebrate.

I moved a table to sit closer to her because I wanted to watch every little reaction and movement from her. My hand grasped her throat, her pulse right there at my fingertips and her little vibrator in my other hand.

I ran the toy through her pussy lips, letting the toy get nice and wet. Her mere excitement for this was a damn turn on.

"Such a pretty little birdie, getting her toy wet for me. I bet you could make it to ten." My thumb rubbed the sensitive spot on her neck as she moaned from the touches. My cock was pressed hard against my jeans, but I wanted this from her. To remind her that I had everything she would need, that she could rely on me there for everything, but also didn't hurt that she was a tempting siren.

How she blossomed into this goddess, I'd never know, but I was thankful.

I teased her inner thighs as soon as I turned on the vibration, caressing her, watching her lean forward for more.

When the toy hit her clit, I squeezed her throat, counting to one. It was quick but she would learn that sometimes I wouldn't play fair. I let the toy come off her clit and eased up on my hand. "Good girl."

I nodded as she stared back into my eyes, waiting for a signal that the next count would be coming. "Do you need me to give you a signal?"

I wasn't that much of an asshole. She nodded. "Okay, here comes two."

She whimpered but held on as the squeeze of my hand and the vibrator returned. Her body clenched from the sensation, after a little slower count of two. Her muscles tightened until I released.

I peeked at the toy as it glistened from the light around us. Between my hand taking her breath away and the toy, I imagined she would be a puddle. She knew how to communicate, but I also knew she would have enough.

"How you doing?" I checked in.

"Please, keep going," she begged.

I listened, and I continued. Her third one was wonderful to watch as she didn't think she just did. But even after three she was close, but holding back. I knew she wanted to hold, prove that she could make it.

"Four," I started as my hand squeezed once more. She held her breath and rode the sensations of the vibrator. I changed from placing it on her clit to rubbing the toy in small circles over her aching clit. She bucked at the first circle. "Four....Three..." I paused waiting for her body to tighten up. "Two. And one."

I released and she took a little gasp of air. "How you doing?"

Her chest heaved. "I didn't say stop."

Well fuck me, little vixen. "Make it to ten and I'll fuck you anyway you want."

Five and six were so fucking perfect to watch her on the brink of coming, Her legs started to shake from the time she was on her knees to the power of the toy and the impending orgasm.

"Doing so well, honey. But you're holding back. Give me everything," I commanded her. Maybe I needed to tempt her; while she was a little stubborn sometimes she did need an incentive. I placed the toy to the side and unzipped my jeans. Melody's eyes widened, her mouth left gaped. I could see the straight hunger in her eyes.

"I want that," she cooed.

"My pants? Not sure you could fit into them."

"I want that monster that you're hiding from me."

"Then give me what I want," I returned. "Seven."

I slowly counted down and by the time I got to two, her body fully trembled as the orgasm erupted through her like a shock wave. Her head was thrown back, sinking into the back of the couch. I caught her before she could injure herself or pull something. Her mewling sounds echoed through my mind. An intoxicating sight.

She muttered something as I dropped everything to hold her. A sense of guilt rushed over me, I should have seen her like this, should have known she might push herself. I shushed her. She was trying for me. She was doing so well.

"Keep going," she whispered.

"It's okay, we don't have to keep going," I told her. But she shook her head. "Melody, I'm not going to push you. You've already pushed further."

She tried to protest, I wasn't having it. I scooped her up, cradling her in my arms. She nestled further into me. "I could have kept going," she muttered, her voice so soft and light.

"I know honey, but you would have gone to a place mentally that I don't think you're ready to go into." I kissed the top of her head as I kicked our bedroom door.

I laid her down amongst the blankets and the pillows. I shucked off the rest of my clothing because one thing I had learned from my girl, she preferred skin to skin aftercare than clothed and cuddling. She needed the warmth, to feel like she was belonging to someone.

As much as the painful ache in my cock begged to just slip in her, this was about her, being the man that she needed.

I wrapped us into a large blanket, pulling her on top. She wrapped herself like a koala. She was still awake but floating between the worlds of sleep. She nuzzled my chest. "Can I tell you something?"

"Anything."

"You smell good."

Okay, maybe that was the delirium speaking. "What do I smell like?"

"Cinnamon. Bourbon." Her dazed gaze stared at me, my hand tracing the curves and the back dimples. "And home."

"Melody," I groaned. She couldn't say those sweet things, because it made it harder to even think that she would be taken from me one day.

She turned her head, looking toward the ambience light on the nightstand. "You make it hard not to fall for you."

My heart skipped a beat and grew a couple sizes. She was falling for me, admittedly. If only she knew sooner that I had fallen for her when she stepped onto that stage. A classic beauty with a dream and a heart.

"Falling for you, Melody, was the easiest thing for me. It was proving to myself that a love for you was what I needed, that was the hardest."

Her beautiful eyes softened. "You love me?"

"Is that hard to believe?" I smiled.

She shook her head. I rolled us over to where she was beneath me. Reassurance was what she needed, and a hidden beast wanted her to hear me for the next part. "Never underestimate what I feel for you. You're mine. Mine to love, to encourage, to fuck, to fill the cunt with my cum until your belly is round from carrying our children, mine to grow old with, mine to sing with."

I pressed a hard kiss before she could respond. I nipped her bottom lip, she sprung fully awake. Her legs fell open and bucked her hips. I knew how she felt but it was up to her to figure out when she was ready.

Her finger delicately traced my chest. "I'm going to make you proud."

"Honey, you've already done that."

"All the work that you've tried to help me with, I'll get up on that stage and show you that it wasn't a waste."

I nuzzled toward her, "I'll let you in on a little secret." she hummed. I leaned toward her ear, "None of it would be a waste."

Just when she gasped from my cock thrusting into her, my phone rang. I tried to ignore it but after two more attempts, I groaned.

I grabbed the phone to see Greene's name. Rage filled my core. Melody sat, pulling the covers over her, watching me stare at the phone, regretting the next part.

"Greene, you must have a death wish to be calling me right now," I snarled.

He didn't take long. "It's happening, Hound."

I knew it meant the only thing that mattered. "Where?"

Greene relayed the details, giving me everything we needed to make sure it happened. I had hoped this was the end we needed to move on and get this threat out of the city, out of our lives. It was wishful thinking.

I silently moved to grab my clothes, as I called up the club for an open invite to see the downfall of the Hogs. I sat at the edge of the bed getting my boots on when I felt the brush of a hand on my shoulder. I guess in my blinded movements I forgot where I was.

"Baby, you going somewhere?" her small voice said. She rested her chin on my shoulder.

"Something's going down across state lines that requires our attention."

She vanished, shuffled off the bed, scrambling around to find a scrap of clothing. I didn't know what thought popped in her head, but I wasn't going to entertain the idea of having her come for that.

"Have you seen my black bra?" she asked as she rummaged through the drawers.

"You're not going anywhere, you're staying here and a prospect will be outside," I told her.

"I swear I had it the other day."

"Now is not the time to be a brat."

"I'm gonna check the hanging rack, I swear I had it the other day or put it away."

Melody ignored me completely as she left the bedroom. My head started to pound from gritting my teeth. "Melody, you're not going."

"Sure I am, I just need to get dressed. You did put my cut in the closet, right? Also how cold is it right now because if we're riding for a long while, I don't need my nips to get cold. I mean I could put the hand warmers in my bra, if I could just find my dang bra." She wouldn't let up.

I grabbed my holster and the pocketknife for the front pocket. "This time, no." Before I could walk out the door, she leaned up on the door, pressing a finger to my chest. I couldn't stop staring. She was glorious in all her naked goodness. Her auburn hair cascaded over her shoulders. She gazed up at me, daring me to keep telling her "no" like if I could tell her she'd cut my dick off and possibly feed it to me.

She batted her eyes, "Now baby, what kind of ol lady would I be if I didn't support my man and the club? If you think I don't know what's happening then think again. B.B and Otis have a big mouth."

"I'm starting to believe that you weren't this shy, introverted beautiful woman, that there was this tiger waiting in the shadows." I groaned.

Her smile curled. "I was waiting for you, baby. Now, either help me find my bra or take me as I am and risk hypothermia." She pressed a quick kiss and vanished again behind me.

I rolled my neck. "Try my top left dresser drawer."

I was that fucker though.

"Why would it be... Nash Lane, why are all my bras in your dresser drawer?" she yelled sternly.

"You really want that answer right now?"

"Later after you have properly fucked me because we weren't finished."

Now I believed that my life could be fulfilled with a good hearted woman and a club behind me. Also, a woman that kept me on my toes and one that Mama really liked, which meant that Pops would like her. The stars were aligned.

Chapter 38

MELODY

I clung onto him as we passed through the borders of Arkansas, a symphony of engines behind me. An orchestra of pure chaos and order at the same time. There was a sense of power that cascaded around the club. And with Hound in the lead, he looked like a damn glorious warrior. It was no wonder why people were drawn to him.

I knew what that phone call meant. It meant not having to look behind me all the time. It meant relief for Hound Dog and the club. A chance to breathe, a chance to build on the relationship and make it feel somewhat normal. I wanted to be a little selfish and wanted Hound for myself, the opportunity to make more memories with him.

His hand laid on top of mine. He gave me a gentle squeeze. It was hard not to just rest my head on him, the way he made me feel like I was the only one for him, that he admittedly said he was falling for me had me blushing like a sinner in church.

His name on my back, tempted me to get something a little more permanent, but I was never one of those girls that got their partner's name inked on my skin. But I know a certain "future in law" as Mama Mary would put it that might be able to help.

Hound tapped my hand for attention, he nodded toward the off ramp we were heading toward.

Why did it make my heart race to know that it was real? Those promises were being fulfilled even though I didn't have that doubt anymore.

The club slowed their pace, Fender led the pack, tackling his duty like it was his life.

He signaled for the all clear and soon we were about a couple blocks away from where Hound said the Hogs would be. A line of bikes formed around me, like an impenetrable wall.

We waited around, as normal life went on around us. My legs started to shake, my nerves ran rapid fire through my body. A hand trapped my knee.

"Sorry." I whispered.

"Nothing to be nervous about," Hound said. He got off the bike, peering down at me. He gripped my hips and pulled me to the front of the bike. I straddled the tank and he sat behind me.

I looked to my right and saw B.B grinning like a cat. He just nodded in agreement, like it was a decision.

"Uh, Hound, all you had to do was tell me to stop shaking my legs," I said.

His arms snaked around my waist, pulling me in tight. I could smell that luscious whiskey and smoke scent.

Why did the sudden feeling of being surrounded by protectors, people that would go to war for me make me feel invincible?

Hound's hot breath brushed my ear. "This is what happens when someone messes with one and or all of us. Watch the world unfold and give you what is needed." Before I could say anything else, a wave of secured vehicles, vans, and trucks came swerving around the corner. Uniforms ran out of the back, surrounding the area. I watched as a rampage of force stalked around the building, the only anticipation was waiting for them to start any action. Guns were loaded, pointed at anything that moved in their direction.

With a final boom, the swarm of dark clothes entered the building, from a couple of blocks away the echo of shouts were heard. I couldn't help but peek at the guys' faces, a few were still stone like but others were dressed with a sinister, happy smile as if justice was served.

Men yelled as they were thrust to the ground, cuffs slapped on their wrists.

Even from far away I could feel the death stares from those men as they peered with anger riddled eyes. They knew exactly who was behind it.

"Watch what power can do for you. To never have to worry about someone taking something from you. To never having to wonder what being weak means again." He kept whispering in my ear. "This club protects its own, and you, my little songbird, are one that will soar. These men are just as much here for you as they are to see that club go down."

To feel loved and to be like a family, that was the greatest gift anyone could give me. To love and not expect anything in return other than loyalty and trust.

"They won't hurt us again," I murmured, praying those words would never prove me wrong.

I couldn't see how many people were on the ground, but I knew it was enough to end an era of terror for Hound, for the club.

The men watched as the Hogs were carted away, knowing that it ended without their blood and sins being involved. No more guilt or shame, no more worrying about if Hound would come home to me. Maybe our happily ever after was just around the corner.

Hound held me close until the last van and officer left. One by one, the men left, and that night Hound fell asleep in my arms, where he would belong to the end of time.

With everything that happened at the arrests, we fell into a normal routine. Hound argued that we were never normal to begin with, but I'd say otherwise. Morning would be the battle that we'd have of leaving the bed, I was the responsible one but Hound made it very tempting to stay. He had such a mouth on him.

When he'd leave for his runs and what he needed to do with the club. I spent time perfecting songs, working on the catches of melody that sounded in my head. Some days I'd take Hound's truck to the compound and make food or talk with a couple of the ole' ladies that were there. Then by night, Hound would want to be sated and craved a lot more than food.

The week before Christmas, I didn't tell him, but I was going to try again at open night. B.B encouraged me one afternoon when he came to swipe lunch.

"Surprise him, that could be your gift," he pestered me.

I shook my head, calling him crazy. Reminding him that he was the reason why I tried the previous time and failed.

He waved it off telling me that it was stress, that I was trying to please Hound. When I winced and said he was sounding like Reverend, B.B said, "Look kiddo, if you haven't learned anything from the old man, learn this. Try just imagining that you're singing to him. Find him in the crowd and sing. If he's the only one that matters, then just set your mind to thinking it's just him."

As simple as he put it, my mind wasn't a one trick pony. It wasn't easy to shut off everything and focus on him.

I thought about it for a moment, really anticipating that it could be a thing, a trick of the mind. I agreed but only if I was one of the first few ones. Less people to think about. Oh, he promised to keep it a secret. I wanted it to be a surprise. Maybe I'd fake being sick, but not sick enough that he would want to stay.

I would be lying if I said that the thought of pulling off a surprise for him made me giddy like a schoolgirl.

B.B and I kept messaging back and forth, planning the details and making sure that nothing would be out of place by the time Open Mic night happened.

Hound's hand rested on my forehead, his face twisted with concern. "You don't feel warm, you sure it's a cold?"

I bundled up in all the blankets I could find, claiming that I was cold like my body was getting the aches. When Hound came home a little bit, I had to make it look real, even if I was fucking burning up like an inferno.

"Maybe I ate something bad," I lied, keeping my gaze away from him.

"Hopefully not because I ate the last big thing from that casserole a couple days ago. And I know it ain't your period." He sat at the edge of the bed.

That got my attention. "Nash Lane, the fuck you mean it ain't my period. Like you've been tracking?"

I whipped back over, facing him, and he sucked his lips between his teeth. The shit was looking guilty with that look on his face. My eyes bugged out of my head. "Why are you tracking my cycle like a caveman.." I demanded. "You were reading one of my books again, weren't you?"

"I have no idea what you're talking about, but it's not my fault that the hockey player bad boy just threw out his woman's birth control."

"I swear to your mother, if you messed with something, I will have her help me bury you. And Memphis will hold the ceremony. Your daddy will just shake his head knowing that it was me that put you in an early grave," I snarled.

But secretly why did I think it was a little hot to think that Hound Dog would go that way, did he have a secret breeding kink and it took a naughty book to unlock it?

"You might not be feeling good, but you still have that feistiness in you. No, I just remember things. But great to know where your head is at in that conversation." He started to rub my legs.

To have a family with him would be a dream, but we just started to be normal in our routine. I mean I could have joked that he was getting up there in age, but didn't. I wanted to enjoy him for as long as I could before we started to think about expanding or even the possibility. I still wanted to be a part of this relationship and still not depend always on Hound.

I faked a couple of coughs. Hound just raised an eyebrow. But he got up and went to the hall closet, rummaging through things making all kinds of rattling sounds. He yelled from the hall, "If you're feeling that bad or feel like you're coming down with something, let's dose you up. Maybe I'll have Shooter come and check you out."

My eye twitched. The man would take care of me if I just wanted a lazy day. He'd even get in my kitchen to heat a can of chicken and star noodles. But that was all he was allowed to do. "I don't need you to call Shooter. I'm pretty sure that man would bill you and overcharge you for the amount of times you have called him because of me."

Hound came through the bedroom door, leaning on the frame. He had a cold medicine liquid bottle in his hand, reading it. He spun it in his hand before twisting the lid and pouring the contents into the measuring cup. The sticky, sweet medicine made my face scrunch up. I shook my head.

Maybe this was why I didn't play hooky from school pretending to be sick, mostly because I was stubborn with my care and believed that I could beat any cold or flu.

Hound stepped to the side of my bed, slowly tipping the cup to my lips. "You gonna be a good girl and take the medicine?"

There was still an ounce of defiance in me but the look in his eyes told me that if I tried anything then he would have other ways of getting the medicine down my throat. I slightly opened my mouth, allowing the medicine to trickle down my throat with a sugary, cherry slickness. I knew that I would have to gargle some throat tea before I left to get rid of that yuck.

Hound pressed a sweet kiss on my lips, taking in the cherry flavor. But when he pulled back, he was too smug.

"Thank you, beautiful," he said as he sat the cup on the nightstand.

I winced and buried myself back into the blankets. My own hope was that the medicine he gave me wasn't the nighttime medicine.

"Well, are you going to be okay if I do rounds tonight?"

Yes, yes, yes, a hundred percent yes.

"That's fine, baby, just don't be mad if I'm passed out. Just be careful," I muttered under the covers.

He whipped the covers off and kissed the top of my head.

As soon he was out the door and I sprung free from the blanket trap I put myself in. I stared at my guitar in the corner of the spare room, I took a deep breath and told myself that I could do this. I messaged B.B letting him know to put my name on the list. I messaged Sadie, letting her know that I would be there.

I needed the support, I needed my people.

Mostly, I was ready to prove myself wrong.

Chapter 39

Hound Dog

Melody had me worried, normally she wasn't sick, maybe injured from bumping into the kitchen corners or being mauled down from a rival gang, but never sick.

Ever since the little talk with B.B, I had started to let go piece by piece on duties. The fool was right about me needing to let go and keep trusting that the brothers would figure it out and I could relax.

It gave me a chance to really think about a life with Melody. Her worry that I was tracking her cycle for my own purposes was cute, but it did get me thinking about "what if" and then images of a very pregnant Melody humming while truly barefoot in the kitchen. I felt wrong thinking of it, but the kitchen was her happy place outside of music.

Whatever made her happy made me happy in the end.

I walked into the Blue Sax after stopping by the other businesses. Friday nights were chances for a brighter future, a step in the right direction. Twitty was behind the bar tonight, and B.B was zooming in and out of the back and up the stairs to the lofted area. Memories of Melody at that piano last time sent shivers down my spine.

"Whatcha want, Prez?" Twitty asked.

"Whatever is on tap and ain't fruity."

He nodded and turned his back on me.

The Blue Sax was getting busier, and people were walking in, trying to find their friends. Most of them probably were attempting their stardom tonight. The look of nerves and excitement spread across the floor. Twitty handed my beer, it's icy cold cooling my hand, shaking the thoughts of wishing Melody would one day be up there.

"If I didn't know any better, you look like a love sick puppy right now, and it's kind of cute." B.B's voice rang behind me as he sat next to me, reaching behind the bar to pull a bottle of whiskey out.

Did I really look like that? Like I longed for someone? Normally that would be something I'd joke with Memphis about. "What can I say? I'm a very lucky, happy man."

"That you are brother, and fucking finally. If I knew that little peach of a woman you got was the answer to so many of our problems, I would've found her quicker. Maybe have her jump your bones sooner. Get that dick wet a bit." He started to ramble on before taking a swig of the amber liquor.

"Careful what you say, she's not a piece of ass or a sweetbutt," I cautioned him.

He waved his hands. "That's not what I meant. She is a saint. You are the burly, grumpy sad sack that didn't know a good thing when it hit him. Now look at you. Hogs are taken care of, the businesses, illegal and legal, are both thriving, mother chapter is happy, and you got a woman that absolutely loves you."

Well that was one thing we hadn't crossed yet. I darted my eyes away from him, but he leaned over, "Oh boy, did I find the Achilles heel? You have said those magical words right? I mean three simple, meaningful words, but I thought it was obvious."

I slammed back my drink and signaled Twitty for another.

B.B scoffed. "Nash "Hound Dog" Lane hasn't said I love you to his woman?"

"She hasn't said them either."

"Oh no, you're not pinning this one on her. You fell for the woman first, and you ain't said I love you. Jesus Hound, seriously, what's the hold up? If I was you I'd be professing my undying love for my woman and sealing the deal." He tried to joke it off and I played along with it.

"That would mean you need to find a woman that will keep up with your antics, and make an honest man out of you," I retorted back.

"Oh, don't you worry about that, and I'm afraid to say it."

"Again that would require you to have a woman."

He deadpanned. "And I said don't worry about that."

The fucker trapped an innocent woman. "You didn't."

"She just doesn't know it yet." He smirked, that cocky bastard.

Fender and Hank came through cocking an eyebrow at the interaction we were having. Fender brushed through his short hair, "I feel like we're missing something."

"Would it surprise you that B.B may or may not have a secret basement and if we hear screaming and begging from somewhere that we should be concerned?" I pushed B.B to the side before he told Fender something.

Fender and Hank looked at each other, even more confused. Hank spoke up. "I mean it wouldn't be uncharacteristic, we all know the fucker is somewhat twisted in the head."

"And yet I'm perfect the way I am," B.B grinned.

A roar of laughter spread amongst us, it felt good to laugh again, laugh with my brothers. We were interrupted when a busty, dark haired woman that looked like she belonged in a dirty magazine under a teenager's bed approached us. Her hips swayed, the curve of her smile tried to charm us, but I didn't like this. She was absolutely nothing I wanted, not here, not anywhere close to me.

Her smoky voice sounded. "What's a big fella like you doing all alone, with no one to be by your side tonight?" she looked to the side before darting her eyes back at me. She completely ignored the rest of the guys. Her attention was on me.

"Not interested," I snarled out.

"Oh, playing hard to get, big boy? That's okay. I know how to change your mind," she hissed as she plunged herself into my lap faster and pressed a venomous kiss on my lips. My hands gripped her upper arms, pulling her off of me. I yanked her off, still face to face.

"Who the fuck do you think you are? When a man fucking says that he's not interested, it's not a fucking invitation," I growled, practically throwing her off of m

The taste of her was like poison, my guts wrenched. I couldn't stand it, my skin crawled, I couldn't think. As I closed my eyes for a swig of a drink, I tried to erase the feeling that lingered. When I opened my eyes, she'd vanished. It had me worried that I was dreaming or it was a nightmare. But when I turned toward the guys, their shocked expressions were confirmation enough.

"I know I was high that time, because what the fuck was that?" Hank bursted out.

I had no idea, and I didn't want to go find out. I mean, it wasn't the first time that a bold, yet desperate woman approached myself or any one of the brothers, but it was the first time that someone violently threw themselves on me.

I tried to push the memory back in my head, afraid that I might need to tell Melody of this, and hopefully she wouldn't be mad at me. Oh God, I feared the wrath of Melody's anger. I learned she could be a quiet anger type of person, but I didn't want to test that theory either.

B.B kept peeking at the door and looking around the place. One by one the singers were getting ready for the night. B.B kept checking his phone, his expression grew from smiling to concerned. Otis made a joke, "Dude, I know that some of the talent needs some work, but why do you look like that?"

"Like what," B.B spat out.

"Like you're waiting for someone?" I raised an eyebrow.

"Don't know what you're talking about." He closed off.

"Let's welcome to the stage, Ms. Melody Rae," the host announced.

B.B's head banged on the bar top, Otis and Hank stood there with mouths agape. My liquor glass fell out of my hands.

"What did he mean by Melody Rae?" I asked calmly before I needed to ask for forgiveness for what would happen if no one spoke.

The host said her name one more time, everyone in the room turned their heads expecting someone to come through or rush to the stage. The host looked around before moving on to the next name.

"Someone better start talking, and now." My voice deepened.

Otis threw his hands up. "Don't look at us, you said she was sick." Hank took a step back, because he knew that I was ready to explode on my supposed VP.

I turned to B.B's direction, the guilt was all over his face. "What. Am. I. Missing?"

He sighed before trying to curve a smile. "She was going to surprise you. She had told me she was on the way."

One thing was missing though. "Where is she, B.B?"

"That is a very good question that I do not have an answer to. I'll call Woody, he was supposed to be watching over her, right?" I could hear the nerves in his voice. As much as I wanted to lay him flat on the ground, I couldn't. Maybe they had good intentions, but why did the guilt of easing up on my ways, trusting that everything would be okay, go against everything in me?

"Um, Prez, don't think you need to call Woody," Hank said, nodding to the back corner of the stage. He was alone. Melody wasn't with him. Woody's eyes found us at the bar, Otis signaled him over. Woody's head hung low like a puppy in trouble.

My heart raced, thoughts rapidly fired in my head.

"Prez," Woody said when he approached the bar.

"Prospect, where is my ol' lady?" I didn't hesitate to ask.

He cocked his head. "She was right there at the door when she told me to go on. I thought she was coming to find you."

Otis chimed in, "Obviously not."

All color vanished from his face. Woody shook his head in disbelief. "No, no sir. She was right there at the door. No, I'll find her. Please. Ah, fuck's sake."

Woody disappeared into the crowd of people before I could say anything. Then it all came together. She ran. If she was standing by the door, she had a full view of the little venomous trap. She saw everything. She ran without confronting me. She thought I'd do something like betray her.

Her worst insecure thought came true without knowing the truth. I tried to call her, but it went to voicemail. I tried and tried again. Sending her countless messages, although I know she was not one to text. I was holding out for hope.

I tried to use the app thing that Blaze put on my phone to track her phone. But it was still saying she was in the Blue Sax.

"We'll find her," B.B said, joining in the search for Melody.

I didn't pray but I hoped that we would find her and I'd make it up to her.

Chapter 40

MELODY

My fingers tapped on the steering wheel when I messaged B.B that I was heading toward the bar. I had everything planned out and I was more anxious to see Hound's face when he saw me on stage. At that moment, I felt good. I listened to B.B's advice about focusing on Hound in the crowd.

Between being confident in myself, in my skills, and knowing that there was only one person I was truly focusing on, maybe it would be my best chance.

I could hear my sister's voice in my mind. You're a star sissy, you are the light on that stage. Maybe after all this time, she was right. I mean, it was what Hound Dog kept telling me, and I'd let my own stubbornness and lack of self-confidence tell me otherwise.

The club was busier than ever, a mixture of tourists and regulars. Nevertheless, it wasn't going to stop me. Heavy with the flow of musicians and people aching to see them perform. I knew tonight was going to be a success.

When I told him we were leaving, he panicked, worried that Hound would wring his neck for not keeping me home. When I had to call B.B and tell him to make Woody calm down, the young prospect eased up and gladly followed along.

I parked his truck by the back entrance and walked out by the front. Woody, the prospect, was trailing behind me. He was a cute kid, like a little brother. His blonde mop still aged him young, but his sincerity and protectiveness made him wiser than anyone his age.

Woody frantically looked around before edging closer to me, like he was in some kind of security detail, afraid that I would be gone in a flash.

"Buddy, calm down." I tried to get him to chill out.

"I'm just trying to keep you in one piece," he blurted out.

I laughed, "I'm not a broken doll anymore. I won't break on your watch."

"I'm just not sure that Hound's going to like this."

"How about you let me handle Hound Dog, and you focus on just making sure we get through the door?" I coaxed him.

He nodded and pushed through people in front of us before coming up to the bouncers to let us in. Without hesitation, we walked through and my hands got a little sweaty. All the plans quickly became real. With my guitar case in my hand, my dress grazing the floor, I dismissed Woody to be free because soon I was going to be in the arms of Hound and soon on that stage that taunted me. Woody was worried but I waved him off.

My eyes scanned around the hustle and bustle of the place trying to find B.B or very least my man. Even in the warm lighting, it wasn't hard to find them as they draped along the bar top.

My heart should have been happy to easily find who my soul was calling to, but it shrank deep in my chest when I couldn't understand what I was seeing.

What I didn't fathom was a woman with a look of fierceness stalking toward Hound. I waited to see how it would play out because I knew he would ignore her or walk away or something. I set the guitar down by me as I leaned against the wall waiting for what would happen next.

I couldn't hear what they were saying, but it was a brief conversation that landed her nearly in Hound Dog's lap. Her lips smashed into his, and for a moment I thought he was going to shove her off even before she had the chance.

I didn't know if it was my mind playing tricks on me, allowing time to slow down, tormenting my mind into believing everything that I feared.

Hound gripped her arms, his hardened expression full of confusion.

Maybe it was a mistake to be there, maybe I shouldn't have seen what I saw. All air escaped my body, finding it hard to stay where I was, feet firmly planted on the ground. I turned and left, pushing past anyone who was at the door. I kept muttering apologies feeling the push back from patrons.

I rounded the corner, back toward a familiar alley that sent shivers down my body. My stomach churned, threatening to release the contents that boiled in the pit of my stomach. Burning tears that bubbled up to the corners of my eyes, I held them back for as long as I could. I breathed, finding the air I had lost.

He would never do that, allow someone to come near him, giving him a chance to dance with temptation. He was mine, he was always going to be mine.

Pull your shit together, go find that fucking bimbo, and pull out those fake extensions. He is yours.

I kept repeating that command over and over again.

I wasn't going to let some cheap trash take him from me. I wiped the tears of confusion and straightened up. My feet were trying to make their way back inside. I would say my peace and then continue what I planned to do.

Turning the corner, I ran into another person, their body felt as solid as a wall. I was knocked back a few steps and uttered a simple apology, only to look up and see the man had multiplied.

"Well, who do we have here? Pretty little thing aren't you?" the deep voice said, breathing his smoked-filled breath in my direction.

The men surrounded me, trapping me into a human barricade.

"Excuse me, I think you got the wrong impression."

"We know exactly who you are." another voice said behind me. "Time would tell when you would be alone, no guard dog following you."

My eyes became clear, looking at the clothing that was in front of me. No longer was it my nightmare, but Hound's. I pushed through them, attempting to yell out for help, but no one heard me. Someone had covered my mouth. I bit them, hard enough for one to grunt and slap me.

The sting of the hit shocked me. And yet the darkness from the very first night I met Hound circled my thoughts.

"Thought this was a simple snatch and grab, Prez never said she would be scrappy," one voice said.

"It's what happens when you become a little club whore, chasing dick, and having to fight for attention," another one taunted.

Any other time, I'd make a teasing comment about I'm only Hound's little slut in the bed, not in the present company.

Blood dripped from my mouth as the ache continued to pulse through my skin. And yet all I wanted to do was look up with a crimson smile on my face, challenging them to keep going because this little birdie had a hellhound that would set the world on fire and give me the match to watch it all burn.

I had to think of something to do, buy me some time until another brilliant idea struck me.

"If you know I'm nothing but a club whore, then why snatch me?" I said, attempting to derail them any further. I had to fight a little longer until someone could notice.

The light from the alley and street never gave me a clear view of who held me hostage, only could hear the gravel voices that made me wince in disgust. "We ain't stupid, if Prez said that you were important, then you're important. Now be a good little cunt and sleep for a while."

Sleep for a while? I didn't know what he meant until something pricked my skin at my neck. I tried to struggle against the two men that were holding me at my sides. My voice yelled, pleading for someone to hear me, save me.

But only one name was on my lips, Hound. I wasn't going to have him think I left him. As much as I was ready to and believe in the bad dream that was before me, I knew it wasn't true. Because in the end, we were in love, and he wouldn't hurt me like that. He wouldn't want me to think that someone else caught his eye, because I was the only one for him.

He wasn't going to know that the only name I said was his and his alone.

My silent screams burned my throat and a whole new darkness welcomed me and I only hoped that the darkness would let me see Hound's face one more time. If it was my time to go, then maybe I fulfilled my purpose of knowing that we were worthy of each other.

> *Never did I think that a man and a woman*
> *Could love each other like a wolf to the moon.*
> *And all I need is to know you howl*
> *Because I'll howl with you*
> *If it meant staying with the moon and the stars.*

He would never know.

Chapter 41

HOUND DOG

The amount of control on how much I wanted to throw everyone out of the club was teetering when no one could tell me where she was at. My brothers were scrambling the premises, and I waited for a sign to show me that everything was going to be okay.

My fingers itched to call in several favors. The phone burned in my hand, egging me on to do anything. Just when I thought I was going to give in, the right person was calling me.

"Greene, actually the person I needed to speak with. Look, we have a problem." I tried to tell him over the noise of the club. I slunk over to the corner, trying to hear him clearer. But I was catching every other word. "Sorry", "bail", "careful", "lawyer".

Nothing was making sense.

"Hold on, let me get out of here," I said, hauling ass outside away from the noise and the interference. "Okay, what were you telling me?"

"I'm sorry, Hound Dog, the Hogs made bail. Somehow they were careful and had a good lawyer or something. I think it was the judge, personally," Greene rambled on the phone.

My world turned to a dark red.

"What do you mean they made bail? The amount of charges on them should have prevented them from doing so." I couldn't understand how, or how deep their pockets were.

"I don't either, that's why I think it was the judge. I just got the news from Officer Daniels. He told me as soon as he found out.

I'm trying to see if we can't get another judge, but Hound, y'all may need to be careful."

I sighed. "Kind of hard right now. Melody is missing. And was just here."

"Here? Where? Hound, they can't have done this quickly. Unless," he said, dawning on the same thought I was.

"Unless they were already planning this in case they were arrested."

"Being proactive, not reactive. Fucking hell, Hound Dog." He groaned, probably just as frustrated as I was.

Greene kept apologizing and ultimately, it wasn't his fault, but the fault of the system that he trusted. Somewhere deep down I knew that it was too easy for the Hogs to go down. The original plan was to let justice work through, but justice wasn't enough. My deepest fear wasn't that the Hogs would come after the club, because hell it would be a battle that they would lose. But the greatest fear was leaving Melody vulnerable, unprotected.

The fear was eating me up inside, clawing through myself.

Greene kept rambling on and on about how sorry he was and that he would make it up to us, to the club. At that moment, I needed him as an ally. "I need you to work with Blaze. I'll have him come to the station, allow him access to whatever he needs. I don't care what strings or warrants you have to pull. Melody is not here and if you're telling me that the Hogs are roaming free, then the worst is already happening."

I hung up before he could protest or keep rambling on.

I couldn't stand there anymore and worry about what happened to her, I just needed to find her. Keep her safe from all these dangers that presented themselves. As I walked, there was something that caught my eye.

Her guitar case.

By the front door. It was true, it just confirmed that she saw everything. But she wouldn't leave her guitar case. Not when it meant so much to her.

What if she stepped out for air before she came back?

As much as I had hoped that would be true, I wasn't sure either. Maybe Melody didn't know what to say, but in the end it doesn't matter because I was bringing her ass home.

I tried her phone again and again, her melodic voice still answering the phone as her voicemail.

Where are you?

"Hound," a small voice called out. But when I turned it wasn't Melody. It was Sadie. "Please tell me I didn't miss her." Her eyes searched for her friend, and I didn't have the guts to tell her she was missing. I think she saw the look in my eyes because she stepped closer to me.

"Where is she, Hound?" she asked again.

I fell silent. Afraid to voice it to another person, making it harder to accept reality. Sadie took one look at my face and could read it like a book. There was no stopping her when she charged at me.

Sadie gave me a shove, her emotions riding high,.I didn't stop her, it wouldn't make up for the fact that I had no idea. "She said this wouldn't happen, that shit was taken care of."

She wasn't mad at me, although that was a contributing factor, she was afraid for her friend and the fate that waited for her.

"I'm sorry, Sadie, I'm trying to figure that out." I grasped her shoulders.

"I told her to be careful, but she assured me that she was the safest in your hands. Hound Dog, I prayed that was true." Sadie seethed with anger.

"Whatever happened to her, I will bring her back," I promised her like I promised Melody that I'd protect her.

I found Woody and instructed him to take Sadie to the compound. At the very least, if Melody contacted her, someone would be close by to deliver the message back to me. Sadie was hesitant, but she went.

My head continued to spiral, waiting on a sign or a plan. My hands itched to strangle someone, to shed blood on them. I was ready to explode.

B.B came running to me, nearly out of breath. He was hunched over, his hand collapsed on my shoulder.

"What?" I said, gruffly.

"Something you need to see," he said, pulling me to the back office.

The darkened office was only illuminated by the light of the main computer. It bright blue screen lit up from someone using it. I turned the corner of the desk, seeing the security screens pulled up. Twelve different angles, spanning from inside the bar to outside near the alley way and out front.

"What am I seeing?" I asked B.B.

He clicked on something and videos started to play out, the timestamp was nearly an hour or so ago. Before any of the musicians were taking the stage. He played one screen to focus on an interaction between the strange woman and a hooded figure, they knew where the camera angles were at, the fucking bastards.

The woman took the money and curled a smile on her lips. The fucking bitch was up to something. Moments passed, she looked at her phone and started to stalk near me. And then the infamous moment happened.

Another screen had shown the worst fear, the shocked, stunned face of Melody watching it all unfold. I saw her clutch her chest before rampaging through people. Her small frame turned into a bulldozer. B.B switched the camera feed to around the corner near the alley way.

I saw all the emotions as though it hit me as well, her chest heaving for breath. Her body was shivering, probably feeling like she was going to bust from all the emotions clawing at her. Then my brave girl stood up, straightening her back. She wiped the tears away before turning the corner. I thought she was a blessed angel, her long dress cascading on the ground. She was a pure vision, but horror struck me.

The chair was pushed forcibly behind me. My fists clenching seeing four men with the Hogs patch on their back, surrounding her like a trap gazelle in a pride of lions. I didn't have the audio, but the fear in Melody's eyes was enough to know they were hurting her.

But one thing, her expression changed from scared to taunting, the same mischievous face when she was up to no good. What she said only pissed whoever the person in front of her off, he laid a forceful hand on her. Her head jerked to the side.

I wanted nothing more than to jump through the screen. Her head swayed back, facing the men. The blood dripped at the corner of her mouth. She struggled against the two guys at her side, fighting with everything that she had.

The Hogs fucking nicked her, they were drugging her. Everything in me wanted to scream, wanted to throw something, break something.

It was a fucking trap, a fucking ploy.

"We'll get her back."

"This is all my fault," I whispered.

"The fuck you mean it's your fault? How?" B.B questioned me.

The running list of reasons why it was my fault

I stormed out, ignoring all the rational thoughts of taking it one step at the time. I was ready to enlist Blaze to help me burn it all down. Allow all the demons in me to take over, that's all I thought.

I got on my bike, heading to the compound to find Blaze, knowing that he and Greene were supposed to be working on finding her. Everything was a blur around me, because I only had one thought, one motivation.

I had gone back to my room, rummaging through the weapons that I had. I was going to get her back, and most likely my way.

It was a war that I was preparing for, and I wasn't taking any hostages.

A light down the hallway caught my eye as I tried to leave.

Why the fuck was Blaze here?

Blaze was engrossed in whatever he was viewing, along with Sadie that sat close to the screens. To have a friend like that, that would just insert themselves to help with anything someone needed, I was at least grateful.

"You better tell me that you have something? A location, a direction?" I demanded, busting down the door to Blaze's room. The room was cascaded in LED lights, his freckled face illuminated by the amount of screens that were running. Blaze was a genius, sometimes a little afraid to speak to me. But overall, he was a good kid, even if I have to worry about him with a matchbook or a lighter.

He looked back at me with his thick rimmed glasses, the curl of a smile told me he found something useful. Sadie shot me an angered look.

A group of footsteps pounded through the hallway, pushing through the doorway. B.B and Fender sounded out of breath. I didn't know anyone was following me, but that's what happens when your body is following the rage in your mind.

"They definitely crossed state lines, I'd been running my program to follow them through the CCTV allowed me access." Blaze pointed out.

"Greene didn't need you at the station?" I questioned.

Blaze shrugged. "You really want that answer, or the fact that we'll have a location in less than five minutes."

Time was already ticking away, and someone once said that it was better to ask forgiveness than permission. All my senses begged for an answer now.

B.B huffed out a breath, "Prez, I'm asking you to stop and think."

"Not this time. How many times has the Hogs been one to cause this much chaos? How many times do we have to look over our shoulder, pausing on our way of life? How many times are we going to allow them to have us worry about another loved one like Melody being taken or worse, possibly end up dead? I am thinking, B.B. And I'm choosing her, I'm choosing the club not having to look over their shoulder every step they take. I choose our city, one that the chapter has built." The words flowed through me like a wave of truth.

"What you're asking is a massacre, ending more than one person's life," Fender defended.

Short answer was yes, I was expecting that there would be no survivors. I'd shoulder that for the rest of my life if it meant the safety of everyone.

B.B shook his head, finding it hard to believe that we'd come this far in our lives. "Well, I don't think a lot of people will have a problem with it?"

I shot him a look. "What the fuck do you mean?"

B.B only nodded down the hallway, my steps were small, afraid to see what he meant. As I approached the common area, a smile couldn't help but be placed on my face.

A united front of brothers, every one of them packing heat. And to my surprise, Greene was behind them as well. My brothers were standing, waiting for an order to move out.

"You really think you'd do this alone?" Shooter asked.

"We all agreed with you," Hank chimed in.

"All you had to do was trust us," Reverend said. I was shocked that he'd be a part of this.

I turned back to B.B as he plastered a cocky grin on his face.

"Sometimes your way is also the way we think, you forget that we are a club, not everything is on you," B.B said.

"Also, she's one of us," Otis added.

"And a woman like that is worth all the consequences, especially if she melted away that frozen heart of yours." Twitty chuckled

"I'm asking a lot, and partially selfish, and y'all are okay with that?" I asked.

They all nodded.

Sadie stepped from the side, her arms folded across her chest. "You underestimate the power she has over people. She's a lot like you, thinking of others before themselves."

Melody was not like me. But if she could take on a ruthless, unhinged motorcycle club and make her mark on us, that was enough for others to not blink an eye for her.

There was no going back. What was going to be done, would be done.

Someone cleared their throat. "Seems like this would be the time to tell you, I got a location, and you're not going to be happy."

Chapter 42

MELODY

I didn't know what was worse, the hangover I got when I turned twenty one, or waking up disoriented, surrounded by a deranged, revenge seeking rival club.

My head didn't know what to think, it was fuzzy. The only thing I could remember was screaming for help and the thought of Hound Dog on my mind.

Oh fuck. Hound. No, this was not supposed to happen.

I forced myself to find the strength to have a clearer mind, wake up my senses, and figure out what was happening to me. I didn't have to think hard about the people that grabbed me, the evidence was on their chest. My hope was that Hound was ruthless enough and blinded enough by love that any moment, as my mind came to be, that he would be blasting through a figurative door and saving me.

That, or I would be woken up from the nightmare of being drugged and taken and welcomed by the sight of him between my thighs with a hunger like no other.

Alas, as my eyesight became clearer, I was still surrounded by darkness. I knew I wasn't blind as moonlight and the faint light across the surrounding area shined in. I felt the tension at my feet and my back. By the sensation I was feeling, I was bound at the wrists and ankles.

Fucking typical. Just like a damsel in distress.

Could no one think of anything else other than to tie the woman up and wait?

I could hear the faintest of water sounds, but couldn't tell whether it was coming from inside or outside. There was an echo, I could hear myself grunt as I tugged on the restraints. It felt like one of those cliches that happens in movies right before the hero came to save the damsel.

And yet there I was playing the role of the damsel. All that was missing was a volcano and a machine that would be lowering me down to my plummeting death.

Melody has an active imagination while doped up.

"I see why Hound Dog would be so infatuated by you," a voice boomed from my loopy thoughts.

I whipped my head around, attempting to find the voice, but not even the shadows came out to be revealed.

A whole new panic spread over me, the fear of dying too quickly. There was a sudden sharp pain in my head, not from someone hitting me, more like a side effect or something. I wasn't a nurse or a doctor, but it certainly was worse than a hangover.

My heart started to beat out of my chest. My muscles were still weak, although they felt heavy like I was carrying around weights.

"What the bitch doesn't have a bite anymore? Pity."

I'd had enough people calling me names for a lifetime, and at that rate it was getting annoying. "You got anything better than "bitch"? Cause just saying bitch sounds outdated and sometimes a compliment. Are you complimenting me?" I laughed, still a little out of it from whatever they hit me with.

"I liked you better when you were knocked out," the voice fought back.

"Yeah, and only a coward would wish someone was unconscious just so they could say they won. Newsflash, buddy, you didn't. Whatever your plan with me is, it won't work," I taunted them.

My hope was that I wasn't proved wrong. I knew Hound would choose me over the club, but his dedication to the club would rule over anything.

A hand splayed through my hair, gripping a handful of it. "And yet I know it will, he would never pass up a chance to take back this sweet ass. He must fuck you like a rag doll."

Fight, Melody, fuck everything anyone has ever said about you. Fight back, don't falter.

The rancid smell from his body hit my senses, making my face scrunch, like it would do it any good. The man sniffed me. My stomach twisted in disgust.

"Well, at least he knows how to use his dick unlike you with your pencil dick." I hissed, and as expected was rewarded with a smack across the face. Then a hand wrapped around my throat, taking all the air from me. My body squirmed, fighting him off. His fingers dug into my skin.

Everything around me became dizzier, the world's most unbalanced carnival ride.

"Enough, Stetson," another voice demanded.

Stetson, the man whose hand was around my throat, only squeezed tighter. His one track mind disobeyed whoever the other person was, challenging him.

"I said enough," the voice growled out.

Stetson let go of my throat, shoving my head forward. My lungs fought back with the inhalation of air. If I wasn't going to die from lack of oxygen, I felt like it was going to be the opposite.

I coughed, feeling even worse than I did when I woke up.

"I'm sorry about him, he doesn't take kindly to a Saint's ol' lady, regardless if they're a little wallflower like you." The other mysterious man came to view.

The man crouched down to look at me as my head still hung over. His finger lifted my chin. A familiar face, I couldn't place him.

He took a cloth and wiped whatever stickiness was on my face, and I felt the lip of a cup touch my bottom lip.

"Take a sip," he demanded.

I wasn't dumb, I wasn't going to take a chance. He saw the stubbornness in my face, and took a sip for himself, showing that it was safe. He pressed the lip of the cup back to my mouth. The cool water slid down my throat.

"You're wasting your time," my voice scratched out.

He smirked. "I don't think so, and we both know that."

"Using me as bait seems a little too obvious, doesn't it?"

"Hound must have done a number on you, they said you were shy, always stuck in the shadows. What happened?" the man questioned.

Just that, Hound opened me up.

"Guess I grew up," I snarked back.

"I like you," the man chuckled, and then started to walk away, "Too bad that tonight will be your last night."

"Kind of figured, you don't seem like the type to just let me go."

The clinking of metal whipped my head in the same direction as him. "Not only that, but there's something poetic about watching the love of your life die before your life is taken."

My heart sank.

"You don't mean that."

There was a clicking of a gun. "Oh, I do. That club has tried to take everything from me, from my club. They were supposed to run away. Leave Memphis, but I think Hound found a little more... motivation. What did they say? That he found a little birdie with clipped wings. That she batted her eyelashes, and captured something precious to him."

The man turned around, the gun flashing under the pale light. Sweat dripped down my back.

"So, in reality, I think that was you. I think that you showed him that he had to go to extreme measures to make sure that you would never be harmed. So, when a little roadblock like you gets in our way from taking over, we just have to take care of it."

I could have begged, I could have bartered with him and then found a way out of it. I could have stood my ground, waited until there was a sign of light.

He kept going on, filling the silence. "You wanna know the moment when the Saints knew that Hound Dog would be their next president?"

He was turning Hound Dog into a villain. Only I knew it wouldn't work. I shook my head to his question. "When Hound Dog took out my president. Killing him in cold blood. When he showed his club that he would do anything for them, even kill, taking the chance to minimize threats, they knew that he would do anything for the club, therefore making him president when it was time. Sure, it's been a couple of years or so, but it only fueled our hatred and our burning desire to take everything from them.

"This would be the part where you beg for a chance to see him again before the lights of your life fade away." He said, dragging the cool metal across my bare skin.

A voice in my head told me that time wouldn't be on my side and perhaps the man wouldn't keep his word. I had to decide whether it was worth Hound seeing me alive but taken right in front of him, or give him mercy and take away the potential scarring memory of watching me die.

I never thought about death, whether I was scared of it or would welcome it. In tense moments and uncertainty, fear won. I guess any normal day I'd say that I'd welcome it, knowing that maybe if it was my time, my purpose was fulfilled.

Maybe I needed to welcome the thought, maybe my purpose was showing Hound that love was possible if you fought for it rather than run from it.

I wanted to buy more time, there was still an ounce of hope.

"Would it matter, in the end my life would be over and you wouldn't have leverage over Hound Dog? Killing me in the end would give you less power over him."

The gun stopped at my chest, my chest heaved and moved the weapon with it. The man thought for a moment. "Sounds like you're stalling."

"Sounds like you want to lose in the end." I sneered back.

"I hold the control," he fought back, pressing the gun into my skin.

"Not if you pull the trigger early. Rookie mistake of a hostage take over. You're living the stereotypical action stories, where the villain doesn't think. If you kill me at all, you'd unleash the beast that's inside him. Think about your former president, think about how you felt and the anger that made y'all relentless. You really want that for Hound Dog and the club?" I tried to appease his sense of purpose, but even as I spoke those words they tasted bitter, so wrong for me to even think of saying them.

The gun lifted under my chin, testing my nerves. I stared into those dark, soulless eyes of my captor.

His dark eyes transformed into something cynical like many ideas rapid fired in this brain.

"I can see why Hound Dog is so enamoured with you, someone so innocent, begging to be a little slut," he said.

Was that supposed to thrill me? Or scare me?

No, it was disgusting.

"Tick tock, buddy." I rolled my eyes.

Tick, tock indeed, because I didn't know how much time was left nor what else was to come from being around this man.

I also didn't know how much more I could show that I wasn't afraid or that I wasn't this fearless person.

Before I knew it, the man's hand wrapped tightly around my throat, and my eyes started to flutter to welcome a new kind of darkness.

Chapter 43

HOUND DOG

I never considered myself a warrior, a soldier. Maybe a protector, maybe a killer. But never one to say I was a soldier ready for a battle, not when I was ready to win a war and take no prisoners.

"An empty warehouse by the river shouldn't be too far. They knocked out any cameras on the property, but nearby street cameras show people by the main entrance, and possibly surrounding the warehouse." Blaze relayed as we mounted the bikes.

The rev of the engines shot a sense of power and avenge. I knew that it would be a bloodbath, one had been coming for a long time. Too much time has gone by since the threat of the Hogs and I wasn't going to have that in our futures.

They took someone that belonged to me, one that I promised to keep safe.

My mind has spun with the past few hours. I could only assume that the woman that threw herself on me was paid off by the Hogs and she waited until they told her when the time was right. The time that Melody would witness everything and make her vulnerable.

She wasn't going to run away, she was going to come back. She was going to confront me, my brave woman. But I wasn't going to let her down again. I was also tempted to never let her go again. Wherever I go, she would go with me. And vice versa.

Fender started the ride, leading us down and out past the city. The parade of chrome shined in the night, sending a message of terror and anguish to all those who watched us.

We had agreed to be down a block or two. Blaze had stayed behind, only to be our eyes when we didn't know where to go, aside from the darkened streets.

There was a fire coursing through my veins.

As we parked down the way from the warehouse, Blaze sent a message stating that the east entrance wasn't as occupied and the weakest in entrances. A quarter of us would take the east entrance and others around the other way.

Reverend had offered to stay behind in case a twist in events were to happen. I didn't know how much pull the Hogs had, or alliances. But I also knew that Reverend wouldn't take a life unless it was desperate measures. But he would take the pain from others or be there to shoulder the "sin". He'd try to keep the peace as much humanly possible.

Shooter offered a sneak attack approach as we dismantled the east entrance, we'd sneak behind and open the other entrance.

All I knew was that I was ready to charge like a bull. A beast inside ready to do some damage.

"There's no going back, Hound. Risk everything for blood and her," Otis reminded me

I looked up from loading my gun, giving him a wide-eyed look, "Never said it wasn't a risk, and I'm sure as hell not turning back."

Otis just nodded, following my lead down the streets along with Hank, Stray, and Blue.

Blaze's information was accurate, the amount of people at the east entrance were limited and easy targets. Seeing their patch swarming the place only made my blood boil. Stray stepped in front of me, propping his weapon with a silencer on a trash can. Stray took a moment to find the aim we needed to start taking them out one by one.

With one slow breath, one of the medium sized members dropped like deer shot in hunting season. The dead member's partner started to whip his head back and forth, looking for a sign of who fired.

Shooter had reminded us that it would be over too quickly, and before we knew it, it would be us that would be kissing the gravel or an early grave. Before the other man yelled for help, Stray popped another bullet, shooting him straight in the temporal lobe. He dropped down to the ground the same as his friend.

There was another one hidden, but they hadn't come into the light.

I was running out of time and patience. The longer we stood there waiting like hunting season, the less time to make sure Melody was alive. My impatience took over, but I was yanked back down before I could bolt.

Blue, a man of very few words, looked at me and just said. "Wait."

I wanted to fight back, but the words never came. That was until the third member came around the warehouse corner, shocked at the sight of two men plastered on the ground. Stray wasted no time and quickly took the shot.

The last member we saw dropped to the ground. No more were coming. I confirmed with Blaze that there were only three over here, and he assured me that there weren't any more.

I knew the Hog's numbers were dwindling close enough for just a board and a few members, but there was only one person that I was concerned about meeting the mouth of my gun.

Saber. The only man that would dare try anything.

The four of us moved quickly, staying somewhat low to the ground. The other entrance was going to be yards away. I signaled for Blue and Stray to move on, to meet Shooter and B.B on the other side.

Otis stood behind me, as I stalked toward a small opening that was a little too quiet for my liking.

"Why does this feeling too fucking easy?" Otis remarked. I couldn't blame his paranoia because I agreed. This opening of the warehouse was a little too easy to get through. Everything in me was shouting that this was a trap, and someone was the bait.

A little light was shone in the entryway, but nothing else mattered as the sight of Melody flooded my mind.

Her beautiful body was limp and bound. Her hair looked knotted like someone touched it, but I couldn't tell her other injuries. For all I knew, whatever she was dosed with may not have worn off. I had hoped she was breathing. I had checked to see if there was anyone hiding before taking a few steps toward her.

I'm here, songbird.

It wasn't until we were halfway in the warehouse that Melody's head lolled from side to side before snapping up to look at us. I couldn't make out her full expression, but I could see her shaking her head.

A clicking of a readied gun stopped us dead in our tracks. Our bodies froze, straightening up to peek at who dared to stand in our way. My way.

But a sinister laugh pulled my attention, Saber switched on a light that shined brighter, illuminating the space, illuminated the rough spots on Melody's body, smears of blood, and her clothes exposing more skin than I liked.

Saber lit a cigarette, finally taking a step from the side, but with a hunting knife by his side. A cloud of smoke swirled around him, as he made his way toward Melody.

Her eyes started to well up with tears. It took everything in me to not dart to her.

"Well, darling girl, I think you were right. It was better to have that power and control. It just feels so good," he said, stepping behind Melody, trailing his hand along her neck and down her torn open shirt. Her body contorted at the touch. "Fell into a trap so easily. You said he'd come and that it was better to leave you alive, using his one weakness against him."

She wouldn't help him. The way he spoke made it seem like it was a long time plan.

"Hound," she whispered, "I'm sorry. I tried to buy you time..." Her voice cracked from the raw emotions bubbling in her throat.

Saber interrupted, "Oh, she's being a little modest. Told me to use her to control you, thought it would be that you'd give up easily. Cause you wouldn't want any harm to come to her, though.," hHe pressed the cigarette still burning in his hand into her collarbone. "She bleeds so easily."

Melody held back the painful screams. The butt of the cigarette burned into her skin. He discarded the stick and pulled the knife to her throat.

"One would say she's a perfect little plaything." He smiled.

I pointed my gun toward him, but the person behind us stepped further to Otis's back. I glanced behind to see Stetson, a troublesome soul, point his gun at Otis's head.

"Let her go, if you want me then take me,." I offered. But he only laughed.

He bent closer to Melody's ear. "What a noble thing. But you know, Melody, why would he say something like that, not when a little minx was sucking face with him, just hours ago. She's more what he wants. More to offer."

"Melody, don't listen to him," I tried to remain calm.

"Oh, but it's true, you saw. I mean, the timing was perfect. I mean almost like fate."

"Honey, you know what I've said. You and me." I couldn't think of the right words.

She cracked a soft smile, she knew.

"You believe this? This man would even let a woman like that girl approach him. He could have walked away."

All kinds of fire burned in me, he was trying to taint her way of thinking. He continued, "I mean, he has you to thank. I mean those messages with B.B, letting us know your every step, made it all the easier to show you the truth."

"What truth?" she asked.

"That bitches are easily replaced, thrown out like trash."

I stepped closer, but Otis grunted as he took a hit to his body. I twisted around, seeing him on his knees.

"I wouldn't do that. It's one thing to choose her over your club, but choosing over a long time friend and brother over a girl you fawned over," he hissed.

I had a few ideas that popped in my head, ones that I didn't know if it would work out.

"Well, now that you're here, let's talk about what happens next. If you want this cunt alive, leave Memphis, I don't care where you go, but Memphis is ours. I'll leave with her and if you follow through then, I'll return her." There was a sinister smile that told me that she wouldn't.

"Not going to happen."

He sighed. "Pity that you had to make this harder than it needed to be."

There was a slight commotion outside of the warehouse. A few guns fired in the background, I snapped my eyes to see Saber worry, almost falter, not knowing if a force would be coming through those doors.

He lowered the knife toward her side, then wrapped his arm across her chest, "No matter what is going on outside, it doesn't mean you win."

I focused on Melody, her eyes stared back at me. Her breathing became steady and her arms started twitching. My gun started to shake a bit in my hands

"There is no way out, you and your men are fucking pathetic thinking that you will win. We built a case with your name in it. It may not be your fault, but your club's name is tainted, for anyone to pin something else on you. We were here long before you, and we'll keep coming back. There is no way out."

Saber sounded like what he was: a desperate man rambling on, trying to grasp a sense of dignity, thinking that in the end he would end this battle, when the war would be over.

She puffed out her chest. Her small voice was powerful against the noise outside. A small smile lit up her face. "Remember when I said that you wouldn't want to unleash the beast if you killed me."

"You're lucky that you're still breathing." He sneered.

"Well, be prepared for a reckoning, you'll need all the air," she said before her arms snaked out from her bindings, wrapping her hands around his hand over the knife.

It was quick.

Melody thrusted the knife, slashing her side along the way, and shoved up into Saber's chest. My voice roared and all time stood still.

I didn't know what commotion was happening behind me, all I knew was that Otis had swept Stetson's legs from under him, and Stetson ended up with a bullet in his skull.

Melody fell to the side, hitting the wet gravel under her. A dark pool of another wetness spilled on the ground.

I rushed to her side, ignoring Saber screaming from the pain, slowly writhing away.

I shook my head, this wasn't supposed to happen. It should have been me in the place, the one lying on the ground. I whipped off my cut and the long sleeve flannel. I rolled the flannel, applying pressure to the wound.

I cradled her head, shook her a bit to wake her up. Her eyes fluttered open, and that beautiful smile warmed me with hope. "Hey baby."

"You realize that was stupid." I choked out the words. I wanted to be mad at her, but she proved that I could never underestimate her.

She chuckled. "Never said I was the smartest. I mean that's not a deal breaker is it?"

"Oh, someone's got jokes." I played along. I should have taken it as a good sign that she was joking, cracking jokes in a time like that.

"Well, if I ain't got the brains, I guess I'll be the funny one in the relationship." She coughed.

I didn't know how else to help her. I needed to find Shooter or Fender. I saw the glimpse of Otis running to the other side of the building, hoping that he was trying to find someone.

"You know I wrote you a song." She broke my attention.

I imagined she was, the way she would stare at me randomly with the lovesick look in her eyes. I nodded. "Yeah. I hoped you did. You gotta sing it for me one day."

She took a ragged breath, "Little girls dream of princes, ones that would whisk to the great unknown.

I kissed her hard, stopping her because I knew what she was trying to do. But I felt her humming against my lips. She pulled away.

"Please," she pleaded.

"No, honey, you'll sing it to me when you're ready."

This wasn't going to be her goodbye.

Her dirty, probably wounded hand cupped my cheek. I leaned into her touch. "Why is it that music has been easier around you?"

"Guess you needed a teacher."

"No, I didn't. A teacher can come and go, but you, Nash, are a forever thing." She continued, "I didn't need a teacher, guess I just needed you, the person that sees me for everything that I am."

I hugged her tighter, keeping the flannel in place.

"Just to think you saved me from fire all those years ago and see you're still saving me."

A thunderous parade of footsteps grew louder. One soul that rushed to the side. A glimpse of Shooter was breathing heavily, a little splatter of someone's blood across his face, and yet the sight of him filled me with joy.

"I'll always see you, Melody." I rested my forehead on hers.

"Hound, I..." she started to say, but I silenced her with another hard kiss, wiping away any thought of her saying she loved me before I could say it first. She wasn't going to say it as if it was her last goodbye.

Because in reality, if she was actually dying, so would I.

A world without Melody would be a world without the sun on your face warming you, giving everything and anything that was good.

"Let her go, man, I got her," Shooter tried to coax me to let go.

One thing was for sure, I would never let her go. I didn't think any one of us would be able to let her go. No one wanted to have the hardest goodbye.

Chapter 44

HOUND DOG

After letting loose of Melody, all the rush of adrenaline returned. My focus turned toward Saber. The pathetic excuse of skin hunched over in pain. A crowd of my men came with a few hostages in tow.

I bent down to the ground, facing toward Saber. Saber tried to scoot away from me, kicking his feet, dragging himself across the ground.

"Why try Saber? You signed your death warrant the moment you threatened my ol' lady," I said.

His soft whimpers attempted to latch on to any kind of hope.

B.B crept up behind me and handed me my gun, the one I had dropped when rushing to Melody. "One of the prospects and Blue's ol' lady are on the way with one of the trucks. Greene offered a police escort, he'll spin a story," B.B said.

It wasn't going to be too long before Melody could get to a hospital. I begged silently that she would be able to hang on long enough. My hands were still painted with her blood, it was enough fire to end it once and for all.

"Make sure they put me down as an emergency contact, I don't need anyone stopping me once we're done here." I commanded.

"What we gonna do about this lot?" B.B's sinister voice echoed.

I straightened up, slowly walked over to Saber. His body trailed a line of blood. "I'm done worrying about every step they take."

I walked past a line of men with their hands behind their backs, with sneers that I was the evil one. And maybe I was because I would unleash a cleansing. Just then, a truer evil thought passed my mind. "Get Reverend, he should be here for the last rites. A true, proper end to the era of the Hogs."

It wasn't a punishment for Reverend, but a chance to ensure true purity would be here. I wasn't playing God, but I did feel close to it.

Before I knew it, Saber tried to find a "weapon" of some sort. I stepped on his wrist. "Still thinking that you can find your way out of this?"

Reverend stepped up beside me. "Prez."

"Do you think there is any redemption in the evil of this world?" I asked.

"Depends on which version of you're asking. As a spiritual leader, I have to have faith that we all can be redeemed. But if you're asking me as a brother, witnessing the pain and truth of this evil, no amount of redemption could save them. Their fate was sealed." Finally he said something we could agree on.

I glanced over my shoulder to see Blue's ol' lady and Woody helping Shooter cart off Melody. Her practically lifeless body sent an ache in my chest. As soon as the tail lights faded in the night, there was nothing that was going to stop me.

I signaled two of the guys to pick up Saber, holding him. His grunts and groans were like a symphony. Blood kept dripping from his chest. The wound wasn't straight to the heart, that would be too good for him. His head bobbed back and forth. His beady eyes appeared so helpless.

B.B and Reverend stood behind me, waiting for orders.

First step would be preparing the bodies and then light the place up like a funeral pyre.

I took his head, pulling it back. Because the last thing he'd see when he meets his end is my face, knowing that the man that he craved to take down would be his undoing.

"You don't deserve any of this, you deserve the levels of hell." I hissed. "Your own envy and pride caused your end. Not me, not my brothers. I wonder what the soul feels when the guilt of your own club dying from your stupidity would feel like."

Reverend started to mutter prayers and rites, but I only asked that the souls be buried down in hell. There was no rite they deserved, not after all blood that they spilled, every innocent life they took by pinning drug overdoses on innocent artists.

One by one, each of the brothers ended each Hog's life. Tears, sweat, and even piss spilled on the floor once each had dropped to the floor. Gunshots echoed in the warehouse, like a clashing cymbal.

Saber struggled against my men holding him. The horror of each one of them dying by our hands finally scared him, knowing that he was going to be next.

When the last member dropped to the ground, my gaze turned to him. Reverend finished his last prayer. I knew one thing for sure, I would never turn back and regret this moment.

As each of my brothers stepped away from the fallen bodies and stood behind me, there was no greater feeling or act of vengeance compared to that.

"I win, motherfucker. Saint's will forever reign in Memphis. See you in hell." With that, I delivered one final blow to his head, the light disappeared from his eyes.

The wash of relief rushed over me. I let go of the breath I was holding back for so long. One that I held the moment Melody came into my life and the moment that I knew trouble was brewing.

I could have released my anger in so many ways. I could have lasted his torture a lot longer.

I holstered my gun.

"It's done, boys," I said.

"Time to light it up," B.B announced. "Y'all know what to do, make the bodies unrecognizable, no traces left behind. In and out."

"We don't need to be here any longer than we need to be." Fender added.

I stared at Saber's body, waiting for a moment of doubt, that I would awake from this dream and still be living in a nightmare. That moment never came.

I knew that our chapter would be like any other chapter, we'd do anything for the club, to show that no one would take what we had away. We'd do anything to show power, control.

I'd beg for forgiveness rather than ask for permission later if needed.

I knew our consequences would come after, I'd be prepared for anything, even if it was the mother chapter coming after my ass for a dumbass move.

Time had passed and the brothers and I stood outside the gates, this would be the moment that everything would be final.

No dead to be risen from their watery graves. No outside threats that we knew of coming after us or pinning something on us.

Maybe for a while, we would go back to breathing without having to glance over our shoulders.

Someone tapped on my shoulder, pulling me from my thoughts. Reverend stood there, with a match in his hands.

"Cleanse by fire?" he asked.

"A means to an end." I said, striking the match and dropping it in the puddle of lighter fluid. I wasn't going to leave until I knew that building would come down.

The fire grew like a hungry monster, consuming everything. Fire blazed across the warehouse, latching on with its fiery hands. The dark red and orange of the blaze sent a rush of heat.

It's wrong to think that this was a glorious sight, but I never said I was right.

It felt like justice. It felt like the start of a new life.

B.B clasped a hand on my shoulder. "Time to go, brother."

"We fucking did it, B.B."

He chuckled. "Wow, did the infamous Hound Dog just say we?

"Asshole."

"Dickhead."

"Do you regret me coming into your bar that night? Pulling you into all of this?" I asked. I'd never asked B.B if he regretted it, but all that we'd been through the past decade or so, I never wanted any brother to feel like they regretted being patched in nor me being president.

"They always said that when opportunity comes knocking, don't ignore it. Well, it was hard to ignore when you busted the hinges," B.B joked. A small smirk plastered on my face. "Listen, Hound. We're given this one life, and we make it the best we can. If that meant that I needed to trust my friend, then I trusted my friend."

"Even when we accidentally set your ass on fire," I couldn't resist mentioning the moment that B.B did question what he got himself into.

"Even then, plus I got a little sexy burn that makes women stop and stare," he said cockily.

"Sure, that's what they're staring at," I joked.

"Oh, Hound, you know what they're staring at." I knew the fucker probably had winked at me. "Don't worry, there's only one person that I'd let stare at me with no limits."

That was going to be another discussion for another day.

I couldn't stay around any longer. I had someone more important to see.

Chapter 45

MELODY

If you'd told me that I'd risk my life more than once for the man I loved, I'd have said that you'd be on mushrooms. But I'd call myself a liar, seeing how my life had unfolded.

All I could remember was the pain in Hound's eyes as he cradled me, trying to stop the bleeding. All I knew was that I tried. I tried to hang on to everything, buy him time to end it all. Taking the knife through my side was not a part of my plan, but when push came to shove, it was the only chance I had.

I knew in the end someone's blood was going to be spilled, I just made the first move. Maybe it cost me more than I imagined but I did it. And most likely would do it again, minus being kidnapped and drugged.

I remembered my "almost" declaration of my love for him, almost singing to him, but after that, my mind went blank.

I never saw a light, or the ghost of Aria waiting for me. I dreamed. My mind played versions of Hound and me in our home, in our bed, in his arms. Dreams of a little one chasing after Hound and breaking his heart when they gravitated toward a drum kit. Dreams of laughter of Otis and B.B being some of the best uncles. Stray and Hank making sure I could still hit hard.

But, one that was always on repeat, was me and my guitar on that stage, and seeing Hound Dog in the audience just smiling, in full awe and wonder.

I didn't know if they were visions or wishes of the heart. Regardless of what they were, they were happy ones, ones that you never wanted to let go or have someone take away from you.

I never had a blood family after Aria passed, never rekindled a relationship with my father. What I did find was a found family, one I never was looking for or thought I desired. I had Sadie and that was all.

Hound Dog was my family.

The Saints were my family.

I didn't want to lose them when I just got them.

The sounds of machines beeping steadily stirred me, my eyes fluttered to the dim lights. Everything was bright and white, easily confused with the "bright light" everyone talks about. My head turned to find a window or something to focus on.

Windows showed the cascade of darkness. Why did everything hurt? I thought I just nicked my side, but it felt like my body was made of stone and every movement I had was harder than the last.

How long was I out? What happened?

A million thoughts swarmed in my head.

"Melody," a sweet voice called.

Sadie.

I tried to find my voice, but no words came out. A vision of dark hair and curves came into view. Sadie's blurred face twisted in overwhelming emotions. She held back a sob. I tried to move my hand to reach out to her.

"Sweet girl," another voice echoed. A voice that was like a warm hug.

Mama Mary.

"O..kay," I croaked out.

"Yes, my dear, everything is okay," Mama Mary comforted me.

"Sa.." I tried to call my friend.

"It's okay, don't try to speak." Sadie sobbed.

Jesus, did people think I wasn't going to make it? It wasn't that bad of a cut. Not like Saber. I hoped that the blade had melted into his chest. A bit dramatic, or maybe that was the pain medicine that I hoped my I.V was hooked up to.

I tried to clear my throat, Mama Mary came to my side again with some water. The cool liquid slides down my throat, it feels weird.

Something was missing, more like someone.

My eyes darted around the room. Mary Mama laughed, placing the cup back on the side table. "Don't worry, I had to send him home briefly, the boy was starting to smell. I mean, it didn't help that he looked rough to begin with."

He was here, he was okay. At least that was what I thought.

Sadie pushed a piece of my curls behind my ear. "You can't do that to me again," she warned. I cocked my head, not understanding. Like I had a choice in the matter. She shook her head, "You can't leave me lonely."

"Now you're sounding like him," I croaked out.

"How?"

"Possessive." I chuckled.

"Seriously, Melody. You can't risk your life anymore. You have too many people that love you and need you."

"Like you?"

"Like me," she said, taking my hand, squeezing it tight.

"She's not wrong. I mean you should have seen the club taking up the entire waiting room. Shooter even had heart balloons and Fender was holding a stuffed animal. Your little nurse, Amelia, had to tell them to leave and make room for the other families." Mary Mama laughed, getting comfortable in the lounger.

"How did you two?" I started, then coughed. Why was it so damn hard to talk?

But Sadie finished, "How are we in the room and not the hulking caveman?"

I nodded.

"We said we were family," Sadie said without missing a beat. She raised her hand. "Sister."

"Mother," Mary acknowledged.

Found family. A love that fills the holes in your heart from the hurt from the past. There was a warmth in my heart.

They would do that for me, be there for me whenever I needed someone the most, and without the expectation of it.

I couldn't hold back my tears, but this time they were tears of happiness.

"When is he.." I started.

Mary finished. "Coming back? As soon as he looks like a human being. As for the others, B.B told them to rest for a while. Everyone needed it."

"How..." I started to ask, but Sadie chimed in, reading my mind, "How long have you been out? Almost two days."

"And we almost lost you on the table," another bright voice chimed in. A small, blonde with a pixie cut and a full arm sleeve of tattoos came to the computer, logged into, then grabbed the stethoscope that draped from the IV pole.

Her badge read "Amelia" and I had to hold back laughter imagining this woman telling a bunch of bikers to leave the hospital. I doubted there was a lot of sugar in her voice.

"You scared off my bikers," I said, my voice still raspy.

"Scared is an extreme way of putting it." She giggled.

"Shooter tried to tell her off, and she stood her ground, had that "go ahead and try me, buddy. I'll kick your ass" look." Mama Mary explained.

Amelia waved off Mary as she took my vitals; the cold metal made me shiver.

While the ambience was nice to wake up to, I wanted one person holding me right then.

"That man of yours, though. Girl, better hold on to him. I mean what a fiancé." Amelia gave me a look of approval, pursing her lips.

Did she say fiancé?

"He's not..." I tried to say, but she cut me off. She pressed a finger to her lips like she knew it was a lie.

When she finished, she crossed her arms, swaying her hips. "So, how about I let your medical team know you're awake and we can do something about that catheter. Cause girl, there's nothing sexy about having that in and reuniting with your man."

I nodded.

Then a flush of embarrassment rushed to me. I didn't think about that, nor felt it. Sadie laughed seeing my face. Her laughter died down when she said, "Don't worry we'll give you a sponge bath before he comes rolling in."

Within hours, after feeling less like a human experiment, and a little more pain medication hitting my system and a sponge bath, I felt... I guess I felt better.

But it wasn't long before heavy footsteps came running in when Mama Mary went to go find Hound and tell him the news. If the man had superpowers, it would be speed. Sadie rolled her lips, snickering as she scurried out. Mama Mary followed behind her, closing the door.

Hound's blue eyes softened as he practically got down on his knees. Here I thought I was the dramatic one in our relationship.

"Baby, get up. Look, I'm fine. I'm alive. You saved me." I coaxed him to get up because he was still too far away from me.

I didn't know whether it was disbelief or sadness or awestruck, but he wouldn't stop staring at me.

"You can't do that again," he softly said.

I rolled my eyes. "Sadie already beat you to the punch."

He didn't move, and if I wasn't in a lot of pain, I would have gotten up and held that man until he believed that everything was real.

"You can't leave me," he said.

"Again. Sadie already beat you to it." I laughed.

Then Hound did the only thing he could think of, he got off his knees, took two big strides, and cradled my face in his hands. "I said, never leave me again." He enunciated the words. And when he finished, he pressed a tender kiss on my lips, taking in all he could for the moment we had. There was a need in his kiss, like he didn't want it to end.

To say he stole my breath was an understatement, he breathed something more into me.

And when he pulled away, it took everything in me not to pull him back. "Can I tell you something, baby?"

"Anything." He sat close on the bed.

"You kept me from telling you something important," I said sternly, but then playfully caressed his beard. I tugged on it, then told him the words that I had I saved in my heart. "I love you."

One of his hands grabbed the back of my head, pulling me closer to his mouth that was spread in a sappy-looking smile. "Say that again?"

"What, that you kept me from telling you?" I grinned.

"Brat."

"Yours though."

"Say it again."

"I. Love. You," I said, peppering a kiss to him at every word.

"You want to know why I kept you from telling me that?"

"Because you wanted to be the first one?"

He shook his head. "Because I wanted to hear them because you were living for me. I wanted to know that you would fight to survive just to tell me you love me because you would be coming back home with me. Never leaving me to worry if I earned your love, let alone deserve it. Everything from the beginning was about your timing, your wants."

The more he spoke, the more I realized that it had been there all along. And yet I still wanted to hear him say it because I knew for a while he was holding back, but never knew why.

"So you wanted me to say it," I teased him.

"So that in return I could say that I loved you the moment you walked on that stage. I loved you when you started to make it feel like home again. I loved you when you walked back into my life from all those years ago," he said as I pulled him into my arms. I ignored all the pain, I just wanted to feel him close.

Chapter 46

HOUND DOG

I had wished so hard that I would see those beautiful hazel eyes once again, that I would hear her laughter, and see that smile once more.

When Mama told me she was awake, I couldn't help but run. The amount of times they said they almost lost her, the rush of guilt and sorrow hit me like a train. I didn't know what to do, and it wasn't like I could dig up a grave and kill the motherfucker again.

I wasn't going to take anymore chances or let Melody take those chances again.

What was done was done and now it was time to move on.

As much as I could, I cuddled with Melody in the uncomfortable hospital bed, knowing that we'd get yelled at by that little nurse.

My woman.

My little songbird.

All mine.

Melody chuckled even though her eyes were closed, I looked down at the smile she was trying to hide.

"What's so funny?"I asked, trying to contain the smile that was coming.

"Something that the nurse had said. Ignore me. Just one of those thoughts that I can't shut up." She laughed.

"Okay, now you have me curious?"

She rolled her lips between her teeth, finally then looking up at me. "She said that *my fiancé* hadn't left the waiting room."

I remained quiet because I didn't want to admit that in a moment of weakness an impulsive thought crossed my mind. Let alone that at that moment I was looking rough and to prevent anyone in the hospital from being alarmed anymore, I called her my fiancée as they tried to look up her medical records for a hint of my name.

I mean, no one in their right mind would say yes when they took one look at me and the brothers that trailed along. Especially to see a woman like Melody. Night and day difference

Maybe the impulsive thought was a dream, a wish, buried deep down until it was ready. I didn't know; she was just the one for me and I knew I was never wanting to go looking again. Especially when she was worth everything in my life.

Pops was right, when you know you know. And for Melody Rae Hart, she was the one that I wanted to spend the rest of my life with, and sure, call me possessive but I wanted her for myself, her body, her soul, her love.

"Baby?" Her small voice broke my thoughts.

"Yeah?"

"You're not laughing." She started to get worried.

"I mean, I didn't hear the joke."

She shot up from the bed, rolling on her uninjured side, my hand draped over her waist. "Did I miss the transition from ol' lady to fiancée? I mean I know my memory is kind of hazy, details come and go, but I hope that I would have remembered that part."

I mean, did I have a ring? Not at the moment. She deserved something special. Something that was a reminder of her and just how unique she was.

"Well, it doesn't sound like you would have said no," I teased her.

"Why would I say no?" she teased right back.

There were so many reasons I wanted to defend why she shouldn't, but she would fight right back and then win. "Well then I'll take it as a yes."

"You didn't ask." she sassed.

"Keep it up, songbird. You really think I'm not keeping count."

Maybe not then, but I knew when it would a real answer.

Her cheeks blushed the reddest shade, reminding me of the color I'd like her other cheeks to be.

She fiddled with my shirt, tracing her fingers on my chest. "You never said if you won."

I took her chin and tilted it up. "*We* won, Melody." She was a part of me, she was a part of the club. We protect our own, and now love even harder and maybe faster.

"It's over?"

I nodded.

"Okay." She released a breath that sounded like it had been trapped for a long time. "Will you tell me what happened?"

I shook my head, it wasn't the place and it wasn't something she needed to think about. I didn't want any more nightmares to plague her. She needed to heal, be ready for the next chapter in her life, in *our* life.

But she teased right back. "What your old man mind can't remember?"

"Careful, this *old* man can edge your ass until you beg for forgiveness for that."

She giggled and she fell asleep resting her chin on my chest. Her soft snores were music to my ears.

Moments later, the nurse, Amelia, came in and stopped short. "I should tell you to get out of her bed, but I think she would put up more of a fight than you."

"Thank you."

"I'm just checking her fluids and vitals."

I nodded.

"She's a fighter, your woman."

"Yeah," I said.

"I didn't ask, but are your guys okay?"

"We're fine," I whispered. Melody started to stir but settled with the smallest moan. It was selfish of me to think that she was having a dirty dream knowing that the next few weeks were going to be a bitch.

Amelia paused at the computer. "I meant your guys. None of them were in the ER"

"Don't know what you're talking about," I sternly said, putting an end to any accusations.

"Greene told me enough, just wanted to make sure she had a strong support system and if one of them is injured. Just saying I can help."

I was going to hurt Greene. "He shouldn't have run his mouth."

"Greene is a good man, he knows who he can trust. Just like I trusted him."

I cocked an eyebrow. "When did you and Greene get buddy buddy?"

"When he's saved me a couple times from... things." Amelia stopped. "Plus he knew I spotted lies, but I went along with it. If you all need anything, a friend of Greene's is a friend of mine."

"A friend? Why would you do that?" My brows knitted.

"Because a group like that who would do anything for a woman like Melody, that's worth protecting. Call it a bleeding heart. I know I would be thankful and do anything in return for people like that."

Amelia turned, but there was a slight sadness in her cheery voice. I stopped her. "Thank you, Amelia, for being there for her."

"Mia," she said softly, turning back to look over her shoulder. "Hurt recognizes hurt, sir. I'll be there for someone else's heal-ing."

I thought what she meant to say was that she was there for someone's healing except her own. She reminded me a little of Melody. I thought about her words the rest of the night while my own woman was sleeping in my arms on her own way to getting stronger.

Chapter 47

MELODY

Healing was a bitch.

It was one thing being watched by Hound Dog when we were alone and he wanted to watch but it was another to be watched like a baby bird trying to break free of the nest and she gets pulled back into the nest at the first instance of wings flapping.

It also didn't help that I was horny like a teenager and wanted to jump Hound's bones but the fucker wouldn't give in. He even hid all the toys. He told me the doctors said that I couldn't do "extraneous" activities for a long while. And I swear that was payback for when I was going to withhold when he was told the same thing when he had his potential concussion.

I was wound tighter than a virgin on her wedding night. I was minutes away from either murdering him or taking matters in my own hands.

He'd say, "I promise it will all be worth it in the end."

I called it a load of crap.

I did my damn physical therapy exercises, and when I kicked Shooter out, during my third week post hospital, Hound and I had an argument which in the end I made him sleep on the couch. And yet that didn't work because the bastard snuck in and I woke up with arms wrapped around me like a koala. I thought I was the clingy one.

I guess being on the brink of death and almost high-fiving Jesus will do that to a lover, make the roles reverse.

In the end, I was welcomed by a better surprise. Mia from the hospital, came by instead of Shooter. She was better company than a grouchy and dark humored Shooter. Though it didn't stop him from being outside the door. I thought about warning Mia away from Shooter, but she didn't really give him the time of day.

That still didn't stop Shooter from watching over her.

Rather than a nurse, I gained a friend. One I knew that I could count on, more than just making sure I was taking care of myself when Hound Dog was called away for business.

In my "second" healing time, I worked on music, submitted songs to a few studios, and found my groove again.

Sometimes I ended up in the kitchen, only to get yelled at when Hound came home and told me I was doing too much. I threatened to tell his mama that he wasn't being a good boy. I blamed it on the sexual tension.

But one night in February, Hound covered my eyes, guided me through somewhere. He told me to get dressed up, that he was taking me out somewhere special. I thought for a second he was trying to take me out for an early Valentine's day dinner or something. My panicked thought was that he was proposing, but that would be weird, especially after the hospital when he didn't talk about it again.

Well, we didn't talk about it again. Never pictured myself married let alone potentially a full life with Hound Dog.

"Hound, you know I'm not fond of surprises." I groaned.

"I promise, you'll like this one," he said so sweetly. So contradictory to his outward appearance and demeanor around others, he was such a cinnamon roll.

A few more steps and we stood still.

I felt his heart pounding against my back. "Ready?" he asked.

"Sure, baby."

He removed his hands and there in total darkness was a dimly lit Blue Sax stage. But not a soul in sight. I hadn't returned since that night.

I took a few steps, my high-heeled boots clicked against the wood floors, they echoed throughout the place. Each step I still felt a twinge of pain on my right side. But it was faint, so I fought against it.

"Is this some sort of lesson? Confronting my demons? Coming back to where it all started?" I said, suppressing a laugh.

"I know that you wanted to sing that night, that you were ready."

My shoulders dropped. "It was supposed to be a surprise. I was gonna show up on that stage, and only sing to you."

I turned around and saw Hound in all his sexiness holding out my guitar. "Then get up there."

"There's no one else here?"

He smirked. "And? You said you wanted to sing to me."

He was cockier when he could read me like a book. "Yes, yes I did." I reached out to grab the guitar. He didn't let go, instead he pulled me in for a kiss. Anytime the man kissed me, it was one of those you couldn't pull away from. It was easy to just melt into him.

I could have gotten lost in that kiss but he pulled away, gently twisting me around, and tapped my ass. "Then get on up there."

He walked away towards the booth. Illuminating the stage, shouting orders to plug up the guitar. As soon as the feedback from the system spooked me. The stage lights were warm, and bright, but I could still see the outline of Hound and his broad shoulders. I knew that it was just him and I, but I couldn't wait to just sing

My heart wasn't racing, I wasn't sweating, worried about what others were thinking about me.

"You ready, little songbird," he asked, stepping down from the booth. He circled around until he reached the soundboard.

I took a deep breath, remembering that months ago this was where it all started. But that woman from months ago was no longer the woman on stage. I looked back at my life realizing I had no regrets.

I was happy. And for once, it was a true statement rather than an empty feeling.

Sure, were there moments that I wish I could go back and prevent myself from getting into these sticky situations? Absolutely.

One thing was sure, I stopped hearing those voices that told me I wasn't enough or I'd never have the talent to go far. It took one man and the second-worst night in my life to put in a line of fate that entwined my soul with my better half.

The man would do anything to keep me happy and keep me feeling loved.

There weren't enough words to tell him how I felt about him, but I knew one way to show how grateful I was for him.

I began my melody, the one that played in my head for months after I looked into those gorgeous blue eyes. It was second nature, almost like a lullaby, one that kept me going to remember what I was living for.

Mama always opened that storybook,
Stories that were filled with dreams and wishes.
Little girls dream of princes,
Ones that would whisk to the great unknown.

Hound couldn't stop smiling. I started to sway with my music. My feet felt in tune with the pre chorus. It was just him and me.

But I was in my own world.
So baby don't be surprised.
If I say yes so fast.
The music grew into a full band in my head.

Because,
Never did I think that a man and a woman

Could love each other like a wolf to the moon.
And all I need is to know you howl
Because I'll howl with you
If it meant staying with the moon and the stars.

I couldn't understand what was happening to me, but it felt like nothing I felt before. The rush, the pride, the accomplishment, the pure happiness of my voice echoing around.

I think the excitement got to me because I was doing it. I didn't have an audience but I got on that stage. I got on that stage and did what Aria said I would do.

I would shine.

I slowed down the last chorus, letting my voice turn vibrato, almost like I was howling like the song.

Corny? Maybe. But what is art but what you make of it.

Because,
Never did I think that a man and a woman
Could love each other like a wolf to the moon.
And all I need is to know you howl
Because I'll howl with you
If it meant staying with the moon and the stars.

I had my eyes closed for a while as I let the notes float out.

When my eyes fluttered open and the last note faded from my guitar string, I heard another sound that I never heard before.

Applause.

More lights revealed a huge crowd that shouted my name, clapping their hands and all. Tears started to well up in my eyes.

I saw the brothers, I saw Mama Mary and Hound's dad, Sadie wiping tears away. I was confused

How?

When?

Why?

All my questions weren't going to be answered right away.

Hound came up on stage with arms wide open. "I knew you could fucking do it."

He gathered my face in his hands and pulled me into a possessive kiss. I could feel his happiness and his pride toward knowing that I did it. His hands gripped me tight. There were more hoots and hollers.

He quickly remembered that we were not alone.

He grabbed the mic, "Excuse me, ladies and gentleman. B.B come entertain these good people and the first round is on us."

Before I could fight back or ask any more of my questions, he hoisted me over his shoulders and carried me off the stage and quickly to the back of the building. I'm guessing the office, but didn't ask as a quick sound of a lock and a small growl before I'm kissed again.

"Hound, hold on baby. Before you give me whiplash."

He brushed a hair behind my ear. That little mischievous smile on his face curled, "Wouldn't want that."

"You are too good to me, baby."

"I beg to differ."

My hand slid down his chest, I had one goal in mind because I deserved this, a release that has been building since I left the hospital. Hound never made it easy around the house looking like a fever smut dream and I couldn't scratch that itch. It felt like the longest game of edge in my life. I thought I was ready to combust.

"You know, when someone does something this nice, this amazing, it must mean they deserve a reward. At least, that's what you taught me," I teased, as my hand played with his waist band to his jeans. Hound groaned under my touch. "Would my Hound Dog like a treat for being so good to his woman, his lover?"

He didn't say anything but when he closed his eyes, I knew I had him under my thumb. I popped the button on his jeans, shimming them down his legs. The man was waiting for me, as if those dirty thoughts that swirled around his head traveled to his hardened cock. My fingers traced along his pelvis, the ripple of his muscles cascading down his body made my eyes widened with need.

I walked Hound back to the couch, having him sit as I sank down to my knees. My mouth watered for a taste of what I had been missing for weeks. This time it was going to be me that was hungry, aching for more.

My hand wrapped softly on his cock; he hissed at the simple touch. I could have had him explode in a matter of minutes, but I wanted my little revenge. "This is mine," I growled with the same amount of possessiveness he showed me.

My tongue traced his tip, giving him the chance to be ready for what I wanted to unleash. I got his tip wet enough for a taste, but I set him off when I stared at him as I sank my mouth slowly down his length. I dared him to break contact, I wanted to watch him squirm, watch him reach for more.

I bobbed up and down as my hand followed up and down, circling around him. When he bucked his hips, I'd pull back and he'd groan, begging me again for my mouth. When he'd get close, when he tried to grab my hair to direct me, I'd pull back. I felt the ache of my own pleasure build, watching him come undone. His body told me everything I needed to know when the wet sounds of my own mouth mixed with my moans. I knew he was loving the sight of me becoming a messy slut for him.

I edged him.

I drove him mad with lust, like he was like a firework ready to take off. I rendered him quiet other than his moans and groans. For a split second, I thought I heard him whimper. For a moment, I wanted him to beg like he made me plenty of times.

The last time I pulled back, I grabbed his attention, gathered a load of spit that was dripping from me, allowing it to drip on his tip. Hound hissed out a "fuck".

His muscles tensed when swallowed him whole, having him hit the back of my throat, hallowing my cheeks to drive him past the breaking point.

I was so lost in the power of feeling like a goddess that I didn't notice him yanking me up off the ground.

No longer was the mess of a man but a crazed man that wanted to devour me. He kissed me hard and fast, tasting himself on my tongue.

He lifted me, whipping off the long dress I was wearing, ripping the panties that were soaked.

"My turn," Hound growled as he impaled me with his wet cock. Between his cock and my soaked pussy, he slipped in quickly. My eyes rolled back, feeling full and needy. "Such a good girl for me, songbird?"

"Yours, always yours."

"And only for me," he groaned, "Show me how much you wanted this." His hand traveled to my throat, giving me a light squeeze.

I wanted it for so long that I didn't need instructions or commands, I was going to take. My hips took over, moving in a way that was just as much as a shock to me as it was to Hound. The tension kept building, reaching the top. I exploded when Hound's other hand pressed on my throbbing clit, circling it, working me into a frenzy. I couldn't stop, I kept moving, thrusting myself on his cock until I was clenching around him.

"Fuck, it feels too good," I whimpered.

"That's it," he groaned, watching his cock disappear inside. "You gonna come for me?"

I nodded, before I knew it a cascade of tingles flowed through me. I screamed his name, taking every ounce of pleasure. Hound never stopped teasing my clit as he chased his own release, lifting me slightly to take control over his thrust. With a roar from him as he couldn't take it any longer, he came hard. The warmth of his cum felt like my own reward, the sense of pride that I made him do that.

I was in control.

The thought of him succumbing to this feeling sent shivers down my spine to my pussy that was still filled by him. Sweat built between us, he pushed my waves out of my face, and the sweet sentimental look in his eyes ingrained in my brain. The soft smile, one of love, one of desire to keep each other.

"Beautiful," he murmured before kissing my forehead.

"Fucking finally." I giggled.

"Was I neglecting my little songbird," Hound cooed.

I pouted. "Never do that to me again."

Hound Dog kissed the edges of my mouth, "Then never try to die on me again."

"And yet you still love me," I said, wrapping one of my arms around his neck and playfully tugging on his beard.

"Always will. Loving you is one of the easiest things in my life." Hound Dog said.

I guess there was nothing wrong with a little birdie loving a hound dog. A hound dog that wasn't afraid to let the birdie fly to her own rhythm and show her the world could be hers.

A love that was stronger than any bullet. A love that was surrounded by music.

Melody's Apple French Toast

INGREDIENTS:

- 3 medium apples - peeled and sliced (honeycrisp or a pink lady, leftovers are for the chef)
- ¾ cup brown sugar (but measure with your heart)
- 4 tablespoons butter
- ½ teaspoon vanilla - divided
- 1 teaspoon cinnamon - divided (again measure with your heart)
- 6-8 slices white bread (Brioche... the fluffier the better)
- 2 eggs - lightly beaten
- ½ cup milk
- 1/3 cup - flour
- optional: powdered sugar (honestly there no option... use it)

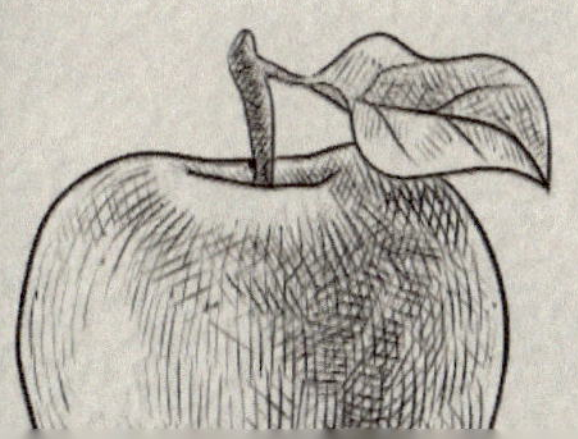

Melody's Apple French Toast

as requested by the mc

STEPS

- Add apple slices, brown sugar, and butter in a medium sauce pan. Cook over medium high heat until brown sugar has dissolved and butter has melted. Add 1/4 teaspoon vanilla and 1/2 teaspoon cinnamon and reduce heat to simmer. Cook 6-8 minutes longer. Remove from heat and allow to cool slightly and thicken while you prepare toast.

- In a large, wide bowl whisk together eggs, vanilla, milk, and cinnamon. Stir in flour and whisk until smooth. Completely submerge one slice of bread in the mixture, careful to coat both sides. Lift the bread out of the liquid and allow to drip off excess.

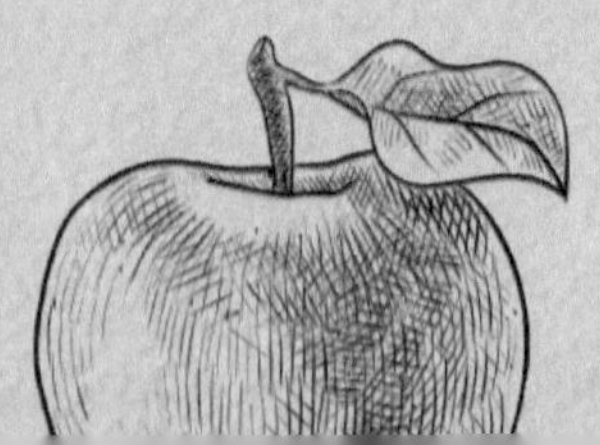

Melody's Apple French Toast

STEPS

- Cook toast in a large pan over medium heat 1-2 minutes until lightly browned, then flip and cook other side 1-2 minutes. Repeat with remaining bread slices. Generously top toasts with apple-cinnamon mixture. Sprinkle with powdered sugar if desired.

- Melody's note: Sometimes I like thick pieces of bacon on the side. There's nothing better than a brown sugared and maple drizzled from the dish to dunk that bacon into.

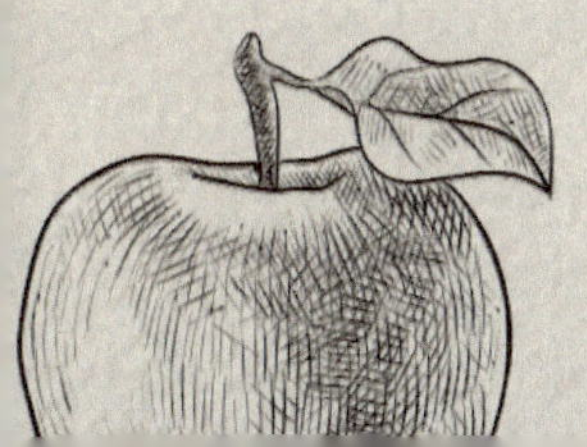

Acknowledgements

A long while ago, I promised myself that I would never set a release date until I was ready and the book was written. I had taken a year off of writing anything new because I was focused on re-releasing Wild Cub and updating Buried in Sins. But my Aunties Cala and Riley approached me with a shared world in my original love series; Motorcycle Club romance. The fact that they entrusted me to be a part of this world with AMAZING authors, I was honored and I knew I would have to work hard and I sure did. Memphis Chapter is also my homage to my childhood spent in Memphis and Millington area. Memphis is birth place of so many amazing art and culture, is was a no-brainer where I wanted my chapter to be placed.

I want to truly thank Cala Riley for pushing me and helping me become the author I am today. Thank you entertaining my questions, my rants, and sometimes my ADHD thoughts, especially if I was worried I missed something. I wanted to make you proud and I hope I did.

Mama and Papa Fritz, thank you for the endless support and love and understanding when I just wanted to spend the day writing. You told me to dream and follow them and look what happened. Also, thank you for sparking your love in that bar in Millington and bringing young "Jamie" to Tennessee and loving it.

My Queenies, My Vanessa and My Deanne, I love you both for loving me and making sure I remember to pick up my crown when I have my rough days. Thank you for loving my stories.

April, needless to say I'd be lost without your friendship and your dedication. You truly keep me going baby girl.

Kayla, ma'am, I can't express how much you have done for me. I never thought I'd find a friend at work that would alpha/beta read for me and tell me "I couldn't stop reading". That comment alone gave me strength, I don't know if you realized that.

Stacey and Jess, thank you for entertaining my "what if" questions and then giving me a laugh when you ask "why are you asking that?" and then playfully wondering how dark I was taking it and trying to get me to make it all make sense. Guess you had to find out right?

To my high school theatre mentors and teachers (VPAA) for always asking me "what is art" knowing that there were a million answers and never any wrong answers. I may not have called to stay on the stage, but you showed me that I could create the words and tell the stories.

Dez, thank you for bringing Hound Dog to life!! And my first cover model cover ever!

Beth, thank you for being so helpful in bringing this baby to life. I appreciate you and cheers to many more.

To anyone who felt like Melody, being told that you'd never amount to anything if you followed your dream, be ready to give them the middle finger and tell them "I told you so." Sing your song, dance with your heart, create for you and the souls on this Earth,

Afterword

There's so much we can do for our community, helping those thrive. You can volunteer your time, donate, or simply educate others around us. If you or anything else is experiencing homelessness, domestic violence, suicide ideations, or anything else please utilize the numbers below.

Homelessness:

- Check out your local shelters or google for a HUD (Housing and Urban Development) phone number.

- Volunteer, donate, advocate

Domestic Violence:
Call or text: 800-799-7233
Visit their website: https://www.thehotline.org/

For Rape, Sexual Assault, Abuse, and Incest National Network
Call: 800-656-4673
Visit their website: https://www.rainn.org/

Suicide Hotline:
Call: 988
For more information: https://www.samhsa.gov/find-help/988

To those who feel unheard, unseen. I see you, I hear you, you are safe with me.

<u>**More books and what's to come**</u>

Grim Wolves MC
Wild Cub
Savage Angel
Rising Dawn (Coming Soon)

The Treasured Outcasts
Buried in Sins
Unearthed Sins (Coming Soon)

Saint's Outlaws MC: Memphis Chapter
Hound Dog's Howl
Shooter's Saving Grace
B.B's Queen (Coming Soon)

About the Author

Jamie Fritz is a full time social worker with her masters in Social Work, that works in various populations such as family services, veterans, homelessness domestic violence, and pediatric health care. She lives in Eastern Virginia, where the weather never is correct.

She is known to write stories with wild, unhinged, burning romance with happily ever afters. She hopes that her writing will shed light into the vulnerable communities that have a special place in her heart. Author of the Grim Wolves MC series, Saint's Outlaws MC: Memphis Chapter series, and the Treasured Outcasts series.

She's still waiting for prince charming but he might have gotten lost or the dragon burned him to a crisp. When she is not immersed in the community and writing, she is attempting to go through her TBR list with her dogs, and surrounded by family. She enjoys a good whiskey and coke, while doing whatever her ADHD tells her to do.

9 798986 728131